LOST SOULS

Born above a shoe shop in the mid-1960s, Neil White spent most of his childhood in Wakefield in West Yorkshire as his father pursued a career in the shoe trade. This took Neil to Bridlington in his teens, where he failed all his exams and discovered that doing nothing soon turns into long-term unemployment. Re-inventing himself, Neil returned to education in his twenties, qualified as a solicitor when he was 30, and now spends his days in the courtroom as a Criminal Prosecutor and his evenings writing crime fiction.

To find out more about Neil go to www.neilwhite.net

By the same author:

Fallen Idols
Last Rites
Dead Silent
Cold Kill

NEIL WHITE

Lost Souls

AVON

This novel is entirely a work of fiction.
The names, characters and incidents portrayed in it are
the work of the author's imagination. Any resemblance to
actual persons, living or dead, events or localities is
entirely coincidental.

AVON
A division of HarperCollins*Publishers*
77–85 Fulham Palace Road,
London W6 8JB

www.harpercollins.co.uk

This paperback edition 2012

1

First published in Great Britain by
HarperCollins *Publishers* 2008

Copyright © Neil White 2008

Neil White asserts the moral right to
be identified as the author of this work

A catalogue record for this book is
available from the British Library

ISBN 978-0-00746-449-2

Set in Minion by Palimpsest Book Production Ltd,
Falkirk, Stirlingshire

Printed and bound in Great Britain by
Clays Ltd, St Ives plc

All rights reserved. No part of this publication may be
reproduced, stored in a retrieval system, or transmitted,
in any form or by any means, electronic, mechanical,
photocopying, recording or otherwise, without the prior
permission of the publishers.

MIX
Paper from
responsible sources
FSC **FSC™ C007454**
www.fsc.org

FSC™ is a non-profit international organisation established to promote
the responsible management of the world's forests. Products carrying the
FSC label are independently certified to assure consumers that they come
from forests that are managed to meet the social, economic and
ecological needs of present and future generations.

Find out more about HarperCollins and the environment at
www.harpercollins.co.uk/green

Acknowledgements

I would like to express my heartfelt thanks to all those people who have offered support and encouragement in my writing endeavours so far. I know who you are.

The staff at the Crown Prosecution Service in Burnley have been very accommodating to me, and even one or two defence lawyers have said kind things, although they were the briefest of moments.

The last year has been very busy, with the release of *Fallen Idols* and the writing of *Lost Souls*, but I know how hard the people at Avon have worked to make the former a success and to bring *Lost Souls* to life. For that I am grateful, and in particular my gratitude goes to both Maxine Hitchcock and Keshini Naidoo, who have consistently given encouragement, sound advice, and, above all else, good company.

My agent, Sonia Land, has been a source of constant support, and knowing that there is someone there to offer not only advice, but the right advice, is a great comfort.

The last twelve months have been exceptionally busy. If I wasn't writing, I was working, and if I was doing neither, I was doing author visits, or radio interviews, or library visits. I have met some very nice people on my travels, and I hope we meet again, but in the background during all of this has been Alison, my wife. She has had to bear the brunt of my distraction, and she knows how grateful I am for that. I promise it will get better ...

To Alison

Chapter One

The old man turned away and closed his eyes, clamped his hands over his ears, but the images were still there, searing, sickening. He tried to shut them out, screwed up his eyes and started to pace. It was no good. He ended up where he started each time, next to her.

She was tied to a chair, her arms behind her back, her wrists strapped tightly to the thin spindles. Blood covered her face and painted her shirt in splatter patterns. He looked at his hands. They were sticky with her blood.

He closed his eyes again, but the sounds were harder to shut out. Wherever he paced, whenever he couldn't see her, the noises were still there, like echoes, constant reminders.

He stopped to take some deep breaths. The woman he wanted to remember was the one he had known in life. She had been fun, vibrant, a face full of smiles. That was the image he wanted to keep, not the one in this room, her face a grotesque mask, nothing left of the person he'd known.

He couldn't shake the image away. He had seen her

face in life; and now he had seen it in death. And it was worse than that, because he had seen her die, her eyes wide open, in pain, in fear, the knife getting closer. She had known what lay ahead of her.

He started to walk around the room faster, tears running down his face. He clenched and unclenched his fingers, looked up and then covered his ears as he walked, as he tried to stifle the sounds that once again crashed through his head. He had heard her last word, forced out through clenched teeth. It had come out as a guttural moan, but he had known what it was. It was *no*. She had tried to say *no*.

He took a deep breath and stopped pacing. He turned to look at her. She was still the same. He put his head back and sobbed, and then he sank to his knees.

He stayed like that, rocking slightly as he sniffed back the last of his tears.

After a few minutes he stood up and slowly walked over to the chair. He put his hand on the woman's cheek and gently stroked it, her skin soft under his fingers. But she felt cold. He leaned forward and kissed her on the top of her head.

'I'm sorry, so very sorry,' he whispered. 'I tried to warn you. I really tried.'

The old man stepped away and looked down at his feet. He could feel the tears trickle down his cheeks, his skin parchment-thin, and as he touched them the blood washed away from his fingertips. He muttered a few words to himself, a private prayer, before reaching for the telephone.

'Police please.'

He waited to be put through, and when he heard the voice at the other end of the line, he calmly said, 'My name is Eric Randle, and I want to report a murder.'

Chapter Two

North or south, murders are the same.

DC Laura McGanity blew into her frozen hands and, just for a moment, dreamt of London. Two weeks earlier it had been her home, but already that seemed like a lifetime ago. She had only moved to Lancashire, a mere two hundred miles from the capital, but it felt like a foreign country as the frigid air blew in from the hills that surrounded the town. She paced along the yellow crime-scene tape and it snapped loudly as it blew in the early-morning wind. She shivered and wrapped her scarf tighter round herself.

It wasn't just the weather that felt alien. It was the quietness. She was standing by an open-plan lawn in a neat suburban cul-de-sac, with the hills of the West Pennine Moors as a backdrop, painted silver as the rising sun caught the dew-coated grass, just the snap of the crime-scene tape to break her concentration. She missed the London lights, the buzz, even the noise. In comparison, Blackley was like a constant hush.

Laura had been brought up in the south and trained by the Met, but love had brought her north. She had arrived in a small town, concrete and graffiti replaced by moorland grasses and dry-stone walls. She knew she couldn't afford a mistake. Her transfer north had been a risk, and she didn't want to destroy her new career so soon. She had seen the looks in the eyes of the other officers in the station. Wariness. Suspicion. She was the girl from the big city, come to tell them their jobs.

She had to be alert now, because there was no time for distraction. With any murder the first twenty-four hours were the most important. After that, evidence on the killer could be lost. Fingernails got scrubbed, hair got cut, cars got burnt out.

She looked up just as Pete Dawson, the other detective at the scene, approached her. He was holding two steaming mugs of coffee.

'You look like you need one of these,' he said.

It seemed to Laura like he barked the words at her, the staccato speech patterns all new, the vowel sounds short and blunt. The London rhythm she was used to had more swagger, more bounce.

She smiled her thanks, and as she wrapped her hands around the mug she asked, 'Where did you get them?'

He nodded over towards a house on the other side of the road, where Laura could just make out fingers on the edge of the net curtain, the light inside switched off so no one could tell that anyone was watching. 'She's been twitching those for half an hour now. I think she's hoping for an update if she gives us drinks.'

'Did you tell her anything?'

Pete shook his head. 'I'm holding out for a fry-up. But be careful. These old mill girls can lip-read.' When

Laura looked at him, confused, he added, 'So they could still talk over the noise of the machines.'

Laura smiled. She liked Pete. He was one of those necessary cops. Precise minds are great – those who can dissect complex frauds or see leads in cases that look like dead-ends – but sometimes you just need someone to kick down a door, or find a quick way to prise information out of someone. Laura reckoned Pete knew many quick ways. He looked one wrong word from hurting someone, all crew-cut, scowl and scruffy denims. He was normally with the drugs squad, more used to throwing dealers against walls than loitering around murder scenes.

She took a sip of the coffee and sighed. It was hot and strong, and she raised it in thanks to the parted curtains on the other side of the street.

'You look like you expected more,' Dawson said, nodding towards the crime-scene tape. 'Not used to the quiet life yet?'

A week before, Laura might have thought he was having a dig, but she knew him better now. Pete's smile softened his words and his eyes changed. They became brighter, warmer, and she sensed mischief in them.

But he was right, Laura *had* expected more activity, the usual commotion of lawns being combed by uniformed officers, or a squad of detectives knocking on doors. Today there was none of that. The body had been taken away, but the first two cops on the scene were still there, an ashen-faced probationer and a police officer not far off retirement. Scenes of Crime officers were inside, their white paper suits visible through the front window, but out in the street Laura felt like she was on sentry duty.

'It doesn't seem like the quiet life,' she replied. 'I moved north for a better life, and I get this,' she nodded towards the house, 'and in the middle of the abductions. It seems pretty dangerous around here.'

Pete shrugged. 'It's not always like this. Once we catch the bastard who has been taking those kids all summer, we'll get more people to work cases like this.'

Laura looked back towards the house. 'And are we any nearer to catching him?'

'Every time there's another one, we're waiting for the mistake, the breakthrough.' He shook his head. 'He hasn't made one yet.'

The abductions had been the big story in Blackley over the summer. The first one only rippled the nationals – everyone thought it was a runaway – but the next one confirmed a pattern and the media all came to town.

Children had been going missing all summer, snatched in the street. They disappeared for a week, sometimes longer. When they were found, they seemed unharmed, but there were things the eyes couldn't see.

There had been seven of them so far, all boys: latch-key kids, early teens, cocky and street-sure. But that was a mask, protection from what they missed at home: love, security, attention. They came back with the mask slipped, and they seemed confused, frightened, days lost with no idea about where they'd been or what had happened to them. They'd thought they owned the streets, but now they realised how vulnerable they were, and that the world could be much crueller than they'd imagined.

They were found stumbling around, confused, lost, like they had just woken up. They were clothed, with no marks or injuries. They had to be examined intimately, just to check for a sexual motive, but there'd been nothing so far. They were sent home, back to the arms of their parents. The boys were all hugged a lot closer after that.

The eighth child was out there now, Connor Crabtree, with whoever was taking Blackley's children. He had last been seen cadging cigarettes in a small car park behind a corner shop, accosting strangers as they went to buy milk or something. That had been six days ago, and no one had seen or heard of him since. The press were on standby, waiting for the inevitable return, something to report; the nation was gripped by the story. The press had even given the kidnapper a name: the Summer Snatcher.

Laura didn't like the name – it sounded corny, no imagination – but she knew that it helped to keep the story in the news. It was more than just a story in Blackley, though. Everyone knew there would be more. Most parents had stopped their children going out, and the streets seemed quieter once it went dark. But the children being taken were the ones of parents who hadn't listened, whose lives were too difficult to make room for their children.

There weren't many clues. There were fibres on the boys, just tiny strands of cloth, from a blanket or something similar, but until they got the source they couldn't get the match. The first two children had dust on their clothes when they were found, small specks of concrete and traces of asbestos, but nothing specific. The police in Blackley were following leads, just to be visible, but everyone knew they were waiting for the return of Connor Crabtree, hoping it would bring fresh evidence.

Laura shuddered as she thought about her own son, Bobby. Four years old, in a strange town and a long way from his real father. She blinked, felt her eyes itch, took a deep breath. It wasn't meant to have turned out like this, but Bobby's father had decided a long time ago that Laura wasn't going to be the last woman he slept with. He'd left, and Laura had struggled on her own for a while, but when she had fallen in love again she was able to give Bobby a family life once more. But it was hard. She needed to be with Bobby in the mornings. She missed seeing his sleepy face, and she wanted to know that he needed her.

'What's your theory about the abductions?' Laura asked.

Pete considered for a moment, his face thoughtful, his hands jammed into his pockets. 'I don't know,' he said. 'Could be a woman. You know, the kids are looked after and then given up again, some nurturing instinct satisfied.' He smiled. 'Not that they'd ever ask me anyway.'

'Why not?'

'I've spoken my mind too often.'

'What do you think about this?' she asked, nodding towards the murder scene.

He exhaled. 'I don't know. Some nutcase is the obvious guess, but there is one thing.'

'Go on.'

'The victim knew the killer. There was no break-in,

9

no sign of a struggle anywhere else in the house. No one reported it until the old guy made the call.'

Laura knew there was some sense in what Pete said. This was no domestic or a burglary gone wrong. It was a sadistic execution. A young woman, Jess Goldie, small and frail, barely twenty-five years old, had been strapped to a chair and strangled with a cord. There were no signs of a fight, no evidence of sexual assault. There was just a chair in the middle of the room, a dining-room chair with strong wooden legs, and she was strapped into it, her wrists tightly bound with thin nylon rope.

But that wasn't what had struck Laura when she first went into the house. It was something else, the sight that had caused the young probationary officer to spend the next hour sitting outside, gulping lungfuls of fresh air in between dry-heaving.

Whoever had killed this young woman had ripped out her tongue and gouged out her eyes.

Laura had methodically examined the scene. She was at work, a detective, so the shock stayed away, her mind too busy to process emotion. It would come to her later, she knew that, maybe when she was in bed or taking a bath, alone and vulnerable.

There was nothing to suggest a struggle, no defensive wounds to the hands, no ripped clothing. But then Laura spotted the marks ringed around the woman's neck, as if the cord had been pulled many times over. It hadn't been a quick kill. It had been dragged out, made to last.

She turned to Pete. 'What did you make of the old boy who called it in?'

Pete stroked his cheeks thoughtfully. 'Eric Randle? Hard to say. He didn't look the sort, if there is such a thing, and the only blood on him looked like contact blood. No splashes or spray. But it's all too neat for me.'

Laura was about to ask something else when she heard a car drive into the cul-de-sac. It pulled up in front of the house, and she watched as a small man in a sharp suit climbed out.

'Oh great,' Pete muttered. 'Now it's all going to turn to shit. Egan's here.'

'Egan?'

'DI Egan,' said Pete, his voice low and quiet. 'Dermot Egan. We call him Dermot Ego. You'll soon find out why.'

As she watched the figure walk towards the house, Laura sensed that he was right.

Chapter Three

Sam Nixon parked his car and looked out of the windscreen. He used to like sunrise – it made even Blackley look pretty – but the view had lost its charm years ago.

Sam's office was in the middle of a line of Victorian bay fronts, with stone pillars in each doorway and gold-leaf letters on the windows, legacies of Blackley's cotton-producing heyday. The town used to rumble with the sounds of clogs and mills, and the mill-owners' money would end up in the pockets of the lawyers and accountants who spread themselves along this street. Blackley's life as a Lancashire cotton town had ended a couple of decades earlier, but it was marked by its past like an old soldier by his tattoos.

Sam could see the canal that flowed past the end of the street. The towpath was overgrown with long Pennine grasses, and ripples in the water twinkled like starbursts as they caught the early-morning sun. The old wharf buildings were still there, three-storey stone blocks with large wooden canopies painted robin's-egg blue that hung over the water, but they were converted into offices now. The sounds of a new day filled the car, the whistles of the morning birds as they swooped from roof to roof, the rustle of leaves and litter as they blew along the towpath. It was heritage Lancashire, lost industry repackaged as character.

But it was the only bright spot. The factories and mill buildings further along the canal were empty, stripped of their pipes and cables by thieves who traded them in for scrap, left to rot with broken windows and paint-splattered walls. Those that were bulldozed away were replaced by housing estates and retail parks.

Blackley was in a valley. A viaduct carried the railway between the hills, high millstone arches that cast shadows and echoed with the sound of the trains that rumbled towards the coast. Redbrick terraced streets ran up the hills around the town centre, steep and tight, the lines broken only by the domes and minarets of the local mosques, the luscious greens and coppers bright dots of colour in a drab Victorian grid.

Beyond those, Sam could see a cluster of tower blocks that overlooked the town centre, bruises of the sixties, dingy and grey, where the lifts reeked of piss and worse, and the landings were scattered with syringes. They had views to the edges of town, but everything looked bleak and wet from up there, whatever the weather.

Sam closed his eyes and sighed. He was a criminal lawyer in Blackley's largest firm, Parsons & Co. As soon as he hit the office his day would be taken up by dead-beats, drunks, junkies and lowlifes, a daily trudge through the town's debris. Criminal law was budget law, the most work for the least reward, so he had to put in long hours to keep the firm afloat. He started early and finished late, his day spent fighting hopeless causes in hostile courts, and most evenings wrecked by call-outs to the police station.

He used to enjoy it, the dirt, the grime. A legal service. A social service. Sometimes both, with a touch of court theatre, just the right phrase or the right question, maybe just a look, could mean guilty or not guilty, jail or no jail.

But then the job had worn him down. He had two children he hardly saw, and he couldn't remember the last time he had hugged his wife.

And he was sleeping badly. He was staying up too late, and when he did finally fall asleep he woke up scared, bad dreams making the day start too soon. They were always the same: he was running through doorways, dark, endless, one after another, someone crying far away. Then he would be falling. He woke the same way each time: a jolt in bed and then bolt upright, drenched in sweat, his heart beating fast.

He opened his eyes and sighed. He rubbed his cheeks, tried to wake himself up. He couldn't put it off any longer: he had to start the day.

His head was down as he walked towards his office and fumbled for the key. He had to put his briefcase down to search his pockets, and that's when he saw him.

On the other side of the street was a man, stooped, old and shabbily dressed, his clothes hanging loose from his body. His hands were clutched to his sides as if he were stood to attention, and his eyes were fixed in a stare, unblinking, unwavering.

Sam felt uneasy. The courtroom usually protected

him, shrouded in respect and court rules, but defence lawyers pissed people off. Victims, witnesses, sometimes just the moral majority. He felt himself grow nervous, checked his pocket for his phone, ready to call the police if a knife appeared. But the old man just stared at Sam, his face expressionless.

Sam eventually found his key. He took one last look into the street. The old man hadn't moved. He was still watching him.

Sam made a mental note of the time and turned to go inside.

Chapter Four

As Egan walked towards them, Laura could sense his self-importance. He was jogger-trim, his nose tight and hooked, his hair bottle-dark and cut just too neatly, not a strand out of place. His white shirt was bright and crisp, to emphasise his suntan, she guessed, which seemed more salon than sunshine.

Pete smiled. 'He's going to be pissed off about this.'

'Why?'

'Because the last time I saw him he was at one of the press conferences for the abducted children, preening himself. There isn't much airtime in this case, and he'll want to get in and out quickly. He won't give up a place on the podium for what might be just a bad domestic.'

Laura looked at Pete. 'If he's involved in the abduction cases, why doesn't he stick with those?'

Pete looked at Laura and said under his breath, 'I suspect it wasn't his choice.'

DI Egan looked around as he took in the scene. He almost stepped on Laura's toes before he noticed her. She saw his quick appraisal, eyes all over her body, ending at her bare ring-finger. Lesbian or prey, in his eyes she could see that she was either one or the other.

He spent too long looking at the identification she had hanging around her neck and then asked, 'So what do we have, Laura?' He looked away before she had a chance to answer, so she ended up talking to the back of his head.

'Deceased is called Jess Goldie. It looks like she died from strangulation, sir, but it wasn't quick,' she said, trying to hide the fatigue in her voice. The early start was catching up on her.

Egan started to show interest. 'What do you mean?'

'I saw her neck before the doctor arrived, and there were a lot of marks, as if she had been strangled over and over.'

'What, you mean sex games? You know, strangle, release, strangle, release?'

Laura thought she saw a twinkle of excitement in his eyes. 'Can't say I do,' she replied, weary of cops who saw the quick thrill in everything. 'She died in her clothes. If it was kinky, it was shy kinky.'

Egan pursed his lips and looked away.

'And there was something else.'

Egan turned back, his eyebrows raised. 'Go on.'

Laura glanced at Pete. 'She's missing her eyes and tongue.'

'What do you mean, "missing her eyes and tongue"?'

'It means that she hasn't fucking got them any more,' said Pete, his voice rich with sarcasm. 'What do you think it means, that she left them on top of the fridge or something?'

17

Egan spun around, eyes angry, so Laura interrupted. 'She was tied to a chair, and her eyes and tongue have been cut out.'

Egan continued to stare at Pete, who just stared back. Eventually Egan turned away. He sighed and then began to chew at his lip. Laura sensed that he had just seen this investigation stretching a long way into the future.

'I bet you could do without this,' said Pete to Egan, as he raised his eyebrows at Laura. 'On top of the abductions, I mean.'

Egan's top lip twitched.

Laura looked down and tried not to smirk. She had quickly figured out that Egan's eyes were on the career ladder. She had seen his type before: delegate everything and then take all the credit. Look pert and enthusiastic in strategy meetings and then ditch the work onto others. She could guess why Pete hadn't climbed very far.

'Is it drugs?' asked Egan, looking around, trying to change the subject. 'Some kind of revenge attack?'

'Doesn't look like it,' Laura said. She was new to Blackley, but she knew enough to know that this wasn't a drug neighbourhood. It was full of new-build townhouses, all shiny red bricks, narrow paths and neat double glazing, brightened up with cottage fascias and potted plants. It was a first-time-buyer estate. Drug dealers don't bother with the housing ladder; they stay low until they can move really high. 'I checked with intel half an hour ago, and she's not on our radar. Just a nice, quiet girl, so the neighbours say.'

'How was she discovered?'

Laura and Pete exchanged glances before Laura

replied, 'The call came around four this morning. Some old boy, Eric Randle, said he went round to check on her. He found her tied to a chair, dead.'

'Went round to check, at four in the morning?'

'That's what I thought.' Laura raised her eyebrows. 'Said he'd had a dream.'

Egan smiled, almost in relief. 'This sounds like a quick one.'

'Maybe, maybe not,' she said. 'I saw the body, and I saw him, and he doesn't seem a likely. But he doesn't have an alibi.' Laura thought back to the meeting she'd had with the old man. He hadn't spoken much, seemed in shock.

'So is he suspect or witness?' asked Egan, watching her carefully.

'Suspect. Everyone is, this early into it.'

'So did you arrest him?'

Laura noticed the tone of Egan's voice, slow and deliberate, making sure it had been *her* decision. He would stand by her only if it looked like she had got it right.

She paused for a moment, thought about what they had in the way of evidence. The old man had been visibly upset, but Laura had checked him out for wounds or scratch marks. Nothing. His clothes had been seized, to check for blood-spray, and he'd agreed to a DNA swab, for elimination purposes she'd told him, along with his fingernail clippings, but nothing in her instincts told her that he was the killer.

'No,' she said, after a moment. 'He's of interest, but no more than that.'

Egan nodded, a thin smile on his lips, and then headed up the path towards the front door.

'Crime scenes are still in there,' she shouted.

Egan stopped, looked back at her. Laura thought he appeared irritated, as if she had somehow insulted him. Before he had a chance to speak, a uniformed officer appeared at her shoulder.

'We've got a neighbour who says she heard something last night.'

Egan looked over and then moved back down the path towards them.

'Who is it?'

The uniform pointed behind him to a house a few doors away, at the edge of the cul-de-sac. On the doorstep stood a woman in her fifties, wrapped in a quilted dressing gown, her hair messy and eyes bright with fear.

'What's she got?' Egan barked the questions, sounding impatient.

'She says she heard a car leave very late, well after midnight. It had been parked at the entrance to the cul-de-sac. A nice car, Audi TT, navy blue. When it left, it screeched away.'

'Did she get the number?'

The uniform held up a scrap of paper. 'Not last night. But she remembered it this morning when she saw the police arrive because it was one of those personal ones.'

Egan looked down at the piece of paper and grinned. 'We need to do a vehicle check on this.'

The uniform smiled. 'Already done it.'

Egan pursed his lips a couple of times, like a nervous tic, and then asked, 'Who's the keeper?'

'Someone called Luke King.'

'Is he known to us?'

'His father is.'

'Go on.' Egan was sounding impatient again.

'He's Jimmy King.'

Egan looked like he'd been slapped.

'Who is he?' Laura whispered to Pete.

Pete sighed. 'Some would say a local businessman, one of the most successful in Lancashire.'

'And what would others say?'

'The most ruthless and sadistic person they have ever come across.'

She was going to ask Pete something else when she noticed that Egan had started to pace. She sensed that if Egan was about to feel the strain, she was about to get even busier.

Chapter Five

It was over an hour before anyone else showed up at Sam's office. It was the same most mornings, quiet until just after eight. He preferred it that way normally, away from the office chatter, but it was different this morning. He was edgy, troubled by the old man outside the office. Every time he looked out of the window, he was there, staring up, watching him work.

And Sam was trying to work. The early-morning office time was important. Being a criminal lawyer could be a full day. All-day courts and all-night police stations, with clients and witnesses to see in between. Sam had a diary full of appointments, although he knew most of those wouldn't attend. They'd turn up instead on their trial dates, expecting him to defend them when they hadn't even bothered to tell him their story.

So the early morning was when Sam caught up, the office fresh with the smell of furniture polish after the attentions of the dawn cleaner. He briefed counsel, compiled witness statements from a jumble of notes, or dictated the stream of correspondence demanded by the Legal Services Commission.

The younger lawyers did it differently. They went for visible overtime, working late into the evening, hoping to be noticed. But it made no difference. Only one thing mattered, and that was the figures. How much money was made. No one asked *when* it was made.

At Parsons & Co, whatever problem needed sorting, there was always a lawyer willing to bill you for it. Crime had always been Sam's thing, but when Harry Parsons had started out, he'd done everything from divorces to fighting evictions. As the firm grew, it sprouted departments. The criminal department was the most precarious, because the work was so unpredictable. Police budget cuts could lead to fewer arrests, or if a lawyer upset one of the bigger criminal families the department would find itself with fewer clients. The claims department was the money-spinner. It used to help people who called into the office, victims of *real* accidents. Now it just handled referrals from those claims farmers who advertised on television, the promise of free money slotted in between debt-firm commercials, and now the lawyers settled claims for people they never met.

Harry Parsons himself still worked in the office, but he didn't venture out much, working instead from a room along a dark corridor of worn carpet and faded paint. A local legend, he'd built up the practice from virtually nothing, but he ran it now from a distance, trusting the departments to deal with the day-to-day domestics. Everyone else was jostling for position: the old man was due to retire in a couple of years, and they were all hoping for a share when he went.

They didn't have the ace card that Sam held, though: he had married Harry's daughter, Helena, and given him two grandchildren. As far as Sam was concerned, he was at the head of the queue.

Sam was looking out of the window when he heard the other lawyers and clerks begin to trickle in. They gathered in a room along the corridor and drank coffee, exchanged insults. Sam would wander in when he finished what he was doing. He was on his third cup of coffee and he could already feel his heart thundering, but he needed the kick. He had a morning in court to get through and the broken sleep was getting to him. He looked round when he heard a knock on the door. It was Alison Hill, the newly qualified lawyer in the firm, spending some time in crime until she decided what she wanted to do with her career. She would move on, he had seen the ambition in her eyes, but until then Sam liked seeing her around the office. She wore her hair back in a ponytail, clasped by a black clip, and her blonde locks gleamed. Whenever they met, Sam automatically toyed with his wedding ring, felt himself smile too much. She was tall and elegant, with a bright and easy smile, her green eyes deep and warm.

He nodded towards the window. 'Do you know him?'

Alison walked over and looked into the street. Sam could smell her perfume, something light and floral.

She shook her head. 'Never seen him before. Why, is he bothering you?'

He shrugged it off, but as Alison turned away from the window, Sam noticed she had a file in her hand.

'Everything okay?' he asked.

Alison looked down, almost as if she had forgotten she was holding it. 'I've got this today, for trial,' she said.

'What is it?'

'Johnny Jones, for assault.'

'What's the problem?'

She looked awkward for a moment, and then said, 'He seems guilty. I've looked at every angle and I can't see a way out. He attacked the karaoke man because he missed his turn. Half the pub saw him do it, and it's on CCTV.'

'Sounds like a classy place.'

She grimaced. 'It reads like the worst night of your life.'

Sam smiled, found himself playing the elder statesman. 'Don't worry about Johnny Jones. He'll be convicted, guaranteed, but he won't listen to your advice. He'll want an acquittal out of pity, but he won't get one. Just call it character-building.'

'How come? It's a complete no-hoper.'

'Would you rather lose a no-hoper or a dead-cert winner?'

She didn't answer.

'Nothing you can do will get him an acquittal,' Sam continued, 'and the prosecution will give him a hard time for having the trial. He will get the verdict he deserves, and maybe even get the sentence he deserves. But', Sam raised his eyebrows at her, 'if you mess up a dead-cert winner, when you have made promises you thought you could keep, you'll see your client's eyes every night when you go to sleep, that look in his eyes as he gets taken down the steps. Fear, anger, confusion. Trust me, that's worse.'

Alison sighed and then smiled. 'Thanks, Sam.'

'Any time.' As she went to leave, Sam said to her, 'Don't forget the magic words, when you get to your feet.'

She looked confused. 'Magic words?'

'"Client's instructions." When you are asked if the "not guilty" plea stands, just say that those are your client's instructions. It just gives a hint that you don't believe in what you are doing.'

'Why should I do that? It won't help Johnny Jones.'

'Forget about your client. You're the one who matters, and for your sake the court needs to know which one of you is the idiot. There is only one thing worse than a lawyer making a hopeless application, and that's a lawyer not knowing it is hopeless.'

'Bang on the table, you mean?'

Sam grinned. He remembered that from law school, the old adage that if you are strong on the law, argue the law, and if you are strong on the facts, argue the facts. If you are strong on neither, bang on the table.

'Bang it hard,' said Sam. 'Take every point, regardless of how pointless, just so that the punter thinks you're a fighter. He won't know you're talking nonsense, but if you fight the case he will think you're the best young lawyer in Blackley.'

Alison nodded, looking more relaxed now. 'Okay.'

'Remember, you're Harry's golden girl.'

She blushed, although they both knew that there was some truth in that. Helena, Sam's wife, had once been a lawyer at Parsons, but had given it up when she'd had children. It seemed like Harry saw Alison as Helena's replacement.

Sam looked back out of the window. The old man was still there.

'If I get killed today, remember his face.'

'Can I have your office?'

'Get out.'

She was laughing as she went.

When he was alone in the room again, Sam watched the street life. The pavement was getting busy with lawyers from other firms, big egos in a forgotten Lancashire town. They barely noticed the drunks who congregated at the end of the street and shared cheap cigarettes and stolen sherry.

He watched the lawyers walk by for a while, waved at the ones who looked up. When he looked beyond them, he noticed that the old man had gone. He checked his watch and then stepped away from the window. He made a note of the time. Like most lawyers, he lived his life in six-minute segments.

Chapter Six

I watched Bobby as he watched television. Parenting was all new to me, but I loved Laura McGanity, and she and Bobby came as a pair.

Ambition had taken me to London a few years earlier, and I had fulfilled that, carved out a small niche in the crime circuit: Jack Garrett, crime reporter. It had come at a price, though, most nights lost chasing down drug raids or shootings, or writing exclusives on scams and gangsters, losing sleep as I waited for the door to crash in.

But then my father was killed a year ago. We had grown apart before that; we were like strangers when I went south, but since his death I had needed to come home to Lancashire. I didn't know why, couldn't work it out. Maybe it was as simple as guilt, trying to make up for the years when I had been away, chasing excitement, chasing dreams. Whatever the reason, I was back in Turners Fold, the small Lancashire cotton town where I grew up, all tight alleys and millstone grit; the town I had worked so hard to escape from.

It was harder for Laura, though. We'd met on a case

– she was one of the detectives, while I was the reporter prying for a story. She was London to her boots, at home in the noise, the movement, the youngest daughter of a City accountant. I had given up a lot to move up north: my social whirl, my contacts, my new life in the city. But Laura had given up everything familiar.

I sat down next to Bobby. His eyes stayed fixed on the television – *SpongeBob SquarePants* – and I wondered how the move would affect him. Laura had divorced Geoff, Bobby's father, not long before we got together and contact had been sporadic at first. As soon as I'd arrived on the scene, things had miraculously improved. But now I had dragged Bobby two hundred miles north, away from the urban clutter of his toddler years and into the open spaces of Lancashire moorland. We had settled in an old stone cottage, with a slate roof and windows like peepholes. At night the cottage seemed to sink into the hillside, the lights from within like cat's eyes flashing in the dark.

I looked towards the window. I could see old redbrick mill chimneys in the town below us, the lines of terraces like slash marks in the hills. The town-centre streets were still cobbled in places, the edges worn smooth by the Lancashire rain. I'd forgotten about the rain. It was the reason for the cotton industry, the moist air good for working with cloth, but the cotton had gone now, leaving damp streets, dark and foreboding against slate-grey skies. Between the town and us was a rich green hillside, broken by dry-stone walls and clusters of trees. This was the Lancashire that people didn't expect, the rolling open spaces. Only the brooding shadow of

Pendle Hill at the other end of the valley broke the mood.

I checked my watch. Bobby had to be at school in half an hour. It was my turn today, Laura had been snatched away by a murder in Blackley, the next town along.

I felt my fingers drum the table. Was there a story in it? I needed something, because a child was still missing. They usually stayed away for a week, sometimes longer. Connor Crabtree had been gone for six days, and the nationals in town were all on countdown. It made it harder for me. I was just a freelancer, trying to sell stories to newspapers who had their own people at the scene, like I was a dog at the dinner table, waiting for scraps. I did best when the press weren't there and I could get the early quotes.

I had sold a few stories though, small articles on the people affected by the abductions, and on the town itself, but they were just padding. Now Laura was at a murder scene and I was at home, doing the school run.

'Are we going to school soon, Jack?' asked Bobby, his voice quiet, almost a whisper.

I looked around, the sound bringing me back. I checked my watch. 'Ten minutes,' I said.

There was a pause, and then Bobby asked, 'How long is ten minutes?'

I sighed, still not sure how to answer these questions. I'd had no training for this. It had been okay when I was just Mummy's boyfriend who sometimes stayed over, but this was different. Now we shared the same house, vied for attention from the same woman.

'A *Postman Pat* story,' I said. He looked happy at that and turned back to the television.

As I watched him, I realised that this wasn't a game any more. Bobby wasn't just the noise in the house. He had to be nurtured, cared for.

I was about to stand up, to finish getting ready, when Bobby said, 'Where's Mummy?'

I stopped, thought about that. As always with children, a version of the truth was best. 'You know she's a police lady,' I said, my voice soft.

Bobby nodded.

'Well, sometimes police ladies have to go and help people. That's where she is, helping someone.'

Bobby turned to look at me again. He didn't look convinced, and already I sensed that his parents' divorce had toughened him up too much for a boy of four. I found myself smiling, though. I could see so much of Laura in him. From the flickers of dimples to his mop of dark hair, stuck up around his crown, and the twinkle of mischief in his eyes.

I winked at him and ruffled his hair. This needed to work, I thought to myself, as much for Bobby as anyone else.

But then I remembered Laura, how she had looked this morning as she threw on her clothes in silhouette, the smell of her warm in my bed, the soft brush of her lips as she'd kissed me goodbye. No, I needed it to work for me, not just for Bobby.

As I thought about Laura, I realised that I needed to start looking for some more work. I'd built up crime contacts in London, people who would look at the stories

I was selling, loose tongues in the police stations and hospitals. I was back at the start again, building up an address book, looking out for the angle the local papers might not report. The abductions would end eventually, but we had a mortgage to pay until then. Laura was at a murder. And where there is a murder, there is always a story.

I picked up my phone and dialled her number. After a few rings I heard her voice.

'I can't talk about the case,' she said quickly.

I laughed. 'Maybe I was calling to hear your voice.'

'You heard it this morning.'

'I'm a reporter, Laura. I've got to report, and I've got a source on the inside.'

'Sorry, Jack, that ended when you saw me naked. It's a rule of mine.'

I whistled. 'Quite a price, but worth every penny.'

I heard a soft giggle, but when she asked about Bobby I knew that I'd had my final answer on the subject.

'He's fine,' I said. 'Don't worry. The school is new to all the kids. Bobby will be no different.'

'What are you doing today?'

'I don't know. I might have a creep around Blackley, see what I can find. Apparently there's been a murder.'

'Jack!'

I laughed. 'If you won't tell me anything, I'll just have to find out myself.'

'How long will you be out?'

I sensed the worry in her voice. Bobby needed collecting from school.

'Don't worry. I'll be back.'

I sensed her relax. 'Okay, thanks, Jack,' she said. There was a pause, and then, 'I'm sorry about all this.'

'I knew you didn't do nine-to-five when we met,' I said. 'Anyway, it's good for me. I've gone straight to the school run and skipped the dirty nappies.'

She laughed. 'I love you, Jack.'

'I've always loved you,' I replied, and then the phone went dead.

I looked down at Bobby, who had been watching me as I spoke. I nudged him lightly on the arm. 'Come on, soldier. Let's get you to school.'

And the glow I felt when he smiled at me took me by surprise.

Laura had gone to a quiet corner of the police canteen to answer her phone, but when she ended the call she turned round to see a grinning Pete holding two mugs of coffee. He was keeping her caffeine levels high.

'That was beautiful,' he said. 'I feel all warm inside.'

Laura blushed and grabbed a cup from him. The canteen was small and busy, the tables filled by the extra uniforms, the footsoldiers, drafted in to help with the murder inquiry. The abductions were still the main focus though. There were posters on every wall and on the door, glossy blow-ups of a small business card, a simple image of large hands over a small head, protective, caring. One had been found in the pocket of each abducted child. The press knew about them but had agreed not to report them. In return they got daily updates. Every police officer in Blackley knew about them too, and had been told to keep a lookout. Every time someone was searched, their wallet and pockets were checked. If someone was brought into custody, their property was double-checked.

'C'mon,' Pete said. 'Leave the bacon for these boys. Egan is about to address his generals.'

It felt quiet in the Incident Room when they walked in. Egan had pulled in a few more muscleheads from the proactive team, those officers who liked patrolling the alleys, watching the active criminals; burglars and dealers would be getting an easier time for the next few days. They found some seats at the back of the room, and as Laura sat back in her chair she looked around.

The police station was showing its age. The walls had been painted many times over, the current version of cream uneven and flaking, with large radiators beneath sash windows. The ceiling was high so everything below it looked jumbled, untidy, just a clutter of desks and paper. There was talk of a new station being built on the edge of town, but that was years away yet.

Egan paced at the front of the room and stroked his chin. He looked tense. He had watched Laura and Pete walk in, the last ones to arrive.

Egan turned to address the room, announced his presence with a cough and started with a summary of the case so far: how Jess's body had been found, the usual list of inquiries. Boyfriends. Money. Stalker. He was a flipchart cop. He had done all the leadership stuff, put pictures of the dead woman on the wall, jotted down suspects and ideas. The others in the room had short attention spans, and Laura could sense their restlessness, as if they knew they wouldn't get the resources to do the job properly. They had to get lucky, and quickly.

And it might take luck, because crime scenes had already reported back and the forensic sweep was looking slim. There were DNA tests to run, fingerprints to compare, but, for a bloody murder scene like that, nothing stood out yet. No bloody handprints on the walls or the doors, or any footwear marks on the floor. The evidence might be there once everything was looked at, but nothing instant had shown up.

Egan paused to look at Laura. 'You spoke with the old man. How was he?'

'Tired and emotional, I suppose. I told him I would call on him later to get a statement. Neighbours confirmed that he was banging on the door not long before the call was made, so we didn't think we had enough to bring him in this morning.'

'But what did *you* think?'

'I don't know. He was there, he was upset, but other than that, I'm not sure.'

'Still no alibi?'

Laura shook her head. 'None. Just that he was at home, dreaming about her.'

Egan looked eager at that. 'Eric Randle has to be our target suspect. I want to know everything about him by the end of today. Where he worked, who he knows, where he goes. I want someone to keep an eye on his house. See who goes in and who goes out.' And then he pointed at Laura and Pete. 'And you two can go get his statement. Once you leave, he might think that's it.'

Laura and Pete exchanged glances. It seemed mundane after the pressure of the murder scene.

'What about Luke King?' asked Pete. 'He was in the area and left in the middle of the night.'

'Make some discreet inquiries,' answered Egan. 'That's your job once you've finished with Randle.'

Pete seemed unconvinced. 'How long do we wait if he realises we're watching him?' he asked. 'There may be the deceased's DNA on him right now. If we wait, it'll be gone.'

Egan took a deep breath, looked as if he was trying to control himself.

'I'm aware of that, but he has no idea that we know about him yet. Let's just keep an eye on him, see what he does.'

Pete didn't reply. He just clenched his jaw and stared at Egan.

Laura knew what Egan really meant: that if they got it wrong against a powerful family, only a confession would save them from a shift back into uniform, riding the Saturday night van for six months, fighting drunks.

Egan split everyone up into teams of two, gave them all a task, and then broke up the meeting.

As the room had emptied, Laura watched Pete as he walked past Egan.

'And what are you going to be doing, Dermot?'

Egan looked him up and down, and then said curtly,

'Taking responsibility,' before he turned and walked out of the room.

When he had left, Laura asked, 'Do you two have a history?'

A smile played on Pete's lips for a few seconds. 'Just flashpoints,' he said.

He sounded calm, but Laura noticed an angry flush on his cheekbones. 'You know what it's like with cops,' he continued. 'You think you've got trust, but as soon as the shit hits the fan, cops like Egan point the finger like they've just seen the end of the fucking rainbow.' He nodded towards the door. 'C'mon, I'll tell you about it another time.'

Laura made a mental note to find out one day. The day was getting long enough without having to spend it dodging bruised egos.

'But what if he's right about Luke King?' she said. 'Maybe Eric Randle should come first.'

'Yeah, if he's right he'll take his applause. But if he's wrong he'll make sure we cop the flack. Just me and the new girl.'

They were turning to walk out of the room together when someone shouted from the back of the room, 'What's the old boy's name again? The one who called it in?'

Laura turned around. Yusuf, a young Asian officer with a soul patch on his chin and thin-rimmed glasses, was sitting in front of a computer screen. 'Eric Randle,' she shouted back.

'In his sixties? Scruffy? Lives on the Ashcroft estate?'

Laura nodded.

'I might be wrong,' he continued, looking up now, 'but I think his name came up in the abduction cases, when the children first started disappearing.'

Laura snapped a look back at Pete. They raised their eyebrows at the same time. This was about to get very interesting.

Chapter Seven

Eric Randle lived in a pebble-dashed semi on the Ashcroft estate, a collection of local-authority cul-de-sacs and high privet hedges. It wasn't Laura's first visit – she had been given a tour of the Blackley trouble spots on her first day – but this was her first incursion as part of a case.

Pete seemed like he knew it well, and as they did the circuit of the estate Laura started to understand why. The neighbourhood grocer had a red neon sign, but it was cracked and dirty, the windows protected by metal grilles during the day and shutters after it closed. Young girls walked the streets, but they weren't the carefree teenagers they should have been, with college books tucked under their arms or heading into town to work in chain-stores on a Saturday. These girls pushed prams, their hair pulled back tightly as their fingers glittered with cheap gold, a ring for each finger, the gleam broken only by the orange glow of a cigarette as the smoke swirled around the next generation in the pushchair beneath. Laura didn't see many smiles, and as Pete drove on she sensed the hostile recognition in their look. They were the police. They were trouble.

'Seems a strange range of suspects,' she said.

Pete looked over from his driving. 'Huh?'

Laura pointed outside the car. 'The son of a local hotshot or this. I'm getting a feeling already which way it's going to go.'

'The kids are ruining this place,' he said. 'It used to be okay, twenty years ago.' He looked over at her. 'But do you know what? There are some good people here. The older ones, the ones who didn't have the savings to get out when it turned to shit, scared to go out, scared to stay in.'

Laura had seen these waste estates in London, but they seemed different there. In London they were more like spots of squalor in a vibrant whole, just part of the London jumble. She had been in the north long enough to know that the affluent areas were usually out of sight, often over a hill or two.

But it wasn't just the housing that gave the estate away for what it was. It was the desolate looks in people's eyes, the hopelessness, the cold northern winds etched into their pale complexions, the hunched shoulders, their hands pink and raw.

'Do you know what the worst thing is?' Pete said. 'There are some decent kids too, whose parents do their best, but they just get swept up by the rest of the shit and end up with needles in their arms or a pocket full of rocks. By then it's too late. Just debris, that's all they are round here.'

Laura looked back out of the window and realised that Pete had described the real poverty she could see. It wasn't about money or housing. It was about hope. Every face she looked into seemed to hold an acceptance that this was it, this was as good as it was ever going to get. It was no wonder they took shortcuts.

'Here we go,' said Pete, and he swung the car into a street of semi-detached houses.

Laura looked at the line of net curtains, at the long, unkempt grass, at the discarded plastic toys on the lawns. There was a dismantled car in one garden, engine parts leaking oil onto the path.

As they got nearer the top of the road, Pete curled his mouth into a snarl.

'The bastard,' he said, his teeth gritted. He banged the steering wheel. 'He's given us the wrong address.'

Laura peered through the windscreen as she felt her stomach turn over. She thought of the dishevelled old man from the murder scene, upset and scared. Could she have got it so wrong?

As the car came to a stop, she saw that the house was boarded up, covered with graffiti. There was a large splash of white on one corner of the board over the main window where someone had thrown a tin of paint.

'But I called it in and he checked out,' she said, her voice suddenly heavy with fatigue. It was still too early for the day to seem so long.

Pete was quiet for a while, but then he started to climb out of the car. 'Don't worry,' he said. 'I could have stopped him too, but I didn't. We'll take the shit two-handed.' He nodded towards the house. 'We might as well take a look now we're here.'

They walked up the short path together. It was cracked and chipped along the edges. There was also a splash of paint on the floor, obviously where the tin had landed. Pete went to the front door and kicked it.

'Pretty solid,' he said.

Laura grabbed his arm. Eric wasn't enough of a suspect yet to arrest him, Egan had decided that, so she knew it was too early to go in uninvited. 'Don't. Let's just take a look around.'

'But he's not living here.'

'Someone does.'

When Pete looked at her quizzically, she pointed downwards. 'Look at the lawn.'

He looked at the small patch of green in front of the house, puzzled. It was a neat square with a line of soil around it.

'It's been cut,' Laura said, 'and there are no weeds in that border. If he doesn't live here, he must have good neighbours, because someone is looking after it.'

Pete smiled. 'If you keep on bringing these clever city ways with you, you'll be my boss soon.'

'Let's try round the back, see what we can see.'

Pete followed her as she went, and Laura sensed curtains twitch in the houses across the road. No one came out to speak to them. No coffees around here.

The back garden was similar to the front. Just a small lawn surrounded by empty flowerbeds, maybe only fifteen yards long. The windows at the back were boarded up as well, but they were free of graffiti. Laura looked round when she heard a noise, and she saw Pete had his head in the wheelie bin at the side of the house.

'Anything unusual?'

He let the lid bang shut. 'It's empty.' He rubbed his

hands together as if to get dirt off them. 'Let's go. He's not here.'

Laura looked around. She wasn't so sure.

'C'mon,' Pete said. 'I'm going to find him. I want to know why he gave you a fake address. That must put him higher up the list.'

Laura was about to say something, when Pete turned to go. She decided that she was too new to object. Instead, she agreed with him. 'I think he was already at the top.'

The boy looked peaceful. His eyes were closed, his breaths soft and light, blond hair splayed out on the soft cotton pillow. The light came from an old paraffin lamp, the flame making the shadows pull in and out and his skin glow and shimmer.

He stood over him, listened to his breathing. It sounded regular. He went to stroke the boy's cheek, but he stopped himself. The boy wouldn't be with him for much longer. He didn't want to leave traces. But as he looked down and saw the warm velvet of his skin, innocent and pure, he knew he couldn't stop himself. He held his hand over the boy's mouth, felt his warm breath, and then he lowered his hand, felt the boy's lips on his palm, felt the breaths get hotter.

He closed his eyes for a moment, relished it, let out a groan of pleasure as his palm became warm. Then he pressed more firmly. He opened his eyes so that he could watch the boy's chest rise. He gave a small gasp as the tiny chest stayed there, as the boy waited to take a breath, for the air to return.

He pressed harder, just a few more seconds, felt the

rush as the boy's face started to go red. He swallowed, felt his own breaths come faster. He could choose. It was entirely up to him. Life or death.

He smiled to himself, almost in congratulation. He chose life.

He moved his hand away and the boy's chest sank. The boy let out a long sigh, and his breathing returned to normal.

He put his cheek near to the boy's, felt the warmth on his own. He sat back and began to laugh, excited. He held up his hands, turned them in the light from the lamp. Healing hands, he thought, laughing louder. Healing hands.

He turned towards the television. It was the morning news that interested him. The old portable television was plugged into a car battery, a long coaxial cable leading out of the room. It threw blue flickers around the dirty walls, making the colour of the boy's face shift and move.

The boy was on a bed by a wall, an old camp bed, a collection of sheets and blankets over him at night. There was a book next to it, *The Little Prince*. He read from it sometimes. The boy had been looked after, and he would be going home soon.

The news started on the hour. The boy had been the lead story for the last week. It was slipping down the news now, often just a tail-end reminder. The parents had done what they could to keep the press interested, but with no news there was nothing to report. The police had done what they always did, released information slowly, repackaged old leads as new ones, just to keep the story alive.

He settled back in his chair. His breathing slowed down, his body became still. He sensed the shadows in the room settle around him, like a cloak around his shoulders, dark and comforting. As the news came on, he closed his eyes and waited.

The boy was the third story in. The parents wept some more. They loved him, they realised that now. But what about when he had taken him? He was just hanging around the streets, close to midnight. Cider and cigarettes. Bikes and skateboards. Not at home. Not safe.

He smiled as the parents pleaded to the camera, felt himself become aroused. They were searching the streets, doing their own door to door. Oh, he liked that. They desperately wanted him back. And he could do that. He could make it better. He sat forward. He wanted to see their eyes, wanted to know that it would be different when the boy went home.

He sighed with pleasure. He had seen it, the pain, the longing, the apology in their eyes. They knew now how much being without him had hurt them.

He looked towards the boy.

'I'll make you rich, Connor,' he whispered, a tear forming in his eye. He leaned forward, so that his mouth was by the boy's face. He spoke softly, tenderly. 'Richer than you've ever been before. Not money,' he said quietly. 'You won't need that. There are greater riches in the world than that.'

He looked back towards the television.

'Just one more day,' he whispered. 'Just one more day.'

Chapter Eight

I made it to the morning briefing on the abductions, held early to give the evening editions and lunchtime television a chance to get their reports ready. There was nothing much that was new so I headed to the Magistrates' Court, next to the police station.

Going to court had been my fall-back in London. If in doubt, go to court, because there was always something to write about. My career had started by writing court reports, when I had worked on one of the local papers based in Turners Fold. All the crime from Turners Fold ended up in the Blackley court – it was the biggest local town – so I knew my way around the courthouse, an old Victorian building, with pillars by the doors and high ceilings that wrecked the acoustics. The magistrates sat high and lofty, looked down on the lawyers perched on old wooden pews, and at the defendants perched high in the dock.

The regular court reporter, Andy Bell, a haggard old smoker with long, grey hair and patched-up trousers, had been hostile at first. He had put the years in, on Fleet Street in his younger days, and, like me, he had returned to his northern roots. But he had mellowed over the last few days. He remembered me from before I moved to London, and he soon realised that we wanted different things. I wanted the angles on Blackley life, the background stories. He just wanted the day-to-day knocks.

It was the internet thieves Andy hated, the ones who scoured the web for his stories when cases first hit the courtroom and then just arrived for the sentence hearings. I didn't do that. He had earned the right to those stories. And anyway, he knew the tricks. If he had a story that he knew would interest the nationals, he would get the local paper to hold it back from the website until after the London deadlines. By then his story would be in London and in print before the internet hyenas knew anything about it.

It was one of those stop-start days, the cells quiet, and I was filling in the gaps by drinking coffee with Sam Nixon, one of the defence lawyers.

Nixon was one of the main players in the courtroom. Tall and dapper, he looked every inch the lawyer. Single-breasted Aquascutum suit, neat and sharp, and Thomas Pink shirt, he shone success when surrounded by failure. The courthouse attracted showmen, those who strutted and boasted, promising clients acquittals they couldn't deliver, but Sam was different. His accent didn't have the polish of his looks, he spoke direct and bluntly and the magistrates liked him for it. If Sam Nixon said it had happened, then it had. The earth is flat? According to Mr Nixon it is, and that's enough.

I was talking football with Nixon and watching the movement from the court corridor, the town's drama.

Young men in tracksuits slouched on hard plastic seats, there to see friends, to socialise, part of their scene. Bad skin. Bad teeth. Bad lives. The older ones sat back and looked bored. The first-timers wore suits and stared at the floor, picking at their nails.

A prosecutor loitered nearby, but he wasn't saying much, more interested in Sam's football tales than his caseload. He was a good lawyer – I had been around enough prosecutors to know that most of them are – but the machinery of the civil service knocked the fight out of them, so that being able to forget about work became the best part of the job.

I turned around at the sound of laughter from a corridor that ran from one of the back courts. A man bounced into the foyer, his arms swinging defiantly, his grin showing off brown teeth and a complexion that looked like he had hovered over too many joints, his skin tarred and lined. He turned in a circle, his chest out, his arms in a come-on pose, and said to Sam, 'She's a fucking star, that one,' before strutting past the glass ushers' kiosk and out of the main door.

The 'fucking star' emerged from the same corridor, a tired look in her eyes. I had met her before but I couldn't remember her name. She was one of Sam's assistants, pretty and blonde and tall, with her hair tied back into a ponytail that swished against the black suit cut tight to her body, her skirt just above her knees. She had the figure to carry it, and I sensed the mob of tracksuits a few yards away turn to gape.

Sam Nixon nodded towards her. 'Have you met Alison Hill, one of the lawyers at Parsons?'

I smiled and held out my hand. 'I've seen you around.' When Alison shook, she smiled back at me, her eyes warm.

'Nice to meet you,' she said. I sensed the confidence that comes from good education and good looks.

I nodded towards the exit doors. 'Looks like someone was happy.'

Alison looked that way briefly, and then she said, 'I lost.'

I thought back to the client as he'd bounced through the court foyer. He looked like he had spent his life being beaten by the system, every loss carved into the anger lines around his eyes. He had lost again but at least he had stood up to it.

'I'm not so sure about that,' I said. When she didn't respond, I asked her, 'Was justice done?'

'Not yet,' interrupted Sam, and he looked solemn.

Alison looked puzzled.

'The bill,' said Sam, and then he began to grin. 'The job's not done until we get paid. *Then* there's justice.'

As Alison rolled her eyes, my eyes caught someone looking at Sam.

He was in the middle of a pack of drinkers. They all looked haggard and tired, their faces much older than their years, red and puffy, their eyes unfocused. Their clothes hung loose and stained, their movements were slow and deliberate.

I guessed that whoever it was, he wasn't pleased with Sam's last effort for him. His eyes were red like all the rest, drunk even that early in the morning, but the focus was sharp and clear. Despite the drink, his stare was hard and direct.

I looked at Sam, who acted like he hadn't noticed him. He was talking to Alison.

I was about to say something when Sam reached down for his phone. When he looked at his screen, he seemed concerned for a moment and then held it up. 'I've got a message to go and see Harry.'

Alison winced. 'So I can have your office after all.'

Sam laughed, but I could tell from the look in his eye that there was some truth in that. I knew of Harry Parsons' reputation, the curse of the local police, and I had heard that he was as ruthless with his staff.

As Sam left, I watched the drunk follow him with his eyes, the glare ever-present.

I turned to the prosecutor, a tall man in a shiny suit, with flashes of grey at his temples, badger-style, and frayed tips on his shirt collars. I didn't know if he earned less or just cared less, but he seemed a fashion rail away from Sam Nixon. 'Who's that?' I asked, as I nodded towards the man in the corridor.

The prosecutor looked for a moment, chewed his lip as he thought of a name, and then said, 'Terry McKay. He's here most weeks. Drunk, usually.' He checked his watch. 'They'll have to call his case soon. If it gets adjourned over lunch, we won't see him again.'

I smiled. Terry McKay. I made a note of the name and went back into court.

Laura sensed Pete's anger as they arrived back at the station. He was gunning for Eric Randle now. She wasn't sure that they had got it wrong, but it had turned Pete silent and brooding. The echoes of their footsteps were the only sounds as they walked along an old tiled corridor heading to the Incident Room. As they got there, Pete spoke in a whisper, an angry hiss. 'Egan will love this,' he said.

There were a few officers in the Incident Room, sifting through information brought in by those cops knocking on doors. As they walked in, someone shouted out, 'Did you get Randle?' and Laura saw all the faces in the room turn to look at them.

Pete threw his coat onto a desk. 'Randle's house is boarded up. He wasn't there.'

All the faces looked back to their screens, glad they weren't the ones who had to break the news to Egan. Some whistled, some smirked.

Pete stayed by his desk and rummaged around in his drawers for something. Laura sensed that it was just to make himself look busy, so she walked on and headed for Yusuf, the officer who had recognised Randle's name earlier.

As she approached, he smiled, almost bashful. He seemed too timid to be a cop, the antithesis of Pete Dawson, but as she heard Pete cursing at the other end of the room she realised that it was no bad thing.

'You said Eric Randle's name came up in the abduction cases,' she began. 'How come?'

Yusuf sat back and nodded, pushed his glasses up on his nose. 'His name comes up a lot,' he said. 'Whenever something happens, a murder or something like that, he calls in with information, reckons he is some kind of psychic. He's done the same with the abductions.'

'Psychic?'

Yusuf nodded again. 'He told us to look near the railway.'

'Is that it?'

'He was warned off, so his calls stopped, but when I show you this, you'll see why.' He reached over to a binder and passed it to Laura. 'I did some digging around after you went to see him.'

'Were you on the abduction cases?'

Yusuf nodded. 'Logging calls, making lists of suspects, trying to cross-reference them. Speaking to the families, just listening out for something.'

'But there wasn't much to hear?'

He shook his head. 'No common theme, except that the kids were from bad families.'

Laura took hold of the binder, and as she flicked through the papers she saw that it contained intelligence reports, all hole-punched and inserted precisely.

'I've put them in chronological order,' he said.

Laura's eyes twinkled with amusement. She'd already guessed that he probably had.

'If you want me to get anything else for you, just ask,' Yusuf continued, and then he blushed as she smiled back.

'Thanks. I'd like that.' She was about to walk away when she thought of something. 'What are you doing on this case?' she asked.

'Calling friends of the victim,' he said. 'I break the news, and when they calm down I ask about her other friends, ex-boyfriends, new boyfriends, that kind of thing. Each call leads to another person, and I research every name I come across.'

'Any other suspects?'

Yusuf shook his head. 'Not yet. She led a quiet life.

Not many boyfriends, and no one on the scene at the moment, although her friends think there may have been someone getting close to her.'

'Did any know Eric Randle?'

'I didn't ask specifically, but a few mentioned that she was a member of a club, used to meet every week, but no one knew much about it, as if she was embarrassed to talk about it.'

Laura picked up the file and nodded her thanks. Back at her desk, she started to read.

The first item was an intelligence report from the eighties. It was a warning that Eric Randle was a problem caller, that he would call the police with information, often about murders or missing children, not always local. He was warned off a few times because he got in the way, turned up at crime scenes, but over time he was regarded as a harmless nuisance and left alone.

Laura leafed through a number of incident logs, created when Eric Randle called the police to provide information. They sounded vague, usually just some idea that someone was in danger. Most had ended with a quiet warning not to meddle.

She looked up when she sensed Egan enter the room. She could hear Pete still sounding off about Randle. Egan didn't say anything. He just listened, and then began to walk around the room asking if anyone had found anything new.

Laura looked back at the folder, and then she saw something that made her forget all about Egan.

Eric Randle had briefly been a suspect in a couple of prostitute murders around fifteen years earlier. Two girls had gone missing from their usual beat, last seen getting into a dark-coloured saloon. They were found on some waste-ground near to the motorway, both stabbed and mutilated. The killer didn't strike again, certainly not in Blackley, and the police thought that the attacker was maybe part of the travelling crowd. But they started to look at Eric Randle because he had called the police and told them things that they hadn't released to the press. He would have been arrested, but he didn't fit the profile. He was too old and had no criminal history.

The killer was still at large.

Laura put the file down and thought about that. Profiling was big back then – the *Cracker* years – and maybe too much weight was attached to it. Profiles never caught anyone. They just eliminated people, and sometimes they were wrong. She made a note to find the file for that case.

Then the next part of the file made her jolt, just as Egan started to walk over to her desk. She put her head down and began to read, just to make sure she had seen it right. She had. A different case, a different time.

She put the folder down and sat back, thinking hard about what she had just read. Five years ago, Eric Randle had been charged with murder.

Chapter Nine

The light around Harry's doorframe glowed along the dark corridor. Sam tapped lightly and went in.

He saw Harry sitting behind his large mahogany desk. It gleamed, dominating the room with its leather top and ornately carved legs. The room was decorated like a Victorian parlour, the wallpaper gold with burgundy stripes, broken up by caricatures of famous judges and paintings of the Lancashire countryside.

Harry stood up when Sam entered, his shock of curly white hair sticking up from his head, his face deeply tanned, the frequent visits to his Spanish villa making him look weathered and kind. It was a disguise. Sam knew Harry was ruthless, determined and cold in all things. He dressed smartly for someone of his age, though. He was a couple of years over sixty, and he wore dark three-pieces, his stomach only just bulging the buttons, with hand-made shirts framing bright silk ties, a flourish above his waistcoat. And he always wore brogues.

Sam had followed him into brogues, but not the three-pieces. Sam went for single-breasted suits, dark and simple. His hair was shorter than Harry's, cut down to a number two, his way of hiding the shrinking hairline and the flashes of grey appearing at the sides. Sam's early-morning walks kept the weight off, but the job gave him blood pressure that scared his doctor.

'Hello, Sam, good to see you.' Harry smiled, but it was quick, functional, lacking in warmth. His voice was nasal, almost a whine. It could wear a court down to his way of thinking pretty quickly.

Sam smiled back, a quick nod. 'Mr Parsons.' It was only 'Harry' at home, never at work.

There were two other people in the room. Sam recognised one straightaway. Jimmy King. They had met a few times, at family events, but it was his reputation that marked him out, ruthless and rich, the first producing the latter. He was dressed in black pinstripes, his hair swept back and dark. Sam wasn't convinced it was natural. When Jimmy smiled his teeth looked bright, too clean.

The other man was much younger, and looked quiet and nervous.

Sam knew Jimmy was a childhood friend of Harry's. He'd heard the story too many times, how they had both grown up in the same children's home, a dusty old Victorian building, forgotten by their parents, beaten by their carers. They had grown up tough, and so Harry and Jimmy had made a pact, and that was never to be beaten, to always look after the other, and to show everyone that they could rise to the very top despite their poor start.

Harry had gone to university to study law, his first

exposure to the middle classes. He scraped his way through on student grants and part-time jobs, and then returned to Blackley with a new accent and a dream of his own practice. Jimmy had gone too, but he found his studies hard. He realised something else, though: that there was money in property, and students needed property. So he dropped out of university, borrowed money and bought a house. He filled it with students, crammed in like inmates, and when the rent started coming in he bought another. When Jimmy returned to Blackley he had ten houses and a desire to buy up the town that had treated him so badly.

Harry and Jimmy had remained close, inseparable. Harry had even invited Jimmy to Sam's wedding, but business commitments had kept him away. Jimmy had sent his apologies and a crystal bowl. It was still in a cupboard somewhere.

Sam could tell that this was more than a social occasion. Something big was happening. He could see it in the way Jimmy and Harry exchanged glances, knowing and wary.

Jimmy King moved towards Sam, his hand outstretched, a disarming smile telling Sam that Jimmy was in charge. 'How is the beautiful Helena?' he boomed, his Lancashire accent strong, although Sam knew it varied, depending on the audience.

Sam wanted to say, 'Drunk most of the time', but he resisted. Instead, he smiled and shook hands, felt King's other hand wrap around his. Sam could feel the control in the man's grip, like a statement of intent, so he shook back hard, tried to feel the crackle of his fingers. King's smile flickered for a moment and he gripped back. Sam felt Jimmy's rings press against his own hand, the gold bands thick and bold. Sam had won the first skirmish.

'Good morning, Mr King,' Sam said simply.

Jimmy King regained his smile and patted Sam lightly on the back. 'Jimmy. Call me Jimmy.'

Sam nodded politely. He sat down and crossed his legs, tried to figure out the reason for the meeting. He knew one thing: he didn't trust Jimmy King. Despite being Harry's friend, Sam knew of Jimmy's reputation, and he saw how the rest of the staff became jumpy whenever Jimmy called into the office.

In the eighties, Blackley had tried to sweep away its past by clearing the slum terraces. Many stood empty, boarded up and derelict. They were sold off at a bargain price; Jimmy King had bought streets of them. He renovated them and rented them out, and was credited with saving communities. Those he couldn't save were bulldozed and sold to developers.

No one mentioned *how* he treated his tenants. The houses were damp and cold, created health problems, asthma and respiratory illnesses. Some tenants tried to take a stand and threatened court action. The visits from Jimmy's men came in the night, when Jimmy was somewhere visible. Not many complained for long.

Sam didn't see a landlord rescuing communities in Jimmy. He knew Jimmy's background, but Sam's wasn't so different. The law had been Sam's way of escaping a derelict council estate: his edges were still rough, his accent strong, maybe his eyes lit by a little more fire than most lawyers. Sam had met the Jimmy Kings of the world many times over, and he saw just another gangster, ruthless and selfish, who used the ordinary people of the town for his own ends.

Sam looked at Harry, who seemed impassive. That was always Harry's way. He would sit and stare, let people talk, so that he made them nervous and they talked when they should really stay quiet.

'A girl was murdered last night,' said Harry eventually, 'on the Daisy Meadow estate.'

Jimmy King sat down and nodded in sympathy.

'It turns out that a car belonging to Jimmy's son Luke was near the scene,' Harry continued, 'so it will help the police concentrate their efforts better if they can eliminate him from the inquiry.'

Sam looked past Jimmy and at the nervous-looking young man. He had a vague recollection of an awkward teenager at Harry's fiftieth birthday party, who'd sat in a corner all evening and watched the girls dance. Adulthood hadn't changed him too much. He was in his mid twenties, his face pale, his eyes heavy under a small blond flick. He was wearing a suit that he couldn't fill, the shoulder pads hanging slack over his lanky frame. He looked at Sam once and then quickly looked away, twitchy. His cheeks looked raw from a shave he hadn't needed.

Sam turned back to Harry. There was a look in his eyes Sam hadn't seen before. Harry Parsons was never nervous. Not ever. But he was now.

'Just elimination?' asked Sam, watching Jimmy King.

Jimmy smiled. His son just looked at a spot on the floor.

'What else?' said Harry, trying to drive the conversation. 'We want to be discreet.'

'Who's in charge of the investigation?'

Sam thought he saw Harry's mouth curl slightly.

'DI Egan.'

Sam realised now why Harry might be nervous. Sam had dealt with Egan a few times, and the DI's big problem was that he wasn't nearly as clever as he thought he was. The son of Jimmy King might get him a press conference, make him a hero with the officers who wondered quietly where Jimmy King's money *really* came from. Sam looked at Luke again. Egan would sacrifice anyone for exposure, and Jimmy King's son was small bait.

'You haven't been arrested,' said Sam. 'If you're just a witness, make him come to you.'

He said it like a challenge, and watched Jimmy shift in his seat. Luke still looked at the floor.

'Civic duty,' said Harry, 'and Jimmy doesn't want his goodwill turned into a media circus.'

Sam noticed a quick exchange of looks. It felt like there was something he was missing.

'How do you know all of this?' asked Sam, curious.

Jimmy's eyes narrowed. 'Let's just say that I know people who know people.' He turned his charm back on, flashed his teeth at Sam. 'It's important that this stays quiet. If Luke's involvement becomes public, everyone will know about it, and he will never live it down.'

'What involvement?' asked Sam.

Jimmy paused for a moment, uncertain. 'What do you mean?'

Sam glanced at Harry. He was still staring, letting him talk.

'Mr Parsons said "elimination",' said Sam. 'You said "involvement".'

Jimmy King twiddled with a ring on his little finger, a cluster of tiny diamonds glinting. 'Semantics, Sam.'

'Semantics convict people.'

Jimmy smiled, but Sam could see that the warmth had gone. 'Yes, of course.'

'If I agree to do this, the only people who go are Luke and myself.'

Jimmy was quiet again, flashing looks at Harry, waiting for guidance. Harry exhaled and then nodded.

'Wait downstairs,' said Harry to Jimmy. 'Ask reception to let you wait in a side room. I'll just have a talk with Sam first.'

When Jimmy stood up, he looked at Sam and then said quietly, 'I give my lawyers some leeway because a rude lawyer is often a good lawyer. But I'll warn you now, if I find out that you are just plain rude, you have made an enemy, whoever your wife is.' He smiled thinly, his stare hard and direct. 'I wouldn't recommend that as an option.'

Sam didn't say anything as Jimmy left the room.

Harry turned to Sam. 'What are you playing at?' He looked angry, his brow furrowed.

'What do you mean?' asked Sam.

'You were rude to an old friend of mine. He has been good to this firm, and good to Helena. I expected better.'

'If I deal with a client, I am in charge. That's the rule. You taught me it, Harry. If Jimmy King hangs around, he will want to run the case his way.'

'There isn't going to be a case.'

'The parents are always best left out. That's the right way, isn't it?'

Harry was quiet. He knew that was his motto. Control. It was all about control. The lawyer had to be in charge, because the line between lawyer and criminal can be a thin one. If the criminal is in charge, he can pull the lawyer over the line with him. No client is worth your career. That had been Harry's mantra throughout Sam's training. Don't run errands, don't pass on messages, don't take anything to them. Stay professional and distant.

And parents were the worst of all, because they controlled the client as well. It didn't matter how old they were, children didn't tell the truth in front of their parents.

Harry turned away to look out of the window. 'At least be polite. For your own sake.'

Sam nodded and then turned to leave the room.

Chapter Ten

Blackley police station was next to the court, so Sam had to run the gauntlet of courthouse drunks and crooks to get there, Luke King tucked in behind him. Sam tried to make conversation, asked him what he did with his life, but Luke didn't answer.

Sam shrugged and gave up. He had just to advise him, not like him. And the day was getting weird. The old man had been outside the office again, staring at him as he left. If he was still there later, Sam would call the police.

They reached the entrance to the police station. It was an old stone building, with roman window arches and block-effect stone on the corners. Steps went up to double-glazed doors and a bright sign, the old wooden doors and blue lamp long gone. Reinforced glass windows lined the building at pavement level, a faint glow giving the only hint that anyone occupied the rooms below. They were the cells, a line of damp, tiled rooms, with an aluminium toilet and a PVC mattress for furniture.

As they were about to climb the steps, Sam turned to Luke. 'Are you okay about this? We don't have to do it.'

Luke didn't respond.

'It's your call, not your father's. If there's something you want to keep from the police, then leave.'

Luke looked towards the police station, and then back towards Sam's office. He saw the group of drunks outside the court.

He turned back towards Sam, and Sam sensed more determination than before. Luke seemed suddenly confident, his eyes less scared.

'There's something you ought to know,' he said.

Sam smiled and shook his head. 'You're here as a witness. I'm not going to change anything you're going to say. I'm here just in case the police think that you're more than that.'

He shook his head. 'No, you've got to know this.' He moved closer to Sam and grabbed his wrist. Sam could smell the office coffee on his breath, could see the gloss of sweat on his top lip.

'I did it.'

I watched Sam Nixon walk by, and I was curious.

I was on the steps of the court, just passing the time between cases, when I saw him, the brightness of his shirt loud in the shadows beneath the old grey buildings. Then I noticed the young man walking alongside him, nervous in a grey suit, the pads hanging off his skinny shoulders. Sam was walking quickly and the young man was struggling to keep up.

As they walked past, I saw Sam glance at me and then walk on. The police station was next door to the court, and I watched them slow down as they got near to the steps.

I was interested. Not many people go to the police station in a suit, and I knew that solicitors didn't go to the police station as much as they used to do. Police-station runners do most of it now, cheaper versions of the real thing.

I had read the reports, that for lawyers crime no longer pays. It is all about volume, so police-station runners handle most of the police-station work, giving the lawyers the time to go to court. The runners only have one choice to make: whether to advise clients to answer questions or stay silent. The suits are cheaper, shinier, the faces younger, but they are prepared to put in the hours, and they are all billable hours.

'Look at the cunt.'

I whirled around. It was the drunk from before, Terry McKay.

'Who?' I asked. 'Sam Nixon?' As a journalist I had learned a long time ago that it was good to listen to anyone who was prepared to talk.

Terry swayed on the steps, and turned to me slowly, his eyelids barely open.

'Who the fuck are you?'

'I'm the person you're talking to,' I said, 'so tell me, who's the cunt?'

Terry turned back to the street.

'Him,' he said. 'With fucking Nixon. Cunt. And Parsons.' His head bobbed as he talked.

I nodded towards Sam and the young man in the suit, who were now by the bottom of the police-station steps.

'Who is he?'

Terry turned to face me. I saw that his denim jacket

was covered in stains, and the sides of his shoes were splitting where his feet were forcing their way out.

'Don't you fucking know, arsehole?' He launched spittle onto his chin when he said this, as his head bobbed and shook.

I grinned. Drunks like him didn't bother me. He wanted to talk. The booze had just made him forget how. 'You tell me, arsehole,' I said.

Terry stared at me, in that way that drunks always do, concentrating too hard. He swayed and his feet shuffled slightly on the steps as he tried to steady himself.

'Fucking King's boy.' He said it with a snarl. 'That cunt owes me.'

'King?'

Terry turned back, his teeth bared in anger. 'Aye, fucking King. Jimmy King, whatever, bullshit fucker.' He clenched his fist, looked like he was going to punch something. 'He owes me, fucking owes me.'

I became alert. I knew of Jimmy King. Local businessman with a bad reputation turned into a pillar of society. Respectable. And his son was being escorted to the police station. Now, *there* was a story.

'What's his name? The son?'

Terry grinned at me. 'Luke,' he said slowly, relishing the sound. 'Remember that name.'

I smiled at Terry and went for a walk, just to see where they were going.

Sam paused for a moment, surprised, not sure he'd heard Luke right. It sounded cold, like they were just words. 'Don't tell me any more.'

Luke shook his head, his eyes wide now, staring into Sam's. 'No, you've got to know. I did it. I killed the girl. And do you know what? I enjoyed it.'

Sam tried to pull away, but Luke's grip was surprisingly tight, strong.

'And do you know what else?'

'Enough,' said Sam, his irritation coming out in a hiss. 'I don't need to know this. Not yet.'

'I'm going to do it again.'

Sam gave his wrist a yank and pulled it away.

Luke stepped in closer. 'I'm going to keep on until someone catches me,' he said, his mouth curled in a grin. 'How will *that* make you sleep?'

Sam was stunned, quiet, not knowing what to say, when Luke walked away from him. He was heading for the steps, then he turned around.

'C'mon, Mr Nixon. It is Mr Nixon, isn't it? Not Sam?' He smiled. 'Catch up. The police want to speak to me.'

And with that, he stepped up onto the last step and went into the police station.

Sam looked around, back at the drunks outside the courtroom. Terry McKay lifted his hand, gave Sam a nod, but there was little warmth in it.

Sam realised then that he had no option. He had to follow his client into the police station. It's what he did. That had always been his choice.

Harry and Jimmy stood at the office window and watched Sam walk towards the police station with Luke. When they went out of view, the men didn't speak. Jimmy tugged at his shirt cuffs and turned away. When he sat down, he crossed his legs and waited for Harry to join him. He watched Harry as he went back to his desk. Jimmy's head was still but his eyes tracked Harry's movement.

Harry sat down and swallowed.

'Can we trust Sam?' asked Jimmy.

Harry nodded slowly. 'He came from the gutter, so he knows how far the drop is. He won't want to go back.'

Jimmy scowled. 'It's even further for us, Harry, so you'd better be right, for your own sake.'

Harry didn't respond. He looked down at his desk and clasped his hands together. He didn't look up again until Jimmy had left the room.

Chapter Eleven

Laura looked through the glass in the waiting-room door. Egan was behind her.

'Is that him?' she asked, nodding towards the lanky kid in the bad suit. He had someone with him. A taller man in a suit. Short hair, flashes of grey around the temples. 'Jimmy King's boy?'

Egan nodded. 'That'd be my guess.' He sounded terse, his plan to covertly observe Luke King thrown away by the unexpected visit. The boy was either playing a dangerous game, or he was innocent. Egan pointed through the glass. 'And he's brought his lawyer. Sam Nixon's not here to carry his sandwiches.'

'Is Nixon any good?'

Egan smiled. 'None of them is good. They're just different shades of shifty.'

Laura looked back through the glass. She knew that most police officers didn't like lawyers, but she knew something else as well: that when they got into trouble themselves, drink driving or with expenses fiddles, they always went to the trickiest defence lawyers in town.

As Laura looked through the glass, she put Eric Randle

to the back of her mind. He had once been arrested for murder, but not convicted. And the scene in the waiting room now made the whole picture look rather different.

'Maybe it's not all bad,' said Laura. 'After all, not many witnesses come to see the police with a brief. But why come at all? And how did he know?'

Egan's lips twitched at that. 'I don't know, but if there's a leak, I'll find it.'

Laura went to press the button to release the security lock, but stopped when she felt Egan's hand over hers.

'Let's make him sweat for a while first,' he said. He left his hand there.

Laura pulled her hand away, and she saw that Egan was smiling. Her phone vibrated in her pocket. Saved by the bell. As she brought it out, she saw it was a message from Jack. *'Is Luke King there anything to do with you?'*

She shook her head and sighed. He didn't miss a trick.

Sam felt edgy as he waited in the police station. He sat on an old orange seat, hard plastic bolted to a hard tiled floor, and he shifted about as he tried to get comfortable. A bored desk assistant trapped behind glass took details of driving documents as people brought them in. Sam watched her, just to avoid Luke's conversation. He had been told too much already.

Sam knew he had to get Luke out of the police station, but Luke didn't seem interested in that. He hadn't said anything since the confession. Instead, Luke sat silently, the tapping of his foot on the floor the only noise. It sounded nervous, but whenever Sam looked across, the boy looked calm, almost happy.

Sam had told him only one thing: say nothing.

Sam turned around sharply when he heard the door open. It was DI Egan. He looked as he always did, quietly confident. There was an officer behind him he hadn't met before. A woman, tall, attractive, with shoulder-length dark hair and dimples. Sam hoped that she might discourage Egan from playing games.

Egan strode towards Luke, businesslike, trying to cut Sam out. Sam stepped in front of him.

'Good morning, Mr Egan.' Sam drew himself up to his full six feet so that he looked down on Egan. He sensed the other cop standing back.

'Mr Nixon, it is so good of your client to come down and help us.' Egan said it with his top lip curled, as if Sam had just pissed on his shoes. 'We need to eliminate him from an inquiry.'

Sam sensed the unspoken words: Why does he need a lawyer if he's innocent?

'Which inquiry?'

'That doesn't involve you at this stage. Mr King isn't under arrest.'

Sam turned round to look at Luke, just to gauge his mood. Luke's eyes betrayed no emotion. They were cold, precise.

'If you want to leave, you can,' Sam said to him. It was a cue, but Sam wasn't sure that Luke understood it: *leave now, while you still have the chance.*

'You do know why your client is here, don't you?' said Egan from behind Sam, sounding hostile.

Sam turned back around. 'You tell me all about it.'

Egan sighed, already tired of the game. 'We would

have come for him anyway. We think young Mr King might have some information in relation to a murder investigation. We were hoping he would help us, so we can eliminate him from our inquiry.'

Sam leaned into Egan, as if to whisper. Egan leaned in too, couldn't stop himself. Sam spoke quietly, almost a hiss, his eyes wide in mock-excitement. 'Did you say a *murder*?'

Sam saw the female officer's mouth flick upwards in a smile, but she stopped herself when Egan stepped back, his anger flushing its way up his cheeks.

'Don't try to be funny, Mr Nixon.'

'There is nothing funny about being linked with a murder,' said Sam. 'Unless you can assure me that my client is not under suspicion, he does not want to speak to you.'

Egan breathed through his nose, his lips twitching, saying nothing. Laura intervened.

'We've received information that your client was nearby,' she said, and she flashed a quick smile at Luke, disarming, friendly. 'He might have seen something that could help us. He could be a vital witness.'

Smart answer, thought Sam. Egan looked angry, like he had lost some ground.

'Hello,' said Sam to Laura. 'Have we met?' He asked because he knew it would annoy Egan.

Laura was trying to look stern as they exchanged details. Sam caught an accent, south of England.

'I've spoken with my client and he has nothing to say.'

'Except when it comes out of your mouth,' said Egan, looking at Luke. 'So why is he here, in his best suit?'

'Because if he hadn't come, you would have hauled him out of bed in his pyjamas, probably with a photographer on your tail, just to get your perma-tan on TV.'

Laura looked down, smirking.

'Look, Inspector,' Sam continued, trying to sound reasonable, 'Mr King has nothing he wants to say to you. If you want to make him, you have to depose him at court. But for that you need to charge someone else, so if you want to hear what he has to say, either arrest him or someone else.'

Sam turned around and took hold of Luke's arm to escort him out of the station. He tried to move quickly, but Egan was quicker, moving fast, gripping Luke's other arm.

'Luke King, I am arresting you for murder.'

Sam was shocked. He could tell from the look in Laura McGanity's eyes that she was too. That was good. It meant that Egan had acted off the cuff. It meant that there wasn't any evidence against King yet. The custody clock would tick away, and it would put pressure on the police. This was a high-profile arrest, and Dermot Egan had made it without any evidence.

If they had done nothing, Egan could have watched Luke at leisure, covertly. Now he had shown his hand, moved too quickly.

Luke looked the calmest of all of them, almost serene.

Sam stood to one side as Egan cautioned Luke, giving him the usual 'right to remain silent' bull. You can say nothing, but if you do, the prosecution will use it against you. Didn't seem like much of a right to Sam.

As Luke was led away, Sam looked down at his hands. Killer's hands. Then he looked at Luke's face.

Luke was smiling.

I moved away from the door of the police station. Laura had kept her back to me, but I could tell that Luke King had been arrested.

And I knew that Laura was dealing with the murder investigation. I smiled to myself. Now that Jimmy King's son had been arrested, the story had just got better.

As I walked back towards the court, I saw Terry McKay again. He was sitting on the court steps, receiving a green bottle from one of the others swaying near him. He barely looked up as I stood over him.

'Where does King live?' I asked.

His eyes focused on me slowly. He shut one eye as if the sun had blinded him, but it was almost certainly the sherry that had made his pupils sluggish.

'Who wants to know?'

I grinned at him. 'I do.'

He looked me up and down, and then laughed to himself. His friends stepped back and looked at me strangely, as if I was from another world. And I suppose I was in a way. They lived their lives in a haze as they stumbled from one bottle to the next, never really taking part in society. They regarded me as an intruder, a reminder of the life they had stopped living when the drink took full hold.

He waved me away and lifted the bottle to his mouth.

I thought our dialogue had ended, and I had turned

to walk away, when he slurred at me, 'Some big fucking house past Whitwell. On the road to fucking nowhere.'

I reached into my pocket and floated a twenty down. I had a sense that we might speak again, so it seemed like dialogue in the bank.

'Get drunk on some decent stuff,' I said. 'No more of that shit.'

Terry didn't look at me. Neither did any of his friends. They were looking at the note, and it was as if all they could see was their next bottle floating towards the pavement.

Chapter Twelve

'How did Egan handle the interview?'

Laura turned to look at Pete. It was the first thing he had said since they'd left the station.

They were heading out to Luke King's house, where he lived with his parents in a palatial new-build many miles from Blackley. They were heading north and were driving along single-track country lanes, over pack-horse bridges, twisting between long hedgerows, the fields dotted by trees and painted in that brighter green which seemed so much more like summer, broken only by the white dots of sheep.

'Egan was like I expected,' said Laura.

Pete laughed. 'Like an arsehole then.'

Laura looked out of the window and smiled. 'Your words, not mine.'

'Any hissy fits from the defence?'

Laura thought back to the interview. It had been like a long fight, starting from when Egan tried to get the defence lawyer to sit in a corner, well away from his client. From then on the defence hadn't co-operated. It was a tricky balance, Laura knew that, the need to throw the defence off-kilter, to try and get a confession, but without turning it into bullying. If it went too far, the confession could be kept away from the jury. Murderers had walked free because of that.

'One or two,' she said. 'Maybe when Egan gets one of his confessions thrown out of court, he'll do things differently.'

Laura turned to look out of the side window. She had taken a gamble in coming up to the King house. The interview with Luke King had ended when a superintendent interrupted and asked to discuss tactics with Egan. Laura had guessed from Egan's face that someone with influence had placed a call, that the tactics were more about getting King out than keeping him in.

For all the things about Egan she didn't like, Laura thought he was right to be suspicious about Luke King. And arresting him would get DNA samples from him, from his hair, his fingernails. Anything else was best to look for while he was still locked up. This was a murder investigation, and Jess Goldie deserved more than favours called in from the golf-club bar. Maybe the inside of the car had blood smeared on the steering wheel or on the seat, or his clothes contained traces of her blood or hair.

Laura had needed Egan's consent to search the house, and he was the only inspector she was prepared to ask. He had nodded quickly, hoping that she would find something to justify his decision to make the arrest. Laura had been ready to go on her own, but she sensed that it would be a no-loser for Pete: he would either play a part in Egan's downfall or he would find something useful. Either way, he would get to raise a glass.

'How was Egan with you?' Pete asked, back to his favourite subject.

'Familiar,' she said, but she sensed that Pete guessed it anyway.

'That'd be about right,' he replied, still staring straight ahead. 'He tries it on with everyone, especially new meat like you.'

'You know how to make a girl feel special,' she said jokingly, but Pete didn't laugh.

Laura watched him for a while as he just stared straight ahead. 'What's the thing between you two?' she asked.

Pete didn't react at first, and Laura started to wonder whether he had heard her, but then he sighed and replied, 'We started as cops at the same time. I ended up on the Support Unit before he did, so by the time he arrived I'd learned a few tricks of the trade.'

Laura raised her eyebrows at that. She knew about the Support Unit. In jumpsuits and boots, they patrolled Saturday nights, looking to split up fights. Or maybe prolong them. The 'distraction strike' was their favourite technique, where an officer under threat could strike the attacker hard, the distraction of the pain making time for an arrest. Best delivered as a hard punch to the nose, it suited those who liked a ruck. As Laura looked at Pete, she guessed that he had fitted in well in the Support Unit.

'Did you have the van door rule?' she asked.

He tilted his head, and then started to smile. 'So they had it in London too?'

Laura looked forward again. 'I've heard of it.' And she had seen it in action, the rule that if the back doors of the van had to open, the cops didn't leave the scene until someone was in the van with them, for the hand-cuffed ride back to the station with plenty of hard braking. The spread of CCTV had stopped much of the fun for the Support Unit, but until they put cameras in the vans, most people would still arrive at the station on the van floor, the victim of one too many emergency stops.

'What did Egan do that upset you so much?'

'He didn't like our methods, so he reported them, and then backed a prisoner up on a complaint.' Pete glanced at Laura. 'Maybe he was right, I don't know, but why didn't he tell us first?'

'What happened to you?'

'I got shoved into Custody for a couple of years. It was only the arrival of civilian jailers that got me out, and by the time I did he had arse-kissed all the way to his pips.'

'So he's not the most popular person in the station?'

Pete shook his head. 'Not below him. Those above him like him, admire him for his courage, all that shit. And let's face it, he's only looking up.'

Laura shook her head and looked out of the window. She felt her phone vibrate again. '*Meet for lunch? J xx*'

Laura sighed. It sounded like a great idea, but she knew it was a no.

She texted back. '*No can do. Off for drive in country. Make sure Bobby ok from school.*'

She put her phone back in her pocket and thought about the long nights in she'd shared with Jack in London just a few weeks earlier. As she looked at the countryside flashing by, they seemed like part of a different life.

*　　*　　*

I smiled when I got the message. I had expected the police to head out to the house. It was a common formula: have an interview to set up the lies, and then search the house to disprove them.

I had parked half a mile from the house. I'd asked at a local garage for the exact location of Jimmy King's house, showed them my press badge and said I was late for an interview. I was still driving my 1973 Triumph Stag, in Calypso Red. It had been my father's old car, washed and treasured by him every Sunday until his death. I loved the car myself now, it reminded me of sunny weekends watching Dad polish it, but I knew that Laura would recognise it in a flash if I parked it too close to the house.

I was sitting in a tree, fifty yards from the house and across a secluded lane. I was looking down into the garden, a long green lawn, striped, with colourful borders all around. Pink, blues, violets. They looked well-maintained, and at the end of the garden were trees, willow and pine, although they were still small, some years to go before they created the country-garden look they were trying to achieve. The house itself stood out against the old stone cottages dotted around the valley. The bricks were fresh and new, with white pillars against the church-style front door and two large gables at the front, so that the house was H-shaped, grand and imposing. I guessed that the grilles on the gate were so people could see in, rather than the Kings see out.

All I had to do now was wait.

Chapter Thirteen

The boy was still asleep, the television off now, just the flicker of the oil-lamp for company.

He leaned forward, watched the rise and fall of his chest, the slight movement of his lips as he breathed. He looked angelic, young and untroubled, a long way from the problems at home. In that light, unaware of his surroundings, he was just another young boy.

He scuffed his feet on the floor, the noise of his soles in the dust loud, as if the surroundings weren't used to sound. The walls were thick with cobwebs, the ones above the oil-lamp dancing in the heat of the flame, grey flicks as they waved in the half-light.

He stood up and stretched. He knew he couldn't stay there all day. He knew the boy would be all right. There was still enough sedative in him to keep him quiet until the next morning. Just one more night and then it would all be better.

He leaned over the boy, watched his face for a moment. His hand reached down and moved the boy's hair to one side, as if to keep it out of his eyes. He smiled, almost paternal, and then leaned forward to kiss him on the forehead. His lips touched softly, just a light brush.

He would be back, to make things right.

'I always knew there was money in property,' said Pete.

Laura looked up, and through the windscreen she saw what he meant.

They were approaching a pair of high steel gates sitting between brick pillars, the central point of long brick walls that surrounded a house she could see at the top of a sweeping gravel drive.

The house stood out as a blemish in a quiet green valley, Laura thought. It was too new for the setting, the ivy planted around the base of the walls not up to the ground-floor windows, so that the brickwork still gleamed. Maybe in a hundred years or so, when the roof had dipped in a few places and the walls had weathered darker, it would look desirable, but Laura thought that it seemed more lottery-win than country-set.

Pete had to bark stern words at the intercom to get the gate to open, but within a couple of minutes his tyres crunched on the gravel and they had parked in front of the large oak double doors at the front of the house. Jimmy King stood on the front doorstep. He was wearing a shirt open at the neck, but the rest of his attire was smart, with crisp pleats in his pinstriped trousers and a deep gleam to his shoes.

'What are you doing here?' he barked.

'Good afternoon, Mr King,' said Laura, stepping ahead of Pete, guessing that her diplomatic skills would be better than his. 'We are currently holding your son, Luke, at Blackley police station, and we just need to have a look around.'

'Do you have a warrant?'

'Do I need one?' It was a clichéd question, but it usually worked.

Jimmy King paused for a moment, and then stepped forward to block Laura's way. 'Yes, you do,' he said, before turning around and walking back into the house.

Laura and Pete exchanged looks, and before she could stop him, Pete was bounding up the steps to the front doors, large and imposing, a stone above the entrance engraved with a motto: *Strength in Unity*. Pete jammed his foot in just as the door was about to close.

Pete grinned. 'No, we don't.' When Jimmy King stepped back, surprised, Pete continued, 'Your son is under arrest and we have the authority of an inspector to be here, so we can do it with or without your co-operation.'

'Which inspector?'

Pete shook his head. 'That doesn't concern you. So it's arrest or search. Which do you fancy?'

'I've met bully-boys like you before,' said Jimmy, his face impassive, his voice cold. 'You need to remember that it's only a job, that you'll want to go home at night and forget about it.' His look hardened. '*I* don't forget anything.'

Pete glared at him. 'And I've met plenty like you before,' he said, and pushed past him and into the house.

Laura shook her head. She admired Pete's style, but she wondered how many complaints he could fend off and stay in the job.

When they went in, Laura saw how unlike a country

house it was. There were no panelled walls or dark corners, no oak beams across the ceilings. Instead, the light almost bounced its way around the house as it streamed through large windows and off the gold stripes on the wallpaper. The stairs went up out of the hall and fanned out to both sides of the house. Laura thought she saw a chaise longue at the top, below a large window that streamed light down into the hall. The rooms on either side of her were carpeted in pristine cream, and flowers adorned every spare piece of surface. It made Laura realise how much she had to do in her own home, with so many boxes still unpacked and none of the rooms in colours she liked.

Laura was pulled back to the reason for the visit by Dawson's growl.

'Where's Luke's car, the blue Audi?'

Jimmy King stared at them both for a few seconds, and then sat down. 'I thought this was a search,' he said, his fingers together, steepled upwards. 'So find it then.'

'I'll show you,' said a female voice from the top of the stairs.

Laura looked up and saw a woman in her late fifties, with bottle-blonde hair swept back into a tight wave. She was wearing a yellow jumper, her shirt collar up, and a string of pearls, like a woman who ached to be accepted for what she would like to be, higher up the social scale than everyone else. It was the unpleasant rise to her smile that gave her away, looking down on Laura like she was trying to sell her lucky heather.

Laura glanced towards the pictures on the wall, dominated by a family portrait: the success story with his society wife and his two perfect boys. Luke King was the youngest, and he looked nervous in the gaze of the lens. The woman at the centre of the picture, sitting on a throne-style chair, was the woman now coming down the stairs towards Laura.

Laura smiled. 'Thank you.'

Mrs King nodded as she passed and then walked towards the back of the house, through a large kitchen full of the stainless-steel trappings that looked like they cost as much as Laura earned in a year, and then into a brick-built conservatory filled with wicker furniture and pot plants.

As they stepped into the garden, Laura saw someone watching them from the end of the lawn, a tall, dark-haired man, lean and fit in his jeans and T-shirt. But he headed off to a brick workshop tucked away into a corner as soon as he saw them. Laura watched him as he padlocked it and then headed back to where he had just been, pocketing the key as he went.

'Who's that?' asked Laura.

Mrs King followed her gaze and then said, 'Danut, our gardener and handyman.'

'Danut?'

'He's Romanian.'

'Has he worked for you for long?'

'Started at the beginning of the summer.'

As Laura watched Danut, she noticed how he avoided her gaze, how he seemed suddenly engrossed in putting his tools away.

'He's a good worker,' continued Mrs King, seeing that Laura was watching him. 'Honest, strong, very good with his hands.' She looked at Laura. 'Do you want to question him?'

Before Laura could answer, Mrs King waved him over. 'Danut, come here.'

Danut stayed where he was for a moment, and then began to walk slowly along the lawn. As he got closer, Laura could sense that he was wary of them. When he came to a stop, he looked at Laura and clenched his jaw nervously.

'These are two police officers,' Mrs King said, 'and they would like to . . .'

'Where's Luke's car, the blue Audi?' Pete interrupted sharply, cutting out any prompting.

Danut glanced at Mrs King, who nodded, almost imperceptibly.

'The blue car is for valeting,' said Danut, his English broken and heavily accented.

'Where is it, though?'

'I just say, I took it for valeting this morning. They wax and polish and I collect soon.' He raised his eyebrows. 'Only twelve pounds, and it come out like from showroom.'

'When did you take it?' Pete barked.

'Early. Before nine.'

'Who asked you to take it?'

Danut looked at Mrs King again before answering. 'Luke. He asked. He said take it for valeting.'

Mrs King looked at the floor as Laura made notes. Pete stepped away, his face screwed up with frustration. He turned round quickly. 'Which valeting place?'

Danut shrugged. 'In town. Small place. I don't know street.'

Pete stormed off and headed back into the house.

'Where are you going?' It was Mrs King, running to catch up. Laura followed.

'To search your son's room.' Pete began to look around him when he reached the hallway, deciding where to go. 'Are you going to show me where, or do I have to go through every room?'

Laura saw how Mrs King looked dejected for a moment, an instant of weakness that passed in a second, and then she hurried after Pete, catching him as he reached the bottom of the stairs.

'I'll show you Luke's room,' she said quietly. Laura noticed for the first time that the rims of Mrs King's eyes were red, as if she had been crying, and she detected a tremor in the woman's hands.

As she passed through the hallway behind the others, Laura saw that there were no other family pictures on the wall, and as she glanced into the rooms she couldn't see any in them either. There were some country views, a hillside and a lake in one, an old hunting lodge in another. It seemed like the family didn't celebrate the ordinary things, the laughs, the unexpected moments. It all seemed too orderly. She could hear Jimmy King hissing into a telephone.

Pete and Laura followed Mrs King up the stairs. As they got to the top, Laura looked out of a large window. She saw Danut staring up at the house.

'What are we looking for?' whispered Laura to Pete.

'Last night's clothes, if we can find them, and check out the sheets and towels. Bag them and tag them.'

'Anything else?'

Pete almost smiled. 'Don't forget we are missing two eyes and a tongue. *They* would be useful.'

As Mrs King opened the door to Luke's room, she stepped to one side.

'Do you want to keep an eye on us, to make sure you're happy with what we're doing?' asked Pete. It was partly a dig, but Laura wasn't sure Mrs King got it.

Mrs King shook her head and stepped away, looking at the floor.

'No, go ahead.'

They walked into a room that seemed to belong more to an adolescent than someone Luke's age. There were posters on the wall, some rock bands Laura didn't recognise, with a large television in one corner and a games console underneath, along with game boxes scattered on the floor. Next to the television was a cabinet filled with DVDs. Laura cast a quick eye over the titles, but they seemed mundane. A few slasher movies and Far East martial arts titles, but the rest were recent classics and *Simpsons* box sets.

They carried on looking, going through drawers and bookcases. There were computer disks and comics, and science fiction figures all around the room. They found diaries, and those were bagged up along with the computer disks. But nothing unusual.

Laura stood by the computer. It was on, a screensaver showing a series of *Star Wars* images in a constant loop. She jiggled the mouse and was greeted by the welcome screen, partially obscured by the password box.

She looked over at Pete, who had his hands in a drawer.

'Anything yet?'

He shook his head. 'Nothing, but maybe he keeps things hidden.'

'Any sign of girlfriends in here?'

'Not a thing. No porno, but no photos or love letters. You'd expect one or the other.'

'Don't judge everyone by your standards.'

Laura looked out of the window and saw Danut still looking up at her. She stopped for a moment and studied him, trying to work out his interest. He noticed her looking and turned to walk away. As he went, his head was down, his pace slow and deliberate. Laura made a mental note to find out more about him.

She turned around when she heard someone else come into the room. It was Jimmy King, and he had a telephone in his hand and a smirk on his face.

'It's your inspector,' he said.

Laura and Pete exchanged glances before she took hold of the phone. 'Hello. DC McGanity here.'

'This is DI Egan.'

Laura pulled a face at Pete.

'You have to leave the King house now,' continued Egan.

'But sir, you gave us consent,' Laura protested.

'It's withdrawn.'

'What about the things we've collected?'

'Anything incriminating?' When she didn't answer

immediately, he barked, 'Leave them,' and then the phone went silent.

Laura handed the phone back to King, who smiled at her. And she knew what it meant, that he had the power.

Pete almost knocked King into the doorframe when he walked out of the room. King glared at him angrily. Laura smiled now. She knew that the best weapon was patience. If Jimmy King's time was due, then it would come.

I scanned the grounds with my camera, said a silent thanks for zoom lenses, and I saw why the garden looked so good. As I looked through the lens I watched a young man walk across the garden. He went towards some concrete outbuildings at the end of the lawn. When he got there, he had a look back towards the house and then slipped into a garage-type building, rectangular pale concrete, with green double doors at the front. I got some shots and then turned back to the house.

I was starting to feel stiff when I saw movement by the front of the house. I raised the camera and zoomed in. It was Laura again.

I saw Jimmy King walk with them. It seemed like he was making sure they left quickly.

I took pictures until Laura left, and then I checked my pocket for the number I had jotted down. One call to some old contacts at the local paper had got me Jimmy King's home number.

A woman answered. She sounded terse.

'Good morning,' I said. 'I'm Jack Garrett, and I'm a

reporter. Do you have any comment to make on the arrest of your son?'

There was silence. And then the phone went dead.

I jumped down from the tree and started to walk back to my car, feeling pleased with myself. Even no comment is sometimes worth reporting.

Chapter Fourteen

As Pete swung the car into the police-station yard, he muttered, 'Today is turning into a fuck-up.'

'Two suspects,' sighed Laura. 'One we can't find, and the other is about to walk.'

'Bad management,' said Pete, and he started to smile. He brought the car to a halt in front of the station and jumped out. 'C'mon, bring your rags with you.'

Laura followed Pete towards the back entrance of the station, holding two large clear exhibit bags, one containing old valeting rags, the other filled with the tissues used to wipe clean the car interiors. It had taken a few circuits of town to find the car valeters, but then she had seen the Audi parked on the street. The owners of the firm were more than happy to help, although the way some of the valeters melted into the spray mist made her think that not all of them declared their earnings. She didn't ask any questions. That was a fight for someone else.

Just before she got to the door, ready to swipe her way in, she felt her phone vibrate in her pocket. When she checked the display she saw that it was Jack. That made her nervous. She was on the first day of a murder investigation, and he was calling far more than usual.

'Hello,' she snapped.

Pete raised his eyebrows as Laura listened, and he saw how she softened during the call. She was smiling when she snapped her phone shut.

'Good news?'

'It was Jack,' she said. 'He's bringing Bobby down to meet me after work.'

Pete winked at her. 'Maybe the day isn't turning out that badly.'

They walked to the Incident Room together, and they detected a sombre mood.

'What's wrong?' asked Laura.

'The preliminaries have come in from the post mortem,' someone said, an eager young detective.

'Go on.'

'Jess was tortured. She was alive when she lost her eyes and tongue.'

Laura took a deep breath. 'So more than just trophies.'

'Seems that way. They were taken out by something sharp, though, almost surgical. There were nicks on the bone around the eye-socket where the blade scraped it.'

Laura winced. And she guessed that her time with Bobby would be briefer than she'd hoped.

'She hardly cried out.'

The voice woke Sam up quickly. He must have fallen asleep. He looked around, scared for a moment as he wondered where he was. Then, as it came back to him, he rubbed his eyes.

He was in a cell with Luke, as they waited for Egan to decide what he was going to do. Sam could have waited outside, or even back at his office, but he knew how cops like Egan operated. He knew there were too many casual conversations with prisoners, just little asides, hints that their lawyer might be wrong.

It had been a long wait, though. The paint on the walls, grey and grim, matched the toilet in the corner. He hadn't used it yet, but that moment might come soon. It was the lack of good light that struck him the most, the windows frosted and small, but it was the smell that Sam knew would linger.

The cells in Blackley police station had a smell all of their own. The police station was over a hundred years old, and the cells felt more like cellars, with little natural light and a position below ground level. A century of damp had seeped into every piece of brickwork, the smell broken by disinfectant and whatever had been left by their occupants, all those weekend drunks, drug addicts sweating their way through withdrawal, old feet. Sam knew it would stay in his clothes and in his hair for days.

'What did you say?' asked Sam.

'She hardly cried out,' Luke repeated.

Sam stood up and stretched. 'Don't say any more.'

'No, I want to tell you,' Luke continued. He was obviously enjoying himself.

'I don't want to hear it,' Sam replied, although it wasn't his conscience that made him say it. There was a corridor full of empty cells, and Egan had marched him past all of them to get to the large one at the end, where there was room for a few prisoners. Sam couldn't see the microphones, but he knew one of the cells was bugged. It had been done a few years ago, when one of the police-station runners was suspected of smuggling drugs into the cells. At first the police had thought he was just providing a good service, when bringing his clients chocolate or sweets. But they'd soon begun to notice that his clients stopped being as eager to get out. So the police bugged a cell. Not to use in court, just for intelligence gathering. They were in the bugged cell, Sam was pretty sure of that.

Luke smiled and sat back, his head against the white tiles.

'Oh come on, you do. You must have wondered what it would be like to kill someone.'

Sam turned towards him, his anger starting to surface. 'I've never wondered that, because I have never wanted to kill anyone. But stay quiet in here because if you talk, they might listen.'

Luke whistled, his eyes wide. He looked around. 'Wouldn't that be fun.'

His smile shut off at the sound of a key in the lock. It was Egan, his jaw set firm and angry. Sam wondered if someone higher up had told him to release them.

Sam had to squeeze past him to get into the tight corridor. He blinked at the bright light, and then felt himself pulled to one side.

'The dead girl's mother is in the waiting area,' Egan hissed. 'Maybe you'll want to look her in the eye on the way out.'

Sam jerked his arm away. 'I'll tell her how you can't

catch her killer, Egan,' he said angrily, and then cursed himself for losing his temper.

Sam didn't wait for permission from Egan. He started to lead Luke away, but he was angry with himself. He was baiting Egan to make himself feel better. Sam had gone into a police station with someone who'd said he had killed and would kill again. Sam had done what he could to get him out. What kind of person did that make him?

Egan glared at Luke all the time he was being booked out of custody. As they went through the waiting area, Sam saw a woman, sitting at the back, a tissue clenched in her fist, her chin puckered, her eyes red. Luke looked away, but Sam saw her watching them, her eyes getting wide, her mouth opening.

Sam looked away and left the station, with Luke at his shoulder.

I was back in Blackley when Sam Nixon came out with Luke King. The best reporting involves patience, although I could tell that the news was already beginning to spread. There was a reporter from the local paper there too, along with a cameraman and a young woman with a microphone.

I saw Sam mutter 'shit' to himself as he came out of the door. He glanced back at the station, but the only way was forward.

I moved forward as the cameraman went towards Sam, who tried to push past, Luke tucked in behind him. The court stragglers spilled onto the pavement and watched the excitement. I thought I heard somebody cheer.

Suddenly Terry McKay appeared in front of Sam. He swayed towards Luke King, his finger in the air, waving in jerky movements.

'You're a fucking wanker,' he sneered, his teeth bared, brown and jagged, spittle landing on Sam's suit.

Sam tried to move forward, tried to push Terry out of the way, but Terry just pushed back.

'They catching up with you?' he continued, shouting now.

Terry turned towards the camera, to make sure he was being filmed, and Sam took the opportunity to slip past him, Luke keeping up with him. The cameraman stepped in front of McKay, leaving him alone on the pavement, confused and angry.

As Sam walked off, he tried to step up the pace, but the cameraman was quicker, blocking his path. Sam realised that he had lost the option of silence, so I watched him as he licked his lips and swallowed. A microphone and my voice recorder were pushed in front of him. He cleared his throat and his cheeks flushed.

'As you might know, the police have been speaking to my client in relation to a murder that took place last night. My client would just like to say that he is mystified as to why the police wanted to speak to him.'

His voice sounded strong, assured.

'He knows nothing about the unfortunate woman who was found dead last night, but hopes that Blackley Police find whoever committed this awful act. He hopes sincerely that the police are now able to devote their time to finding the killer, and that they stop trying to achieve quick publicity by pursuing an innocent young man just because he happens to have a well-known father.' Sam smiled. 'Thank you. That's all.'

And with that, he walked away, Luke close behind.

I watched them go, noticing how Luke kept his eyes down, not wanting to meet anyone's gaze. I thought about Sam and the few conversations I'd had with him. Did I know him well enough to get the inside track?

I checked my watch. I still had some time before I had to collect Bobby. And I wouldn't know until I asked.

I had some research to do first, though.

Chapter Fifteen

Sam didn't pause in reception. The seats were full of people ignoring the no-smoking sign, but he couldn't face seeing any clients. Let the caseworkers speak to them. They spent their days working the files, visiting crime scenes, seeing witnesses, harassing the prosecution. And when the prosecution ignored the letters, they harassed them some more.

Sam wouldn't ask the Crown Court runners to speak to anyone in the office. They weren't employed for the daily grind. Harry recruited them for the flash of their legs, nothing more, to brighten the lives of prisoners and take notes in court. The word soon got around the pubs and estates in Blackley that if you wanted to see a pretty girl when you were stuck in a prison cell, you went to Harry Parsons & Co.

When Sam got back to his office, he sank back into his chair and shut his eyes for a moment. It was the old moral question, the one he tried to avoid. How could he defend a killer? The answer was easy: the judicial process would decide how to treat him. It was a cop-out, an excuse, but it was the only thing that helped Sam sleep. When he ever did.

But what happened when his client said he would do it again? *That* wasn't in the script. Sam had the power to stop it. The Law Society rules allowed him to breach client confidentiality if someone's life was at stake. He rubbed his hands over his face. He knew he couldn't do it. Luke King wasn't an ordinary client. And that sickened him.

Sam still had his eyes closed when he heard his door click open. When he opened them, he saw Harry standing there.

Sam wasn't surprised. Although Harry never came to his office – he called Sam to his – Sam guessed that Luke's case might make a few things different around here.

'Something wrong?' asked Sam.

Harry shook his head. 'I was just passing when I saw you.' He tried to look casual, but Harry Parsons didn't do casual. 'How did it go with Luke?'

Sam saw Alison looking into the room.

'He's still got his liberty, if that's how we measure these things,' Sam said.

Harry didn't answer, so Sam played him at his own game. A few seconds passed before Harry spoke.

'Tell me what happened.'

Sam sat forward and rubbed his eyes, and then he told Harry all about Egan getting frisky, seeing a big name, a headline.

'So is he out now?' Harry asked.

Sam nodded. 'He's got to go back, but he knows that Egan will be watching him.'

Harry stayed quiet for a moment, his eyes down, thinking, and then he nodded. 'Thank you for looking after him,' he said, and then turned to walk away.

As Harry was about to leave the room, Sam shouted after him. 'If he is taken in again, I don't want to act for him.'

Harry turned back round, and Sam noticed that his cheeks were flushed. 'Why ever not?'

Sam tried to think of a way to answer that sounded reasonable, but there wasn't one.

'I just don't, that's all.'

Harry was about to respond when there was a light tap on the door. It was Karen, Sam's secretary. She looked nervous.

'Excuse me, Mr Parsons,' she said, her voice quiet. 'Sam, there's someone to see you. He's in reception.'

'Has he made an appointment?'

She shook her head. 'He says it's urgent. He's been hanging around the office all day.'

Harry turned to walk out. 'Stick with it, Sam,' he said quietly, 'for all our sakes.'

And then he left the room. As he went, Sam saw that Alison was still outside his office, but as Harry passed her, she turned and walked away.

For all our sakes. What the hell did he mean by that? Sam didn't know, but he was sure he had seen something in Harry's eyes he hadn't seen before. Fear.

Chapter Sixteen

The old man had been seated in a room by the time Sam got there. It was one of the older interview rooms, with woodchip and ancient desks, not for the best clients.

Sam was hit by the smell as soon as he walked in. It was as if the old man had slept in his clothes for days, a musty mix of sweat and damp. From the back, Sam saw straggly grey hair over a dirty old grey overcoat, tide-marks along the collar. As he went around the desk, Sam recognised him straightaway. It was the old man who had been staring up at his window that morning.

Sam sat down in front of him.

The old man was in a chair without arms, and he looked vulnerable, scared. His knees were together, his hands over them, and he looked defensive. Under his coat he wore a shirt, but it looked creased, as if he had found his only clean one under a heap of others and made a special effort. There was a film of grey bristles over his cheeks, and his dark-rimmed glasses were held together by tape over the bridge. His eyes had once been bright blue, Sam could tell that much, but now they looked tired, ringed by dark circles.

Sam didn't try to put him at ease. The old man had been watching him all day, and Sam wanted answers, although he wondered now how the old man had ever made him nervous.

'Hello, my name is Sam Nixon. How can I help you?' It came out brusque, unfriendly.

The old man looked surprised. He watched Sam for a moment, and then looked down. Sam realised that he'd just ruined the prepared speech.

'My name is Eric Randle,' he said quietly, his voice sounding hoarse, 'and I have dreams.'

'We all have dreams,' Sam snapped back. He looked at his watch. At the moment this was all free of charge.

The old man ran his finger around his collar, and then said, 'I dream of the future, and it comes true.'

Sam started to twirl his pen between his fingers, a habit he had when he wasn't sure what to say.

'I paint them,' Eric continued. 'My dreams, I mean.' He shifted in his seat. Sam didn't say anything. He just looked at the old man, let him talk.

'I've always painted, since I was a child,' Eric carried on, leaning forward in his seat, 'but then I started getting these dreams, strong, vivid, violent dreams.' He rubbed his eyes. 'I knew they meant something, but I didn't know what.' He shrugged. 'So I started painting them.' He sat back and smiled, a nervous smile. 'I paint my dreams, and then they come true.'

Sam tried not to smile with him. 'What, you influence the future?' He put his pen down. 'I saw it in a film once. Richard Burton. *Medusa* something.'

'No, no,' Eric said, his eyes wide now. 'You don't

understand.' The old man took a deep breath and rubbed his forehead. 'These aren't normal dreams. These wake me up, and I'm crying sometimes. I know I've seen something terrible, something that will kill people, but I can't do anything about it.'

'What kind of things?'

Eric began to clench his jaw, his eyes distant. 'Disasters, murders. I've seen plane crashes, earthquakes, bombings. And I can't do anything about it, because I don't know when it's going to happen, or where.' He looked back at Sam, his eyes almost pleading. 'Sometimes I'm too scared to go back to sleep. So I get up, no matter what time of night it is. I get up and paint my dreams. And then they come true.' He wiped his eyes. They looked damp, his lip trembling. 'And I know all the time that I could have stopped it, if I'd just known more.'

Eric looked at Sam expectantly, as if he suddenly thought that Sam might have an answer. But Sam had his mind on something else.

'Why have you been following me today?' asked Sam.

Eric sat bolt upright and wiped his eyes, looking more focused. He reached into his coat pocket and produced a roll of paper. 'I painted this a few months ago,' he said.

He passed it over, barely rising from his seat; Sam had to lean over the desk to get it.

Sam unrolled it carefully. It wasn't cheap paper. It felt thick, luxurious, not the glossy white of office paper. It seemed completely at odds with the man's appearance.

It wasn't a painting as he expected it. It was more of a collection of jottings, of images. There was no structure, no form, but the images immediately got his interest.

Sam could tell the old man had talent. The human figures were drawn with swift lines, almost scribbled, and the colours overran, but the figures had astonishing movement, action.

It was the image in the middle that drew Sam's attention. It came at him like a shot of adrenaline, recognisable straightaway. It was a woman, petite, young, tied to a chair. There was something hanging from her neck, like a rope, and her chest and face were painted bright red, with crosses over her eyes. Sam hadn't seen the pictures from the scene of the murder, but he had heard Egan describe it over and over during the interview as he tried to rattle Luke.

Sam looked up at the old man, who smiled, just a nervous flicker of his lips.

Sam looked back at the picture.

There was more in the picture, and when Sam saw his own name scrawled across the top corner he felt his chest tighten. There were two people painted underneath his name, standing in front of a statue, of some old Victorian dignitary on a six-foot plinth. Sam recognised it. It was a statue near the court. The faces of the people in front of the statue were empty, but Sam could tell it was two men from the width of the shoulders and the suits.

Sam sat back and folded his arms. 'What does this all mean?'

'I don't know.' Eric looked at Sam, his eyes wide. 'Sometimes I don't know until afterwards.'

'Until after what?' Sam was getting frustrated now.

'Until after it comes true.'

Sam put the picture down. 'Mr Randle, this is all very interesting, but I'm a lawyer. I deal with legal problems.' He gestured towards the picture. 'I just don't see how I can help you.'

'I didn't come here for advice,' he said softly. 'I came here to warn you.'

Sam felt a flutter of nerves. 'Warn me of what?'

The old man shook his head slowly, sadly. 'I don't know. But you've been in my dreams all the time lately, and they're getting stronger. Really strong.' He rubbed his eyes and his voice came out in a croak. 'I haven't slept well in months. I keep hearing things, awful things, people crying, screaming.' He rubbed his eyes again. 'And I hear children, but they don't say much. But I feel their pain, like they are lost and can't get home.'

Sam wondered what to do. He could ring the police, but then what would he say? An old man had painted a picture and dreamt about him?

But then Sam remembered how he had been waking up every morning lately, bathed in sweat, the same dream making him wake up scared, bolt upright. A dark house. A boy crying. Doors, lots of doors. Falling.

Sam held up his hand.

'Mr Randle, I don't . . .'

'You've got children, Mr Nixon,' he interrupted. 'That's right, isn't it?'

Sam felt a burst of anger. This was more than a passing client. He had researched him, looked into his life before he came to the office.

Sam stood up quickly and got ready to march Eric Randle to the door.

'It's got a scientific name,' Eric said as he looked up. 'Precognition. It's not just me, you see. There are a lot of people like me. Some people write things down, some of us draw. Some people just forget their dreams, until something happens and they think it has happened before.' He leaned forward and became animated. 'Have you ever had a dream that something awful was going to happen, and then, not long after, it does?'

'I can't say I have.' Sam spoke through clenched teeth, one hand already on the door handle.

'Perhaps you just don't remember.'

'And perhaps I just haven't. Look, Mr Randle, you've got to leave. And if you don't, I'll make you.'

The old man looked anxious, waiting for a response. Sam didn't give him one.

Randle stood up, moving more quickly than Sam thought he would. 'You're in danger, Mr Nixon,' he said.

Sam stayed by the door, his eyes blazing now.

'Keep that,' Eric said, pointing at the picture. 'It might mean something soon.' He started to leave, and then stopped. 'We have meetings.'

'Who does?'

'The people who have these dreams. We meet up and tell each other what we've seen.' He put a leaflet on the desk. It had been done on a home printer, the colours dull on cheap paper. 'The girl in the painting was in our group.'

Sam looked at the piece of paper again, curled up on the desk. 'What, the dead girl?'

Eric nodded. 'Her name was Jess Goldie. She used to write down her dreams. She had seen it coming, we both had, we saw it in a dream, but we hadn't known it was her.'

'When did you paint this?'

'There's a date on the back.'

Sam walked over to the desk and turned the paper over. The picture was over three months old. Or so the date said. He looked at Randle, who shrugged his shoulders and then set his jaw as he clenched back a tear.

'She was my friend,' he said, 'and I couldn't stop it.'

'So what do you want me to do?'

'I just want you to be careful, Mr Nixon, and promise me that you'll listen to me if I call you.'

Sam thought about it for a moment, and then he realised that it was a cheap promise, one he could always break if he wanted.

'Okay,' said Sam. 'Promise.'

Eric looked happy with that. Sam watched him as he gathered himself and then shuffled out of the office. When he had gone, Sam felt his forehead. He was sweating. He looked at his hands. They were trembling.

He laughed nervously. The day had turned into a strange one.

Chapter Seventeen

Sam watched Alison as she drank her beer. She licked her lips whenever she took a sip, and ran her fingers through her hair as she laughed at one of Jon Hampson's anecdotes. Jon was the ex-detective who ran the Crown Court department at Parsons & Co. Some cops just couldn't let go, as if they missed the dirt when they retired.

Sam looked away. They were snatching a quick drink before heading home. For Sam, it was just a way of putting off the evening round of arguments with Helena, but he wasn't in the mood for Jon.

Jon Hampson had been a scruffy cop, but his switch to defence work after his retirement the year before had changed him. He was small and round, his face pale, the cheeks marked by broken veins, but he had started to speak in a deep bumble, an affectation that helped him play the part. He peered over his glasses and his suits were now three-pieces, always with a bright handkerchief to match his silk tie.

'Can we give the war stories a rest?' pleaded Sam. 'I've come here to get away from work, not revel in it.'

Jon stopped talking and exchanged raised eyebrows with Alison.

'Is everything okay?' Alison asked.

Sam looked at her and saw the concern in her eyes. She was young, pretty and funny, just about everything his wife used to be, and he felt bad for snapping.

But the day hadn't been good. It had started with Eric Randle watching him from the street, ended with a warning, and had a killer in the middle. And Sam knew that he still hadn't caught up with his paperwork. The day had had too many distractions, and it would get no better when he got home.

Sam held up his hand in apology. 'Yeah, I'm sorry. I'm just tired, that's all.' He sighed. 'I just wonder sometimes about the point of it all.'

Jon didn't answer at first, just watched as a waitress came over, bringing three more beers but no smile. He looked back at Sam. 'What? This, now – café culture? Or life itself?'

'No, no,' said Sam, banging his bottle on the table. 'Law. What I do. And what you do. Intruding. What is the point of it all? Of any of it?' He rubbed his eyes and felt the skin sag under his fingers.

Jon laughed, too many cigarettes turning it into a wheeze. 'You *have* had a bad day.' He looked at Alison. 'Has he been like this all day?'

Alison started to grin, but Sam shook his head. 'There isn't a point, and that is the *whole* point.' He moved his beer around on the table, making small circles in the condensation from the bottle. 'Seriously, why do we kid ourselves? I pretend I'm helping people.' He shook his head. 'That's just bullshit. I help crooks stay free. Nothing more.'

'Whoa, Sammy boy,' said Jon, his hands held up in surrender. 'It's taken you this long to work it out?' He winked at Alison. 'Maybe it's time for a holiday.'

'Are you okay?' repeated Alison, her voice concerned, quiet.

Her hair hung forward as she leaned over the table, her hand out. Sam wanted to take it, just hold it in his fingers, feel her warmth, a woman's touch.

He looked away as he thought about Helena. She had once been warm like that. Then the drinking had started. Just social at first, a glass of wine with dinner, and then the bottle. He knew it was partly his fault, because he was never there to give her something else to think about. Their lives didn't feel good. It was all routine and arguments. Sam hid at the office. Helena hid in the bottle.

'Typical liberal lawyer,' Jon said, as he warmed to his theme. 'You came out of law school to change the world, but then you met the crooks and realised that they don't want change.'

'That's a dismal view from an ex-cop,' said Sam.

Jon waved him away. 'You enjoy your conscience while you can, because it will wear you out. Me? I'm just out to make money.'

'Didn't you care when you were in the police?' asked Alison, her eyes full of innocence.

Jon snorted. 'I did thirty years and made no differ-ence. I just helped move the money around. All those wages. Prosecutors, court staff, ushers, forensic scien-tists . . . An economy all of its own.' He tipped his bottle towards Sam. 'Even those ambulance-chasing bastards are doing the same thing. You know the ones. A firm dealt with a case last year, a bus crash. By the time the claims people had been round the estate, two hundred people had been on that bus. They must have been hanging off the fucking roof. If someone crashes into you, take a picture, because by the time it gets to a claim, the other car will have been full. But the money keeps swirling. Insurance assessors, claims farmers, lawyers. Don't forget the lawyers. And when the damages cheque arrives, it's spent. The shops stay busy, the taxes get paid, the country stays afloat.'

Even Sam was smiling now. Jon had that knack. 'So I'm being patriotic?'

Jon shrugged. 'You're in it for the money, for the glory. For this,' and he waved his hand around, 'sitting in a pavement bar that can't decide if it's in Paris or Blackley, paying more for your beer because the girl who brings it to your table has got bouncy little tits and an arse you want to grab the next time she goes past.'

'You must have had a conscience once?' asked Alison.

Jon smiled at that. 'I watched them all walk free. Rapists, child-killers, robbers. All set free by some clever defence work, and the lawyers were the ones going home in the Mercs. Maybe I just thought it was my turn.' He raised his eyebrows. 'Just take the cheque, Sam.'

Bobby held my hand as I waited outside the police station for Laura.

It felt strange – his fingers were tiny in my palm – but nice, secure.

It had been an interesting afternoon. I had finished it off in Blackley library, trying to find out what I could about Luke King. It was a gamble, because if he was charged with murder then the story would die until the court case had finished, and by the time I could use it most of the hacks in London would have paid for the research, cued up old school friends to say how they always thought that things weren't quite right with him.

I needed Luke to be dropped out of it, and then find out why he was ever linked to it. There might be a bad rich-kid story in there.

Nothing came from a Google search, but the library had been quiet, just a few pensioners browsing the alcoves, and so I had a free run at the microfiche scans of the local paper. They were stored in boxes for each year, with a daily copy fitting onto one piece of film and sorted into individual months. I was able to go back eighteen months before I ran out of time, but there was nothing really to get excited about.

As I went through, the abduction stories became a constant headline. I became distracted, and printed off some of those stories to see if I had missed an angle.

I had seen the same image each time. A distraught mother, her features embattled, almost broken down by life, often alone. I wondered if the lack of interest for the first missing child was because of how they looked, in tracksuits and in poverty. No one asked the question about why the children had been out so late, but it was implicit in the tone of the pieces.

But when I got to the reunion pictures, the families looked different. The smiles were broad, the relief obvious, but there was something else. It looked like thanks for a second chance, and the hugs from their missing offspring looked special, as if they were the first they'd had for a long time.

I felt Bobby pull on my hand. As I looked up, I saw Laura. I felt my breath catch. Her dark hair bounced lightly as she walked, and I could see her dimples flash at me as she got nearer. I let go of Bobby and he ran towards her, and, as she picked him up to swing him round, I saw many emotions flicker across her eyes. Relief, happiness, sadness, guilt.

When she reached me she leaned across to peck me on the cheek, but she couldn't get close enough for Bobby leaping around. I made do with a smile.

'How was your day?'

Her smile faded. 'Varied, and not ended.'

'Made any progress?'

She shook her head and looked straight ahead. 'Let's eat,' she said, but she didn't look at me when she said it. 'Fancy pizza, Bobby?'

I looked down as Bobby grabbed my hand again, and he started to swing between us, his legs kicking up high, squealing and giggling. It seemed like pizza was fine, and I sensed Laura's mood brighten again.

We headed towards an old cobbled square, near to the legal quarter. As we got closer I saw Sam Nixon at a small steel table with Alison, the young lawyer from court earlier, and an older man in a suit and bright tie. It was packed at the end of the working day, somewhere for young suits to buy wine and talk loudly, laugh even louder, and watch the married ones shuffle towards their cars. It was different to the pub across the road, where skinny men in football shirts and grubby jeans drank out the day.

As we got closer, Sam Nixon looked up, and he appeared surprised. But I realised that he was looking at Laura.

'Good evening, Detective. End of a long day,' said Sam.

Laura slowed up and smiled.

'Hello, Mr Nixon.'

'Sam.'

'Okay, Sam,' she said, and smiled. 'How's young Mr King? Do you think he'll sleep easy?'

'I'm sure he will.'

Laura was about to walk on when Sam stopped her, his hand resting lightly on her forearm. 'Have you heard of Eric Randle?' he asked.

I thought that Sam's eyes looked worried. I glanced at Laura, but her gaze betrayed little.

'Why do you ask?' said Laura.

Sam shrugged. 'I can't say. Client confidentiality.'

I saw Laura's eyes flicker at that. She paused for a moment, and then said, 'Eric Randle discovered the body. He's the one who called it in.'

I looked down, tried not to take part in the conversation, but my mind couldn't help but process the details.

Sam began to shake his head, smiling to himself. 'At least that clears up one mystery,' he said. 'Thank you, detective,' and he raised his bottle in a salute.

I felt Bobby tug at me as Laura set off again.

'I'll catch you up,' I said.

Laura looked uncertain for a moment, and then she turned away with Bobby.

'How's your day been?' I asked Sam.

He looked up at me. 'Not a bad set-up there,' he said. 'She does the groundwork, you get the story.'

I started to say it wasn't like that, but then I realised that it was *just* like that.

'What about Eric Randle?' I asked, curious.

Sam looked at me for a moment, and then he pulled out a piece of paper from his pocket.

'He paints his dreams,' he said, throwing it onto the table. 'Just for a moment, I thought he was genuine.' He sighed and drained his beer. 'I'm going home.'

I picked up the piece of paper and looked at it. I took in the images, the flashes of colour, and then my eye was caught by the television, a flat screen mounted high behind the bar.

I pointed. 'Could I have your autograph on this before you leave?'

He followed my gaze. The TV showed an interview, two men standing in front of a statue. It was the one near the court. The interview was the pavement scene I had witnessed earlier, with Sam and Luke King. I looked down at the painting again. One of the images on it was like the picture now on the television screen. Eric Randle's painting had turned into real life.

I watched as Sam became transfixed by the television, and then I patted my pocket as I turned to walk away, where I had just put the painting handed to me by Sam.

Chapter Eighteen

Sam's house was in semi-darkness when he got home. He'd stayed out later than he intended.

It was a detached house, with a gravel drive and a neat lawn at the front. Bay windows jutted out from either side of a porch, and a double garage stopped anyone seeing round to the rear, to the long stretch of lawn and neat shrubs. It was a suburban dream, a long way from the place he had grown up in, a run-down council house with mould on the ceilings.

As he went in he could hear the television blaring, and as he looked down the hall he could see the flickering blues, the rest of the room in darkness.

He tried not to make too much noise. When he went into the living room he saw Helena asleep in the chair. There was an empty bottle of wine on the table next to her, near to a glass with a thin layer of red in the bottom. He hoped the bottle was her first, but these days he couldn't be sure.

He knelt down next to her. She was breathing softly, and her cheeks had a soft flush, the effects of wine and struggling all day with the children. He looked to the ceiling, towards his two boys in the rooms upstairs. They'd be asleep, another day when they hadn't seen him.

He moved some strands of hair that had been lying over Helena's face. Her skin felt soft and warm, and he gently ran his finger along her cheek. Being asleep took ten years off her, nearer to when they'd first met at university.

Being Harry's daughter had got Helena a rich accent and a private education, her teenage years spent at boarding school. She had liked Sam's rough edges, so different to the boys she had known when she was growing up. And Helena was a world away from the girls Sam had grown up with – bitter beyond their years, their youth and vitality obscured by teen pregnancy and hopelessness.

Harry hadn't been happy to see Sam arrive on the scene. He saw Sam for what he was: a rough kid aiming too high. As far as he was concerned, Helena was way too high for Sam. Maybe Harry saw in Sam too much of himself.

But Sam and Helena had stayed together, maybe because of Harry's protest, not in spite of it. They got their law degrees and went to the College of Law together. When they both emerged, Harry gave them both jobs, perhaps scared that Sam would get a job away from Lancashire and take Helena with him.

It backfired on him. Sam and Helena moved in together, and then Helena became pregnant just when she was starting to build her career. Zach came first, the wedding much later, followed by Henry. After that,

Helena gave up the law, time with her boys more important than anything her job could give her.

Sam leaned forward and kissed his wife on her forehead. He remembered their first kiss, her lips soft like rose petals, warm breath on an April midnight, tentative, careful. He remembered how she had looked the first time he saw her naked, on a sweltering summer night just before their exams, her skin soft, warm, her murmurs of pleasure like lullabies.

These days it seemed like they had forgotten how to know each other, kept together only by children and habit. They didn't speak much, just household conversations, and their infrequent lovemaking had become functional, empty.

Helena murmured and shuffled in the chair. He thought he saw her smile. He reached underneath her and picked her up, and as he stood she burrowed her head into his neck. She was light, had hung on to her slim frame, even after two children and a diet wrecked by booze. As he lifted her, he saw the second empty bottle tucked into the sofa. He sighed.

He took her upstairs and put her on the bed. As he looked down he was gripped by sadness. The girl he had fallen in love with had been happy, always smiling. Why had their life together turned out so different to how he had imagined it would?

He covered her over and kissed her on the cheek. 'I miss you,' he whispered.

He looked in on the boys. As always, they looked serene, their sheets pulled tight under their chins, their breaths soft and deep. He felt the ache he always felt when he hadn't seen them that day. But they had to live and suburban dreams cost money. A lot of money.

He thought back to Jon and what he had said earlier. Was it all just about the money? Had that been Sam's reason for going into law? He'd chosen criminal law because he could relate to the people, or so he told himself. His own upbringing hadn't been much different from his clients', on a concrete estate, brought up by his mother after his father chose booze over her. Sam had got lucky. His mother had been desperate for him to get away, to make a better life for himself than she had, and so had held down two jobs to keep him in education. But had he really chosen criminal law because he felt a bond? To his clients he was just another suit. Or was it because he was too different from those in the glamorous jobs, in corporate or banking law? Maybe he had never really escaped the estate.

He went back to the bedroom and lay down behind Helena, so that his arm rested on her. He closed his eyes. Perhaps tonight he'd actually sleep.

He was jolted awake by the ring of his mobile phone. He looked at the clock. Thirty minutes had gone by. He put his head back and thought about not answering, but as he let it ring Helena started to move.

He reached into his pocket and recognised the number. Blackley custody. Why hadn't they called the firm's out-of-hours number? Let a runner get out of bed.

He stepped out of the bedroom and answered the phone. Terry McKay had been arrested. And he was insistent that he had to see Sam.

Sam exhaled. He remembered how Terry had been earlier, drunk, aggressive. Sam thought about not going, Terry didn't deserve his time, and he was tired. But he knew he had no choice. His job had been his choice, and for as long as Terry McKay drank, there was money in him.

Sam closed the door and headed out.

Laura shushed me quiet as I passed her a glass of red wine. She had kicked off her shoes and was relaxing on the sofa. Bobby nestled in her arms, just drifting off to sleep.

I kissed her on the cheek, and I could smell Bobby, took in a deep breath of washed hair, that infant smell, the ultimate clean.

I flopped onto a beanbag, the last remnant of my bachelor furniture. It was still chaos inside the house. Boxes lined the walls, the contents still not unpacked, and most of Bobby's toys were piled in a corner. We hadn't done the territory thing yet, worked out whose favourite pictures were going on the wall, and which were going to be relegated to my study. I could guess the answer. Laura just hadn't told me yet.

'How is he?' I said, nodding towards Bobby.

Laura stroked his hair.

'He's been a good boy.' We were talking in whispers, letting Bobby fall into a deeper sleep before he was taken upstairs.

I smiled. 'He'll be fine. And how was your day?'

She closed her eyes. 'Too long.'

I took a drink and sat back, but then I remembered

something. 'Geoff called. He wants to know if he can have Bobby this weekend.'

Laura sighed. 'I'll think about it,' she said, and then hugged Bobby a little tighter. I could see worry in her eyes, that Bobby would become the object of a power struggle.

'I was near the station today,' I said casually.

Laura looked at me. She shook her head. 'Don't, Jack.'

I shrugged, tried to look innocent. 'What?'

She raised her glass, now empty, rather than answer. As the wine I poured glugged to the top of the glass, she said, 'No point in grilling me for news. I'm not going to say anything that isn't approved. We've got an unsolved murder and a team made out of those not good enough for the abduction cases. And we're no nearer to solving either.'

'Is that a quote?'

She drew a finger across her neck in a cutting motion. 'Off the record, journo.'

When I smiled, Laura said tensely, 'I mean it, Jack. Things are different now.'

'Why?'

Laura looked around the room. 'It looks sort of obvious. We live together now.'

'But it worked before.'

Laura shook her head. 'Before, well, we were just in contact when we felt like it, and most reporters have police contacts. This is different. They'll think it's pillow talk and I've worked hard for this.'

I knew she was right, and I knew how much she had

fought for her career. Her parents were good people, her father in the City, her mother doing voluntary work, but they thought Laura had been destined for better things. A lawyer. Doctor. But Laura wanted to do a job that excited her, and she had been right. She was a good cop.

'Okay,' I said, smiling in defeat. 'It'll be okay, you know.'

Laura looked quizzical. 'This,' I said, my eyes flitting around the room. 'Us, in the north. It'll work out.' I leaned down and kissed her on the top of her head. '*We'll* work out.'

Laura leaned back, closed her eyes. I scooped Bobby into my arms and made my way to the stairs.

He lay down next to the boy, a collection of blankets keeping him warm. He could feel the summer coming to an end. The walls became damp as the temperature dropped, the moisture dirty, making grey streaks around the room and the ceiling drip as the heat from the oil-lamp went upwards.

He shivered. The boy's breaths were inches from his face, soft flutters over his cheeks. He reached across and moved the boy's fringe out of his eyes.

'Nearly there,' he whispered, and then wrapped himself up in the blankets. 'New start in the morning. You'll see.'

He closed his eyes, felt the excitement in his stomach, sensed his pulse quicken as he thought of it. He almost laughed out loud. He wished he could tell people what he did, could see the gratitude in their eyes as he explained how he changed their lives, reminded them about loving, about caring. The ones affected would know, but he knew that not everyone understood.

He settled down and tried to get some sleep. They had an early start.

Chapter Nineteen

I was alone downstairs, surrounded by papers, Laura asleep upstairs. The radio was on, just a soft background noise. I'd been using the internet to research Eric Randle, and the results were now spread over the table, a cold beer acting as a paperweight. In the middle of all of it was Eric's painting.

I felt frustrated. I had spent the day hunting a story on Jess Goldie's murder, but now it felt like I had pieces of two but not much of either. Luke King's arrest had been promising, but then it went cold when he was released. Anything more I could have got was lost when I was sidetracked by Randle, the story of a man who discovered a body, who then painted it and passed it off as prophecy.

I thought I heard a creak and glanced towards the ceiling. I hadn't shown the painting to Laura. I was worried that she would think I was working against her. When I was working, I had to be the journalist, not the copper's mole.

I picked up the painting. I knew from the media whispers that Jess had been found strangled, and that her eyes and tongue had been taken. That could match the painting. The eyes were crossed through – clear symbolism – but it could mean many things. I had seen the picture of Jess released to the media, small and demure, with a shy smile and straight dark hair, bookish and awkward. The figure in the painting was indistinct, lacking in detail. That was the trouble with the premonition business: it takes a maybe and turns it into a definite.

But what about the image of Sam Nixon being interviewed alongside Luke King? Was that a coincidence too far?

And there was a connection. Eric Randle had found the body in the picture, and Luke King had been arrested for the murder.

I took a mouthful of beer. I didn't have to prove it was true. All that mattered was whether it was a good story. It was certainly interesting. But I wanted to write the truth, as much as I was able. If my name was the byline, I needed to justify what I had written.

I leaned forward and began to move the papers around. For all the benefits of the internet, nothing seemed quite the same unless it was on paper and in my hand.

I had Googled Eric's name and found a lot of matches. One was a mathematics professor from a university in Southampton, and another an author of a book on the history of Weybridge. But as I scrolled through, I began to pick up more relevant hits.

The Eric Randle I was looking for came up first on dream sites. I should have expected that. But it seemed that Eric came towards the novelty end of the spectrum.

The serious stuff came first, Freud and Jung. It seemed like Freud never got past the sexual, trains in tunnels, junior school metaphors like that. Jung got nearer to the current scientific view, that dreams were the mind's way of sorting its problems, that when we wake up our minds throw all of our thoughts together into a jumble, and we remember them because they are our waking thoughts.

But if that was the case, just a subconscious spring clean, then how could Eric Randle dream of the future and get it right?

As I flicked through the scattered papers, it seemed like the whole dream scene had been hijacked by paranormal cranks and mystics. I could buy sleep supplements to make my dreams more vivid, or so the advert said, or I could learn techniques on how to remember dreams, because most of the ones I had were forgotten within a couple of minutes. But could I find a way to predict the future?

I saw the term 'quantum physics' used a lot. I didn't fully understand it – the theory that everything exists all at the same time, so that visions of the future were really just insights into another plane of reality – but I didn't buy it; it seemed like real science had been used to dress up crackpot theories.

But it was in these sites that Eric Randle's name had started to appear: just small articles, written by people who wanted to believe in him.

I drained the beer bottle and stretched, let the soft flutters coming out of the radio soothe me, and wondered whether I was wasting my time. The police suspected Eric Randle, I had guessed that much, and if he was charged with an offence, sub judice would keep the detail out of the papers for months. But still I was drawn to it.

There was a whole scene out there that I realised I knew nothing about. It was an industry, a belief, many would say a proven truth, and I realised that Eric Randle was far from unique. Precognition was the scientific word for it, direct knowledge of the future obtained through extra-sensory means, mostly through dreams. It had even bagged an American president. Not long before his death, Abraham Lincoln dreamt that he came across a guard of honour in the East Room of the White House, standing to attention around a corpse on a raised platform, wrapped up in funeral vestments. When he asked who was dead, he was told that it was the President, and that he had been assassinated.

I went back to the computer and carried on scouring the web. It seemed like the supply of dream sites was endless. Dream submission sites, analysis sites, premonition sites . . . And every so often Eric Randle's name would appear. He had been painting his dreams for years, and people all over the world, it seemed, were interested in him.

Then I found something.

Tyrone Tyler had been the first boy to go missing in Blackley, right at the start of the summer. The earliest pleas to find him got plenty of internet coverage, and one of the articles mentioned Eric Randle, a local psychic who pledged to use his talent to find Tyrone.

Now I'd heard his name come up in two of the local

big stories. As tiredness took over, I knew what I had to do in the morning: seek out Eric Randle.

Terry McKay was already in the glass booth when Sam was shown through to him.

Blackley police put prisoners on the other side of a glass screen, with just tiny holes to talk through. Sam wasn't sure if it was to stop lawyers passing things over or so that the police could listen to lawyers shouting their advice.

Sam tried to look friendlier than he felt and asked Terry if he knew why he had been locked up.

'Cos I smashed a fuckin' window.' His voice was slurred, his eyelids heavy, but Sam knew that Terry's drunkenness wouldn't be enough to get him an acquittal.

'Why did you smash a window, Terry?' Sam rubbed his eyes as he asked the question. He needed sleep. He checked his watch. It was close to midnight.

Terry nodded gently. He began to smile, a slow, hostile smile.

'Because I wanted to speak to you,' he said. 'Alone.'

Sam exhaled. 'You could have made an appointment,' he said.

Terry shook his head and glared at Sam. 'Can't do that. Harry Parsons won't let me.'

'What, Harry won't let you into the office?'

Terry nodded, still glaring.

Sam knew that the local drunks and real down-at-heel junkies were sometimes thrown out when they came into the office begging for money. Client care could only go so far.

'You can come to the office, okay, so if that's what this is about, let's get on with it and go home.' Sam was watching him all the time, not making notes. He noticed the look in Terry's eyes come alive.

'You were with Jimmy King's boy today,' Terry said quietly, deliberately, his voice becoming clear.

Sam felt his lips twitch. 'You know I can't talk about other clients,' he said quietly. 'I wouldn't talk about *you*. It's the rules.'

'But *I'm* talking about me.' He dipped his head towards the holes in the glass. 'Jimmy King owes me, and so does Harry fucking Parsons. Owes me big.'

'Owes you for what?'

Terry jabbed the glass with his fingers. The fingertips were black with grime, the nails brown with nicotine.

'He owes me for the last two years of my life, and he won't pay.'

Sam felt his interest dip, the interview sounding like a complaint that was too old to worry about.

'Let's get on with this, or I'm going home and you can do the interview on your own. I'm sure Harry did his best. If you've got a complaint, we have procedures.'

Terry leaped to his feet, the chair clattering onto the floor behind him.

'That fucker ruined my life,' he shouted. 'Everywhere I go, they call me a rapist, a killer, a beast, and I've done nothing wrong! That fucker promised to pay me, and he hasn't. All my old friends, they won't talk to me. The police bully me all the time, always checking up on me, watching me whenever I go for a sleep somewhere.'

'And who is the "fucker"? Harry Parsons or Jimmy King?'

Terry laughed, but it was rich with bitterness. 'Both.'

'So you got me down here just so you can tell me that you hate my boss?' Sam stood up as if to go. 'You're wasting my time, Terry.'

'You fucking sit down!' He was shouting, banging on the glass.

Sam paused and turned round to listen.

'You tell Harry and that fucking King I want my money.'

'You're not going to get any money from Harry. Don't do the crime, and all that shit, Terry. See you. I'm going home.'

'I didn't *do* the crime,' Terry said in a snarl, spittle peppering the glass.

Not another convicted innocent, Sam thought, and sighed. He turned back. 'Just tell me, Terry, quickly, before I go, why Harry owes you money.'

He simmered for a few seconds, and then he whispered, 'Harry told me that I'd get five grand if I lied about the person who attacked that girl.'

'Which girl?'

'A couple of years ago. A nice girl, so the police said, walking home from work. Someone dragged her into the church grounds and strangled her.'

Sam remembered the case, but he couldn't remember Terry McKay being dragged into it. It was all over the papers for a couple of weeks, but then the story had died away, just another lost victim.

'So why were you involved?'

'Because someone gave me a purse, told me that they had found it and that I could get a reward.' Terry sat down. 'I took the cash and threw the purse away. I sold the credit cards on. Someone used them, and when they were caught, the trail came back to me. And then the purse was found. My prints were on it.'

'But they didn't charge you with the murder?'

Terry shook his head, his mouth set hard.

'They wanted to, but all they had was the purse.'

'So why does this involve Harry and Jimmy King?'

'Because when I told the police who had given me the purse, I lied about it. I told them it was a Paki.' He looked at me, direct. 'But it wasn't. It was no Paki.'

Sam sat back down again. 'Why did you lie?' asked Sam tentatively. He had a feeling he was about to hear something he didn't want to.

Terry wiped his mouth on his hands, looking suddenly nervous.

'Harry Parsons told me to, when he came down here.'

'Harry did what?' That took Sam by surprise. Harry never went to the police station. He employed people to do that.

'He told me that if I lied about it, I'd get five grand. Five fucking grand.'

'I don't believe you,' said Sam.

Terry banged his fist on the table again. 'You check it out,' he shouted. 'Five thousand pounds. Never saw a fucking penny.' He pointed. 'He owes me money, and I want it.' Sam thought he could see tears in Terry's eyes. 'Do you know what I could have done with that money? I could have made a brand-new start.'

Sam knew there would be no new start. Terry lived in the Orchard Hotel, but it was no country idyll, more of a fifteen-room hovel in the red-light area, occupied by the town drunks. The owner charged as much as the state would pay, provided basic furniture and a bed, and turned a blind eye when the residents spent the evenings drinking stolen booze in the lounge. In return, the residents ignored the damp in the carpets and the mould on the walls. No amount of money would have changed that. It would have gone down his throat. Nowhere else.

'So you let a murderer go free for the promise of five grand?' Sam couldn't hide the contempt in his voice.

Terry laughed, but Sam could hear the scorn wrapped up in it. 'Yeah, I know you charge more than that when you do it.'

Good shot, thought Sam. Straight to the conscience.

'So who was the person who gave you the purse?'

Terry leaned forward so that his mouth was right up to the glass. His lips looked dry, the skin pointing flakes towards the glass, a white line of dry spittle marking them out.

'It was the King boy,' he said. 'The one you were with this morning, looking all proud in his suit.'

'Luke King?'

Terry nodded. 'Did someone else die?' he asked.

Sam exhaled. The day was getting worse. His job was not to care.

But Sam cared, and that had always been his problem. Now Luke King was linked to two murders, and he knew about both. 'Let's get you out of here first,' said Sam, 'and then we'll talk about how to get you your five grand.'

Terry eyed him with suspicion.

'No one saw you smash the window,' Sam continued. 'Just make no comment to any questions.'

'What about forensics?'

'What, glass samples for analysis?' Sam shook his head. He knew there would be fragments from the window on Terry's clothes, but the police were unlikely to pay for a forensic report in a simple damage case. 'We'll worry about how strong the case is if you get charged. If you admit it, you're guilty. If there's forensic, you're guilty. If you keep your mouth shut, you might just have your day. I reckon you're due one.'

Terry started to calm down. And if Sam could get them to start the interview soon, there was a chance he'd be home before sunrise. Just in time to leave for work.

Then something occurred to him.

'Why me, Terry? What do you expect me to do?'

Terry shook his head. 'Nothing.' Then he smiled, a warm line of brown teeth. 'I just wanted to warn you.'

'Warn me?'

'Yeah, warn you. I saw you with him today and he's trouble.' He shrugged. 'You've always been all right with me. Just be careful.'

Sam scratched his head, almost laughed. It seemed like everyone in Blackley was worried for him.

Chapter Twenty

He shivered as dawn came around. The morning chill had a sharper kick than usual.

He sheltered under blankets, and as he tried to get warm he looked at his hands, the tips of his fingers grey and cold. They looked thin, he thought, the skin sharp and raw. Healing hands. He needed to take greater care of them. He saw a fly buzz around in the light from the oil-lamp in the corner of the room and then come towards him. He swatted at it, felt it bounce off his knuckles.

He groaned as he sat up. The room swayed for a few seconds, but when it righted itself, he rubbed his face, felt his stubble, and then brought the oil-lamp closer. He checked his watch. They would be leaving soon.

He looked over at the boy, his breaths coming out as thin vapour trails. He reached out and stroked the boy's cheek. It felt cold, soft. He smiled down at the boy and then stood up. His back ached, and he groaned as he stretched.

He started to pace. He tried to shake himself alert. He needed to eat. He felt weak, and now was not the time for lapses of concentration.

His thoughts stopped dead when he thought he heard the boy sigh. He went over to him again and checked his pulse. There was a quickening. When he opened the boy's eye, the pupil reacted more quickly.

He felt a moment of panic. He had to act quickly. The boy was coming round.

Sam woke up gasping, his forehead damp. He looked around frantically and took in the sight of his bedroom, Helena asleep beside him. He flopped back onto the bed, his chest heaving.

It was the dream again, the same one as always. It came in flashes. He was running through a building, the walls dirty, the rooms empty, his head filled with echoes. He was tired, but still he kept running, through doors, his quarry always running through the opposite door. He was panicking but he didn't know why. He was just chasing something he couldn't catch, trying to escape from something behind him. And then he was falling.

He looked at the clock, five thirty. Helena had hardly moved. He stared at the ceiling, tried to calm himself down, but he could feel his heart beating fast. His eyes felt heavy, the skin under them sore from lack of sleep, but he knew that he wouldn't go back to sleep.

He got up and crept downstairs, trying not to wake anyone. He made a coffee and felt some of the tiredness lift, but he knew it wouldn't last. The dream had been waking him for weeks. Not every night, but more than was good for him, so that he yearned for sleep during the day. As he sipped his coffee, Terry McKay came back to him.

Clients never blamed themselves. Sam knew that. It was either the police, or the judge, or the lawyer who prepared the case.

But this was something different. Terry was genuinely angry, resentful. Terry was saying that his father-in-law was involved in a conspiracy to conceal a murder. He could accept that Terry had been set up, an easy fall guy, some drunk sleeping off a bottle nearby, but by Harry Parsons? Never. Harry's mantra had always been the same: be ruthless, but be honest.

But Sam couldn't shake it off, because Terry had blamed Luke King, and Sam knew something about Luke that Terry didn't.

He couldn't speak to Terry for a few hours yet, even if he had wanted to. There had been a warrant for his arrest as they went to leave, for non-payment of fines. He was staying in the cells until morning.

Sam looked in on Helena before he left. Terry had been talking about *her* father, the grandfather of *his* children. Helena murmured and pulled the sheets down. Sam watched her breasts rise and fall and wished he could just climb back in with her. But he knew what would happen: he would be pushed away.

As he clicked the front door shut and blipped off the car alarm, Sam knew he would be looking further into what Terry McKay had said. He just didn't know why.

I was up first, toasting bagels and filling a tray with a teapot and glass of orange juice. The air smelled of warm butter. Bobby watched me as he worked his way through a bowl of Ricicles. I winked at him. 'Do you think Mummy will like this?'

He smiled at me, his eyes still sleepy. 'How do you do that?'

'Do what?'

'Blink with one eye.'

I raised my eyebrows. 'Practice,' I said, full of adult mystery, and took the tray upstairs.

Laura murmured when I opened the bedroom door. The sunlight was streaming through the curtains, giving the room a hazy look.

'Good morning,' I said. 'Thought you might like a pick-me-up.'

She smiled, her eyes still half-closed. 'You mean a get-me-up,' she drawled, and then pulled the sheets back. 'You could get in.'

I sighed, seeing her naked body against the sheets, long and slender, but as I leaned towards her I put the tray there instead. 'Bobby's downstairs.'

She groaned and turned over. 'Just food then.'

I started to pull on my shoes. 'I've got to go out,' I said. 'Can you take Bobby to school?'

She sat up and wiped her eyes. 'Of course.' She leaned forward and wrapped her arms around my neck. I could smell the sleep on her. 'Where are you going?'

'Just a feature I'm working on.'

'Can't you tell me?'

I lifted her arms from me, and then kissed her on the nose. 'Confidential,' I whispered.

She smiled as I left the bedroom. I skipped downstairs,

and when I headed for the front door, I saw Bobby blinking hard.

'Just one eye,' I shouted.

'I can't,' came the shout back.

'Keep trying!' I was still smiling as I climbed into my car.

Chapter Twenty-one

Sam was at his desk, the first to arrive, as ever, but he couldn't work. Every time he thought of something to do, his mind kept on going back to Terry McKay.

McKay was a drunk. McKay was a thief. McKay was dishonest. No prosecutor would build a case based on his evidence.

Sam sat poised with his hand on top of a file that needed work. The rest of the office was in darkness, the computer monitors blacked out, the soft tick of the clock in reception the only sound in the building. Sam wasn't paid to care. Ignore Terry McKay, he told himself. He should process the damn police-station file and do some billable hours at his desk. His job was not to investigate. His job was to earn money for Parsons & Co.

He rubbed his cheeks. He hadn't shaved that morning, hadn't wanted to wake Helena. His second coffee of the day was on his desk. He felt anxious, edgy, but maybe it was the caffeine.

He powered up the computer, the terminal clicking and stuttering, until the XP logo flashed up followed by the blue desktop, the screen uncluttered, just a few icons aside from the standard Internet Explorer and My Documents. Lawtel, Criminal Law Weekly, Westlaw, widely used legal search engines providing access to the latest authorities. Being a lawyer wasn't always a huge skill. It was often just about knowing where to look for the answers.

Sam clicked on the PMS icon, the Practice Management System. It threw up the server page, and in the middle was a search bar. He looked at the file in his hand, ready to type in the name, when he paused. He took a gulp of coffee. He typed in Terry McKay instead and pressed return.

A list came up. Terry wasn't the only McKay to use Parsons, but when Sam clicked on Terry's client number, it was obvious that Terry was the main one.

The entries were all repeat nuisance offences. Drunk and disorderly, damage, minor public order offences, thefts from shops. It was the routine work that provided cash flow. Offend, arrest, court, guilty, bill. Nice and regular, and Terry McKay had troubled the courts and police for fifteen years. The last five of them were recorded on the computer.

And then Sam saw it, standing out above the rest of his skirmishes. A murder, from two years ago.

Sam made a note of the reference number and the storage location and headed out of the room.

The dead files were stored in the dark basement in order of month of destruction and then reference number, lined up in red jackets on metal shelves. They gathered dust and then they were shredded as soon as the Law Society rules allowed. A marker moved along every month, showing the next series of files for destruction.

He had to fumble for the light switch at first, his shoes loud as they shuffled on the concrete floor. The strip lighting flickered into life, and then as he searched his nose began to itch, his hands throwing up dust. It only took him a few minutes to find the file, and he was soon back at his desk, the file lying on top, wiping his hands clean on his handkerchief.

He looked at the cover for a few minutes, a red front with Parsons & Co across the top. He was nervous about opening it; Terry McKay's anger was still fresh in his mind. But then he realised the obvious: that he wouldn't know the contents if he didn't open the cover.

He turned the cover slowly, and the familiar look of a police-station attendance sheet was the first thing he saw, all made out in Harry's neat script. It was a form that all lawyers had to complete, just so that they could satisfy the bureaucrats that they had asked all the right questions. It didn't seem to matter whether or not the right advice was given.

That shocked Sam. Terry had been right; it had been Harry who had gone to the police station. But Harry hadn't been for years. What made this case so special?

As he went through the form, Sam read a story just like Terry had told him the night before. He had been drinking and was sleeping it off somewhere when he was approached by a man. He was given a purse so that he could claim the reward. Terry said yes, just because you didn't say no to much when you were down to sleeping off booze in parks. Even when drunk, Terry could still plan how to pay for his next bottle. He described the man as an Asian man in his thirties, stocky build and a scruffy moustache. That was as far as the description went.

It seemed that Terry had said nothing in his police interview, just relied on a pre-prepared written statement that said all he had told Sam the night before, except that the attacker was described as Asian not 'Paki'.

Terry McKay was locked up for thirty hours before he was eventually released. The police got an extension, were getting ready to charge, but then the prosecution said that they wouldn't run it. The whole case was based on possession of a portable item: the purse. Terry went from suspect to witness, and the murderer was never caught.

Sam put the file down. He didn't know what to make of it all. The story Terry had told him was contained in the papers he'd just read. There was nothing to back up Terry's revised story other than his word. And the word of Terry McKay wasn't worth a great deal.

But then Sam looked at the file again. There was something about it that looked strange. He went through the pages again. There was the front sheet, the one that contained all of Terry's personal details. Then there was a middle page, which contained Terry's story. On the back page, there was space for signature, and a box underneath to write in the attendance times.

Then he spotted it.

The middle page looked different. The paper was brighter, cleaner. The attendance sheets came as a three-page pack, stapled together. They shouldn't be different colours. And the ink looked different, the blue slightly darker.

Sam tilted the back page to the light coming in from the window, tried to see if he could spot the indentation of what had been written on the middle page, just to see if they were different. He thought he could see something, tiny grooves, but he couldn't make out what they said.

Sam remembered the look in Terry's eyes, the anger, the certainty. Clients lied, they lied all the time, but he could usually tell. Sam had believed Terry.

Had Harry re-written Terry's instructions? The pre-prepared statement was the easy part. Harry would have read that out, with the barest of detail, and from then on Terry would have made no comment to the questions. It was the re-written sheet that contained the detail, the words which would protect Luke if Terry tried to go back on the story and help the police.

As Sam looked at the page, saw how Harry's neat script told a coherent tale, he realised that Harry could have done just that. Which meant that his father-in-law had bribed a drunk to cover up a murder.

Chapter Twenty-two

The first part of my journey from Turners Fold was through green fields, the early-morning mist sitting between the trees, picking out the hills like paper cutouts. By the time I reached Blackley the dawn light was making the copper dome of a local mosque blink flashes of light over the terraced streets.

I skirted the town centre, and headed towards a complex of flats just where the ring road made the houses dirty. I drove around a few streets and saw the same thing, decay, until eventually I came across a collection of u-shaped blocks, three storeys high, with balconies running around the two upper floors. Some of the windows were boarded up, and others were covered by metal grilles. I could spot the drug dealers: they had metal doors held fast by large locks. It marked them out, but stopped a quick entry and gave them a tactical advantage. I spotted a couple of men hanging around between the blocks, eastern European, dark-haired and twitchy. I knew how it worked with the dealers: they preyed on the needy to do the street stuff, usually asylum seekers, and paid young mothers a small rent to store the drugs in their lofts. The police swept up the street dealers, but every time they raided those higher in the chain they came back empty.

I eventually found the address I was looking for and parked next to a basketball court. The roads were starting to get busy with cars, people from other parts of Blackley heading into work.

I looked again at the cutting that had brought me to this address. It was the one I had seen the night before. Darlene Tyler's son, Tyrone, had been the first boy to go missing during the summer. He had been playing with his friends but became separated. His friends wouldn't say much about what they had been doing, and for ten days the local paper was filled with images of Darlene looking distraught.

But that wasn't why I was here. I was at her address because in one of the pictures there had been an old man, looking nervous, as if he was avoiding the gaze of the camera. There was a sidebar on him, and it was Eric Randle, described as a local psychic trying to help the family.

I folded the cutting and put it in my pocket. Eric Randle's name had cropped up in the two biggest stories in Blackley. The town wasn't big, but it wasn't *that* small either.

Darlene's home was on the first floor and in the middle of a long balcony. The stairs didn't smell good, but I had been to worse places in London. At least I didn't need a lift.

When I reached the door, I listened for a few seconds. I could hear the sound of laughter inside. I was about to knock when the door was flung open and a young teenage boy ran past me.

As I watched him go, I saw that he was smiling,

turning round to wave, his school bag over his shoulder. I looked back towards the doorway and saw a woman in front of me. Darlene Tyler.

As Tyrone disappeared down a stairway, she turned to look at me. She was suspicious straightaway.

I smiled and held out my press card.

'Hello, I'm Jack Garrett, I'm a reporter. I'd like to talk, if you have a moment?'

At first I thought she was going to tell me to get lost, but instead asked me to come in. We walked along a small hallway, marked out by a 'murder carpet', as the police call them, of patterned brown swirls. Most dead bodies are found on carpets like that.

As we got into her living room, she turned to me and smiled. 'I didn't used to like the press – vultures, or so my dad used to say. But,' and then her face softened, her eyes watered, 'they helped me get my Tyrone back, so I suppose I owe you one.' She lit a cigarette. 'What do you want to know?' she asked, blowing smoke out of the side of her mouth.

As I thought about how to start, my eyes took in the details of her lounge. Whether the article needed any social commentary depended on who bought it, so it was better to have it and not need it. There were some trophies on the mantelpiece, darts tournaments, and on the wall were two Samurai swords, crossed over one another. The settee looked threadbare on the arms, and the carpet looked worn near the large television, gleaming silver in the corner of the room.

But the place looked clean. Darlene looked after her home the best she could.

'I was reading some press clippings from when Tyrone was missing,' I said, 'and I wondered if you would mind giving me an update.'

'What sort of update?'

'Just how your life has been since you got Tyrone back.'

Darlene sat down and started to tell me, and I let her. The art is to get people talking. The right talk can come later.

Darlene told me how she lived alone with Tyrone, how his father had gone to prison a few years earlier. Darlene had two jobs, cleaning work in a couple of the town-centre pubs, and then bar work in the evenings.

'I won't go on benefits,' she said determinedly. 'I pay my way.'

'How did Tyrone fit in with your jobs?'

Darlene took a hard pull on her cigarette.

'He didn't,' she said. 'And that's why he went wrong.' She shook her head and looked down. 'I should have been there for him, but I wasn't. I trusted him to go to school on his own, but he didn't. I trusted him to stay in, but he went out. You've seen what it's like round here. It's hard enough when you try to do the right things. To do the wrong things round here, well, it's always easy.'

She wiped her eye, a stubby nicotine finger taking away the tears.

'I let him down,' she continued, her voice breaking. 'I know that now, but I wanted to give him the same things his friends had. I got it wrong, because all he really wanted was for me to be home.'

'So you don't have two jobs any more?'

Darlene shook her head. 'I work for an agency now. They get me jobs when they can, just odd days in different places, but only ever during the day. I'm home when Tyrone is. It's like he's learned how to smile again. And he's going to school every day,' she added proudly.

I watched her and I sensed an uncomfortable thought in her, that Tyrone's abduction had been the thing that had saved him. And her. It had given them a second chance.

'What can you tell me about Eric Randle?' I asked.

She stopped smiling, her expression growing uncertain.

'He was an oddball,' she said. 'Came round and told me about how he had dreams and he could find people – people who were missing.'

'Did you pay any attention to him?'

She stubbed out her cigarette in an old Boddingtons ashtray. 'Not really, but you've got to try everything, haven't you?'

'I saw the article with you and Eric in it. He seemed like he was pretty involved.'

She scowled. 'Once Tyrone was found, he stopped coming round.'

'Sam?'

Sam opened his eyes. He was in his office. He looked around quickly, checked his watch. How long had he been asleep?

It was Alison. He looked down at himself. His shirt was dirty from the archive cellar and he looked un-usually dishevelled.

He nodded. 'Sorry. Was at the nick late last night.'

'Terry McKay?'

He was about to respond, but then stopped himself. 'How did you know?'

Alison went red and looked away. 'I heard one of the clerks mention him. Why? Is he a problem?'

Sam tried to gauge whether she was testing him, fishing for something. 'No,' he said eventually, watching her carefully, 'he's just a town-centre drunk. But he pays the bills.' He looked towards the open court diary on the corner of his desk. 'What have you got today?'

Alison smiled, and looked more relaxed. 'A flasher. Spends his afternoons dressed in bras and panties, masturbating at his window.'

Sam smiled with her. 'What's the defence?'

Alison shrugged. 'He told me that if a man can't play with himself in his own home, where can he?'

'What about the bras and panties?'

'He's trying not to think about that. And neither am I.'

'Does he look the sort?'

Alison nodded. 'Oh yes. Overweight, single, milk-bottle glasses.'

'Trousers too short?'

'I could see nearly all of his white socks. I reckon he's got enough porn to make him a champion arm-wrestler.' She held a hand up. 'Don't wish me luck. Just pray that I don't start laughing.'

Sam laughed. Alison didn't look like the sort of woman to be having this conversation.

'Are you okay with doing this sort of case? I mean, don't you find it embarrassing?'

She blushed a little. 'I try not to think about it. I've banned my mum from ever coming to court. And I think the defence will sound better coming from a woman. You know, if it's not a problem for me, then why should it be a problem for anyone else?'

Sam nodded approvingly. She was already thinking like a lawyer.

He picked up the court diary.

'What are you doing?' she asked.

Sam had decided to handle the overnight work. There wasn't much in. A couple of people had breached their bail conditions, some warrants for people who had missed their court appearances.

But it was Terry McKay who was drawing him to the overnight work. Sam still had the old file in front of him, and he felt compelled to talk to him again.

'Just the cells,' said Sam. 'They need emptying.'

Sam was about to say something else when he saw Alison's eyes move to the door. It was Harry.

Harry flickered a smile, a momentary thing. 'Morning. If I might just have a word with Sam.' He kept his eyes on Sam all the time.

Alison nodded. Sam wondered if he saw something, an acknowledgement, a sign. He tried to clear his mind. He was in danger of becoming paranoid.

When they were alone together, Sam gestured to a spare seat.

'I'll stand,' replied Harry, and then, 'Are you going to court like that? You look a mess.'

Sam glanced down at himself, saw the dirt and creases on his shirt. Before he could respond, Harry said, 'I was

151

checking the diary on the computer and I saw Terry McKay in there.'

'He was locked up last night,' Sam said. 'He smashed a window and asked for me. He's been kept in because of an old fines warrant.'

'So why are we doing it? We won't get paid for a fines warrant.'

'Goodwill.' Sam looked Harry in the eyes so that he could check for a reaction. 'After all,' he said mildly, 'next time, he might kill someone.'

From the twitch of his eyes, the quick blink, Sam knew he had hit home. He felt anger start to simmer. 'I'm over there on something else, so I'll soak it up in that bill.'

Harry said nothing for a few seconds, and then he nodded and turned to leave the room.

As Sam listened to Harry's footsteps receding down the hall he saw Alison walk quickly past. She had been listening.

He was about to go after her when his phone rang. It was reception. Eric Randle was downstairs again.

When she had first arrived in Lancashire, Laura had enjoyed the drive to work.

Rush hour in London had been a crawl and snarl, one long queue between traffic lights, barely faster than walking. Using the tube had been quicker, but she had stood at the edge of a platform too many times with a crowd behind her, just one surge from a trip onto the tracks, or felt hands on her rear too many times to be a coincidence. Sometimes it was worse than hands, the excitement of nearby commuters pushing into her as the train rocked and rumbled.

It was different this morning. Jack was interested in the Goldie murder, and that made her nervous. She knew that Jack had to write – they needed the money, they couldn't live on her salary alone – but she still had her *own* job to think about. If Egan suspected that her sweet nothings were about work, her move north would be much shorter than she'd planned.

She spotted Bobby in the rear-view mirror, looking suddenly grown up in the blue sweatshirt and grey trousers of his school uniform. That outfit had wiped out all those years of dependency and cuteness and replaced it with a boy going out to find his place in the world.

As he chattered in the back, telling Laura about the boys in his class, she noticed his accent, the chirp of the south. She wondered how long it would last. How would her ex-husband cope with a northern son? He was a proud Londoner, had talked about Saturdays at White Hart Lane with his boy. Was she being cruel taking Bobby away from all that?

She had little traffic to cope with, and the views as she drove, the green of the Ribble Valley, the fringes of trees, reminded her why she had moved to Lancashire. The town of Turners Fold dipped in front of her, the lines of terraces different to the streets from her own childhood. The doors opened straight onto the street, and they all ran towards the town, down steep hills, marking out the route to work for the cotton workers of years gone by. Now they were starter homes, the first step on the ladder before people graduated to the open-plan estates on the edges of the town.

As they passed Victoria Park, a small collection of large trees which horseshoed around sloping grass, cut neat, broken by flowerbeds, Bobby shouted, 'What's that boy doing in the flowers?'

Laura's eyes flicked to the mirror, and noticed Bobby look back towards the park.

'What boy?'

Bobby turned back. 'There was a boy, lying down near the flowers.'

'What was he doing?'

Bobby shrugged. 'Don't know.' His interest had already waned.

Laura drove on for another few seconds, but then she slowed down, her tyres scraping against the kerb as she stopped.

'You're not messing around, are you?'

Bobby shook his head. 'I saw him.'

She checked her watch. She was already pushing her goodwill at the station to be taking Bobby to school, everyone working long hours on both cases.

She had no choice, she knew that.

She turned around and drove back towards the park. She stopped by the war memorial, a stone needle on a wide plinth etched with the names of the fallen, and looked among the green.

She couldn't see anything at first, just grass and trees and coloured dots of flowers, but then one of the colours slowly moved.

She stepped out of her car, locking it to keep Bobby

154

safe, and began to walk slowly towards the moving shape. Then, as she got nearer, she started to run. It was a boy, around twelve years old, dressed in just T-shirt and tracksuit bottoms. He looked like he was just waking up. But what was he doing there?

She knelt down, tried to see if he was injured. Then, as he turned over, she saw his face and recognised him.

It was Connor Crabtree, the boy who had been missing for a week. As he rolled over, something slipped out of his pocket onto the grass. It was a business card, showing large hands over a small head, protective, healing. The same as the ones found with all the other boys.

She glanced over to her car. Bobby had his face pressed against the window, looking out.

Laura reached for her phone and dialled 999. Bobby was going to be late for school.

Chapter Twenty-three

I sat in my car and looked at the piece of paper in my hand, the painting given to me by Sam Nixon the day before. Eric Randle painted dreams, he had said. Maybe he did, maybe he didn't, but I got the sense that Randle was getting himself involved in the case, and that usually meant something. He'd found Jess Goldie's body and then bothered the lawyer acting for the first suspect. He had involved himself with Darlene Tyler. People like that don't give up.

I needed to speak to him. What type of feature depended on his co-operation, but I knew one thing: I was going to write it.

So I waited in my car in a parking slot, just thirty minutes allowed, and kept watch for Nixon. Maybe he could provide the link.

I didn't have to wait long.

Sam bounded down the steps to the street, an old man shuffling behind him. I got just glimpses, the pavements busy with lawyers walking towards court, buff files tucked under their arms, weaving between builders and workmen eating breakfast from a sandwich bar, but I saw the old man produce a piece of paper.

I jumped out of my car and walked over to them. I heard Sam say to the old man, 'I've told you: this is not a legal problem.'

I thought Sam looked harassed, his voice tetchy. The old man looked disappointed.

'Hello, Mr Nixon,' I said.

He turned round and looked at me in exasperation. 'Here,' he said to the old man. 'The press are here. They'll listen to you.'

Sam thrust a piece of paper back into the old man's hands and walked away, bumping into my shoulder as he went.

I looked at the old man and knew straightaway that I was looking at Eric Randle. I recognised him from the Tyrone Tyler article.

I smiled to myself, unable to believe my luck. The old man looked forlorn as he stared down at whatever Sam had thrust back at him. I saw that his suit was shabby, cheap and grey, with the cloth worn around the pockets and shiny along the arms. He looked like he'd had a shave, though, judging from the pieces of tissue with dots of red stuck to his neck. The collar on his shirt was frayed, but he looked more like someone who had made a special effort than someone who didn't care.

He looked up as I stood in front of him, peering at me through thick lenses, the bridge of his glasses held together by clear tape.

'Hello, Mr Randle. I'm Jack Garrett.'

He shrank back, suddenly scared. 'How do you know my name?' He looked around and started to inch away along the pavement.

I did my best to look friendly. 'I heard about the poor woman you found yesterday. It must have been a terrible shock.'

Eric looked down and I saw his chin tremble. And I wondered if he was shivering. He wasn't wearing a coat and he looked like he was trying to stay warm. He was thin and frail.

'We could go somewhere,' I said. 'Get some breakfast maybe?' When he looked unsure, I added, 'On me.'

He stopped and gave me a thin smile, his eyes weak and yellow-tinged. 'I don't know you. Why should I trust you?'

I looked up towards the Parsons offices, at the gold-leaf letters on the windows. 'I know Sam Nixon.'

Eric nodded slowly, as if I had said enough, and then turned to walk in front of me. As I got alongside him, I tried to sound like I was making idle conversation.

'What's that in your hand?' I asked.

He looked at the paper as if he had forgotten it was there. 'It's just a painting.' His voice seemed quiet, unsure.

'Of what?'

There was a long silence and I didn't push him. Then he said quickly, 'I paint my dreams.'

I feigned surprise. 'That sounds interesting.'

He looked up at me, and his wariness started to fade. I pointed him into a café behind a Victorian shop-front, with sauce bottles on the table and stewed tea served in chipped white mugs. He looked hungrily at the menu, displayed on white plastic behind the counter, so I ordered two teas and a full English for Eric. I stayed silent as he ate, his eyes never leaving the plate, the beans and tomatoes mopped up by thick white bread, until eventually he pushed the plate away and adjusted his glasses. He looked sheepish, as if I had caught him at a weak moment.

'Why do you paint your dreams?'

He looked embarrassed. 'Because they come true.'

I laughed politely. 'If only we could *all* say that.'

He shook his head. 'No, not like that. These are bad dreams, and later on, they come true.' He licked his lips and rubbed his forehead. There was a film of sweat there.

'Why does that concern Sam Nixon?' I asked.

He studied me, as if he was trying to work out how much I knew.

Then he smiled properly, but I detected sadness, his eyes moist, and he looked away.

'He's in them,' he said quietly. 'In my dreams.'

I paused for a moment as I remembered Sam's re-action when he'd seen the television pictures, a replay of the painting he had given me.

'How did you know it was Sam?'

Eric stared blankly at me and said, 'I've seen him on the news before, on the court steps, things like that.'

'What was he doing in your dream?'

'I see him running,' Eric said, his nervousness dis-appearing, his eyes becoming more focused, direct.

'Through doors, one after the other. It's dark, but still he just keeps on going. He is panicking. I'm chasing him, running harder than I've run in years, but I can't catch him up. I'm screaming, screaming really hard, stop, stop, stop, but no one listens.' Eric banged his fist hard on the table, a flash of emotion, and his drink spilled onto the faux marble surface.

He looked up at me, panting, and then he wiped his mouth on a dirty white hanky he'd dragged out of his pocket.

'I'm scared, Mr Garrett,' he said.

'Scared of what?'

Eric gulped, his gaze flickering around the café. 'I don't know. Scared of what I see, I suppose. Of what I hear.'

'How long have you had these dreams?'

'For as long as I can remember. It was only when I started painting them that I realised they were coming true.'

As he spoke, he looked lost, bewildered.

'How long have you been dreaming about Sam?' I asked gently.

Eric exhaled and looked about us again. The tables around us were full, but no one was talking or smiling. They just stared into a dead space in front of them, as if this was just part of wishing the day away.

'A few months.'

'Why have you come forward now? Why not earlier?'

He swallowed. 'The dreams are brighter than before, noisier, more vivid.' He rubbed his chin. 'I'm scared to go to sleep now, but I always do – until I wake up shouting.'

'And Sam Nixon is in those dreams, when you wake up?'

He nodded. 'And I am too, but when I'm there, I always bolt awake, and I feel like I can't move, my stomach churning, my throat tight, like I can't breathe. I feel scared.'

'But you've had similar dreams before?'

He nodded. 'But not like this.'

'Why are they different?'

He adjusted his glasses again, a stalling tactic. 'They just are,' he said.

I was interested. Not because I believed what he was telling me, but because it was an interesting story. The truth is only ever a bonus.

'Sam Nixon won't listen?'

Eric shook his head. 'Most people don't.'

'I'll listen,' I said, my voice low, reassuring, 'and I'll write about it if you like. I'll tell the world about your dreams, and show them your paintings.'

Eric held up his hand. 'I've only got this one with me.'

I smiled and pulled out the piece of paper from the day before. 'And what about this one?'

He looked at my hand, and then at my face, and looked scared again.

I leaned forward. 'Don't worry. Sam gave it to me.' When he didn't answer, I said, 'So you drew a picture of Sam and Luke King in front of that statue. That doesn't prove anything.'

'It proves you recognised the picture,' he said.

That stalled me. I took a drink so I could think. 'You could have drawn that after seeing him being interviewed in the street,' I said. 'You could have guessed they would show it on TV later.'

'And what about Jess Goldie, the girl who was killed yesterday? She's in the picture.'

'You found her, Eric. You *saw* how she looked.'

He looked down. I knew more about him than he realised.

'How do I know you haven't seen those things and made up the pictures afterwards?' I pressed.

'You've got good contacts,' he snapped.

We considered each other for a while. 'I want to write about you. But if you'll let me, you've got to be honest with me.'

Eric swirled the tea around in his mug thoughtfully. 'I just want people to know that I'm telling the truth, and one day they will.'

I nodded towards the piece of paper in his hand. 'What did you paint?'

Eric passed it over.

As I unrolled it, I saw that the paint looked fresh, the colours bright. The main image was of a young boy. I couldn't make out his age, but he looked small, scared. He was pictured sitting in a park, a line of trees behind him, tall conifers, with small dots of colour denoting flowers peering through the green. There was a block in the background, like a square building, but everywhere else was just green.

I looked at Eric. 'When did you dream this?'

'This morning, in the early hours. It came in flashes, like when someone takes a picture. A bright flash, catching the boy like I've painted him. Nothing else.

I thought I could hear crying, but I couldn't tell where it was coming from.'

'I thought you had a dream about Sam Nixon.'

'I did, but I didn't paint it. I painted this and fell back asleep. *That's* when I dreamt of Sam.'

'But you didn't paint Sam?'

He shook his head. 'I was too frightened. I thought I would come and tell him about it first.'

I held up the painting. 'Can I keep this?'

Eric nodded grimly. 'Keep it somewhere safe. You might recognise the picture one day.'

I smiled my thanks. 'Tell me about yourself.'

And he did. He told me how he had grown up in Blackley, had worked as a hospital porter before he'd lost his job. He had a daughter, but she lived with her husband on the other side of Blackley. He wasn't very good at filling his days since his wife had died.

As he talked, I sensed how lonely he was, fearful at how his life was going to end. He must have had some hope at some point in his life. When he paused, I said, 'Tell me more about Jess.'

Eric's eyes narrowed and he looked down. 'I paint my dreams. Jess wrote hers down.'

'So who was she? What did she see?'

Eric sat back. I thought he was going to cry. He took a breath and composed himself.

'She was a lovely, sweet young woman, not like a lot of them you see now. She liked books and flowers and beautiful things. She came to our group a few months ago.'

'Group?'

Eric looked down, embarrassed. 'People like me, we

meet every week, just to talk, so we don't feel alone. Jess had been having awful dreams, and not just when she was asleep. She worked in the library, and sometimes, when it was quiet, once all the college kids had gone, she would get flashes, just images, pictures. But each one frightened her, made her sit up. She told me that it was like she was doing something, and then for a few seconds she would forget where she was. Then the images would be gone, and she would be left gasping, scared, sweating.'

He smiled.

'She was terrified she had a tumour or something at first, even went to see a doctor, but then she just knew to come to our meeting. Most people we have at our meetings just come along, something tells them to. We don't advertise.'

'Why were you there, at her house?'

Eric lifted his glasses to wipe something from his eye. 'I had a dream, but this time I knew it was happening right then. I could feel it. When I got round there, Jess was already dead. I called the police and that was it.'

'You know that Sam Nixon represents Luke King? He could make out you're the killer to get him off.'

'So you think he killed her?'

'What?'

'You said "get him off". If you thought he hadn't done it you would have said "prove his innocence".'

I shook my head. 'I don't know any more than you do.' I pulled out my press cutting. 'What about Darlene Tyler? And Tyrone? Did you dream about them too?'

Eric looked betrayed, hurt.

'This is your chance to get your story across,' I reminded him, 'but you'll understand my interest.'

He looked at me for a few seconds. No, it was more than that. He *studied* me.

'I had been dreaming of boys, helpless boys. I thought I might be able to help.'

'The police might think that you're just a glory hunter.'

'There was no glory in finding Jess like that.'

I couldn't argue with that.

Eric looked down, and it seemed like he now regretted talking to me. I knew I had pushed it as far as I could, but also that I might have to speak to him again.

'Can I get back in touch?' I asked.

Eric nodded uncertainly, but he gave me his address anyway. I reached into my pocket and produced a ten-pound note. 'And have lunch on me.'

Eric sat back, unsure, too polite to say no, too polite to accept. Then I saw his reality take hold and he took the note, whispering a quiet, 'Thank you.'

I turned to leave when I remembered the group Eric had mentioned. 'When do you meet, this group of yours?' I asked.

'Every Wednesday at eight. Sometimes there is only me there, but I like to go just in case I'm needed.'

'Today is Wednesday.'

He didn't answer so I stood up to leave. I thought I saw movement just outside the window. I looked back to Eric. He hadn't seen anything.

I walked quickly out of the café and looked down the street. There were people milling around, but nothing unusual. Pushchairs pushed by young girls in tracksuits, blue-ink tattoos on their forearms like broken veins. But no one who might have been watching us.

I looked back into the café. Eric had gone.

Chapter Twenty-four

When Laura walked into the Incident Room, she was met by applause.

She smiled as she saw Pete coming towards her, holding a silvery plastic statuette, a poor replica of an Oscar.

Laura put her hands on her hips and scowled playfully. 'Go on,' she said warily. 'For what am I owed this dubious pleasure?'

He tilted his head, amusement twinkling in his eyes. 'We award it for fuck-ups, you know, like forgetting to caution prisoners when they are interviewed, or losing exhibits, and we think you've done just enough in your first fortnight in the job to deserve it.'

'Like what?' she said, punching Pete on the arm.

'How about losing the number-one suspect? Or pissing off Jimmy King?'

'Hey, that was you as well.'

'But what about pissing off the abduction squad? Overnight heroine. On this misfit squad and then you just stumble over the missing child.' He grinned. 'Priceless.' He thrust the statuette into her hands.

Laura didn't know what to say. She looked at the statuette and saw all the scuff marks from previous recipients.

She looked up.

'I couldn't have done it without Pete Dawson,' she said, in mock acceptance. 'He has taught me how to fuck up royally in my brief time here.'

The room roared with laughter and Pete put his hand up in appreciation.

'And I know I couldn't have got by without you lot,' and her hand swept the room. 'The biggest bunch of fuck-ups I have ever worked with.' She grinned and bowed. 'Thank you.'

As Laura carried the statuette to her desk, she felt slaps on her back, whispers of 'nice one'. She felt good. Fitting in was hard but she finally felt like she was getting there.

Just as she got to her desk, she heard the room go quiet. 'McGanity. Come and see me, please.'

She recognised Egan's voice. When she saw Pete's scowl, she said, 'Hey, at least I got a "please".'

It was mid-morning before Sam walked out of the police-station yard with Terry McKay.

Terry's fines had been cancelled. He had been a few hundred pounds in arrears, but the court weighed it against the night he'd spent in a cell. It was the way the justice system worked, trapped by targets. People like Terry made the court look bad, because he made the books look bad, so they helped him, found short-cuts to make the figures work.

But still Terry didn't seem happy. Maybe because he knew that he would run up a few more fines soon, whenever he next took a trip on the justice roundabout.

'Did you speak to Harry?' he asked, as he wiped his nose on his hand.

Sam stopped. 'Look, Terry, will you just drop this.' His voice was raised, and people outside the court looked round. 'I've done my part, the legal part. Anything between you and Harry is nothing to do with me.'

Terry shrugged. He was holding a plastic bag, bound at the top by a red tag, his belt in there, along with the scraps of change he'd had on him when he was arrested.

'Is that it?' Sam asked, and stepped closer. He could feel his temper rising. No sleep and too much coffee. 'You drag me out at midnight and pester me, and you end it with a shrug? For fuck's sake!' He stormed off.

He heard someone outside court jeer. He stopped. He took some deep breaths, tried to tell himself not to do anything, not say anything. But he couldn't stop himself. He could feel his heart beating, the adrenaline racing through him.

He turned back to Terry. 'Don't make me a laughing stock,' he hissed through gritted teeth. 'Do you know what it is like to be with you in the middle of the night when I should be at home?'

Terry didn't say anything. He looked at Sam and swung the bag he was holding over his shoulder.

Sam stepped closer. Terry didn't flinch. Instead, he stared back at him and said, 'I'd swap my life for yours.'

Sam looked at him, surprised. Then he looked down at Terry's worn-out shoes, at the skinny arms, legs, the boozy flush to his cheeks. He felt ashamed, embarrassed. What was he doing, shouting at people like Terry McKay, at his clients?

'I'm sorry,' said Sam. 'It's just been busy lately, you know, I'm a bit tired. If there's anything else I can do for you, you know where the office is.'

Then he stopped when he realised that Terry wasn't listening.

'Are you okay?' asked Sam. He saw that Terry was staring straight ahead, his jaw clenched, his cheeks paler than before. Sam turned to where he was looking. Luke King. He was leaning against a wall, his arms folded. He was smirking.

Terry swore under his breath and then turned to walk away.

Sam walked towards Luke, angry. 'You could have made an appointment,' he said sharply.

Luke laughed. 'Good performance. Do you treat all your clients like that?' Before Sam could respond, Luke looked past him and said loudly, 'Maybe it isn't you I've come to see.'

At that, Terry looked back again and quickened his pace.

'Stay there, Terry,' Sam barked, but McKay was not going to stop.

Luke watched Terry McKay disappear around a corner and then he turned back to Sam. He smiled arrogantly. 'Of course it's you I want to see.' Luke nodded to where Terry had gone. 'He seemed twitchy.'

'Next on your hit-list?' asked Sam sarcastically.

Luke shook his head. 'I'm your client. You can't speak to me like that.'

'No, not any more you're not,' Sam said firmly. 'You stick with Harry.'

'But it's you I want, Mr Nixon. You helped me.'

Sam felt his fingers tighten over the file he held in his hand. He could feel anger surge through him again. He pushed past, felt his shoulder hit Luke's. He didn't look back, his mind racing. What did it all mean? He had seen how Luke had looked at Terry. To Luke, Terry wasn't just another down-and-out.

Sam walked quickly, wanting to get away from Luke. The route took him past the court again and then along a small parade of shops: an insurance broker's, a sandwich bar, and then, just before a small roundabout, a television shop.

He walked past the shops deep in thought. But then something caught his eye, made him stop. It was the television shop. No, more importantly, it was the television in the window, showing images of a park behind crime-scene tape. It looked familiar.

Then he heard a voice behind him.

Egan closed the door as Laura entered. He sat on a desk in front of her, one leg on the floor. She wasn't sure if she was supposed to find it alluring. She didn't.

Laura stood, and Egan realised that she was towering over him, so he went and sat behind the desk.

'I just wanted to check on how you are doing,' he said, and pointed towards the Incident Room. 'You need to keep away from that canteen culture crap.'

Laura smiled as sweetly as she could muster. 'Thank you, sir. It must be worse up here than the ten years

I had in the Met. For you to warn me like that, I mean.'

Egan paused, trying to work out if Laura was laughing at him. His lip twitched.

'I want you and Dawson to watch Eric Randle today. You lost him yesterday. He's been found. There are two officers watching his house. You know, the same one you went to yesterday. Relieve them, and stay on him all day. Follow him, wherever he goes. Report back to me every hour.'

'What about Luke King? Is he still a suspect?'

'I'll look after Luke King. I think that situation needs a bit more, shall we say, finesse.'

As she re-entered the Incident Room, she realised that it was universal, the yin and yang, that for every Pete there had to be an Egan. Laura knew which one she preferred.

'Looking for a new one?' I said to Sam, as I saw him transfixed by a bank of televisions in a shop window, all showing the same image. I had been to the library, and my hands were full of photocopies. I had been checking the other abduction stories for links to Eric Randle, but there were none, and I felt frustrated.

Sam turned around, and I was shocked by his appearance. There was stubble on his cheeks and his tie wasn't quite straight. But worse than that were his eyes. They were red-rimmed, and as he looked at me I thought I saw something in them, just for a moment. Sam looked scared.

He looked down, stumbled for a response, but then

the image on the screens caught my eye. It showed a park in Turners Fold. I recognised it straightaway, from the brick block of the old burnt-out aviary to the sweep of the trees along the top of the park.

But it was something else that caused the flutters of excitement in my stomach. I pulled the painting from my pocket, the one given to me by Eric. I looked at the picture and then back at the television screen. As my eyes were drawn back to the painting, I began to recognise things in it. The square block in the middle. The trees, the way they curved around the top of the park in a high crescent. The shape of the lawns.

I held it out to Sam. 'You recognise it, don't you?' When Sam ignored me, I pushed it nearer to him. 'You saw it this morning, when Eric showed it to you.'

He looked at me, his eyes wide. 'It's the ramblings of a silly old man,' he said quietly, and then he walked off, head down.

I rushed into the shop and barely noticed the looks of the shop staff as I went over to one of the televisions inside and searched in vain for the volume control. Why did everything have to be on a bloody remote? It was the tail-end of the report, and I recognised Turners Fold, but it was all in silence.

I looked at the painting again. It looked like the same park, and there was a small figure lying down.

A spotty youth in a shirt and tie appeared at my shoulder.

'Can I help you, sir?'

I looked around and pointed at the television. 'What's this about?'

He looked confused. 'About twelve hundred pounds. To be exact, eleven hundred and ninety-five.'

'No, the news item. What have they been saying?'

He shrugged. 'We sell them, we don't watch them.'

Then a picture of Connor Crabtree appeared on the screen. I realised that either Eric was telling the truth, or I held in my hand a painting by the kidnapper.

I left the shop as quickly as I had gone in. I needed to see Eric Randle again, before the police got there.

Chapter Twenty-five

The town centre faded quickly in my rear-view mirror as the Triumph Stag climbed the long lines of terraces, with dusty windows and stone doorways right by the pavement. The streets were busy with Pakistani women in billowing silk clothes, some with veils, glittering brown eyes peering out. The cars on the street were mainly new, with alloys and chrome, spoilers and bright paint, magnets for the young men who stood around talking.

Once the terraced grid faded, I turned into an estate, a collection of cul-de-sacs coming off a circular road. One route in, one route out. The faces on the pavements became white, and hostile eyes glared out from under the peak of a baseball cap or a hood, with tracksuits wrapped around skinny legs and tucked into socks. No one walked. They either bounced or they slouched, some attached to vicious-looking dogs with bow legs and jaws like bolt-cutters.

The houses were mainly semi-detached and well-spaced, with dark brick at the bottom, grey pebbledash at the top, behind straggly privet hedges with beer cans wedged at the bottom, blown there by the wind, the colours faded by the summer sun. England flags hung from some of the windows, dirty with the rain, almost like a warning. The cars along the kerbsides were old and worn. Pool cars, the police called them, ragged old Vauxhalls used by local youths, none with insurance, most without even a driving lesson let alone a licence.

It was a desperate sight, but one that made me realise how lucky I had been. I hadn't grown up wealthy, but I had grown up loved. On this estate I saw just hopelessness and anger. But then I saw something else, something which made me think that maybe there was some fear as well.

Among the collection of grimy semis were the occasional spots of colour, flower baskets and double-glazing, with well-kept gardens and neat brick walls. They were islands, pockets of hope, but their children hung around in the same neighbourhood, were bothered by the same dealers, made to run in the same pack, their dreams of a better life stolen by those who didn't dream at all.

I found Eric's street eventually, tucked away at the top of the estate, backing onto fields. I crawled up slowly in the car as I tried to work out the address from the numbers on the doors.

I stepped out of my car and looked around. I noticed a small group of teenagers leaning against a wall, looking like they weren't interested, passing a cigarette between them. But I could tell they were watching me. I patted my wallet and phone subconsciously.

I looked back at the address given to me by Randle. The brickwork was splashed with paint and someone had painted 'peedo' in large red letters over the board.

It would have had more impact if it had been spelled correctly. As I looked up, I saw every window was boarded up, no sign of life anywhere. The numbers on the door were chipped and broken, and the letterbox was nailed shut.

I heard the teenagers approach me.

'Nice car,' said one, in a way that told me that it might not stay nice for long.

'Looking for Dirty Eric?' another asked, blowing smoke towards me, the cigarette almost down to the filter.

I turned around. 'Does someone still live here?'

They all laughed. 'Yeah, the fucking nonce,' one said, and another said, 'We tried to torch the fucker's house,' and then threw a stone at the boards as if to emphasise the point.

'You the police?' It was a girl, her eyes bagged by dark rings, her tracksuit stained and grimy.

I shook my head. 'No, I'm a reporter.'

'What's the dirty perv done now?'

'Nothing. I just need to see him.'

Some of the group walked off and picked up pieces of brick from the front garden. They made thuds as they threw them on the boards over the windows.

I looked back towards the house. 'So he's got it all boarded up because you little wankers keep on breaking his windows?'

They stopped what they were doing and looked at me, surprised. Then they started to look uncertain. They were in a pack, but I was bigger than all of them, fitter than all of them, and older than all of them.

'Who you calling wankers?' said one, but he was at the back of the group, and mumbled it quietly.

I smiled, but I packed it full of menace. 'Work it out. Now, tell me what Eric Randle did to make you want to burn his house down, and then watch my car while I'm in there. A tenner if it's good, and my car is still how I left it when I come out.'

The girl at the front held out her gold-ringed hand. 'Money first.'

I shook my head. 'Info first, and then look after my car. Then you get your money. You'll get enough cider and fags with that to see out the rest of the afternoon.'

The group started laughing, flicking their fingers and bouncing on their heels.

'He got locked up for murder, man,' said one, a skinny blond kid with his head shaved around the sides and a fringe gelled flat.

I tried to bluff my surprise. 'Shit, and you want to mess with him?' I said, my voice filled with sarcasm.

'Yeah, but he got off with it.'

'So he's not a paedo?'

He looked sad. 'I don't know. But he's not right,' and he jabbed his temple with his finger.

'How long ago was this murder?'

The group looked between each other, and then the kid at the back said, 'A few years ago, when I was still in juniors.'

I winked at them. 'Cheers. Now for the next part. I won't be long.'

I walked up the path and someone shouted, 'Do we still get our money if he's not in?'

I didn't answer, but I smiled to myself. At least it showed a spark of initiative. I banged on the door and stood there for a while, waiting, and then looked back when I heard the sound of a key being turned. 'You're going to have to work for it.'

As I turned back to the house, I saw Eric's face appear, blinking in the sunlight.

My eyes struggled to adjust to the murkiness as I went inside. I turned around fast when I heard the door slam shut and the key quickly turn.

'You saw it,' said Eric, his voice snapping out the words.

'What did I see?' I asked, squinting.

I was aware of Eric moving in front of me, like a shadow, the slow shuffle of his feet betraying his whereabouts.

'You saw the news,' said Eric. 'Where that boy was found. It was in my picture.'

I smiled to myself. I had been right. I had started to see through the darkness better, and I thought I could see Eric grinning. 'Why is your house all boarded up?' I remembered the words of the teenagers outside and wanted his version.

Eric's grin twitched and he turned away. 'The local kids don't like me.'

'Why not?'

He shrugged. 'I live on my own. I just sit in here and paint. If I don't have the boards up, they brick my windows or put petrol through my letterbox.'

I stole a glance towards the front door. I could make out charred floorboards.

'There's more to this than that,' I said. 'Kids don't pick on old men because they're old. You've got "peedo" painted on the boards. What's that about?'

Eric turned away and walked across the room, glanced towards a framed photograph of a young girl. She looked young, maybe fifteen.

'Because when people go missing, I tell the police about my dreams. But that makes me a suspect.' He went quiet for a moment. 'Sometimes suspect number one.'

'So the police don't believe you?'

Eric shook his head.

'But if you went to them again, they might believe you this time.'

'Or I might just become a suspect again.'

I sighed and began to walk around. The place was bleak. There were no carpets on the floor, and the boards on the windows blocked out most of the light, so it seemed like a cave. The living room contained an old electric fire, a plastic cover with log shapes moulded into it, brought to life by the light underneath. Elsewhere there was an easy chair with worn arms, and a table upon which there was a book, open and face down, a lamp, and a small colour television.

'Why do you stay here?' I asked.

Eric looked down and spoke quietly. 'If they drive me out, the house will stand empty. The kids will play in the house, it will become somewhere to drink and take their girlfriends. Some older ones will come along and rip out the bathroom, take all the pipes. It won't take long to turn this into an empty shell, and I won't let them do it.'

'But Eric, why should you care? Ask for a move, get settled somewhere else. You're too old for this crap.'

'This is my *home*,' he said angrily. 'I've lived in this house for forty years. It used to be nice round here, with good people. There are still some good people, but more bad than good now. It's my home, I've got some good memories, and I won't leave.'

He stood there, his chest heaving with emotion. 'So are you going to write about me?'

'I'd like to, if it's a good story. But a lot of people won't believe you.'

'It's difficult for people, I know that,' he said, nodding. 'If I didn't have the dreams, *I* wouldn't believe it.'

'Do you believe in God?' I asked.

Eric looked confused. 'What do you mean?'

'Just that. Do you believe in a celestial being, a force, something that guides us, determines our life?'

'That's not God. That's fate.'

'You can't have one without the other. Fate is a pre-determined end. Someone or something has to pre-determine it, some force. If you don't believe in God, you can't really believe you dream the future.'

'I don't believe in it; that would make it a faith. I just sort of know it. I have dreams, I paint them, and then they come true.'

'There is another possibility,' I said, watching Eric carefully.

Eric said nothing, perhaps guessing what I was going to say.

'That you are responsible for what is in the pictures,' I continued.

'If you think you are the first person with that idea, you are wrong,' he said.

'I've got to ask the questions the readers will ask. Some will be suspicious.'

Eric smiled softly. 'That depends on how you write it.'

'Show me where you paint,' I said, worried that I had lost his trust.

Eric looked at me for a moment, as if he was wondering why he had to humour me, but then he shuffled towards the kitchen. As I followed him, I noticed a small door between the two rooms. I paused for a moment, it looked like a cellar door, but I looked up when Eric shouted, 'No!'

'What's wrong?' I asked, startled.

Eric looked apologetic. 'I'm sorry, but it's dark down there, and I don't want you to fall.'

I glanced at the door. As Eric nodded his insistence, I followed him into another dark room, wooden boards covering the windows at the rear too. I could see some cupboards around the walls, and then a stainless-steel sink and a grubby gas cooker. Right in the middle of it was an easel. On it was a pad of paper. The top sheet was blank.

'Ready for the morning?' I asked.

Eric nodded.

'Have you got any other paintings involving Sam Nixon?' I asked.

'It's not as simple as that,' he said. 'I dream a lot of things. I don't always know who or what it is.'

'What about Luke King?' I asked. 'He was in the first

picture you showed to Sam, the one with Jess. He was interviewed about her murder. Did you know it was him?'

Eric shook his head slowly. 'No, I had no idea. I knew it involved Sam Nixon, but that's all.'

'But you knew it was Jess?'

'Come with me tonight, to my group. You might understand then.'

I was surprised. 'Are you sure?'

He looked pleased. 'Of course. You can meet others like me.'

I smiled at Eric. 'Thank you.' And as I pulled out my notepad and camera, ready to begin the interview, I thought that he looked truly happy for the first time since I'd met him.

Chapter Twenty-six

Luke King's old school loomed in front of me, at the top of a hill, with views over Blackley. It was redbrick, with Gothic ramparts and high lattice windows, large stone doorways marking the ways in. It comprised two blocks, with ivy over the first, so that from the town it seemed to sink into the hills. Long green fields ran in front, with rugby posts on one side and hockey goals on the other. There was a roped-off area between the two pitches, and I could tell from the shorter grass that it was a cricket square.

The school had history and heritage, and had churned out over a century of politicians and lawyers, accountants and industry leaders. It seemed so different to the one I had gone to, with its flat roofs and tarmac grounds, two soccer pitches marked out in wobbly white lines. As I looked around I also realised it must have been different to Jimmy King's old school, on the rougher edges of town, where all the kids from the children's home went. Maybe that was the whole point.

I would write up my interview with Eric later, but he had painted something connected to Luke King, so I thought it was time to look into Luke, just in case the connection firmed up. And I knew one thing: people don't become murderers overnight. There were one-off crimes of passion, or fights gone wrong, but what I had gleaned about Jess's death was that it was vicious, brutal and coldblooded. So, *go back to the start* was my theory, just to see what came up.

I parked outside the school gates and walked up the drive, underneath an avenue of trees, sycamore and horse chestnut, which swept around the sports pitches. I could hear the soft hum of traffic, but it seemed rural, tranquil. The breeze made the branches creak, and the leaves rustled as I got near the car park.

I followed the signs to the main entrance and found myself outside the secretary's office, facing a sliding glass window, the chatter and noise of a school just a corridor away. I could see the secretary on the other side of the glass, and I knew she had seen me, but she made me wait. Obviously, I didn't look like a prospective parent.

When she slid open the glass, she gave me a frosty look. Glasses hung from her neck on a thin silver chain, gleaming like a necklace against her turquoise jumper.

'Can I help?'

She said it in a way that sounded like she very much doubted it.

'Hello,' I said. 'I'm writing an article on James King, the local businessman, and I'm hoping to build up a family profile. I believe that his children attended this school, and I wondered if the headmaster would be prepared to talk to me.'

She looked me up and down and then placed the

glasses onto her nose, just so she could peer over the top of them at me. She pointed to some chairs further along the reception area.

'Sit down, please. I'll speak to Mr Hawarth.'

I took my place and waited.

As I looked around I could almost hear the echoes of Blackley's past. I faced a trophy cabinet, filled with sports awards. Framed rugby jerseys lined the walls, donated by former pupils who had played at a higher level after leaving. A crested wooden board dominated the centre of the wall, a list of honours on one side, head boys on the other, all painted in white. It told parents one thing: pay for your son's education and great things beckon. I scoured the names quickly.

A caretaker loitered nearby as he collected rubbish in a large black bag. As I waited, he glanced at me and then went outside.

I was kept waiting for twenty minutes; maybe in hope that I would get bored and go away. When it was obvious that I was prepared to wait, a door opened at the other end of the room and a tall man with a grey moustache appeared. He had a military look, from the proud burst of his chest to the firmness of his jaw.

I stood up to greet him and held out my hand to shake. He gripped it and gave it a sturdy pump.

I introduced myself, but I didn't get any further than that.

'I'm sorry, but I cannot discuss former pupils.'

'So Luke King is a former pupil?' Sometimes the only way to get people talking was to get them answering questions.

His eyes narrowed. 'As I said, I'm not prepared to discuss former pupils.'

I nodded acceptance. 'So the interview is over?'

He gestured towards the door. 'Please, Mr Garrett.'

'What do you think about Luke King being a murder suspect?' I asked, and ignored his outstretched hand.

The headmaster stopped for a moment.

'Didn't you know?' I continued. 'He was arrested yesterday. Quite a brutal murder.'

'Thank you, Mr Garrett.' The headmaster tried to sound firm, but I sensed a quiver to his voice.

'What was he like when he was here?'

I got a stern look, and saw the headmaster's hand come towards me again.

'So you've no comment to make?' I persisted. 'Nothing to contradict the suspicions?'

'Mr Garrett, please leave this school now.' The command came out with a growl attached, and I knew I would get nothing further.

I turned to go. Then I stopped at the honours board and pointed at a name from nine years earlier.

'Thomas King? Isn't that Luke's brother?'

The headmaster took a deep breath, tried to control his anger. 'Please go, Mr Garrett.'

He held out his hands as if to usher me out.

'Was Jimmy King an involved father?' I asked. 'Parent evenings? Sports day? Bet he was proud of his son being head boy.'

'Ask him.'

I nodded and turned back towards the door.

'Thank you, Mr Haworth. Sorry to waste your time.'

Then I emerged back onto the school drive, my eyes adjusting to the sunlight.

I hadn't made many friends, but I felt like I had the germ of a story.

As Pete pulled in behind the other police car on Eric's street, he peered up towards the house. 'Must be a dismal life behind those boards.'

Laura looked up, saw the kids hanging around on the street, circling between the kerbs on small bikes. 'It can only be because it is even worse without them.' She raised her eyebrows. 'That's the real tragedy.'

They both got out of the car and walked towards the other one. When they tapped on the window, the officer jumped, and from his bleary eyes Laura guessed that he had been enjoying a nap.

'Not much going on?' she asked.

The officer smacked his lips together and yawned. 'No,' he said blearily, 'hardly a thing. We're making the natives jumpy, though.' As he rubbed his eyes, he added, 'There was *one* visitor.'

'Who was that?' asked Pete.

The officer shook his head and shrugged. 'Don't know. Some bloke in a Triumph Stag.'

Laura felt herself sag. This was going to get tricky. 'A red one?' she asked.

The officer nodded.

Pete looked at her. 'You know who that was?'

Laura nodded slowly. 'Yeah, you could say that.'

* * *

I was speaking into my Dictaphone as I walked back through the school grounds, the sunlight flickering like a silent movie as I moved between the trees.

As I passed an old cricket pavilion, painted green, the felt roof covered with lichen from the nearby sycamore trees, I heard someone say hello. As I turned, I saw the caretaker.

I walked towards him. As a journalist, I knew that if someone wanted to talk to me, I would have to be *very* busy to walk away.

As I got closer, I saw that he was younger than I'd first thought, maybe in his forties. His hair was grey and short, and his face was getting that leathery look from too much sunlight, but there was a sparkle to his eyes, his body still lithe and fit.

'I heard you asking about Jimmy King's son,' he said. His voice sounded blunt.

I nodded. 'Do you know him?'

The caretaker nodded, but I could feel his nervousness. 'My brother used to live in one of Mr King's houses.'

'Good landlord?'

The man took a deep breath, and I saw the wariness replaced by anger, memories darkening his face. 'He killed him.'

I paused, tried to work out what to say next, when the caretaker added, 'As good as, anyway.'

'Tell me the story,' I said.

The caretaker began to talk. His brother had rented one of Jimmy King's terraced houses when he'd first left home. He hadn't expected much, just wanted somewhere to call his own. But it smelled bad. A damp, rotting smell came from the floor. It got into his clothes, his shoes, turned his record covers mouldy. He complained to his landlord, who promised to come down and have a look. When he did, he brought two thugs with him. His brother was given a choice: leave or put up with it.

He'd chosen to leave, but then Jimmy King had told him how much it would cost him to do so. Severance of contract, he'd said.

The caretaker's brother had left in the middle of the night, hoping that no one would know where he had gone. He'd misjudged it. The door crashed in one night, and he was beaten in his bed, told that if he didn't pay up, they would come back. And they did, nocturnal visits when he least expected it. He was also told that if he went to the police, they would come back more often.

'Did he pay up in the end?' I asked.

The caretaker shook his head. 'They found him, after he'd overdosed, blood dripping from his nose, the left-overs of his last visit.'

I didn't understand. 'Jimmy King didn't need that amount of money.'

The caretaker sneered. 'It was the message, not the money. His houses were dank and derelict, and any one of the tenants could have gone to the County Court for a damages claim. None did. The tenants were too scared. They were all on benefits, and so he charged whatever the system would pay.'

'What did you think when his kids turned up here?' I asked.

The caretaker snarled. 'I almost left. It wasn't right that those kids should get what they were on the back of that murdering bastard.'

'What were his two boys like?' I asked.

The caretaker considered, his hands in his pockets.

'Different,' he said eventually.

'What do you mean?'

'From each other,' he said. 'Thomas had left by the time Luke arrived, but he'd been head boy. He was like bloody all of them. Good-looking, full of himself, competitive. Young Luke had a tough act to follow, and he was just different. He was a geek, would hang around with the chess set. Smaller, weedier – it was almost like they had different fathers.'

'Did either of them ever get into any trouble?'

The caretaker shook his head. 'Thomas was too popular for that. Everyone's favourite, including the teachers.' He gave a small laugh. 'I ended up feeling sorry for Luke. He was in Thomas's shadow, and I don't think he liked it.'

I nodded, understanding. But I thought about that shadow, and wondered whether Luke was trying to come out from it with a bang. 'Did Luke get into trouble when he was here?'

'What like?'

'Bullying? Cruelty?' I queried.

The caretaker laughed to himself. 'Luke? He was the victim of bullies plenty of times, but I don't think he had the balls to give it back.'

I looked back to the school. 'A lonely place.'

The caretaker twitched a smile. 'It creates winners, this place. It doesn't cater as well for losers.'

I thanked him for his time and headed back down the drive. I wasn't sure if the story had got better or worse, the school loser ending up as a murder suspect – or maybe even a murderer?

Chapter Twenty-seven

Sam sat up straight. He long-blinked, felt a start, a moment of panic. He had seen it again, the building, tall and dark, filled with shadows. And then falling. The dream came at him quickly, the same one as before. He looked at the clock. He'd lost two minutes.

He stood up and walked around his office, took some deep breaths to wake himself up. It was time for another coffee, but he could feel heat in his cheeks; it wasn't good for him to have more caffeine. He looked down at the files on his desk. They needed work, and if he didn't do it then it would just be a late finish another day.

But then he saw that something was missing.

Terry McKay's file. It had been there earlier, before Sam had gone to court, on the corner of his desk.

He scattered the files, looking for it. A cup fell on the floor, his drink gone cold. Sam could tell that Harry had known about Terry. Was Harry tracking his computer entries? Then he saw Alison go past his door.

'Where is it?' he shouted.

Alison turned and went into his office.

'Where's what?'

'Terry McKay's file. It was here earlier. You saw it.'

'I've been at court with you.'

'No,' Sam snarled. 'You set off after me. In fact, you were late. The ushers were looking for you.'

She pursed her lips, and Sam thought he saw her eyes fill with tears. 'I was in the cells,' she said, her voice measured and slow, her lip trembling slightly. 'I was with Ben Thompson. He was moaning, like he always does, so I spent some time with him. Okay?'

And with that, she walked away from his office.

As he watched her go, Sam was angry. Go on, he thought, report back, keep Harry up to date, one more point for the golden girl.

He looked around for the file again, but it had gone. He noticed his cup. As he bent down to pick it up, he saw there was a crack in it. 'Fuck!' He felt his rage build up. He could hear chatter outside the door, secretaries gossiping. As his door clicked shut, he threw the cup against the wall, and he heard the talking stop.

'So what do you think of Eric Randle?' asked Laura.

Pete looked up towards the house. 'He doesn't get out much. I think we'll be here all day.'

'Had you heard of him before?'

Pete shook his head.

Laura sat back in her seat and closed her eyes. 'I'm surprised at that.'

There was a silence, and Laura tried not to smile. She knew Pete wouldn't let it stay there.

'What do you mean by that?' he asked eventually.

She opened her eyes to answer. 'Jess's wasn't the first body he discovered.'

He turned round towards her. 'Go on.'

'Five years ago, a girl went missing from a playground in Audley Park. She was found in a shallow grave in some woods a few days later.'

Pete looked at her for a few seconds, and then looked back towards Eric's house. 'Young blonde girl? Emily something?'

'Emily Parker,' said Laura.

Pete nodded to himself. 'Yeah, I remember her now. Sweet-looking girl. Long hair and really bright eyes. That's what I remember about the press picture: the bright eyes.' He shook his head and smiled. 'So Eric found her?'

Laura nodded. 'There was something about it in the file I was looking at earlier.'

'Didn't we have a suspect for it?'

Laura pointed towards Eric's house. 'Number one,' she said.

'Shit,' Pete whispered, and leaned forward against the steering wheel. 'He was the one?' he said again, his voice slow, his eyes open wide. 'He's either very unlucky, or . . .'

'Or he's as guilty as hell,' said Laura.

Pete looked back at Laura. 'Did the file say why he was a suspect?'

'He'd called in too many times for his own good, so he was watched. He started going for walks in the woods. Then, a few days later, he started digging at the ground, pulling away leaves, and there she was, Emily, strangled and sexually assaulted.'

'So he was arrested?'

'More than that: he was charged. Classic behaviour, putting yourself into an investigation, calling in with information. When the girl wasn't found, he had to make sure she was discovered, just so we could all admire what he had done.'

'But the CPS didn't fancy it?'

Laura shook her head. 'The report didn't really say, but it sounded like he was locked up at first, did a couple of months on remand, but as the trial got nearer the prosecution dropped the case. It sounded like they hoped that something else would turn up to make the case stronger, but it didn't. So that was that. Case over. He walked.'

Pete whistled.

'Emily was an eight-year-old girl,' said Laura. 'The killer is still free. Now children are going missing again. I'm getting a bad feeling about Randle, aren't you?'

Pete didn't answer. Laura could tell what the answer would be: that if those higher up had some balls, then maybe Eric would have been put away the first time.

Laura turned to look out of the window. She knew that was always the way.

Chapter Twenty-eight

Sam flung his door open. Some of the clerks had come out of their offices at the noise. Jon Hampson was one. Two secretaries stood and gawped, their arms filled with files.

'What!' Sam bellowed.

'What's eating you?' said Jon, his eyes filled with amusement.

Sam didn't answer. He was taking deep breaths, trying to calm down. Then he caught a view of the car park through one of the windows at the back of the office. There was a Bentley, deep red, and from the personalised plates Sam knew one thing: that Jimmy King was with Harry.

Jon saw where he was looking. 'Maybe he wants to know why you've sacked your client.'

Sam sneered. 'Yeah, just fucking maybe.'

He was about to go back into his room when Karen appeared in the corridor behind him. She cleared her throat, sounding scared. Terry McKay was downstairs.

He walked quickly along the corridor, ignoring all the faces in front of him, the people who had stuck their heads out of their offices, peering round doorframes, and made his way downstairs. As the reception area came into view, he saw Terry sway against the counter. The receptionist was young and pretty, Harry's idea – a distraction for the clients who didn't like waiting. She was standing guard, making sure that Terry didn't wander. She looked up at Sam and he could see the distaste in her eyes.

Terry had someone else with him, a woman with two missing teeth and cuts on her face. Sam had seen her at court, a prostitute and occasional thief. She had the same vacant look that Terry had, that one day she would sober up properly and wonder what she had done with her life.

He had seen many prostitutes in court, and none had looked like Julia Roberts. They all looked riddled with bad luck, worn down by substance abuse or just hard living, and they all ended up bearing the scars of their nastier clientele.

As Sam approached, Terry looked round. When he let go of the counter, he stumbled slightly. He had quickly got into that state. It had only been a few hours since Sam had last seen him.

'Terry, go,' Sam said urgently.

He glanced towards the woman to his left, who looked at Sam with suspicion.

'She knows about the King boy,' Terry said, his voice slurred, the smell of cheap sherry tumbling out as badly as every word.

Sam looked quickly at the seats in reception. He knew that the other departments wanted the criminal department to have a different waiting area – this was the quickest way to lose wealthy divorce clients. With relief, he saw that they were empty.

'I don't care, Terry. I just want you to leave, now. For your own good.'

'He wanted to strangle me,' said the woman, her voice gravelly. It came out with a whistling lisp as her tongue found the gaps in her teeth.

Sam put his hands up, palms outwards. 'There is nothing I can do for you. Please leave.' His voice was getting louder.

'He said he wanted me to die, and that he would bring me back to life, just so that I would treasure life more. Healing hands, he used to say.'

'Terry, get out! Jimmy King is here somewhere, and, trust me, you do not want to be here if he sees you.'

Terry started to say something, a sneer on his face, when Sam saw him step back, his eyes wide, looking past Sam.

'Too late,' said a voice.

Sam whirled around and saw Jimmy King walking slowly down the stairs, a thick-set bald man just behind him. Jimmy looked at Sam briefly, but Sam couldn't work out his mood. The bald man just stared at him.

Jimmy walked slowly towards Terry and then stopped just in front of him. Then he smiled, but it was cold, his lips tight and thin.

'Good afternoon. What is your name?'

Terry pursed his lips, and Sam thought he was going to attack Jimmy, but he didn't. Jimmy had a presence, a calmness, hostile and still.

'You want to talk to me,' Jimmy hissed. 'Here I am.'

Terry swallowed. Sam looked towards the receptionist, who was sitting down again. She looked nervous now, her precious self-assurance gone.

Jimmy took a step nearer. They were now nose to nose.

'I'm sure I heard my name. Was I wrong?'

Terry started to walk backwards, but the woman didn't move.

'You owe him money,' she said defiantly. 'Five grand.'

Jimmy looked her up and down, glanced over at Terry, and shook his head slowly. 'I don't think so.'

Sam stepped in.

'Leave him alone, Mr King.' Sam's voice was hesitant, but his message was clear: Don't be a bully.

Jimmy turned around to look at Sam. Then Jimmy smiled, his teeth white.

'I'll tell you what I'll do for you,' Jimmy said slowly. His smile stayed wide. 'I'll meet you later on, and we'll talk about your problem.'

'Terry, you don't have to do this,' Sam warned, sensing the threat. He saw the menace behind the smile.

'I just want my fucking money,' was Terry's reply.

'Meet me later, and we'll try to sort something out.'

Terry looked suspicious, and looked across to his friend, who shrugged, her eyes still blazing.

Jimmy held out his hands. 'If I give you some money, you won't bother me any more.' He sighed, and looked weary.

Terry nodded slowly, unsure.

Jimmy clapped his hands. 'Good. Nine o'clock. Where will you be?'

Terry pointed towards the street. 'In the park, at the end.'

Jimmy nodded and turned away. He looked at Sam, and from the look in his eyes Sam knew that Terry wasn't going to get what he wanted. It was what he was going to get instead that worried him.

As Sam turned away he saw Alison at the top of the stairs. As their eyes met, she turned away.

Chapter Twenty-nine

Pete Dawson yawned as he sat back in his car seat.

He and Laura had followed Randle to an old scout hut in a rundown part of town, where Pete's old Fiesta blended in perfectly. The door pocket was full of chocolate and crisp packets and the front seats bore the stains of spilled coffee.

'How long do we have to wait here?' he asked.

'Until we are told to leave, or Mr Randle decides to go for a midnight walk.' Laura looked around, noticed the shadows, the lack of life. 'Can't be too long now. I can't see the tea-dance set liking it round here later?'

Pete sat back and closed his eyes. 'There might be a market for that.'

Laura smiled at him. She was warming to him, there was something about his gruff honesty she liked. She recognised some of Jack in Pete.

'Do you think he did it?' she asked. 'Killed Jess, I mean.'

Pete opened one eye. 'Hoping for glory?'

'No. I'm just curious. He doesn't look the sort.'

'There isn't a sort. Get used to that idea pretty quickly.'

Laura knew all of that, but it wasn't a good time to talk up her CV. 'But his name keeps on coming up.'

'It's a small town,' Pete replied.

Laura felt her phone vibrate in her pocket. It was a picture of Bobby in his pyjamas with a simple message underneath: '*Goodnight mummy. x*'

She put the phone away and chewed on her lip. The message was from the babysitter, Martha, an old friend of Jack's father. Jack said he had some work to do, Bobby would be asleep soon anyway, but it didn't make her feel any better. There was no point in looking at her watch. She didn't know when she would be back.

'Missing the family?' asked Pete, his voice quiet.

'Why do male cops always assume that we would really rather be with our children?'

Pete looked away. 'Why do female cops always think that we wouldn't rather be with ours?'

Laura didn't reply at first, just looked out of the window, but then said, 'Do you have kids?'

Pete nodded. 'Four, all under ten.'

Laura gasped. 'That's a handful.'

'Don't I look the type?' He gave a small laugh. 'It's worse for my wife. I'm here, watching a clapped-out Portakabin with a grumpy cockney cop, instead of helping her out.'

'Hardly a cockney. I'm from Pinner.'

'Get below Luton and you all sound like the Artful Dodger.'

Laura laughed. 'Cor blimey,' she said, strangling the vowels.

Pete closed his eyes again. 'What brings you to the north anyway?'

Laura thought about that. Love, she supposed. Maybe more than that. A new start, away from the baggage of her London life.

'The usual,' she said. 'A man.'

He smiled. Laura was starting to see something of the old romantic in him, and was about to say so when she saw movement out of the window.

'Look at this. We've got a rush.' They both wiped the condensation away from the windscreen.

But when Laura saw who was arriving, she groaned.

'Bad news?' asked Pete.

'You could say that,' she said quietly.

I parked my car under one of the few streetlights and climbed out. The old scout hut was a grey Portakabin hidden by razor wire. The street was quiet, too quiet, and although the lights of the town centre were bright over the rooftops, the area seemed dark and derelict. I could see a woman working a street corner fifty yards away, but aside from that there was no one else around.

I'd driven quickly to get there. I knew what sort of neighbourhood I was in, and I didn't want my registration number noted as a kerb crawler. The streetlights had thinned out and the shops dwindled into open spaces, where women with skirts up to their curls tried to look into my car as I went past.

My footsteps sounded loud as I walked across the road and my feet crunched on loose gravel. The scout hut was unlocked, and as I opened the door I was struck at how empty it looked. The floor was all scuffed and scattered with metal chairs. The walls were dirty, the marks old, black streaks from shoes or old Sellotape markings. There were a couple of holes, maybe where boisterous young scouts had stuck a foot through. The hut looked uncared for, almost abandoned, and I wondered if I had got the wrong place. But then I heard a noise, a soft chatter, and then there was movement behind a serving hatch at the other end of the room. There were three women, all pension age, fussing around a kettle.

The women stopped when they heard the door shut. I shouted out, 'Hello.'

One of the women put her head through the serving hatch. The other two appeared in the doorway and looked blankly at me. I wanted to say that surely they must have known I was coming, but they didn't look the laughing type.

I waved. 'Hello there. I'm Jack Garrett.'

As I spoke, Eric appeared behind them.

'I didn't think you'd come,' he said, walking slowly into the room. The three women watched me until he turned around to them and said, 'This is the reporter I was telling you about.'

The three women looked suspicious, but they came forward and shook my hand.

'Why do you want to write about us?' one asked.

'Because it's an interesting story.'

'You're not going to make fun, are you?'

I shook my head. 'No, I'm not. I just want to know more about you all. What you do and how you do it.'

'Do you believe in spirits?' asked another.

I wasn't sure what answer I was supposed to give. 'Well, no, not really. I mean, I'm not sure.'

All three women looked at each other and raised their eyebrows.

'I'm Lily,' said the woman who had just spoken, and then she pointed to the other two. 'This is Bessie and Maggie.'

The other two nodded smiles, and then Lily said, 'That is one way we work.'

'I'm not sure I understand,' I said.

All three women shook their heads, smiling.

'That's one way in which we can do it,' said Bessie, her voice stronger, more challenging than Lily's. They all looked formidable, but Bessie was the biggest of the three, her face round under her short hair, the grey hidden by chestnut streaks. 'It's called trance-channelling.'

I tried to hide my disappointment. The meeting had already descended into hocus-pocus. I glanced at Eric, but I saw that he wasn't really listening.

Bessie folded her arms defensively. 'A spirit entity can only communicate by entering the human form, and to receive the messages, the person has to be in a trance.'

'What, you speak to ghosts?'

Bessie shook her head. 'No. It's more physical than that. An entity. Spirit guide. Shaman. Call it what you will, but some of us receive messages from someone in the spirit world.'

'So what Eric paints is what the spirit world tells him to paint?' I asked. I struggled to contain my frustration. Eric looked over when I spoke, and I guessed that he sensed my feelings.

'And what's wrong with that?' asked Bessie, and then she leaned forward. 'Do you know better?'

'Why did you come here?' asked Maggie, her voice quieter, revealing more wariness.

I looked at Eric. 'I was shown paintings that appeared to predict future events.' I thought of a way to dress it up, but there wasn't one, so I added, 'If that is true, then it is one hell of a story.'

'Do you believe Eric predicts the future?' It was Maggie again.

I thought about my answer, but then decided that I might get more out of the group if I was honest.

'No, I don't believe he dreams the future, because that would suggest that the future is pre-ordained, and it isn't.'

'How do you know that?'

'I don't, I suppose, but it doesn't make sense. The future happens because unforeseeable events collide. If it was any other way, it would mean that someone was controlling everything, like some kind of . . .'

'God?'

I sighed. 'I'm not sure I meant that. But it just doesn't fit with what I know.'

'Do you think Eric is a liar?' asked Bessie.

I looked at Eric, and I thought about our first meeting. He was a little strange, lonely maybe, but he seemed genuine.

'No,' I said quietly, 'I don't think he tells lies.'

'And he told you that his paintings were old paintings?' continued Bessie. 'That they weren't new ones pretending to be old ones?'

I nodded. They were probing my doubts, and Eric was coming out of it best.

'But how many paintings has he done that haven't predicted anything?' I asked. 'It could just be a co-incidence. Probability says that, now and again, there will be a match. It's pure chance. Take an earthquake. I could paint one tonight, and there is a good chance there'll be one within a year.' I smiled in apology. 'I'm not saying I have the answers. If I did, I wouldn't be here. But I am finding it hard to believe.' I turned to Maggie. 'How long have you known that your dreams were important?'

'Since I was a teenager,' Maggie answered. 'But I was much older before I realised what they were.'

'Do you think it was a puberty thing?' I asked. 'Something to do with heightened senses?'

Maggie nodded slowly. I detected embarrassment, but she answered me anyway. 'Teenage years are strange, full of intense feelings, and in our dreams too, but not many of us think anything about it.'

'When did you realise your dreams were coming true?'

Maggie leaned forward and took hold of my hands. They were cold and soft.

'When I recognised them,' she said in a soft croak. Her eyes went hard for a moment. 'Do you remember the Moors murderers?'

I nodded. I hadn't been born then, but the press had made them notorious, keeping them in the news for decades, endlessly recounting how they had snatched five children and murdered them, four of them buried on the barren moorland above Saddleworth, just thirty miles from Blackley.

'I saw them,' she said quietly. 'I saw them a long time before their pictures appeared in the newspapers.'

'Tell me.'

Her fingers gripped mine a little tighter.

'I had been having violent dreams for a while. I would wake up shivering, like I had been out in the cold all night. And my head hurt, and I hurt down there,' and Maggie nodded towards her groin, her eyes looking away briefly, the words almost whispered. 'I would have the dreams for a few weeks, nearly every night, and then they would stop as suddenly as they had started. There would be nothing for a few months, and then they would start again, that terror, that feeling of cold, such cold. And I would wake up crying, really crying, screaming for my mother.' She looked bashful. 'I hadn't been married long, and it used to worry my Len, but then the dreams would stop, and he would think it was just a woman thing.' Her eyes were intense now. 'But I knew something bad had happened, as sure as I know I'm looking at you, and I didn't do anything about it. I woke up screaming, sobbing, and then they stopped, just like that.'

'How did you feel when they stopped?' I spoke quietly, and I felt the space between us shrink.

'Not like I should have done,' said Maggie. Her voice sounded sad, some of its force gone. 'I should have been happy they'd stopped, but I wasn't, because I knew I'd missed something.'

Maggie looked down and I saw her eyes moisten. She spoke quietly, not much above a whisper, and I had to strain to hear her. 'It had been really bad one Christmas. Through most of December I woke up every night and ached all over my body, and when I woke up I felt ashamed, dirty. I didn't go to work, I was just too tired.

209

I almost lost my job, but it was the sixties and there was plenty of work to be had. I woke up on Boxing Day with someone's hand round my throat, gripping tight, screaming in my ear, pure hatred. And cold again. So very cold. But when I opened my eyes, all I could see was Len looking at me, scared.'

'How can you be sure it was Hindley and Brady?'

A tear ran slowly down her cheek and meandered around the creases.

'Because I saw them in my dreams. Her hair was down, not like that hatchet beehive she had in her police photograph, but looser, more relaxed.' Maggie wiped the tear away. 'He was vacant and sullen most of the time, sort of angry, but she was just full of hate, all excited, screaming in my face. In my dreams it seemed like he was there because he had just decided to do whatever he had to do, but her,' and Maggie shuddered, 'she was there because she liked it.'

I must have started to drop my hands, because I felt her jerk them, pulling me towards her so that I was looking right into her eyes.

'I know what you are thinking,' Maggie said, her voice stronger now.

'What am I thinking?'

'Why do people like me only dream of famous things?'

I didn't answer.

'Most people say that,' she continued, 'but I had been having dreams like that for a long time before I recognised one. Maybe I only recognise the famous ones. I had no reason to make it up, and I wouldn't recognise the ones that weren't in the news.'

'Did you come forward?'

Maggie shook her head. 'People would have laughed at me. I was scared. I wasn't sure what was happening myself, so what could I tell anyone? It was only after Aberfan that people like us were taken more seriously.'

'Aberfan? Why?'

I had heard all about Aberfan, when a mountain of coal slurry slid down a Welsh hillside and covered a school, back in the sixties. One hundred and sixteen children died underneath it all.

'I dreamt it, just like a lot of other people,' said Maggie. 'The dreams were just dark, like smothering blackness, black peaks, moving, shifting. Then loud sounds, like the sound of aircraft, would snap me awake, and I would be struggling for breath, sobbing for my mother. I would hear children crying out, trying to get to the light, but I was pushed down, trapped, unable to move. And I could taste it, the dirt and coal, and my fingers felt raw. The dreams just got stronger and stronger, and then on that day, when the coal slid down that hill and covered that school, I cried. Everyone cried that day, but I knew I had seen it, had tasted it, had been there almost, but hadn't been able to stop it. Can you imagine how that felt?' She dabbed at her eyes with a handkerchief, a small piece of white cloth embroidered with flowers that she had retrieved from the cuff of her cardigan. 'Those were the worst dreams of all,' she said croakily, tears masking the milky blue of a few minutes earlier.

'But what could you have done to change it?' I asked, moved by her despair.

Maggie's fingers dug deep into mine. 'All I know is that I did nothing, and all those children died.'

'There were others.' It was a male voice.

I whirled around, surprised. I had forgotten for a few seconds that other people were there, transported by Maggie's story, and when I looked I found myself staring into deep brown eyes, hostile behind dark-rimmed glasses.

Chapter Thirty

Terry McKay was dozing, sitting on a bench, a bottle of sherry on the floor, when he felt someone kick his feet.

He opened his eyes slowly, squinting as he tried to focus. He saw a figure in a black suit.

'What?' Terry growled, and reached down for the sherry.

He wasn't fast enough. A foot kicked it away. What was left in the bottle spilled onto the ground and ran towards the small patch of grass behind the bench.

Terry stood up quickly, swaying, and then shouted, 'What the fuck are you doing?'

'Are you waiting for Jimmy King?' came the question, the voice hoarse and low.

Terry stopped, surprised. 'Yeah, where is he?'

The figure in the suit laughed. 'Did you think he was going to sit in public with you, with that cheap shit next to you?'

'So what the fuck is going on?'

'You come with me and speak to Jimmy in private.'

Terry chuckled, and spittle jumped onto his lips. 'What, like a date or something?' He waved his hands

213

in the air in mock excitement and screamed in a falsetto screech, 'I'll have the lobster, Jimmy.' He was the only one who laughed.

The figure in the suit turned to walk away. 'Your five grand, mate, not mine.'

Terry watched him retreat. He looked back at the floor. His mind worked hard as he thought about how he was going to replace the drink. The shops knew him now, and so it was hard enough to steal when he was sober. Drunk, he had no chance. He looked again at the figure in the suit. He was shrinking into the distance. He knew it was dangerous, had heard all about Jimmy King. But his thoughts turned first to the money.

'Wait!' he shouted.

The figure stopped and then turned around slowly. Terry held out his arms to steady himself and then he set off towards him.

'What do you mean there were others?' I asked.

The man with the deep brown eyes came around to face me, his eyes never leaving mine. His jaw looked set firm, his mouth curled downwards in a snarl.

'Who are you?' he asked. He said it like a challenge.

I introduced myself and held my hand out for him to shake. He didn't take it or smile but sat down and eyed me with suspicion.

'I'm Billy Hunt,' he said, as if I ought to recognise his name.

Then I noticed two others in the room, a tall man in his late twenties, well-built with an easy smile and short blond hair, and a woman who was slightly younger. Her short hair was dark and spiky with red flashes, and she wore mock-combats and a tight white T-shirt. When she smiled, her eyes flashed like silver buttons.

'And I'm Dan,' the blond man said. 'Dan Kinsella, and this is Charlotte.'

Charlotte grinned as she shook hands with me. 'Call me Charlie.'

'Billy is right about Aberfan,' said Dan. 'People did dream about it before it happened, but they only came forward afterwards. Have you ever heard of the Central Premonitions Bureau?'

I shook my head.

'Not many people have,' Dan continued, 'but so many people dreamt about Aberfan before it happened that people started to take it seriously and the Central Premonitions Bureau was set up. People were asked to register their premonitions, just in case someone might spot a pattern. Aberfan broke everyone's heart, and if people had known what the dreams meant in advance, then those children might not have died.'

I scribbled it all down in my notebook. 'Don't people always come forward with tales of premonitions when disasters happen?' I said. 'But what about all the un-fulfilled premonitions? A few hits and millions of misses is nothing at all. It's just coincidence.'

'It wasn't nothing to me,' said Maggie.

'Some lived a long way from the village,' said Dan, 'but there was one little girl from Aberfan who dreamt about it just two days before it happened. Eryl Mai Jones. Ten years old. She had a dream that the school was no longer there, that something black had come down over it. Just two days later, it did.'

'But that could just be the overactive imagination of a child,' I argued, trying not to sound scornful. 'Just think what she went through. Her mind would have been all over the place.'

Dan looked at me, a sad expression on his face.

'She didn't come through anything,' he said softly. 'Eryl Mai Jones died at Aberfan. It was her mother who told everyone about her dream afterwards.'

I couldn't respond to that, didn't even try. Dan nodded at me, like he understood why I was lost for words. Then he clapped his hands.

'C'mon, everyone, let's get this meeting underway.'

There was a scraping of metal as chairs were pulled into a circle, and then the main lights were turned off, so that the only light came from candles that Charlie had placed by the serving hatch. They made the faces of everyone become distorted in the light, flickering shadows like Halloween lanterns.

It was Dan who led.

'Before we start, let us remember poor Jess,' he said. 'If everyone can be silent for a minute so that we can all remember how she was in life, before we talk about what we may have seen of her death.'

Everyone looked down. I saw two of the old ladies pull handkerchiefs from the sleeves of their cardigans. When I looked over at Eric, his eyes were trained on the floor. I listened to the noises in the room, the sniffles, the sighs, everyone wrapped up in their memories, but Eric remained stock still.

It was Dan who spoke first, his voice tender.

'We will need to talk about our dreams,' he said. 'We need to know whether anything else is going to happen. Jess was one of us and she's dead. Is anyone else in danger?'

I heard the old ladies gasp, not having made a connection between Jess and the gift they all allegedly shared, but I sensed guilt from the others in the room, as if somehow they had missed an opportunity to prevent the murder.

Dan held his hands out. 'Who wants to go first?'

It was Lily who spoke up.

'I've been sleeping badly,' she said. 'I wake up in a big house, and I can hear a child crying. I try and help, follow the sound, but I never get there. It's always just through the next door, in the next room, but I'm too scared to go on, too scared to go back. I don't know how I got there, but it feels like I am looking for something I can't find, and I'm crying. Maybe not out loud, but in my head I am screaming.'

I noticed that Eric was staring at her, transfixed, and then I remembered that he had told me something similar in the café. 'What happens next?' I asked quietly, pulled in by her tale.

'I feel like I'm falling and then I wake up,' she said.

'Who do you think you are in the dream?' I tried to sound disinterested, just polite, but I had noticed the effect it had had on Eric.

Lily shook her head, and I saw fear in her eyes. 'I don't know.'

The rest of the group exchanged glances, but no one

else spoke. I could sense the nervousness in the room. Dan broke the silence by asking, 'Did anyone else dream anything unusual this week?'

Billy Hunt spoke up.

'I saw a tramp hanging,' he said.

Everyone looked at him, surprised.

'A tramp?' asked Charlie.

Billy scowled. 'Yeah, that's what I saw, and it made me shoot awake. It came at the end of a normal dream.' As he looked around, he held up a scrap of paper. 'I wrote it down,' he said, and when no one responded, he coughed lightly and began to read:

'*Parachuting. Climbing a mountain, maybe a hill, surrounded by friends. And then I'm soaring, on a parachute, the world below me. Everything is small, but I am gliding, not coming down, just flying along. But then I get lower, and the world gets bigger. And the little dots on the floor become people in the world, and as I get nearer they are pointing at me, because I'm flying above them. But I'm getting lower, lower, all the time getting nearer. And they point more. But they are smiling, not laughing.*'

Billy looked up from his piece of paper.

'Then it changed really quickly,' he said, and carried on reading.

'*As I came in to land, it got dark and cold, and there were no more people. The street was long and thin and quiet, and then at the end, just in midair, a worn-out man is hanging, his legs limp, his head loose on one side.*'

'Who did you think it was?' asked Dan.

'I don't know. I couldn't see his face, but I could see

his feet swinging, and I could tell that he was dead.' He looked away defensively. 'Then I woke up.'

'When did you dream this?'

'This morning.'

Dan sat back and looked around the group. 'Anyone had anything similar?'

Everyone shook their heads.

'Did you have any idea of where this person was?' asked Dan.

Billy shook his head. 'I knew it was something bad, but I can't tell you anything else. I didn't recognise anything, or anyone.' He sat back, his arms folded. He seemed hostile, defensive.

I watched Billy Hunt carefully. He had opened up briefly, had become animated, but now he was back to the surly person he had been a few moments earlier. I looked back over at Eric, and I remembered how he had been when I'd first met him, a scruffy, frightened old man. Was he the tramp? Then I looked away when he glanced in my direction. Maybe it was nothing.

Sam turned on his engine when he saw Alison's car pull out of the car park.

He had been waiting for her, wanting to see where she went. He checked his watch. A late finish, even for the golden girl. A late-night meeting with Harry? She had been in his office a lot more than usual, and whenever Harry appeared it seemed like she wasn't far away. Solicitors were manoeuvring for position at Parsons, with Harry's retirement imminent. Harry had found out about Terry McKay quickly enough, and now the file was gone. And Harry had a vested interest in making the file go away. Was this Alison's way of nudging herself forward in the queue for Harry's affection?

Alison lived in an apartment in a converted wharf building, a short drive from the office, with hardwood floors and a balcony view over the canal. He let her get into the traffic flow and then went through a red light so that he was just a few cars behind.

She did the short circuit of the ring road. He gripped his steering wheel in anticipation as she approached the turning that would take her on the road towards Harry's house, but she kept going straight ahead.

He settled in behind her, just one car between them. He saw her turn left at some traffic lights, and he realised that she was heading home. He thought about turning around, but he wanted to see if anyone would visit.

He slowed down and saw that she had parked near the front entrance to her apartment building. He drove past and then came to a stop quietly further along the street. He turned round in his seat and watched her as she climbed out of her car and then fished in her bag for her keys.

Sam turned off his headlights and the street turned ominously dark.

I watched Billy as the meeting wound up. He hadn't said much after the account of his own dream, almost as if he was embarrassed. He didn't seem to fit in as well as the others.

I went to speak to Eric, who was cleaning the kitchen. 'We can use the hut for free,' he said, 'provided we keep it clean.' He finished wiping the surface and then turned around to face me. 'What did you think?'

I leaned against a work surface, a small patch of fake granite. 'I'm not sure.'

'You're not a believer, are you?'

I shook my head.

'But you came here, to hear things you don't believe?'

I shrugged at that. 'I don't have to believe it to write it.'

'But if you tell it like you believe it, isn't that like lying?'

'Only if it's untrue.' I paused, and then said, '*Is* it untrue?'

Eric put the cloth down. 'Sam Nixon is in danger. I feel it as strong as anything I've ever felt. I just don't know why or when.'

'I don't think he's the tramp,' I said jokingly, but Eric didn't smile.

'Don't worry too much about Billy,' Eric said. 'He doesn't contribute much. He's just lonely, I think, which is sad for a man his age. He goes along with it, but I don't think he gets dreams like we do.'

'Why do you say that?'

'Because he doesn't describe the emotions everyone else does when we have the dreams. It's not just the images. It's the feeling of dread, the panic, the knowledge that you have seen something. Billy has never said what he feels; just what he sees. He just dreams, like most people do.'

'So it's a gift the rest of you have?'

Eric shook his head. 'No, a curse.'

'It's a curse for us all,' said a voice.

I whirled around. It was Dan.

'Why do you say that?' I asked.

Dan snorted a laugh. 'Can you imagine what it feels like to see something you couldn't do anything about?' He went to help Eric tidy up. 'I'm glad I found these people. I thought I was going mad.'

'But maybe they were just vivid dreams. You don't really know they predict the future.'

Dan's eyes narrowed. 'I have normal dreams too. Not every dream is precognitive. But I can tell the difference. I can feel them, see them clearly, almost feel the pain in them.'

'So how did you find out about other people?'

'My doctor,' Dan replied. 'I was desperate when I went, but he knew people who'd had similar experiences, and he directed me here.' He smiled. 'It saved my life.'

I saw that Eric had turned away, found some more cleaning to do that stopped me from seeing his face. 'When Lily described her dream,' I said to him, 'with the big house and the falling, I saw your face. I saw something – fear, I thought.'

Eric didn't respond. He just carried on cleaning, but I saw his hand slow down.

'Were you scared, Eric?' I asked.

He turned round to look at me and said quietly, 'I've been having that dream. It wakes me up, just like it does with Lily.'

'Does she know you have it too?'

He shook his head.

Dan looked towards Eric, and then winked at me.

'Time to go,' and then he walked away, back into the room.

I watched Dan wave goodbye to Lily, Bessie and Maggie, before linking arms with Charlie as they went outside. Billy didn't go with them. He watched the door close and then turned back into the room, and there was sadness in his look. I recognised it: he liked Charlie.

'How much have you told the police about your other dream?' I asked Eric. 'The one about Jess?'

Eric stared at me with suspicion, but then he looked down and shook his head. 'Nothing yet.' Then he looked up. 'Are you going to write about me?'

'I think so,' I said. 'Can I speak to you again?'

Eric smiled and nodded. 'Yes, of course, but promise me one thing.'

'Go on.'

'Tell Sam Nixon to be careful.'

Chapter Thirty-one

Terry looked out of the car window as they headed out of Blackley, to a network of tight terraced streets, redbrick, derelict, the windows boarded up. There were still some families left, waiting to be re-housed, but this was an area ready to be flattened. It was Jimmy King's domain, whole streets bought up and sold for redevelopment. Anyone who resisted a move out received advice they couldn't ignore.

Terry looked at the back of the driver's shining bald head, his skin gleaming deep red, his neck wide, the folds at the back of his head thick. Terry looked at the hands on the wheel, large callused knuckles, the grip tight, the shirt-cuffs straining against his forearms.

'Where are we going?' asked Terry suspiciously.

'Like I said, to meet Jimmy,' came the voice. It was quiet, with a measured menace.

Terry looked out of the window again and his hand flicked at the door handle. Locked.

The car turned into a narrow housing strip, the houses separated only by a thin line of tarmac that didn't go the full length of the street. There were still cobbles at one end, and over a wall there was the viaduct, the curved rail tracks that ran high above the town.

They stopped outside a terraced house at the end, the bricks daubed with graffiti, the tags of local kids. The windows had chipboard covers over them, one downstairs, two upstairs. Terry's door opened, and he felt a hand grip his shoulder.

'C'mon, let's talk about your money.'

Terry was pulled out of the car and then pushed towards the front door. He stumbled to his knees and gasped. He looked down the street quickly. There were streetlights, but all the houses were dark. He thought he saw a figure in the shadows further away, maybe a dealer, lurking in the alleys. Then the door to the house opened, and he felt the hand behind him lift him by his arm and push him inside.

He stumbled again. This time his hands hit the floor, and he ended up with grit in his palms. The York stone floor had been removed, leaving just dirt and pieces of broken brick. He looked up, scared, and saw Jimmy King. He was sitting in the corner, on a plastic picnic chair. He looked immaculate in his suit, his legs crossed, his hands placed neatly on his thighs, a ring cluttered with small diamonds on his little finger, catching the light from the builders' lamp next to him.

Terry hauled himself to his knees and wiped the dirt from his chest. His mouth had turned dry, his chest was tight.

Jimmy King grinned, his teeth glinting in the semi-darkness.

'Hello, Terry. Shall we talk about your money?'

Sam was running through the building. He shouted out, but the shape ahead kept on going. It was dark, hooded, pushing through doors, always running away. He reached out, pleaded for the shape to stop. Someone was crying, begging for help. Then he was falling.

He jumped as he woke up. His shirt collar was damp, his forehead wet. He looked around quickly, tried to remember where he was. It was dark. He took deep gulps as it came back to him. He was in his car, outside Alison's apartment.

He loosened his collar and rested his head on the steering wheel. How much longer would he be plagued like this?

He eventually looked up. His windows had misted up. He wound his window down and looked back towards Alison's apartment building, and then he started as he saw an empty space where her car had been.

'Oh fuck!' he shouted, his eyes wide. He thumped the steering wheel. 'Shit, shit, shit!'

He tried to calm himself down. Think, he told himself. Where would she have gone? He checked his watch. It was after nine. She wouldn't go to Harry's house, not this late. What about the office?

He grinned. That's where she would go, back to the office. Harry was probably there now, waiting for the latest on Terry McKay. And Sam knew why: because Harry had lied to save Jimmy King's son.

And now it was Alison who was doing the dirty tricks, selling out her colleagues to get her leg up the ladder.

He turned on the engine. He was angry now. All the hours he had put in for Parsons, all snatched away because of one case. It wasn't going to happen.

He mounted the kerb on the opposite pavement as he accelerated hard and headed back to Blackley town centre.

Terry cried out when the first kick landed.

He curled himself into a ball, tried to protect himself, but the kicks still made it through. To his stomach, to his face. He was yelling, 'Stop it, stop it,' but blood splattered his face as his nose took a hit. He felt it crack, sensed the room go quiet as he reeled from the pain, the noise muffled. He felt like he was elsewhere, felt himself slip from the room.

The haze slowly cleared, and he started to feel the blows again, now punches, methodical and slow, hard and on target.

He tried to ride it out. He had been there before, the victim of gang attacks by restless teenagers. But he sensed that this one wouldn't end when the man in the suit got bored. If he ever did.

There was a pause and Terry tried to look up. He couldn't do it. He rolled onto his back and tasted his own blood in his throat. He coughed. He tried to roll over, but the pain made him gasp. He sank back again and looked towards the ceiling, his chest sucking in air fast.

'Now, Mr McKay,' King said, the tone gentle. 'You said that I owe you some money. Is that right?'

Terry nodded, but his hand shot to his head as the pain in his nose almost made him pass out.

'Good,' said Jimmy. 'I wanted to make sure I heard you right. Five thousand pounds, you said. Who else have you told about this misunderstanding?'

Terry shook his head and coughed.

'No one?' said Jimmy in mock surprise. 'Just that whore you presented to me this afternoon?'

Terry nodded, more slowly this time.

'And what about Sam Nixon?'

Terry said nothing at first. He looked up at the ceiling. The state of his life flashed through his mind. The drink. Prison. His digs. The promise he'd had as a young man. Nice clothes. A car. Girls he'd known. Pretty ones. He shook his head again, this time ignoring the pain. 'I just want my money,' he said quietly.

He heard Jimmy sigh, and as he turned to gaze at him, Terry saw Jimmy look at the man in the suit and nod.

Terry shrieked when his wrist was twisted as he was dragged across the floor. His feet scuffled in the dirt, and then he cried out when his left hand banged against a radiator, the pipe squashed against his fingers. He tried to kick out, but he felt something wrap around his wrist. He tried to pull against it, but the hand holding him down was too strong, too determined. Terry strained, tried to wriggle free, but when the pressure eased he realised that he couldn't move his left hand. As he looked, he saw that it was tied to the radiator pipe.

He reached round with his other hand to get to the knot, but it was kicked away.

He heard Jimmy stand up, his leather soles making light crunching noises in the dirt. Jimmy stepped over to him. As Terry looked up, he realised that he was trapped. He couldn't move away from the wall, and he was in a derelict street where no one would find him. Or hear him.

'I grew up on this street,' said Jimmy, his voice calm and deliberate. 'The old children's home just across the road. Me and Harry Parsons.' When Terry looked up at him, he nodded, a smile teasing the corners of his mouth. 'Surprised? About me? Or is it Harry?'

Jimmy shook his head. 'You're a greedy little bastard, Terry McKay,' he said. 'You take everything. You give nothing back. And we're all supposed to feel sorry for you. '

Jimmy tapped him in the ribs with his shoes.

'You live like a dog,' Jimmy said, and then knelt down, and Terry sensed that it was so Jimmy could see the fear in his eyes. 'How did you get to this?'

Terry tried to scuttle backwards, away from Jimmy, but he couldn't. He was jammed against the wall. 'Don't leave me here,' he pleaded. 'I'm sorry, Mr King. I won't ask any more.'

Jimmy smiled, and then chuckled. 'That's not enough. You're frightened now. You'll say anything to get out. But when you get out, you'll go back to living like you do and forget about this, about what you tried

229

to do to me.' He raised his eyebrows. 'How you threatened me.' He shook his head. 'You need something to remind you, every waking moment of your pitiful life, drunk or sober, that you never, ever threaten me with anything.'

Terry was breathing heavily now, his mouth open, his nose blocked by blood. He saw Jimmy look at his hand, the one bound tightly against the radiator, and then back to the man in the suit.

'Burn it off,' he said.

Terry began to moan, tried to pull again at the bindings around his wrist. The man in the suit nodded and went over to the corner. He picked up something that gleamed metallic in the light from the builders' lamp, and then pulled out a cigarette lighter from his pocket.

Terry cried out when he heard the soft hiss of escaping gas, and then the small flicker from the lighter turned the gas into a blue flame. He began to shake, felt his legs go warm as he pissed himself, tried to pull himself away from the radiator. His eyes opened wide as the man came towards him, the blowtorch in his hand. He tried to cover up his face with his free hand, but the man grabbed it. Before he could cry out with pain or beg or plead, the air was pushed from him as the man knelt on his chest.

He felt the flame get nearer, felt the heat on his palm. His mind raced, driven fast by terror. He screamed, 'No, no, no,' but still the heat got closer. It was just to frighten him, he thought, to hurt him, just to make sure he wouldn't ask again. He wouldn't, he knew that now. He had learned his lesson, not to cross Jimmy

King. 'Let me go,' he tried to scream, but no sound came out.

He bucked as the flame hit his hand, his eyes wide, his mouth open, screaming, crying. It was searing, not stopping. Then he couldn't think any more, his mind overtaken by pain.

Chapter Thirty-two

Sam had parked down the road from Parsons & Co. He hoped to see a light on, just proof that someone was there. He checked his watch again. It looked all in darkness, but maybe they were just being careful. He thought about checking the car park, but he wouldn't be able to see the cars until he was right there, and then he would be in full view of anyone in the building. No, it was better to wait, to catch them unawares.

He took a mouthful of the energy drink, a mix of caffeine, sugar and chemicals.

He waited thirty minutes and still the office was in darkness. He knew he had to take a closer look.

The street seemed quiet when he stepped out of his car, just a sweep of dark windows opposite orange street-lights. Sam didn't want to go to the front of the office; it was too well-lit. There was an alleyway that ran behind the street and separated the offices from their car parks. He walked quickly and ducked into it. The crunch of his shoes resounded as he entered the shadows. He thought he heard breathing, but maybe it was just echoes.

The alleyway was long, just a brick wall on one side

that stretched as far as he could see, broken by gates from the office yards, and on the other a low wall, just a short step into the firm's car park, nothing but a patch of gravel.

Sam jumped as the security light flashed on. He stopped, tried to listen out for movement. Had someone heard him? Then he saw something, just a dark shape in the corner of the car park.

He stood still and the light went off. He tried to peer into the shadows. What had he seen? There had definitely been something.

Sam took a deep breath and then walked slowly forward. His shoes crunched loudly on the gravel, the only sound he could hear. He stepped over the low wall and tried to stick to the edge of the car park, to keep out of range of the security light. There was a glow from the streetlights that ran along the other side of the car parks. Sam could see a mound, a bundle of rags. He edged forward. It was someone lying down. He could hear moans, rasping and low. It was only a few feet away now, and he reached out, ready to touch it. Then he recognised the shape. The streetlights caught the coat he had seen earlier in the day, the worn-out shoes, with the sole flapping away from the cracked uppers. It was Terry McKay.

Sam rushed over and knelt down.

'Terry!'

The security light flashed on, blinding him for a second. He heard a moan.

Terry turned towards him, and Sam saw blood on his face. Then Terry started to raise his arm, opened his mouth as if to say something. There was a gurgling sound. Sam saw blood in his mouth. As Terry turned, his left hand came into view, catching the beam.

Sam spluttered as he saw the hand, the searing taste of vomit in the back of his throat.

There wasn't much left. It was black and swollen, pieces of charred skin hanging down, ragged in places, red and raw in others. Sam thought he could see bone, like white spindles, visible through the flesh.

Sam stepped away quickly, kicking gravel as he went, and vomited at the side of the car park. Terry McKay looked at him, shuffled forward, tried to speak, his eyes pleading, in pain.

Sam whirled around quickly. Who else was there? Who else had seen him? Then his mind flashed back to what had been said by Jimmy, that arrangements had been made to meet. If Sam spoke to the police, he would tell them that. But as he looked down at Terry, he saw exactly what happened to people who crossed Jimmy King.

He wiped his mouth and rushed out of the car park. He didn't look around, not wanting to see Terry looking at him, begging for his help. He looked ahead instead, focused hard on getting away.

Chapter Thirty-three

Sam rushed straight to the bathroom when he got home. He sat on the edge of the bath, his head in his hands, his fingers gripping his hair.

What had he done? Why had he allowed Terry to antagonise Jimmy King? It had been his job to protect Terry. He tried to tell himself that it had been Terry's choice, that it had been nothing to do with him. But then he remembered how he had left him in the car park, desperate, in agony.

He rushed to the toilet and heaved into it, but there was nothing left in his stomach. Cold sweat prickled his forehead and he took in big gasps of air. His hands were shaking.

Sam slumped backwards and looked around, at the expensive Italian mosaic tiles, the power shower, the decadent toiletries Helena loved. Had he left a man desperate for help for all this? Financial security, a world away from his mother's struggles, her worries about the bills or whether her son would mess up his chance to get away from the estate. He thought about Terry McKay. About Jimmy King. About Eric Randle, and Harry

Parsons. And as he heard someone turn over in bed, the lightest of creaks, he thought about his children, beautiful young boys he loved but never saw.

And then he thought about Helena. Beautiful Helena. He'd thought once that all he needed was Helena. Her laugh. Her look. That tease, playful and girlish. When was the last time he had seen that? Or her naked? Not just without clothes, but naked with him, wanting him, needing him?

He put his head back and thought about how she was now, cold when sober, angry when drunk. It wasn't meant to be like that.

He wrapped his arms around his knees, started to rock backwards and forwards, just lightly at first. But then he got faster. Before he had a chance to stop himself, he had his head buried into his knees, sobbing like a lost child.

Kyle was dodging the streetlights, ducking his way through the back alleys. He was out too late, had been told to be back indoors three hours earlier, it was too late for a boy his age. His footsteps made soft pat-pat noises, his trainers creeping along the bricks in the alleyway.

He had to get back, he knew that, but he didn't want to. He was in trouble already but it was nothing new. Ever since his mum's new boyfriend had moved in, he had gone from one argument to another, sometimes beatings. And what was there to go back for anyway? His damp bedroom, in a building covered in graffiti? And his mum? She was drunk all the time, or worse.

Kyle remembered how she used to be, just a year

before. She had hugged him, cuddled him. She had always smelled of drink, and she fell down sometimes, but she was worse now. The flat was always filled with smoke, and with men who sat around and said little, just listened to loud music and giggled at each other.

He had stepped on a damp carpet a few houses back, and he crinkled his nose at the smell – damp, almost like sewage. The alley ran between the two streets of terraces, about four feet wide with a streetlight at each end. The bricks had a wet look and shone back the orange light, the gutter that ran along the centre not much more than a dip in the bricks. The walls were over seven feet high, with tall gates, padlocked, guarding small concrete yards overlooked by narrow, dirty windows. He knew he could cut across the main road at the top and work his way home.

He sneaked along, enjoying the furtive excitement of it. His footsteps were the only sounds he could hear, just soft slaps on the damp floor. He stopped whenever he saw a headlight go across the top of the alley, but otherwise he had the night to himself. He pushed at gates as he went, just to see if they were open. He might find an unlocked bike, maybe even a moped. He wouldn't steal one. He would just take it for a few hours in the fields, and then he would leave it so that it could be found.

A headlight flashed, then the sweep of a beam. He stopped and flattened himself against a wall, faded into the brickwork. It might be the police. He had done nothing wrong, but the police wouldn't think that. They had taken him home a few times. The last time they had

237

visited, a social worker came with them. She'd said he might get taken away if it happened again.

He watched the shadows for a while, but they remained still.

Kyle stepped away from the wall and listened. There was no one there. He walked a few more yards, and then he stopped. He had to cross one of the cut-throughs that connected the two streets. It was wider than the alley he was in, and light filtered through from the street. He stopped, peered around the wall, but couldn't see anything. No police. No one else.

He bolted across the gap and back into the alley on the other side, into darkness once more.

He stopped, felt his breath catch in his throat. He almost laughed at himself for being scared. He set off walking again, pushing at gates, looking out for faces at the windows.

He had only walked a few yards when he thought he heard something, a breath, the sound of a shoe on the bricks. He listened out for it again but there was nothing there.

Kyle set off once more, but more slowly now, rattled, suddenly wanting to be home. Then he heard it again. He turned around quickly, tried to place the sound. But he couldn't. He didn't know if it was in front or behind, or anywhere at all. He looked back down the alley, back to where he had come from, watching for movement, a shifting of the shadows, but he couldn't see anything. He looked the other way, to where he was headed. It was just blackness. The streetlights at the top made it seem darker everywhere else, just shadows until the top of the alley.

He couldn't go back, maybe the noise he had heard came from there. He turned into the darkness. He walked forward slowly and listened for a noise. He was holding his breath, he realised. He felt a tingle down his neck.

As he walked, the lights at the top of the alley got nearer, so he started to walk more quickly. It made his footsteps louder, but each step took him nearer to the main road at the top. He looked around. Some of the back windows were lit, flickering blues from late-night television.

He started to run.

The main road seemed just a few yards away now. He felt scared, something about the darkness felt threatening, hostile. He thought about his mum. He wanted her, needed to feel the wrap of her arms, realised that he wanted to be home, safe behind a locked door.

He was almost at the main road when the figure stepped in front of him, blocking his way. Kyle yelped, started to walk backwards, but a hand snapped forward and gripped his jacket. He tried to pull against it, was about to shout out, when the figure's other hand went over his mouth. He didn't have time to move or dodge, to sprint away. He felt the warmth of a cloth and suddenly the panic went. He started to feel calmer, and then it felt like he was being pulled downwards as the darkness of the alley became complete.

Chapter Thirty-four

Sam woke up with a gasp. He looked down, remembered that he was at home. The clock read 5.45, the digits bright red in the dark room. He was panting, the sheets tangled around his legs. He looked across at Helena. All he could see was a shape, but she appeared still, and her light breathing told him that she was asleep.

He lay back and sighed, rubbed his face. His heart was beating a fast rhythm. Every night was the same, another trip into a nightmare he couldn't control. Why the same dream, night after night, making him wake up like this, his stomach churning, his heart racing? And they were getting stronger, each one worse than the one before, the feeling of dread so real that he could still taste the fear.

He took deep breaths and wiped his forehead. What should he do? He thought about Eric. What would *he* do? How many times had *he* woken like this, drenched in sweat and fear? Sam knew he hadn't given Eric much time, but still he knew the answer: he would paint.

But Sam couldn't paint; he'd never had the talent. If

he wanted to make it real, he would have to do something different, something of his own. Then he thought about his job. He was a lawyer. He used words.

He climbed out of bed slowly, trying not to wake Helena, and crept downstairs, his bare feet quiet on the carpeted stairs. The only sound he could hear was the ticking of the radiator pipes as the central heating slowly warmed up the house. He went to the cupboard under the stairs, where the children put their toys at the end of the day, and rummaged around until he found a drawing pad and a Parsons & Co pen, a cheap corporate giveaway.

He thought about Terry McKay from the night before, wondered how he was, but he shook it away. He tried to hang on to his dream instead, just so he could make some sense of it.

He made himself comfortable in one of the kitchen chairs and thought back on his dream. It started to feel more distant, almost as if it was slipping away with every conscious minute that passed. He began to write quickly.

'I'm inside. It's cold, dark outside. Lots of doors inside. And cold walls. I'm running, and the rooms never end, just doors, shadows in front, shadows behind. I'm chasing. I can hear sounds and I'm desperate. I'm out of breath, but I'm getting no closer, and the doors keep slamming shut in front of me, the walls moving faster, the darkness ahead getting closer, making it hard for me to see where I'm going. I'm shouting out but I can't make out what. I can see a figure ahead, dark, just a shadow, and it's moving ahead of me, faster than I can move, and he is younger, stronger, but I keep going, always chasing, never catching.

I can hear crying, a child. The figure I'm chasing is a man. He's holding something, and it's bright, golden, but he won't let me see it. I'm sure it's a man, although I can't see the face, but the feeling is of evil, of malevolence. But I have to catch him, I'm desperate to catch him.'

Sam stopped writing and sat back as he tried to remember more detail, but it was getting harder. He closed his eyes and tried to picture the clothes he was wearing in his dream, and even whether he could be sure it was him. He started to write again.

'It is me, I know it is. I can tell from the strength of the feeling, like despair, panic. When I felt it in the dream, I felt it in real life. I'm wearing my work clothes, a grey suit, a shirt and tie, but they are soiled and dirty, like I've been running and chasing for a long time. And then I'm falling, can feel the air rushing past me, and I'm screaming. Falling a long way.'

'What are you doing?'

Sam looked up, surprised.

Helena walked into the room, wrapped up in a large white dressing gown, her eyes red and tired-looking. Sam could smell the stale booze on her, it drifted over as she walked in, and her cheeks were flushed.

'I'm writing down my dreams,' he said.

Helena rubbed her eyes. 'You're doing what?'

'Someone came to see me, and he paints his dreams. He says that they come true.'

She sighed. 'So it's to do with work,' she said, 'even at this time of the day.'

'What do you mean?'

'It's always work,' she said bitterly. 'If you're not there, you're wishing you were.'

She sat down at the dining table, a large beechwood oval they'd bought on one of their few shopping trips together. She watched Sam as the pen dangled over the page, and then she asked, 'Where were you last night?'

Sam sat back and thought about his answer. 'I was at work,' he said, which was a version of the truth.

'Who was she?'

Sam didn't answer.

Helena folded her arms. 'Does she make you feel guilty?'

'*I'm* not the one with the secrets.'

Helena shook her head, curled her lip in disgust. 'Don't take me for a fool, Sam. If you're going to have an affair, just tell me and get out.'

Sam said nothing for a few seconds, and then he replied quietly, 'I am not having an affair.'

Helena didn't answer at first. She sighed heavily, and Sam saw a tear trickle down her cheek. 'Why aren't you around more then?'

Sam felt his own eyes begin to prickle. He knew what she was thinking. Harry had rarely been there during Helena's childhood, spending all his time at the office, building his empire, and Sam knew how she felt about it. But he wasn't like Harry. Sam had listened to Helena talk about her childhood, and Sam had sworn never to be like that. Harry lived for the firm, and lived for the law.

But there was still a mortgage to pay, and school fees, and two cars to run.

Helena must have guessed what he was thinking, or maybe it was because they'd had the discussion so many times. 'That isn't what we used to talk about when we were younger,' she said, and her voice started to crack. 'When we swapped dreams, we never said that one day we'll be unhappy just so that we can pay a mortgage. I thought maybe we'd spend time with each other, you know, actually be together, rather than this,' and she waved her hands around as if to indicate everything.

Sam had known that she was unhappy, but to hear her say it came at him swift and hard.

'You say things like that when you're young,' he said, his own voice also a croak. 'This is real life now.'

Helena didn't answer.

'Are you unhappy?' He asked the question nervously, not wanting the answer. He had expected this conversation at some point, had even prepared his answers, but now it was here, he didn't want it.

Helena nodded, looking down, and Sam saw she was sobbing. He didn't go to her. He felt stuck, unable to move.

'Why?' he asked.

She looked up and laughed, but it was bitter, her cheeks wet with tears.

'Why do you fucking think?' she snarled. 'You spend all day at the office, and all night, and then spend the evening running around with some young tart.'

'There isn't some young tart,' he snapped back, his temper rising. 'I was working.'

'No, you weren't!' she screamed, and banged her fist on the table. 'I came by the office to take your sons out for something to eat. It was dark, no one was there.'

Sam didn't answer. What could he say? That he was sitting outside a young woman's apartment?

She stood up and went to a cupboard, began to search through it. Sam grabbed her arm.

'More booze?' he said.

'Fuck off.'

'And the dream I had when we got married wasn't that you would drink yourself into an early grave,' he said, sadness replaced by anger. He grabbed her arm and pulled her towards the hall, pushed her in front of a mirror. 'Look at you. You're a mess.'

She pulled against him. 'And that's why you're playing around?' she shouted. 'Doesn't she look quite as fucking messy?'

'I'm not playing around with anyone,' he shouted, and then he pushed her away. 'Helena, I have not been unfaithful to you, I never have.'

'What about you never will?'

Sam didn't reply.

'And what about the love and cherish part?' she said, before pushing past him as she went back into the kitchen and grabbed a bottle of vodka.

Sam followed her and saw her slam the bottle down on the table and unscrew the top quickly. 'Is that it?' he said. 'Daddy's girl not getting enough attention?' His voice sounded cruel, even to him. 'So you drink. Well done. A real grown-up response.'

'Maybe I just need you around more,' she screamed, and poured a thin layer of vodka into the bottom of the glass. 'You know what,' she said, 'I really don't care any more. And I don't think you do either.'

He reached forward quickly and grabbed her glass. He couldn't think straight. He was angry, tired, upset.

He threw the glass against the wall, bared his teeth as Helena screamed. He picked up the bottle next. Helena moved towards him, so he threw that as well. He turned towards her as pieces of glass fell to the floor and vodka splattered over the wall.

'Try doing without for a day,' he sneered at her, and then he walked over to the piece of paper he had been writing on. He snatched it up and slammed it onto the table. 'Have a read if you like,' he said, and then he left the room.

As he turned to go up the stairs, he looked back. Helena had her head in her hands. The vodka was starting to pool on the floor.

He started to walk upstairs, but stopped when he saw Zach at the top.

'Are you and Mummy arguing?' he asked, his voice coming out in a whisper. He looked worried, too much so for a boy his age. His hair was sticking up and his pyjama bottoms were slack around his waist.

'We've just had a disagreement,' he said, his voice thick with emotion.

'Are you going to work?'

Sam nodded, unable to answer. Zach came down the stairs towards him, and Sam held out his arms. He needed to hug his son, wanted to feel him bury his head into his shoulder.

Zach walked past him and carried on down the stairs.

Sam watched him go, and he realised that he had a wife he still loved and two beautiful children. And that he had never felt as lonely in his life.

* * *

246

The room was lit by the old paraffin lamp. It made the shadows dance as the wick flickered with the flame.

As he walked in, he felt the cold settle around him. Summer was fading and the nights were getting colder. Condensation fell from the ceiling as the wood stove made heat bounce back from the cold ceiling. His feet scraped along the ground, small stones and debris stuck under the soles of his shoes.

He'd found an old wood stove the day before. He put some logs into it and held out his hands as they crackled in the flames. His fingers ached.

As he warmed his hands, he looked to his right, saw the small boy lying on the old camp bed, cobwebs dancing from the ceiling above him, blown by the waves of heat. He seemed so much at peace, so different from the troubled young boy scampering through dark alleyways the night before.

He knelt down by him and smiled.

'It'll be all right, little prince,' he cooed. 'You won't be here long, and then it will all get better.'

The boy's fringe was lying across his forehead, so he blew it away, just soft breaths. He adjusted the blankets he had placed over him during the night. The boy had seemed cold so he had wrapped him up and pulled him closer to the stove, leaving it burning through the night.

He stood up and went to his usual chair. He checked his watch and switched on the television, watched the boy's face as the colours made his skin flicker, his soft pale skin becoming green and blue as he waited for the news bulletin. The old car battery had seen him through most of the summer, but he realised that he would have to get another one soon.

As the news started, he smiled to himself again, pleased, content. It would be a long journey for the young boy, and he might never realise what had been done for him, but one day soon it would all get better. He remembered how the boy had been the night before, skulking through alleyways, sullen and lost-looking. Asleep, the boy looked different. His lips looked soft and his eyelashes were like long blond curls.

The noise of the television drowned out the whistle of the wind. He closed his eyes, satisfied. The boy was the fourth story in, and as he heard it start he felt himself grow hard.

Healing hands.

But then he twitched, opened his eyes. Something wasn't right, something he'd heard. He had felt his heart jolt, a prickle of panic.

He looked at the screen. It was the usual scene, a shot of the alley where the boy had been taken. He glanced over to the boy, and then back at the screen. Kyle Shadsworth. The bulletin had given him a name. But it wasn't that. They'd all had names.

But then he saw the patch on his arm, the fentanyl, the sedative that kept him asleep, knocked him out for days on end, a flow of anaesthetic. He had checked the dosage the night before. The boy seemed tall, and had been out close to midnight. He had guessed his age as twelve, maybe thirteen.

But Kyle was nine, the news now said.

He leaped to his feet. He looked at his hands. They

were trembling. The boy asleep on the rickety old camp bed was nine. Now that he looked again, he could tell. The skin still looked so soft, like baby fat, had felt so smooth under his touch. He looked back at the screen. Kyle's mother was on television, in tears. The hypocrite. Where had she been the night before?

He looked over at Kyle, and saw the wood stove again. And the blankets. He started to get short of breath. The heat would make him absorb the fentanyl quicker, and already the dosage was too high, designed to knock out a boy much older.

He stepped closer. Kyle looked peaceful. His eyes were closed and his lips were parted, but he couldn't see any rise and fall in the boy's chest. He flipped his wrist over and put his watch over Kyle's mouth. When he turned it back, praying for the face to be misted over, the boy's light breaths blocking out the thin black hands, he saw that it was as clear as when he had last looked at it. He reached forward and touched the boy's cheeks. They were cold. He felt for a pulse.

He fell to his knees, put his head in his hands.

His eyes flashed back to the television. Kyle's mother was giving the usual speech, how she wanted whoever had him to return him, safe and well, like all the rest.

He sat down. There would be no happy ending this time, no tearful reunion. He put his head back. It wasn't supposed to happen like this.

Chapter Thirty-five

It was seven o'clock in the morning when Laura's phone rang. I put my head under the pillow, still tired, but then I sensed her become more alert.

When Laura picked it up, her voice still a low drawl, she sounded reluctant. I had fallen asleep before she'd got back last night, and it seemed like her day was starting again already. Laura listened for a while, and then she hung up, fell back onto the sheet. She rubbed her eyes and checked the time.

'Going in early again?' I asked. I felt her warm skin against my own and pulled her towards me. I could taste the night's sleep on her lips and I felt her respond when our hips came together. I was surprised when she pushed away.

'What's wrong?' I asked.

She shook her head and said, 'Nothing. It's just work.'

'Will you cut me into it later?'

She threw the sheet back angrily and climbed out of bed. 'I thought you wanted off the crime scene for a while? Are you missing the action?'

I watched as her body framed itself against the

250

sunshine showing through the curtains. Her dark hair shone out bright against the paleness of her back, and when she turned around I could see the faint marks on her stomach, like scratches, her reminders of when she'd carried Bobby. She looked beautiful to me, and, like I always did, I felt privileged to watch her naked. 'Yeah, because I meet people like you when I do.'

Laura slipped on a dressing gown. 'I saw you last night, going into that hut.' Her voice was clipped, sharp.

I didn't answer, was unsure what to say.

Laura shook her head. 'You're making it hard for me.'

'How come?'

'Don't be stupid, Jack,' she snapped. 'I've given up everything to come up here. I'm in a new job, with new people. This will be a short stay for me if you start interfering.'

'We've got to eat,' I said lamely.

Laura pulled her hair back and gave a small laugh. 'So far I'm the only one bringing in real money, and you're doing your best to stop that. And what about Bobby?'

'What do you mean?'

'Like, isn't it too soon to be relying on Martha, that maybe we should be looking after him? I go to work, put in long hours to pay the bills, and you just dump Bobby on people he doesn't know so you can chase some hint of a story?'

'We had this out last night. You said it was okay.'

'But I didn't know then that you wanted Martha to babysit so you could trample all over my case.' Laura was shouting, her hands on her hips.

251

'So that's it,' I said, my voice harsher than I wanted it to sound. 'I get it now. It's not about Bobby. It's about me getting in your way.'

Laura didn't reply. She glared at me.

I stared back. I wanted to say something, but I stayed quiet, wanted to win the argument.

'"Sorry" would have been nice,' Laura said bitterly. '"I won't do it again" would have been even better. But you'll do it again, won't you?'

Once more, I didn't reply.

'I'm going to have breakfast with my son,' she said quietly, and closed the door.

Sam was drinking from a Styrofoam cup when he went into his office, a hot Americano, good and strong. He stopped when he saw Alison there. She was sitting in his chair.

'What are you doing?' he asked.

'Don't you think I should be asking the questions?' she said. Her voice was quiet.

He laughed, cold and harsh. 'Send Harry down,' he replied, angry. 'Or are you his spokeswoman now, as well as his favourite?'

'What are you talking about? Do you really want me to speak to Harry, after what you've been doing? He'll tell Helena. Do you want that?'

Sam looked confused, didn't know how to respond.

'I saw you,' she said.

He turned red, thought about denying it.

'I was frightened,' she continued.

'Frightened?'

252

She stood up. Her eyes were cold, filled with contempt.

'You followed me home,' she said to him. 'You waited outside my flat in your car. What else have you been doing?' She took a deep breath and glared at him. 'For Christ's sake, Sam, you scared me!'

'Well, you tell me something,' Sam responded, getting angry himself now. 'Why do you think I would be following you?'

She shrugged theatrically. 'I don't know. Why do older men follow younger women around?'

That surprised him. He knew how it sounded, how it looked. 'No, no,' he spluttered. 'That's not what I was doing.'

She went to walk out of his office. 'I came here to warn you, to give you a chance. I don't know what is going on in your marriage, and I don't want to know, but following me home so that you can gawp at me as I get into the shower will not make things better.' She stood close to him as he struggled to think of a response. 'If I see you near my flat again, I will call the police. Or Helena.'

He took some deep breaths. He felt embarrassed, ashamed, stupid even, but he couldn't think of an appropriate response.

Alison looked at him. It seemed like she was waiting for an answer, an apology or something. When nothing came in response, she stormed out of Sam's office.

Sam dropped his coffee, felt it hit his shoes. He put his head in his hands. I just need some sleep, he thought to himself. Just some sweet, uninterrupted sleep.

* * *

Laura was pouring milk over Bobby's cereal. I made myself a coffee as they chatted, just new-school talk about Bobby's new friends. I tried to join in, but when I looked round I saw that Laura was avoiding my gaze.

After a few minutes of silence, I heard Laura ask, 'So how *is* Eric Randle?' She didn't look at me when she said it.

I took a sip of the coffee, felt the caffeine kick me awake.

'He's fine. Still a bit shaken by what happened to Jess.' I knew to go no further on detail around Bobby.

She turned to look at me, waiting to see if I would give anything else up. She kissed Bobby on the top of his head and came over to where I was standing.

'What's your game, Jack?' she asked quietly. 'You're running around with a murder suspect.'

'So he's a suspect? Can I quote you on that?'

'Don't play games,' she hissed at me, her voice low, trying not to let Bobby hear.

'But why does only your job matter?' I whispered back. 'I've got to tiptoe around yours, but you can trample all over mine.'

Laura turned away, and I saw that she had tears in her eyes. I looked upwards and sighed.

I put my arms around her, pulled her back to me and put her head on my shoulder. She was cold at first, but then I felt her sag, and I was aware that she was crying. I buried my face into her hair. 'I'm sorry, I don't want to argue.'

I felt her hand come to my face. 'I know,' she said, and then she looked at me, her cheeks streaked. 'It's not

254

just that. I've come a long way, given up a lot, and I had to fight to get this far. You know that my father was against me joining the police, and he didn't want me to come north. Imagine what he'll say if I have to go back because I messed up.'

'It wouldn't be your fault, though,' I said.

'He won't see it like that.'

I stroked her hair, twisted it round in my fingers. 'Do you really think it would be so awful if I keep chasing the story?'

She raised her eyebrows. 'I heard yesterday that you were at Eric's house. Then I watched you walk into that hut. We're watching him, and we even lost him for a while, and then it turns out that my boyfriend is his new best friend. There aren't many ways I can come out looking good in this.'

I knew Laura was right. But Eric had trusted me, and I had to respect that; a journalist never gives up a source.

But then I thought about Eric. He was a suspect. He had told the police he had seen Jess in a dream, and he had told me nothing more than he had already told the police on countless occasions.

'Have you heard of precognition?' I asked.

Laura looked confused.

'Premonitions in dreams,' I explained. 'Seeing the future and all that.'

Laura nodded. 'He's still spinning that line?'

'He's sincere.'

'Do you believe him?'

I considered for a moment. 'I believe that *he* believes he dreams the future.'

Laura started to smile. 'One of my aunts used to say that she did.'

'You've never mentioned that before.'

'It's not why I remember her, but she used to tell me that she could see into the future.'

'And could she?'

Laura shrugged. 'She never won the lottery, and she didn't see that stroke coming.'

'But you knew that *she* believed it.'

Laura nodded slowly. 'She lived in Devon, so we didn't see her often. Just Christmas and birthday cards, and an occasional trip to her house. But my father believed in her, still does. I thought he would be more rational than that. You know what he's like. She would go into a funny trance and mumble to herself, and then she would rush out and write things down.'

'So if you don't believe Eric, you're saying that your aunt was a liar too.'

Laura sighed at that. 'I'm not sure.'

'Do you know why I was at the hut?' I asked.

Laura shook her head. 'We know that Jess went to some kind of club, but nothing more.'

I smiled. 'It's a dream club.'

Laura laughed. 'What is that?'

'Just like it sounds. They all meet up and discuss their dreams, try and work out if they are premonitions. Jess was a member.'

I went towards the stairs to get dressed, Laura still smiling to herself, when I asked, 'The meeting didn't go on that long. How come you got back so late?'

'They found an old wino with his hand burnt off.

It looked like he'd been tortured. Why don't you look into that instead?'

'What was his name?'

Laura started to load the dishwasher; Bobby was quiet as he ate his Ricicles. 'Terry something.'

I whirled round. 'Terry McKay?'

'That's him. I didn't see him, but we were asked to drive around, to look for a gang of kids.'

'They think it was kids?'

'It's a possibility, so it was worth checking it out.' She raised her eyebrows. 'Bit of a local sport round here, they tell me, beating up tramps.'

I ran upstairs, my heart racing. That was two violent incidents linked to Luke King. And I remembered the words of Billy Hunt from the night before. *A tramp hanging.* Not quite the same, but it might be close enough.

I could hear Laura calling my name, but my mind was rushing through the facts, drawing all the links together.

There was something going on, and I wanted to be the first one to find out. I felt something like a buzz of excitement for the first time since I'd moved back.

Chapter Thirty-six

Pete was waiting for Laura as she hurried into the squad room. People had already begun to arrive, a couple of the junior detectives talking over a coffee by the window, but the room looked like it hadn't really kicked into action yet. Pete was at his desk, leaning back in his chair, two mugs in front of him.

'Glad you could join us,' he said, looking pleased with himself.

She raised her eyebrows at him. 'I could say the excitement is killing me, but I think it's more the early start. So what have you got?

Pete picked up some clear plastic bags and tossed them over towards Laura. 'We found these in the drawer next to Jess's bed.'

Laura picked up the bags and sat down. She stretched the plastic tight to try and better see the contents inside. 'What are they?' she asked.

Pete exhaled. 'Diaries, but not quite. They're a bit weird, like she was jotting down random thoughts.'

He took a drink and then pulled at his lip. He looked bashful, as if he didn't believe what he was about to say. 'It reads like she foretold her own death,' he said.

Laura closed her eyes for a moment, thinking about her conversation with Jack at breakfast. When she opened them, she tried to look surprised. She began to count the plastic bags in her hand, each with an exhibit reference on one of the corners. There were about twenty in all, but not all contained simple pieces of paper. One held a notepad, like a small journal, and Laura put that to one side.

Pete leaned over and shuffled through the bags, and then put one in front of Laura.

'You need to read that one.'

Laura pressed the plastic against the paper inside and the handwriting came into focus. It was in blue pen, scruffy and disjointed, different to how Laura had expected Jess to write. Her house had seemed very orderly and neat. This handwriting was jagged, almost as if the person was writing it when she was drunk – or tired.

'Are we certain it's Jess's writing?'

Pete nodded. 'As certain as we can be.'

Laura pressed the plastic against the paper again and began to read.

'Can't see, can't talk, can't move. All I can see is red. I can hear someone, though, it's a man, and he is laughing. I'm hurting, and I try to get away, but I can't move my arms, my legs. I turn my head to try and see, try to open my eyes, but there is nothing there. Just a red mist, but it seems dark, forbidding. I try to scream for help but there is just a noise I don't recognise.'

Laura looked at Pete, who raised his eyebrows and grinned.

'What do you make of that?' he said.

Laura didn't answer. She didn't know what to make of it. It all fitted, though. The redness. The 'can't see, can't talk, can't move'. Just like she'd been found. But what could it mean? Were these fantasies, some kind of strange sado-masochistic games, where people wanted to be tortured? Was Egan right, after all? Was Jess's death just playtime gone wrong?

Laura didn't think so. But if it wasn't that, then Jess had seen something before it happened. And from the conversation that morning, Laura sensed that she knew how.

'Do you believe in people who can see the future?' she asked.

Pete shook his head slowly. 'Not a chance. If you could see the future, you'd alter it to make it better, which would mean that it would be different, so you wouldn't have seen it at all.'

'That's a pretty skewed way of looking at it.'

He grinned. 'I'm just saying that it's mumbo-jumbo bullshit.'

Laura pointed at the piece of paper in the bag. 'So what about that?'

'There's more than just that one.'

Laura put the first bag to one side and looked at the one underneath.

'Help me, help me, help me. No one is coming, no one is helping. I'm sitting down, and I try to stand and I try to move but I can't. No one can hear me. I can't see

260

anything, don't know where I am, but I can hear footsteps moving around me, feel someone watching me. I struggle, I try to get away, but I can't. And I'm cold. I feel so cold. And weak.'

'What the hell is all this about?' asked Laura.

Pete shook his head. 'Can't say I know, but the notebook is just as freaky. Lots of stuff about trains crashing, planes falling out of the sky, things like that.'

Laura reached over for one of the mugs and took a gulp. She ran through what she had just read. None of it made any sense. She looked over at Pete. 'What would you say if I said that she had actually predicted the future, even her own death?'

'I'd want to know who had been taking drugs, you or her.'

'But do you remember what Eric Randle said when we got there?'

'Yeah, he said he'd had a dream about her.'

Laura nodded towards the plastic bags. 'And she's writing down her dreams.'

Pete's expression didn't change.

'Do you remember last night?' she went on. 'Those people going into that hut.'

Pete nodded.

'It was a premonition club,' Laura said. 'Weekly meetings to talk about dreams.' As Pete laughed, Laura asked, 'Did you recognise one of the people going into the meeting?'

He raised his eyebrows. 'Billy Hunt. Local oddball. Got himself into a bit of trouble a couple of years ago, when he fixated on a young girl who worked in a bookshop in town. He started waiting around for her, turning up when she went out, things like that. She caught him hanging around in the street outside her house one night, just looking up at her bedroom window. She called the cops, and when we searched his house we found videos of her all over the place. He had even filmed her through a gap in the curtains, getting undressed, things like that. He's got a restraining order now.'

Laura took a long swill of coffee and then put the bags of exhibits into her desk drawer. 'We'll go and see Billy Hunt, see what he has to say. He can tell us about their little club. If he thinks he's a suspect, he might tell us more than we expect.'

Pete stood up. 'Didn't you recognise someone there as well?'

Laura turned away and avoided the question.

'Have you told Egan about these diaries?' she asked, as she tried to change the subject from Jack.

He shook his head. 'That's *your* job.'

'My job? Why?'

'Because if I tell him, he'll dismiss it. He hasn't got the imagination. However, if you whisper it into his ear, he might just pay attention.' He winked. 'Give it a nibble, throw in some sweet nothings, and he'll do whatever you want.'

That wasn't advice Laura *ever* wanted to rely on.

As I drove towards Eric's house, I saw two men in a car further down the street. If it was police surveillance, it wasn't discreet. At least it wasn't Laura.

I wanted to ask Eric about Terry McKay. What did

he know? Had he had dreams about him? Had Billy Hunt's dream been about him? I looked up at the house as I parked my car. It looked just how it had done yesterday, desolate and dark.

I looked around as I walked up the path, and when I knocked on the door it sounded muffled, the sound deadened by the thickness of the board.

I listened for a while, but no one came. I banged on the door this time, but still there was no answer. I looked back down to the men in the car, but I couldn't see them any more. They were obviously waiting for Eric to come out, not looking for who went in. I turned back towards the door and turned the handle. The door started to swing open.

I looked around, wondering if anyone else was watching. The windows opposite looked empty, no movement behind the nets. It didn't feel right. A person doesn't board up his windows to protect his house and then leave the front door unlocked. Nerves crept into my stomach. I pushed the door open a fraction more and stepped inside.

The house was in darkness, no sunlight penetrating the boarded-up windows.

'Eric!' I shouted. No response, just my voice as it bounced back at me. I went to the stairs in the corner of the room and shouted again. Nothing.

Something was wrong. I could sense it in the silence, the echoes.

I crept up the stairs, one at a time, ready to apologise when he appeared from one of the bedrooms. But he didn't.

I looked around. There were two bedrooms and a bathroom. It was clean but bare. One of the bedrooms was empty, nothing there behind the wooden boards. The only light upstairs came from the bathroom, the windows there left uncovered.

Eric's bedroom was functional. An old self-assembly wardrobe was in one corner of the room, and on the floor was a mattress, a couple of old blankets cast to one side. I noticed a drawing pad on the floor, and some coloured pens next to it.

But no Eric.

I went back downstairs and looked around some more. My mouth had gone dry. The hairs on my arms were up, my hearing straining to pick up any noise as I tried to take in the house, to look for something that had changed.

I walked towards the back of the house, towards the kitchen, through the living room and into the small recess between the two rooms. I went past the small door, and I remembered how Eric had shouted the day before, anxious for me not to go in there. That it was dark, that people had fallen. But as I looked, I felt my breath escape in a gasp. There was a sliver of light.

I reached for the handle and wondered whether I should go down. I was snooping around in Eric's house. What would he think if he caught me?

But then I reminded myself that I was chasing a story, not making friends, and there was something wrong, I knew that.

I turned the handle and opened the door slowly. The light made me blink, a sudden burst into the dingy house.

There were stairs going down into a cellar, the light from below reflecting brightly off the white walls. I glanced into the kitchen. I noticed a cup on the side, with the string from a tea bag hanging over the edge. It looked like Eric had just abandoned the place.

I paused by the door. If I went down, I could get trapped, the stairs being the only way out. I thought I heard a creak upstairs, but I knew there was no one there. My pulse quickened, and I went onto the first step carefully, waiting for someone to shout out from below. I coughed, just to give Eric a chance to hear me. I went down one step further. My whole body was on the stairs when I sensed the door behind me swing shut. I glanced back at it, worried that it would lock itself. Or that someone would lock it and leave me trapped.

But I had to keep going. I knew that. Something was making me go on, almost as if I was drawn to go down.

I edged my feet down the stairs, as they opened out into a bigger room. The noise of my shoes rustled like I was stepping on sandpaper. I saw something, a shadow. I crept down another step. I saw a foot, someone asleep. One more step and I would be able to see all of the room.

I took another step, my hand against the wall. Then the whole room came into view.

I took a sharp breath, and then I slumped back against the wall. I fumbled for my phone, but then I sat down. I could tell it was no good, that it was no emergency. Too late for that.

There was a boy on the floor, lying down, grey, lifeless. There was no colour to his cheeks, and his lips looked pale. He was dead. His body looked unnatural, posed. I'd heard about the missing boy on the car radio. As I looked at the figure in front of me, I knew that I was looking right at him.

But it wasn't just that.

As I looked to one side of the boy, there was a chair, a rickety wooden thing, cast to one side on the floor, as if it had been kicked over. But it wasn't the chair that grabbed my attention. It was what was swinging above it. Or rather, who.

Chapter Thirty-seven

I was in the garden of a nearby house when I saw Laura arrive.

A young woman with a swarm of kids had made me a cup of sugary tea. Other neighbours stood at their gates as they smoked cigarettes and enjoyed the ringside view.

I watched Laura get out of her car with a gruff-looking man in a leather coat. I guessed that was Pete Dawson. She'd talked about him. Nicer than he looks, or so she said. The officer further along the road pointed me out to them. Pete began to stride over, but I watched as Laura slowed when she saw me.

I smiled sheepishly. Laura took a breath and clenched her jaw.

As Pete got close, he looked suspicious of me. He scowled.

'Nice to meet you, DC Dawson, how are you?' I said.

He looked surprised. He was about to respond when Laura intervened.

'It's all right, Pete,' she snapped. 'I own this one.' She had her hands on her hips. 'This is Jack Garrett, and, for better or worse, he's my partner.'

Pete looked me up and down, and then glanced at Laura. 'What were you doing in Eric Randle's house?' he asked, but his voice was more shocked now than angry.

Laura spoke quietly, but it came out in a hiss, her eyes fiery. 'Yes, what the fuck were you doing in Eric Randle's house?'

I thought back to our conversation earlier in the day, and I knew what Laura was doing. She was angry, but she was asking me to protect her, to let everyone know that it had nothing to do with her. I didn't have Eric to protect any more, and so, apart from Laura, there was just the story to look after. I knew which was most precious to me.

'Chasing up Eric's story,' I said to her, made sure that Pete could hear. 'I'd told you all I knew. I was trying to find out more.'

Pete smirked. 'Your boyfriend is your informant?'

I gave a little laugh. 'I know, it sounds stupid, but he told me that he dreamt the future and painted it. It was a good story.'

I noticed Pete and Laura exchange glances. Then I saw movement over Laura's shoulder. 'Looks like the big chiefs are arriving,' I said.

I saw Pete and Laura deflate. I heard Pete whisper, 'He'll love this.'

'What do you mean?' I asked.

Pete nodded towards Eric's house. 'We had him the other day, when we found Jess. Now this. Turns out that he's the Summer Snatcher, and we let him slip away. Worse than that, if we hadn't been looking for hoodies for attacking a wino, we might have caught him in the act.'

'If it *was* him,' argued Laura.

'What, you think someone else is hanging from that rafter? A case of mistaken identity? And I heard there is a small pile of calling cards, just by Randle's feet.'

I interrupted them. 'Is this Egan?' I asked.

Pete sighed and nodded.

Laura had told me all about him. Just an ego and pinched, rat-like features. 'Look, I know you're both angry with me,' I said, 'but if I get back to you with something, will you talk to me?'

As Egan approached, Pete watched me, and then looked at Laura. 'It depends on what you've got,' he said, and then snorted a laugh. 'It might need to be career-saving.'

Egan sauntered his slow way towards us. Other people stood at their gates, intrigued by the new developments. From the words painted on the boards that covered Eric's window, I guessed that not many people around here would mourn him. As Egan got closer, it seemed like the residents just melted back into their houses.

'I'll cut him off,' said Pete, and he left me with Laura.

There were a few moments of silence, and then she said, 'Be careful, Jack, for both our sakes.' When I didn't respond, she asked, 'Are you all right?'

'Most dead bodies I see are in photographs,' I said. 'Even as a seasoned crime reporter, most corpses are bagged and gone by the time I get there.'

Laura softened. 'Never been to a post mortem?' she asked.

I shook my head. 'It's weird, but it never seems real

when it's part of a story. Maybe it's inhuman, but the bodies are just a detail. Until you see one.'

'Was Eric Randle a killer?' asked Laura.

I looked over to the house, with the word 'peedo' daubed across the front.

'Do you think the people around here know more about who is doing what than you or I will ever know?' I asked.

Laura followed my gaze. 'If you mean do they know who is dealing drugs, or beating their wives, or selling stolen car stereos, then I suppose you're right.'

'It's sat-navs now, so I hear,' I continued. 'They look for the sucker marks on the windscreen. If a car has those, there's a sat-nav in the glove box.'

Laura smiled. 'It has a certain poetry to it, doesn't it, that people who don't go anywhere have all the means to get there. What are you getting at?'

I exhaled loudly. 'I don't know really. I suppose I'm just thinking how I thought I knew about crime, knew all the cons, the tricks, and then this.' I looked at Laura and I knew that my eyes betrayed my sadness. 'I believed him. No, it was more than that. I believed *in* him. I thought he was a nice old man who maybe thought some strange things. I would never have guessed this.'

'Did he say anything to you that made you think he could have done this?'

I shook my head. 'Just that he had dreams, and his dreams came true.'

Laura raised her eyebrows at me, and I sensed that we both saw the road ahead getting stranger.

Chapter Thirty-eight

Laura leaned against the wall at the back of the training room at the police station. It was like a classroom, with chairs set neatly in rows and a whiteboard and flipchart at one end. It was also the room they used for press conferences, so there were hoardings at the other end, large foldaway boards in bright white, emblazoned with the Lancashire Constabulary logo, the helmet crest against a blue ribbon. In front of those was a table, the tablecloth bright white and supporting a microphone in the middle. A reporter was attaching his own to the front of the table. Framed against the backdrop was Egan, taking a drink of water. Laura saw him gargle, and it seemed like he had been home to get changed. He hadn't been wearing that suit at the crime scene, and she was sure his hair was neater, a bit glossier.

'I'm not sure about this,' she said, almost in a whisper.

Pete didn't answer at first. He just watched the reporters as they got ready for the official press conference. They had been looking tetchy for the last few weeks, just a succession of worried parents to fill the pages, and then the relieved parents as the child was returned. But they had to be ready for the capture shot, the news of someone under arrest. They couldn't leave, couldn't rest. There was a buzz now, as they sensed something had changed, that there was something more than just another anxious mother. The television cameras were set up at the back of the room, and the seats were full, all of the nationals represented.

'Don't worry,' said Pete eventually, 'I overheard the press officer. They're not going to say much.'

'No, just that Eric Randle was the abductor and that he hanged himself.'

'Is that wrong?'

Laura looked at Pete. He could tell from the uncertainty in her eyes that something wasn't right.

'What is it?' he asked.

Laura chewed on her lip. 'I don't know, but something is too neat here.'

A flash of my press badge got me into the news conference.

I took a seat at the back, not too far from Laura, and she watched me sit down.

I heard footsteps behind me, and then I smelled something familiar. 'Are you going to behave yourself?' whispered Laura into my ear.

'I'll try.'

I heard Laura sigh. 'Just remember me, that's all,' she said, and then she backed away to the corner of the room.

I looked to the front as I heard the other reporters come in. I could smell the cigarettes on them, the last-minute smokers. It reminded me of nights in the pub with the journalists I knew in London, back when a drink made my clothes smell and my eyes red.

The room was packed, the air-conditioning working overtime. The abductions had taken over the media, daily updates on the news, conspiracies and guesswork on the internet. Seemed like everyone knew someone in the police who knew the real identity of the kidnapper. It was all bullshit, just speculation to keep the story in the head-lines. The abductions sold newspapers. Any angle would do, the truth of it the least important thing. The usual television and radio reporters were there, all thinking of the killer question that might get their name on the national news. The internet leeches were also there, as usual. It seemed like everyone had cheered up, like there might suddenly be a purpose in staying in this backwater Lancashire town. But I had the best story of all: I had found the last victim, and spent time with the chief suspect.

But as I remembered the last victim, young Kyle Shadsworth, his features grey and lifeless, it didn't feel like much of a victory.

My musings were interrupted by the arrival of the detec-tives from the abduction squad. The Senior Investigating Officer, Mark Vaughton, had been at all of the press confer-ences so far, along with two of the assistants. He had been the voice of the abductions throughout the summer, giving the updates needed to keep the story in the public eye. Egan looked round at them and straightened his tie, beaming. The other three men looked less delighted to be there and did their best to keep the mood sombre.

Everyone settled themselves down at the table, and when the press chairs were quiet, the SIO spoke.

'Good afternoon, ladies and gentlemen. As some of you have become aware, a young boy was found this morning. With the greatest of regret, I have to inform you that he was dead when we found him. We cannot say too much this early into the investigation, except to confirm that the little boy is believed to be Kyle Shadsworth, who went missing last night. This press conference will mainly take the form of a statement, and then a very brief question and answer session.'

I noticed the SIO steal a glance at the men on either side of him before he continued. It seemed like a pause for effect, although I detected a slight tremor in his voice.

'Kyle Shadsworth was found in the cellar of a house on the Ashcroft estate. Also in that cellar was the body of a man known to us as Eric Randle. His death appears to have been caused by hanging. However, we are not ruling out any possibilities, and at this stage we must keep an open mind. We pass on our thoughts and condolences to Kyle's family in this time of grieving, and I would ask that you respect their privacy.'

There were murmurs around the room, and the constant noise of camera shutters. The SIO took a drink of water, and then invited questions from the audience.

'Did you know of this Eric Randle before today?' one of the radio reporters asked.

The SIO swallowed, barely visible, but I noticed.

'We will go through the information we have in our possession, and we will check whether we have missed something we shouldn't have.'

Delaying the bad news, I thought, but it sounded like he believed that Eric was the abductor.

'So you think this is it then?' asked another. 'You think the Summer Snatcher has finally been identified, and that he is dead?'

'That is a tag used by the media, not by the police. As I said earlier, we are keeping an open mind.'

So far, so predictable. I stood up quickly and managed to attract the SIO's attention. When he nodded at me, I directed a question at the man who I knew would not keep quiet.

'Detective Inspector Egan, as an experienced and senior officer, do you have an opinion on whether it looked like the suicide of a desperate murderer?'

I saw Egan clench his jaw as he recognised me, but I could tell he wanted to answer, to have his fifteen minutes of fame. He leaned forward and eagerly took the mike. 'As my colleague has said, we are keeping an open mind, but,' and then he smiled, too pleased with himself to stop the words, 'we have no other suspects in mind at this stage.'

I thought I heard someone chuckle behind me as the SIO butted in, 'Although I must stress that we don't know for sure what caused the death of Eric Randle.' I spotted the rebuke, and I saw the flush it brought to Egan's cheeks.

'So, Detective Inspector,' I continued, 'why didn't you stop Randle when he befriended Darlene Tyler when her son was still missing?'

Someone next to me winced.

One of the other detectives opened his mouth to speak, but Egan butted in.

'Eric Randle had been a suspect,' he said, 'and now those suspicions have been confirmed.'

'But not before Kyle Shadsworth died,' I said, running

with the scent. 'That could have been prevented. And am I right in saying that he was also a suspect in the murder of Jess Goldie, the young woman found dead a few days ago?'

The SIO held up his hand and tried to force out a smile. 'I can understand the extreme media interest in this, but we are very early into the investigation.'

I had said what I wanted to say. I let the other questions go on without interruption. As I looked at the officers on the podium, I sensed smugness, a certainty that the problems of the summer were coming to an end. I didn't see it that way. There was something not right, but I just couldn't nail down what it was. All I knew was that someone I had spoken to in the previous twenty-four hours was dead, and another man, Terry McKay, was seriously injured. Even the most committed pessimist would see that as too much of a coincidence.

As the press conference came to an end, I felt my phone buzz in my pocket. It was a number I didn't recognise.

'Jack?' an anxious voice said. He sounded slurred. 'It's Sam Nixon.'

'Sam, what can I do for you?'

There was a pause. All I could hear was him breathing. Then he said, 'I was sorry to hear about Eric Randle. I know I put you on to him. It wasn't too upsetting finding him, I hope.'

I grimaced when I thought of the scene.

'All in a day's work,' I answered flippantly. When Sam didn't respond, I asked, 'Is that all you wanted?'

There was another pause, and then he said, 'I've just had a call from Eric's daughter. She wants to speak to you.'

'To me?'

'She wanted to talk to me, but I told her that you had spoken to him more recently. Is that okay?'

I was a reporter. It was always going to be okay. 'Thanks, Sam,' I said, and he gave me the number. Before I had a chance to respond, I realised that he had hung up.

I smiled. The story was starting to write itself.

Sam clicked his phone shut and closed his eyes. Eric was dead. He didn't have time to think about it, as the court usher tapped him on the shoulder and told him that the magistrates had come back into court.

Sam went into court and sat at the front, on an old wooden bench that was screwed to the floor, the ornate back uncomfortable to lean against. The prosecutor looked him up and down, saw his clothes, creased and unkempt, and whispered under his breath, 'Been doing the gardening?'

Sam closed his eyes at that. He felt like he was somewhere else, distracted. Every time he closed his eyes, he could see Terry McKay's hand. He heard someone arrive in the dock. It used to be small and wooden with a brass rail, but there had been too many jumpers. They always came back, though, the escape bids ending when they realised that they hadn't planned what to do when they returned to the streets. They were normally found at home, waiting to be collected. But one escaper was dragged back in by a couple of prosecutors, and when he woke up in a prison cell the next day, he killed himself. After that, the high glass boxes went in. Now, no one got out.

Sam could hear voices, and then banging noises. He

heard someone say his name. He looked up. It was the chairman of the magistrates, a car salesman in a pinstriped suit whose reputation for toughness made for long mornings for defence lawyers. There were two women on either side of him.

Sam stood up slowly. 'Can I assist your worships?' His courtesy was on auto-pilot.

The chairman nodded towards the glass box. 'Your client wants a word.'

Sam looked back to the dock. The chairman had made his views known. The defendant was a client, not someone with a name.

Sam shuffled out of the bench and went to the dock. He put his ear to the small slit in the glass, just big enough to hear through, sometimes just big enough to pass small white packages through.

'What do you want?'

'Is my girlfriend here?' the prisoner asked.

Sam looked around. The public gallery was empty. 'This is fucking glass,' he snapped back. 'Have a look yourself.'

'Mr Nixon!'

Sam looked around. It was the chairman.

'Yes, sir?' asked Sam, the snap of his voice showing little respect.

'Your language, Mr Nixon, is not what we expect to hear in a court of law.'

'I was having a private consultation with my client, and its contents are privileged. If you want me to speak to him more privately, please stand the matter down and I will do so.'

278

Sam saw the shocked look in the court clerk's eyes. The prosecutor looked amused. He had a large pile of files in front of him, and all day to wade through them in court. Sam was adding entertainment.

'No, thank you, Mr Nixon,' said the chairman, his eyes angry, his voice full of censure. 'We'll get this over with.'

'Oh, fucking nice one, Nixon,' came a growl from the other side of the glass. 'Piss him off, well done, you prick,' and the prisoner sat down with a slump.

Sam turned back to the dock. He was angry now. He could sense it was unstoppable, too many late nights working and fragmented sleep suddenly surfacing.

'Look, shithead,' he shouted through the slit in the glass, 'if you stay in, it's nothing to do with me, or him,' and Sam tilted his head towards the chairman, who he could hear shouting his name loudly. 'They gave you a chance, put you on bail. You were supposed to stay in, you had a curfew, but you couldn't even manage that.'

The prisoner was up on his feet again, his face at the glass, the white-shirted security guards trying to pull him back.

Sam stepped away and bowed theatrically at the chairman, who now just stared at him. 'This defendant', said Sam, 'no longer has a solicitor. At least, not this one.' And then he picked up his files and stormed out of the courtroom.

Chapter Thirty-nine

Laura was sitting at her desk when Egan walked back into the Incident Room, her attention drawn by a murmur. He looked nervous, his eyes darting around the room as he saw all eyes turn to him. Laura saw the press officer behind him, her face flushed and angry. It was obvious that they'd had words.

Laura looked over at Pete, who had been thumbing his way through incident reports and logs of crank calls. Pete smiled, just a twinkle.

They both turned to the front of the room as they heard Egan clapping.

'Can I have everyone's attention?'

No need to ask, thought Laura. You had it as soon as you walked in.

Egan let the murmurs die down and then cleared his throat.

'Some of you may have seen the press conference,' he said, ignoring the smirks around the room. 'And some of you might have wondered why I said what I did.'

No one said anything. It was like watching a public suicide.

'Although I told the press conference that it looked as if the person who had been abducting children was now identified, you will remember that I didn't confirm any link between the abductions and the murder of Jess Goldie. There are two reasons. Firstly, there is no *real* proof of a link. We can speculate and guess, but there is nothing but coincidence so far. And secondly, and more importantly, by not publicly linking them, we might draw the real killer out. He will want to take his bow.'

There was a murmur again, but louder this time. Then Pete shouted out, 'Is drawing the killer out another way of saying that we let someone else die just so that we can get some fresh forensic?'

Laura watched Egan take a deep breath. He was angry with Pete, but she guessed that he was angry because he knew that Pete was right, that Pete had guessed the truth: Egan had messed up, and he was covering up to protect himself.

'If you have any queries about the publicity decisions,' Egan said, the words coming out slowly, 'speak to the press officer here, but I have come here to explain the strategy. Privately, we consider a link. Publicly, there is no such thing.'

'Are we keeping the two teams separate then?' someone asked.

Egan's lips twitched. 'Yes, for the moment, but that is being kept under review.'

Pete sat back, irritated now. Laura guessed that he was angry because Egan had landed on the best solution by chance.

Egan smiled and thanked everyone, and then left the room.

'Did you ever hear such crap?' spluttered Pete.

Laura shrugged. 'It didn't sound like a bad plan.'

Pete threw down his pen. 'He always comes up smelling of fucking flowerbeds.' He looked at Laura, and then held up a pile of incident logs – the crank calls and witnesses were growing by the hour. 'And we have to wade through this shit, without any help,' he barked.

Laura toyed with her pen for a few seconds as she thought. 'I'm going to look at Jess's dream diaries.'

'Why?'

'Because she had dreams of the future as well. The key to all of this is what connects it all: their dreams.'

Pete shook his head. 'The world is going mad,' he muttered to himself.

When Sam left court, he knew where he was headed. He was going to help Terry. He knew he was in the right place when he saw two policemen smoking in the hospital car park. He walked over to them and tried to look relaxed.

'You here for Terry McKay?' he asked.

They exchanged glances and looked at Sam's grubby shirt and bristled chin. 'Been working too hard, Mr Nixon?' one said, his mouth in a smirk.

Sam looked down at himself. He knew how he looked. He started to walk away, his fists clenching, knowing that if he started to say something he could spend the rest of the day in his own cell.

'If you speak to him,' the other one shouted back, 'tell him to make a complaint.'

Sam turned around, shocked. 'He hasn't made a report?'

'No, and I don't get it. Someone burnt his hand off. It looks like a fucking lacrosse racquet, just spindles and bits of flesh.'

Sam turned away quickly. He felt light-headed again. Terry wasn't making a complaint. Had someone got to him?

He rushed into the hospital reception and found out the name of Terry's ward. Visiting hours were nearly at an end, but Sam negotiated the corridors quickly; the hospital was Blackley's new monument, and so the signs were all bright and bold. When he found Terry's ward, he stopped. What if Terry remembered that he had left him? He took some deep breaths and looked at the ceiling. *Don't be a coward.*

He walked through the ward. He could see Terry at the end, a heavily bandaged hand raised in the air. He was about to say something when he saw that Terry had a visitor already. He slowed down as he recognised the person by the bed. It was Luke King. He was talking to Terry, and Terry looked like he was listening attentively.

Sam walked up to the bed quickly and grabbed Luke by the collar. He spun him round fast.

'What the fuck are you doing here?' spat Sam.

Everyone on the ward turned to look.

Luke shrugged off Sam's hand.

'Don't touch me, Nixon.'

'Checking up on your family's dirty work?' and he nodded towards Terry, who looked away, fear in his eyes. Sam turned towards the rest of the ward. 'Take a good look,' he shouted. 'This is what you get when you cross his father.'

Luke didn't react.

Sam looked at Terry, but Terry was still looking away.

'Don't let them get away with it,' warned Sam.

When Terry didn't respond, Luke smiled, his eyes narrowed. 'Looks like you got your answer,' he said.

Sam looked around the ward again, all eyes still on him, and he saw the white shirts and shoulder flashes of two security guards heading for him. He held his hands up and walked out.

When he got outside, the two officers were still there. 'Any joy?' said one.

Sam shook his head. 'None at all,' he replied.

Back in his car, he looked down at his hands. They were shaking. He glanced in his mirror and saw Luke King watching him from the hospital entrance. Sam could see that he was smiling.

He was about to turn the ignition when his phone rang.

'Helena, everything okay?'

Sam sat up straight when he heard that she was crying.

'Helena, are you okay?' he repeated. His hands were clenched around the steering wheel. 'The boys, are they all right?'

'I've had a crash in the car,' she said, the words coming out between sobs.

Sam gasped.

'We're not hurt, but they say I was drunk. But I wasn't, I promise.'

'Where are you?'

There was a pause. 'At the police station.'

'Have you been on the intoxilyser yet?'

'Yes,' she said, her voice almost inaudible. 'Blew eighty-five.'

Shit, that was high, he thought. The legal limit for alcohol in breath was only thirty-five.

'Wait there, I'll come and collect you.'

He drove off, leaving Luke standing there, staring.

Chapter Forty

I met Eric's daughter in the Eagle and Child, an old Tudor pub on the road out of Turners Fold, tucked into a dip, away from the dark grids of the nearby towns. Smoke drifted from the cluster of chimneys in the middle of its roof.

Mary Randle was sitting at a table in a corner when I arrived. I wasn't sure at first if it was her, but as I watched her I saw traces of Eric. Her voice on the phone had been quiet and scared, and she seemed the same in person, looking around as if she was prey, her eyes darting, wary, alert.

I introduced myself and sat down, but when I saw how quickly her smile flickered and died I knew I would have to do most of the work.

'I don't know if the police told you,' I said softly, 'but I'm the one who found your father.' I paused. 'I'm so sorry.'

She looked away. She took a few seconds to compose herself and then asked, 'How did he look?' It came out almost in a whisper, but as she wiped a tear from her cheek she laughed to herself, bitter and full of hurt.

'He looked dead, I suppose, but what I mean is, did it look like he had suffered?'

I gave a thin smile and shook my head. 'It looked like a simple hanging.'

She nodded. I noticed that she was holding a white handkerchief crushed between her fingers.

'He didn't do it,' she said, her voice more strident now. 'You know that, don't you? He didn't hurt any of those children. He didn't take any of them.'

I reached out and put my hand over hers. I felt her hand tense, but then she gripped mine with her other hand. I looked into her eyes and saw an intense look, belief.

'I know,' I said softly. 'I know he didn't. And do you know what, I don't think the police believe that either. Not really, deep down.'

'Then why did they go on television and say that they had caught the Summer Snatcher?' she pleaded.

I held her hands, pumped them as if to make her stronger. 'If you know the truth, hang on to that. The police don't always get it right.'

She sighed and let go of my hand.

As she dabbed at her eyes with her handkerchief, I looked at her and tried to work out her story. She was his legacy, but she seemed reluctant in that role. She had that same look as her father, like some kind of lapsed academic, with her hair short, soft and mousy, her eyes grey. She was wearing a lilac jumper and blue jeans, pressed so that she had a crease down the legs. She looked bookish, and it was hard to believe she came from an estate where tracksuits were the norm. Maybe that's where she got her wariness from – a childhood of not fitting in. Her eyes constantly darted around the room, always looking for the threat, and her fingers played nervously with her leather purse.

'Why did you want to meet me?' I asked.

Mary took a quick sip and licked her lips. Then she said, 'About a week ago my father called me and asked me to contact Sam Nixon if he died.'

I raised my eyebrows. 'He thought he was going to die?'

Mary nodded. 'He thought that often, but he seemed genuinely scared this time round.'

'Did you call Sam Nixon?'

'Yes, as soon as I found out about my father, but he said he wasn't interested.'

'But he told you I was.'

Mary nodded again.

'Did my father tell you about his dreams?' she asked quietly, embarrassed.

I nodded. 'He seemed scared, just like you said, but he told me his story. I wanted to write about him. I still do.'

'He used to paint his dreams. He's done it for years. Often I would go downstairs to go to school and he would be painting in the kitchen. It would take him a few minutes to even notice I was there.'

'I've got a couple of his most recent ones,' I said, as if I was talking about a well-known artist. 'They were painted just before he died.'

'Did you recognise anything in them?'

I smiled. 'I can't believe I'm going to say this, but yes, I did.'

She began to cry, her face crumbling with grief.

'Hey, hey, don't cry.'

'My father died today,' she said, her voice thick with tears. 'I'm allowed.'

I gave her that one. I remembered the feeling all too clearly myself. I sat there for a while, letting her compose herself. One of the first things I had learned as a journalist was to listen. If she wasn't ready to talk, then I would wait as long as it took.

Mary's orange juice must have been getting warm. The ice cubes had long gone. I looked around the pub. The windows were small and the walls were painted Elizabethan cream, above mahogany wood panels that went all the way around the room. The rest of the character was long gone, though, all the rooms knocked through, as it tried to re-create the history that had been ripped out during an earlier refurbishment. Wooden beams painted black ran across the ceiling, the lines broken by witticisms painted in white.

As the silence lingered, I sensed Mary begin to relax again.

'I've got a box of his paintings,' she eventually said. 'I don't know what to do with them.'

'And you think I will?'

'You might do. They go back years, decades.'

'Why don't you want to keep them?'

She snorted a laugh. 'You've seen the house he lived in.' She went quiet, took a deep breath. 'The house he died in.' She paused as a sob choked her up, and then she continued, 'Those paintings ruined his life. Mine as well, if I'm honest about it.'

'They defined his life,' I argued. 'He thought he had a gift and wanted to share it to protect others.'

'No, no, no. He stopped living his life, so obsessed was he about his dreams. You saw his house, all boarded up.'

'It was his home.'

'It was his dream studio. He said he didn't dream when he slept away from that house, and so he worried that if he left he would stop having them.'

'I didn't get the impression that he enjoyed having them.'

'He didn't, but he thought they meant something important. He trained himself to remember his dreams, so that when he woke up he could recall them for longer than most people.'

I looked into her eyes and tried to work out her thoughts.

'You sound like you didn't believe his dreams were of the future,' I said.

She shook her head. 'I wanted to believe him, but I didn't want to encourage him either.' She considered for a moment and then asked, 'Did you believe him?'

I smiled apologetically. 'I'm a reporter. I can write it and not believe any of it, as long as someone buys the story.'

She looked away for a moment, and I could see her trying to hold on to the tears.

'So do you think he was misguided, that he wasted all of those years?' I asked.

She looked back at me and watched me for a few seconds. It seemed like we were the only people in the pub at that moment. She looked down as she began to shake her head.

I reached out to her again. 'It's okay. You're entitled to your own opinion.'

She looked up again as she tried to blink away her tears. 'Oh, it's not that,' she said. 'It makes me so angry because it ruined his life. And it ended it as well. It wasn't always like that. Nor was the house. It used to be a normal house. I grew up there.'

'What about your mother?'

'She died years ago.' She smiled, looked almost wistful. 'If she had been alive, she would have told him to keep quiet about it all. When she died there was no one to rein him in. So he got a name for being the estate weirdo, talking about seeing the future, going down to the shop to get himself photographed with his paintings.'

I looked quizzically at her.

'To date them,' she said, by way of explanation. 'There's a clock on the wall with the date on it. But word got round and the kids would taunt him. And then he started calling the police, trying to tell them what he had seen whenever anyone was killed or abducted. So he became a suspect, and the local kids thought he was guilty. I've seen him spat on, shouted at, mothers with their children screaming at him in the street.'

'And so he boarded himself in?'

She nodded.

'It was the murder of a little girl that caused the problems – they didn't get anyone for it. Dad called the police every day to tell them what he had seen, and then when they saw him looking around where they found the body, they locked him up so fast.'

'But he was released.'

She shook her head. 'After a few months. The kids on the estate don't see that as a declaration of innocence. Most of them get away with crime. There are *no* falsely-accused there. They either get caught or get away with it, nothing in between. So I knew where they thought my dad fitted into the picture. His windows were smashed. Things thrown at the house. The door was always being kicked in. I couldn't stand it any more so I left, and I tried to get him to come with me, but he wouldn't.'

'If you don't believe that he dreamt the future, why did you want to speak to me? You could have stopped at Sam Nixon when he said no.'

'Because it's what Dad wanted. He told me to speak to Sam Nixon if he died, as if he might know what to do. Sam passed me on to you. I'm just following the trail, just so that I can tell myself that I did what I was asked.' She smiled now, the first real smile I had seen from her. 'He was a good man. Misguided maybe, but kind and gentle, all the things a father should be.'

'I'm going to write about him. Are you okay with that?'

Mary nodded. 'He would have wanted you to.'

'If I write the story, it will be the one I want to write, though, which might not be the same one you want. You understand that?'

Mary nodded.

I realised that I needed the raw materials. The paintings. The photographs. Mary must have sensed what I was thinking, because she said, 'They're in the boot of my car. I've put them in date order, and every time something happened that he thought he had seen in a dream, I cut it out of the paper and put it with the painting.'

I started to smile. 'You didn't believe any of it, but you helped him catalogue it.'

'He was my father. I loved him.'

'There is one more thing I need from you,' I said. When she raised her eyebrows in query, I continued, 'I need to know more about your father. And not just the dream stuff. I want to know about Eric Randle the man.'

She nodded at me. 'I can do that.'

Chapter Forty-one

Jess's journal and notes were spread out in front of Laura. They'd been checked for prints and there was only one set on them. Jess's.

Laura picked up the one containing the pieces she had read that morning.

'Can't see, can't talk, can't move. All I can see is red. I can hear someone though, it's a man, and he is laughing. I'm hurting, and I try to get away, but I can't move my arms, my legs. I turn my head to try and see, try to open my eyes, but there is nothing there. Just a red mist, but it seems dark, forbidding. I try to scream for help but there is just a noise I don't recognise.'

Laura shivered and wondered whether Jess had known at the time that she was the woman in the dream. She looked at the other pieces of paper and saw that they were similar in style, but only one other sounded like it foretold her death. None of it made any sense, but Laura knew that there was something there that provided a clue. She sighed. She just couldn't see it.

She picked up a small black book. It was about the

size of a pocket diary, but it was thick and worn. The spine was all ragged and sticky tape held it together at the top and the bottom. Laura opened it.

On the inside, in juvenile pink pen, were Jess's name and a date: 21 December 1994. Underneath were the words '*Dream Journal*' and a simple drawing of a flower. Laura thought about the date and realised that Jess would have been in her early teens, just making her way through puberty. Laura thought back to herself at the same age and remembered the turmoil of those years. The worries, the discoveries, the whole confusion of it all. She thought she could remember vivid dreams herself, often nightmares, a mind made too busy by hormones racing through her system. Jess must have started the journal when she thought her dreams were more than just normal.

As she started to read, Laura noticed that the entries were dated. They were like the notes she had read before, disjointed, but they were more obviously accounts of Jess's dreams. As she flicked through, she started to notice that they had a theme: disasters and death. No happy dreams, or odd dreams, or even erotic ones.

Laura started at the front, a description of the first recorded dream.

21 December 1994
I'm in bed, shaking, moving from side to side, first one way, then the other. House moving. I get under my covers – hear window smash. Shaking stops and I run to window. Broken glass. Doesn't hurt. Scared.

Look out window. See road-bridge moving. It turns over, like a spoilt child kicked it over. Fires starting. Families in street. Seems like half town is rubble. When I woke up, thought bed was moving. Wasn't.

Laura's attention was drawn to the bottom of the page and '*Kobe 17/1/95*' scrawled across it. The body of the text had been written in the same pink gel pen as the inscription on the inside cover, so Laura could tell that they were written at the same time. But the words '*Kobe 17/1/95*' were written in ragged red biro.

Laura chewed on a fingernail. Was it someone's name, or a message? Then she remembered, and she felt her mouth go dry. It was an earthquake, in Japan. She remembered the footage now, the images from shops as shelves collapsed, the buildings moving around like someone shaking a box. Thousands had been killed.

She thought about Jess, wondered how heavily this had all weighed on her mind. The dream had been vivid enough to scare her, but then not long afterwards it had come true. Had there been something in the dream Jess had missed that might have saved some lives? How would a teenage girl cope with that?

She turned through the pages and read abstract accounts of dreams. Nothing jumped out, but then her eye was caught by an entry the following year.

3 April 1995
Big bang, then silence. Screaming. Women covered in blood, men stunned, shocked. Face wet with blood.

Hurts. Where's my baby? Windows smashed, part of ceiling gone, part of floor. People shouting for children. Where's mine? Feel pain. His. Mine. Looking through dust. People dead.

I get out. Dark inside. Dusty. Choked. Can't breathe. Outside warm, sunny. Building big. Many floors. But front missing.

Two men staring. One in orange jumpsuit. Everyone is crying. He isn't. He isn't doing anything. Not smiling. Not crying. Just passive. And he looks at me. He scares me. Cold. Other man dark-haired. Moustache. He speaks with accent. Continental. German? Then turns away.

Laura put the book down. Jess believed she was having premonitions. Then she noticed the words '*OKLAHOMA 15/4/95!*' written in large capitals along the bottom.

Now Laura could recognise the description of the Oklahoma bomb, when a truck rented by neo-Nazis took off the front of a federal building, killing workers and children. She guessed that Jess wouldn't remember the fine details of the dream later that month when the bomb went off in Oklahoma, but the orange jumpsuit? That was a telling detail. Laura remembered the pictures of Timothy McVeigh being led away – it was the main image people still had of him, the defiant ex-soldier in chains. In some ways that must have been harder for Jess to cope with than Kobe, which would have happened anyway, a natural disaster. If there had been enough clues, the Oklahoma bomb could have been stopped.

But who would have paid any attention to a teenager from Lancashire?

Laura sighed and smiled to herself. She was starting to believe in this herself now.

She turned over the page and saw that the entries carried on. Not all of them had notes at the bottom, and many seemed not much more than the strange and vivid dreams of an imaginative teenager. But the ones with red annotations at the bottom were all events she recognised. Plane crashes. Earthquakes. Murders.

She flicked through the journal, trying to find something relevant to the case. There was nothing. The last page had an entry dated 16 December 2004.

On beach. Beautiful. Palm trees. Happy. Sea calm. But then it disappears. Goes out long way. Sea just keeps going out. But then it comes back hard. And just keeps coming, over beach, through streets. Am swept away. Hang on to tree. Being bumped around. Water heavy around head. Which way up? Dark but silent. Chest gets heavy. Have to breathe. Can't.

Laura felt her breath catch. She didn't need to read the note at the bottom to know that Jess had dreamt about the devastating tsunami that had struck ten days later.

She put the journal down and wiped her eyes. She felt tired, the words in front of her flooding her brain too fast, making it too hard to see what it was that troubled her. She felt that the answer to Jess's murder was in front of her, written down somewhere. But she had gone through everything and nothing seemed real. Maybe it was too cryptic, or something was relevant but all mixed up.

She shook her head. It felt like the answer was almost in front of her, tantalisingly close.

She looked up when Pete came into the room. He was holding pieces of paper.

'I don't think Egan liked me smiling,' he said. 'We've got to go and speak to all these people.'

'Who are they?'

He waved the papers in the air. 'Witnesses. Those people who rang in with information about Eric Randle and Kyle. We've got to go and speak to them, take their statements.'

'I thought we were on Jess's murder investigation,' said Laura.

Pete gave a small laugh. 'We're part of the merged inquiry team that's pretending it hasn't merged.'

Laura opened her mouth to speak, and then stopped. An idea started to form, some glimmer of light in her head, glowing, getting brighter all the time.

'You okay?' said Pete.

She looked up at him, her eyes sharp now, focused. 'Are there any more of these?' she said, holding up Jess's dream descriptions.

Pete shook his head. 'I don't think so. Everything from her bedroom cabinet is there.'

Laura picked up the journal and turned it over in her hand. 'This is full of dream descriptions,' she said. 'Ten years of them. I don't think she wrote down every dream,

299

the book wouldn't have lasted for ten years if she had – it must just be the important ones. And they are orderly. They are dated, and she went back to the ones she saw come true and made a note. She was going to some kind of support group when she died, so she still thought it was important.' Laura held it up like a preacher. 'These dreams were a big deal to Jess.'

Pete shrugged. 'So what's the problem?'

Laura opened the journal to the back page. 'This one is full. Look,' and she flicked through the pages so he could see. 'Every page filled up.'

Pete began to chew on his lip. 'Sorry, Laura, I'm not there with you yet.'

Laura's smile widened. 'If this one is full and ends back in 2004, where is the journal she was writing in before she died?'

A flicker of a smile crept over Pete's face as he sat down and looked through the journal.

'You might have something, but,' and then he nodded towards the pieces of paper, 'then again, maybe she got sick of keeping a journal so she used just any old piece of paper?'

Laura shook her head. 'No. You saw how neat her house was. This journal is the same. Each entry dated. All the dates follow. She didn't just open the journal at any old empty page. She went to the next one, so that it all followed chronologically. And don't forget that she will have been writing these as soon as she woke up. No, this girl was orderly, neat.'

'But what about the scraps of paper?'

'She might have used those when she didn't have her

journal with her. Maybe she was away from home when she wrote those, on holiday or something. She wouldn't take her journal with her because it was too precious. What if she lost it?'

'Do you think we should go back to her house to search for it, see if she had it hidden away somewhere?'

Laura looked doubtful. 'It would only be in one place: next to her bed. She would have to be able to open it as soon as she woke up. And it's not there now.'

Pete put the incident reports on the floor. 'Are you thinking that whoever killed her took it?'

'I think more than that,' said Laura intently. 'I think her killer went in there to get it.'

Pete furrowed his brow. 'Why would he do that?'

'Because there must have been something in it that he didn't want anyone to see?'

Pete sat back and exhaled. 'Jesus fucking Christ. Dreams. Premonitions. This is Blackley, a crappy old mill town. It's not *The X Files*.'

Laura grinned at him. 'Do you remember why Eric Randle was there, at her house, at that time of the morning?'

Pete nodded and laughed. 'He'd had a fucking dream.' And then he pointed at the journal. 'And you think that if Jess had written down something that made her killer get twitchy, maybe something her killer had done, or was planning to do, then her killer wouldn't know exactly how much she had seen? Or would maybe see again in another dream? So she had to be silenced.'

Laura smiled, her dimples flashing. 'I'm thinking something like that.' She looked at the journal in her hand. 'There must be something in the missing journal that caused someone to get jumpy.'

Pete sat back and rubbed his face with his hands, as if he was trying to wake himself up. 'So she dreamt of her killer?' he asked.

Laura shook her head. 'No. Why would she let him in if she had seen his face in her dreams as her killer? No, I think she dreamt about something else, and I think I know what it was.'

'Go on.'

Laura raised her eyebrows, her eyes mischievous now. 'I think she saw who was abducting those children.'

'You've lost me again.'

Laura laughed.

'C'mon, it's not that difficult. Who is the one person that connects Jess and the abductions?'

Pete thought for a few seconds, and then he said, 'Eric Randle,' his eyes widening.

'You're getting there, Sherlock,' said Laura. 'And if there was a journal that gave a clue about the abductor, then it must rule out Eric as the abductor.'

Pete shook his head. 'How did you get to that conclusion?'

Laura shrugged. 'It's simple: why would he go to all that effort to avoid detection and then call the police with some story about having a dream? If Eric had killed her, the last thing he would do is start talking about dreams.'

'But that means something else is all wrong,' said Pete.

Laura nodded. 'I'm already there,' she said, tapping

her head. 'If the abductor wasn't Eric Randle, then it was no suicide today. It was murder.'

Pete began to smile. 'And do you know who was friends with both of them?' he added excitedly.

'Go on?'

'Billy Hunt.' Pete put the papers on the desk and then pointed to the door. 'Time for a visit, Watson.'

I hadn't been to the graveyard since I had arrived back in Turners Fold.

My father had died the year before. He had been a policeman, just an ordinary everyday bobby, one who needed nothing more than to do his job, take his pay, and look after his family.

I was an only child, and the family had got even smaller when my mother had died, taken away from me in my teens, cancer robbing her of the fizz that she had, a bounce that had carried her through her life. It toughened me up, but it destroyed my father. By the time he got through the grief, I had grown up and moved on, heading for London with my head filled with dreams.

I loved London – the buzz, the noise, the movement. But it wore me out. I missed the green spaces, the talk, the smiles.

My father had died trying to do what was right. He'd made an enemy he couldn't fight and died for his trouble. Now I was walking towards his gravesite. I was feeling scared.

It was in a beautiful place, at the back of an old blackened church with castellated walls and a high slate roof.

Entry to the churchyard was through an old stone gate, and clematis climbed over like bright flops of cloth in summertime. Turners Fold was in the valley below, my new house on the opposite hill.

The day was clear and I could see for miles, the hills in the distance picked out in sharp relief. I could make out people moving about in the town below, just tiny shapes, and a tourist barge cruised along the canal in the middle of town. A hundred years earlier the town would have been under a pall of smoke, just the hills around clear. Now the industry had gone, the whole town came into view.

As I got nearer to my father's grave, I had to steel myself. I had learned to do that after my mother died. Take a deep breath, don't let the emotions get near. I did the same again now. But as I saw his name it became hard to control. The letters were still bright gold in the black granite, the words simple. '*Robert Garrett. Husband and father, policeman. Killed in the line of duty. Lest we forget the sacrifice he made. You will be missed.*'

Killed in the line of duty. Sacrifice. He hadn't wanted that. He had wanted to get to his retirement and enjoy his life. Would he have done the same again? I didn't know, but I remembered the look in his eyes when he realised that justice had to be done.

I felt the same passion again. Sometimes it was about doing the right thing. I hadn't written much since my father died, just scraps to keep the money coming in. Now, I felt like I was on the verge of a big story once more.

I thought about Laura. I loved her more than I had ever loved any woman. But then I thought about Mary, how her father's memory would be sullied by press speculation. And I thought about Eric, someone I had known so briefly. I knew they deserved justice. All I could hope for was that Laura would still love me when I had finished.

I reached out and touched the gravestone. It was just a stone, nothing more. I smiled at it and headed off.

Chapter Forty-two

There was a pack of kids outside the shop as I arrived. They were dressed all in black, some racing around on bikes, all with their hoods up even though the evening was warm. They were like a pack of rats as they scurried around. The bright red Stag stood out as I parked it, and I wondered whether I ought to get myself a different car, maybe a beaten-up runaround, for days like this.

I sat in my car for a few minutes and pondered where I was going with my story.

I liked the Darlene Tyler angle. It had everything: the horror of the abduction, the joy of the return, the happy ending. It would be good for the glossies. Eric as the abductor would help that story, because he had put himself into it. Proving that Eric had also been a victim would change that.

But then I thought about Eric the father, Eric the husband. And I thought about Mary. Since my father had died, I put greater store on the human side.

I saw the kids look over as I got out of the car, but I caught their eyes and gave them a silent warning.

As I walked towards the doorway I sensed the darkness inside. The windows were protected by metal grilles, so that the glass behind looked grubby. As I walked in, the sunshine outside was replaced by dim yellow artificial light. I saw that the shop was empty. There were two long aisles running away from the door, with the till nearest the exit, the alcohol on shelves behind. No one self-served booze in here. As I looked, it appeared the same went for razor blades and batteries.

I looked down the aisle and saw the clock Mary had talked about, large white digits on a black background, those that turn over like old railway destination boards. The date was correct.

I turned towards the till and saw a large man behind the counter, his stomach inflated like a football under his jumper. He was Pakistani, with a bushy moustache and his hair swept to one side, his fringe decorated with strips of grey. I noticed him watching me so I stepped up to the counter and introduced myself.

'I'm writing a story on Eric Randle,' I said. 'He used to come in here and have photographs taken of his paintings.'

The man looked at me for a few seconds, as if he was trying to reconcile my presence with the news about Eric's death, and then nodded. 'I remember. He come in here maybe four, five times every year. But he had been coming in here more than that in the last few weeks.'

His accent was thick, a mix of Kashmir and the Western Pennines. He looked towards the calendar.

'He never bought anything,' he continued. 'Just got

307

me to take a picture of him holding up some damn painting.'

'Didn't you mind?'

He shook his head. 'It's not worth making enemies round here,' he said, and he glanced outside.

'Do they give you a hard time?' I asked, following his gaze.

'They laugh at my sons because they don't drink and work hard at school, but maybe they would have better lives if they did the same.' He looked back to me, and I sensed disappointment. 'I love England. It has given me things I could not have had in Pakistan, and so many people are nice. But so much of it is bad. It's like they can't see how good it is and want to destroy it.'

'Or themselves.'

He nodded at that.

'Why do you stay here?' I asked. 'You could have got a shop in a place where you wouldn't have to protect your windows with cages.'

He laughed. 'Not at this price. And I charge a lot for the vodka. If I can stop them from pinching it, I make a good living.'

I smiled at him. He was working in a fortress but I could see that he had an exit strategy. Make the money, bring up his children and then get out. As I listened to the kids outside, swearing and shouting at each other, it struck me that none of them had one.

'Did Eric come here often to have his photograph taken?' I asked.

The man shrugged. 'Once every few weeks. I've been here ten years, and it seems like he has been coming all of that time. He came in more when I was first here, but then he stopped for a while. In the last two or three years he has been coming back. He told me he used to come into the shop when the last owner had it.'

I pointed at the calendar. 'Has it always told the right date?'

He looked over towards it. 'Always. It never breaks down. And the clock is always right. That's why I've kept it.' He glanced out of the window again. 'I would get back to your car. It's a nice car and they spoil nice things.'

I looked out through the open doorway and saw the kids looking through the side windows of the Stag. I thanked the shop-owner and went outside, and they all stepped back as I approached. A couple of them smiled. In a different neighbourhood I would have taken it for friendly interest. Maybe I was wrong to think of it as any different round here.

As I reversed away, the pack began to circle the pavement once more.

Laura and Pete arrived outside Billy Hunt's house, a semi-detached bungalow on a low-rise estate on the edge of Blackley, with views towards the retail parks, the neon and glass bright against the dark green of the countryside backdrop.

'Remember, he might be just a witness,' cautioned Laura.

Pete looked doubtful. 'I know Billy Hunt. He'll only help us if we scare him into it.'

When they got to the front door, Laura went to ring the doorbell. Pete stopped her and banged hard instead on the glass in the door, two panels filled with patterned glass that bounced in the frame. After a few seconds, Laura saw a blurred shape appear behind the door, and then, as the door opened a sliver, she saw frightened brown eyes blink behind small round glasses.

'Billy Hunt,' bellowed Pete. 'It's the police. We need to speak to you about Jess Goldie's death.'

The eyes blinked rapidly again, and then the door closed. Laura was about to turn around when she heard the chain come off the door. It was opened by a small and chubby man, with a dark side parting, his cheeks ruddy. He looked dishevelled, his eyes red, his jaw unshaven.

'Billy?' Laura asked. When he gave a nervous nod, Laura smiled at him and asked, 'Can we come in?'

Billy scowled, his lips pursed together, but then he opened the door. He didn't move, so that Pete and Laura had to sidle past him. They went into the front room, and Laura stopped, surprised. There was a woman lying on the sofa, her hair grey and thin, her scalp showing through. She was wrapped in a crocheted blanket, and when she noticed Laura, she looked up slowly. Laura saw tiredness in her eyes.

Laura nodded and smiled. 'Mrs Hunt.' There was a large framed picture of Billy above the fireplace. She knew she'd got it right, because the old lady smiled back, watery and weak.

'Hello, love,' she said quietly as Billy appeared behind her.

'Not in here,' he barked, and ushered them both into a dining room at the back, separated by doors filled with

310

frosted glass. When he shut the doors, he asked, 'What do you want?' His tone was unfriendly, curt.

'Calm down, Billy, we just want to ask you a few questions,' said Pete.

'I want to call my solicitor.'

'I didn't say you were a suspect, but if you're feeling guilty, go ahead.'

Laura looked down, embarrassed. She didn't mind that Pete bullied his way through the job, but sometimes tact got further.

'Is that your mother, Billy?' Laura asked, her voice full of concern.

He turned to her and his mood softened. 'Yes. She's got cancer.'

Laura thought she saw tears flash into his eyes. He blinked them away.

'Does anyone help you look after her?'

He shook his head. 'It's just us two.' He glanced towards the door. 'She gave me everything. I can't just leave her so someone else can look after her.'

'There must be someone else? You can't bear all this on your own.'

He smiled thinly and shook his head. 'I know it sounds sad, a grown man like me, but she's all I've got.' He gulped and clenched his jaw. 'It'll seem quiet when she's gone.'

'Is she in much pain?'

He shook his head. 'The hospital gave us plenty of things to take the pain away. But it won't get any better, I know that.'

Laura glanced at Pete, who looked confused, but she

sneaked a quick wink, letting him know that she wasn't just passing the time.

'I hope you don't mind me asking, but we're just enquiring about Jess. I know she used to go to your dream group, but how well did you know her?'

Billy blushed, and then he went to sit down. He looked at his hands, seemed nervous.

'Did you like her?' Laura probed. 'I mean, really like her?'

He looked up, and then nodded slowly. 'I know that I don't have much to offer, but I think we would have been good together.' He pushed his glasses back up his nose. 'But I don't think she felt the same way.'

'You must have been disappointed. Hurt, maybe.'

'Not hurt enough to kill her, if that's what you mean,' he sneered.

Laura didn't respond. She let the words hang there, watching as Billy squirmed and pushed his glasses back up his nose again, like a twitch.

'How did Jess record her dreams?'

He thought for a moment. 'I think she used to keep a diary. I saw it at the meetings sometimes.'

Laura felt Pete watching her. 'Do you know where she kept it?' she asked.

He shook his head. 'I don't know.'

'Have you ever borrowed it, Billy, or is there any reason why you might have it?'

He shook his head again, more slowly this time. 'I've only ever seen it in her hand at the meetings.'

'Is it the sort of thing that she would lend to anyone?'

'No, it isn't.'

Then Laura smiled. 'Thanks, Billy. You don't mind if we call back sometime?'

Billy watched her, nervously.

Laura turned to go, made Pete turn with her, but then she looked quickly back to Billy. 'Who do you think killed her, Billy?'

He looked surprised, his eyes wide behind the lenses, but then he looked hurt. 'I don't know,' he said quietly. 'I don't know who would hurt her. She was a lovely person.'

Laura watched him for a moment, and then she nodded. 'Thank you, Billy.'

And then she turned to go, Pete alongside her.

'What was all that about?' he whispered.

'Just trying to get the measure of him.'

'And what was it?'

Laura looked back towards the house, saw Billy watching through the curtains. 'He doesn't seem like a killer, because I don't think he would leave his mother alone.'

Pete climbed into the car, Laura with him. 'Where now?' he asked.

Laura twitched her nose as she thought, and then said, 'Drive around the block so it looks like we've left, and then park up further down there,' and she pointed along the street.

'You're not sure about him, are you?'

Laura shook her head. 'We watch, just in case. Whoever killed her took that dream diary. We've asked about it. If he has it, he'll get nervous and want to get rid of it.'

And there was another reason why Laura was unsure, and that was because she thought she had seen something else in Billy: desire. He had been in love with Jess. Laura had seen how he lived, trapped by his love for his mother, and Jess had been free. That troubled Laura, because unrequited love can lead to hurt, and unresolved hurt can end in murder.

Chapter Forty-three

I hadn't been home long when Laura got back. I was sitting on the floor with Bobby, playing KerPlunk, pulling straws out of a tube. Bobby was concentrating hard, his tongue flicking at his lips, pulling out a straw slowly, but as soon as the key turned in the lock, he jumped up and set off towards his mother. He was at that age where he ran everywhere, walking was just too little effort, and so he ran towards Laura, his arms outstretched. I heard him squeal with delight.

When she came into the room, she had Bobby in her arms, his legs wrapped around her waist. I looked up and smiled. It still felt good to see Laura walk into *our* house, the excitement was still there. She walked through to the kitchen, which had an open-plan farmhouse look, lots of oak and a range cooker in the old chimney breast. When I saw her sniff the air, I shrugged apologetically. My dinner preparation hadn't gone beyond a trip to the freezer.

Laura didn't look angry, though. She just looked tired. She came back into the living room, still holding Bobby, and sat down in the old armchair. 'Hello, Jack,' she said, and I sensed she was too worn out to argue. 'You've been upsetting people today.'

'I don't do it to upset you. You know that, don't you?'

She nodded, and then pointed towards the box on the table, the one filled with Eric's paintings and photographs. 'What's in the box?'

I was about to answer when the phone rang. Laura went to it, Bobby under her arm, giggling as she went. I saw her face harden as soon as she answered it. I guessed who it was: Geoff, Bobby's father.

'Bobby,' I called over, 'come and help me with this.'

He trotted over, and I went to get the plates and cutlery, anything to keep him busy. As I handed him things to take to the table, I listened to Laura hissing down the phone. I knew how it went. Geoff wanted Bobby when it was convenient for him. Laura wouldn't say no, because she wanted Bobby to see his father, but not like this, with calls coming in unexpectedly. I knew how Geoff wanted it to happen: he got all the fun days, Laura got the grind.

When she put the phone down, she turned to Bobby, her face filled with mock delight, but I could see the anger behind her eyes.

'Guess what? You're going to see your daddy tomorrow!' she said, her voice excited. When he ran off whooping, she turned to me and said, 'He's collecting him from school.'

'Quite a drive.'

'He wants to see what kind of school it is.'

'And if he doesn't approve?'

That's when I saw the tears in her eyes. I knew then that he was going to make it tough for us.

I wrapped her up in my arms and she sank into me. Nothing was easy.

Laura was upstairs reading a story to Bobby when I started to go through the box of pictures. I glanced outside. The sky was darkening into indigo blue, the lights of Turners Fold flickering into life, the narrow lines of streets glowing orange. I could hear happy murmurs from Bobby's room.

I turned back to the box. It was heavy, crammed to the lid with brown envelopes. I reached in and pulled one out carefully. The corners seemed fragile, as if it had been opened too often over the years, the colour faded through time, yellowed like old newspaper. As I lifted the flap and looked inside, I saw two pieces of paper. I tipped the contents out onto the table: a painting and a photograph.

I looked at the painting first.

It was a picture of a volcano, the lava picked out in bright red as it headed towards a small settlement, palm trees at the base, represented as light green flicks. Eric had a certain style, sort of frantic, as if he was trying to get the picture done as quickly as possible, but I could tell that he cared about a likeness. The sides of the volcano were painted in charcoal and black, setting out the rock in relief, and he had drawn the settlement in little stone blocks. But I could sense the tiredness in his picture, the lines more jagged than smooth.

I looked at the photograph.

It was in colour, and it showed Eric in front of the clock in the shop from his estate. He looked younger, his hair showing shades of darkness, and there was a brightness to his eyes, as if he was a little less worn down.

I looked again at the painting. It didn't mean anything to me. Maybe Montserrat, but volcanoes erupted all the time, and if he painted one as a premonition it would certainly come true eventually.

I put both pictures back into the envelope and put it to one side. I wasn't convinced yet.

I opened the next envelope, and when I saw what was inside, I shivered.

I recognised the scene straightaway. A football ground, the terraces marked out by long, dark lines, the centre circle and the goals making it clear what it was supposed to be. There were a few figures, stick drawings, but they weren't playing football. Instead, they were grouped into a cluster on one side of the pitch.

It was the terrace running along the other side that told the real story. It was painted in bright oranges, reds, flashes of blue, flames licking the underside of the roof. There were some other pictures painted in the corners, separate from the main image. One was a figure in dark clothes, and it seemed like he had flames coming from his head.

It was the Bradford football fire, when the stand had caught fire and fifty-six people died. I was a young boy when it had happened, but it was one of those events etched into my memory, like Heysel and Hillsborough.

I looked inside the envelope and found the photograph. It showed a younger Eric, his hair dark and bushy. He was smiling, a strange lopsided grin, like he felt silly standing in the shop. I wondered whether it was his first time. I peered at the calendar in the background and saw that it said 14 April 1985.

I shook my head and felt for Eric. True or not, he had suffered for more than twenty years. The shop didn't look like it had changed much, with the same dim lighting and cluttered shelves, but the Eric I had met had altered almost beyond recognition. Stress and anxiety had ground him down, until he'd ended up as a shadow of his former self.

I looked back into the envelope and saw some newspaper clippings. I let them tumble out onto the table, the pages brown and dry now. As I looked through, I saw many similar images, pictures of the flames roaring under the roof as people stood on the pitch.

But then, as I flicked through the newspaper images, I saw a picture that took me by surprise.

I picked up the painting again and looked at the dark figure with flames coming from his head, and then back at the newspaper. I checked the date on the newspaper. It was after the painting. Four weeks later.

In the newspaper there was a picture of a policeman. He was running away from the stand, and his hair was on fire.

I sat back and ran my hands through my hair. It was incontrovertible. Eric Randle had painted a picture that foretold the Bradford fire four weeks before it had happened.

I turned to another envelope, lost in curiosity now.

This looked just as old, but again I recognised it immediately. It showed a field fringed by trees, the branches bare. Winter. In the middle of the field was the front of an aeroplane, a large one, but it was on its side, the cockpit windows looking strange against the grass. The rest of the plane was gone. I peered closely and I saw what I was looking for. There were dots of colour in the field, like red and blue swirls. Clothes, suitcases. I felt sick. Lockerbie, when Libyan terrorists exploded a Pan-Am flight over a small Scottish town.

I looked for the newspaper clippings, and I saw straightaway that I was right. They showed the same image, from the same angle.

The photograph confirmed what I already suspected. It showed Eric holding up his painting in front of the shop's calendar. He looked more serious in this one, as if the Bradford painting had made him think that he had been right once, and he was now nervous that he would be again. And the date on the calendar proved so. October 1988, two months before the atrocity, the walls behind covered in fireworks posters and Halloween masks.

I heard footsteps behind me, and as I looked round I saw Laura coming towards me, her eyes red.

'He needs to see his dad,' I said softly as I put the picture down. 'Every boy needs his dad. I can't replace him.'

Laura nodded. 'I know, but why does he have to make it so difficult?' she asked, her voice strained.

'Because he can,' I said softly, and I stood up to pull her closer to me. 'Things will even out. Just give it time. If Geoff is doing this to get at us, he will get bored. If he is doing it to see Bobby, we can sort out more formal arrangements when the fuss dies down. For Bobby's sake, though, don't make it into a battle. Geoff wants a fight. If you don't give him one, he'll calm down.'

Laura hugged me, and as she buried her head into my chest I could smell the mustiness of the police station on her. I kissed her on the top of her head.

'Don't worry,' I said. 'We've got Nostradamus on the table here.'

Laura looked over. 'What are all those?'

So I told her about my meeting with Mary Randle and how she had given me all of Eric's paintings.

Laura then picked up the pictures I had already taken out.

'What are you up to, Jack?' Her voice sounded suspicious.

I tried to look innocent. 'I was curious, that's all.'

'Is this just for a story?'

'Yes, because it's a good one. Local misfit turns out to be the Summer Snatcher, ended by a sad suicide.'

Laura looked at me, and I could sense her working out what she could tell me and what she couldn't.

'That's right, Laura, isn't it?' I said. 'Just the result of a guilty conscience?'

'You found him,' was all she said in reply, and she sat down. I joined her after I'd gone to the kitchen and come back with two glasses of red wine.

As she took a sip, she leaned back and kicked off her shoes. I could see her looking at me, at what I was studying, the pictures and clippings strewn across the table.

I nodded towards them. 'Do you want to see what I've got? Quid pro quo?'

Laura watched me, and I could tell she was tempted. I saw her sigh and smile, and then she said, 'If we share information, it's off the record unless I say otherwise. And you keep your sources secret.'

'My first rule, you know that.' I nodded towards the box of papers. 'But you know that these aren't exhibits yet. They go in my story and then back to Mary, and if she lets the police have them, that's her choice.'

Laura stretched as she stood up, and I noticed that her wine had already disappeared. She agreed and joined me at the table, but not before she had topped up her glass.

I showed her the two paintings I had looked at so far. She scratched her chin.

'Could be coincidence so far,' she said.

I agreed. 'Let's see what else there is.'

We started opening envelopes, one at a time, checking the photographs and the paintings. Some didn't have clippings with them, some did.

'There must be a few hundred in here,' she said.

'We've got them going back to the early eighties, so that's still just ten a year.'

'And not all get hits,' she replied. Then she stopped. 'Look at this,' she said, her voice hushed.

Laura handed me a picture filled with columns, a long row of them, white against a grey background. In front of them all was a car, black, mangled and bent. A photograph of Eric holding it in front of the clock dated it in April 1997.

I looked up and shook my head. I didn't recognise it.

Laura handed me a clipping from August 1997. I recognised it straightaway. It was a picture of the Pont d'Alma tunnel in Paris, in which the Princess of Wales died, when the hired black Mercedes crashed and sent the world into shock.

'It's a bit of a stretch,' I said. 'It's not specific enough. A car crash. It could have been anybody at any time. He just got lucky that it happened in the same year.'

'But look at that,' and Laura pointed to a scrawl in the top corner of the page.

I looked closer, and saw that it was the number 13, written in a rush.

When I looked up at Laura, she pointed at a sentence in the newspaper clipping. I read it and whistled. The car crash that killed the Princess of Wales happened when the hired black Mercedes crashed into the thirteenth pillar in the Pont d'Alma tunnel.

'He gets a few hits,' I said, smiling.

Laura frowned and pointed at the envelopes we had opened where there had been no clippings. 'But look how many he doesn't get hits on. Maybe if you paint enough, you'll always get hits.'

'Maybe, but do you know what gets me: he often predicts the media images, not just the events.'

'What do you mean?'

'I could maybe accept some kind of mass telepathy,' I said, 'because a lot of these have human intervention. These were the days before suicide bombers. People put bombs on planes. Maybe people had been talking about old wooden football grounds and fire risks. All of that is possible.'

'Telepathy?' Laura queried, opening envelopes at the same time.

323

I laughed. 'I can't believe I'm saying that, but I suppose it's the most logical explanation. But what no one could have guessed was how the press would report it. On these, he has predicted not just the events, but the way they were reported. That is something way beyond telepathy.'

I stopped talking when I saw Laura's face drain.

'What is it?'

She held up a painting.

As I took hold of it, I saw a line of buildings standing high above a thin ribbon of blue water. Right in the centre of the picture were two tall grey towers. The World Trade Center. Eric had clearly known this location, because the buildings were so recognisable, as if he had tried to make sure everyone would know that it was New York. But it was something else that drew my eye. Right in the middle of the sky was an aeroplane, a passenger jet, if the white body and blue stripe was anything to go by. And it was heading right for one of the towers.

I exhaled. 'There's no mistaking that one.'

Laura looked grim-faced. 'It's not just that,' she said, and the photograph floated down to the table.

As I leaned in for a closer look I felt a cold prickle run down the back of my neck.

In the picture, Eric was standing in the usual place, in the middle of a dingy aisle and in front of the calendar. The calendar that was never wrong. He didn't look happy. I sensed a real tiredness in his eyes, as if he had been missing sleep, and his clothes looked dishevelled, much more like the Eric I had met.

But it was the date on the calendar that had stopped the joking between us. In bright white letters: 11 September 2000.

I looked at Laura, and I saw how she looked nervous now.

'He dreamt it,' she said quietly. 'Exactly a year before it happened.'

'Mary said he hadn't done any paintings for a few years,' I said, 'and that he had started again recently.' I pointed to the painting. 'I bet that was the reason he stopped. When the towers went down a year later, he knew he had seen it and had done nothing to stop it.'

'But what about the rest?'

I shook my head. 'He knew where this was going to happen. There is nothing specific in the other paintings, but there's no mistaking that this is the Manhattan skyline.'

We stared at each other for a few moments, both of us remembering how we had felt on that terrible day, full of disbelief, how the world had suddenly seemed a scary place. And what if we had known it was coming, but just not when?

We both turned back to the box and began to lift out more envelopes in silence.

Chapter Forty-four

It was just past midnight when I finished going through the envelopes. Laura had given up an hour earlier, tiredness taking over when she had a run of no-hitters.

I had made a list of the pictures, just brief descriptives and whether or not there were any clippings in the envelope. Three hundred and twenty envelopes. Fifty-three hits, and some of those seemed speculative, but I had to admit that I was impressed. I was still a sceptic, but things had happened that I couldn't explain.

There had been a gap, I was right about that. It seemed like Eric had done nothing for around five years after the 9/11 attacks, but then the dreams seemed to return. In those dreams, there was a theme. There were no hits, no matching press coverage, but it seemed like he had been dreaming of a building, maybe a house, dark and foreboding. The building was large, with two peaks at the front, like gables, and dark all around it. In others, there were just doorways, with someone silhouetted in them, but again they were lacking in detail. The theme was the same though, just a large house, shrouded in darkness. I remembered Lily's dream from the meeting, running through a large house, always chasing.

I sighed. My story was getting strange, but it was getting interesting, and that was the key to any piece.

I went to the My Pictures folder on my laptop. I wanted to remind myself of what I had seen. If I was going to write the story, I had to confront all of it. Before the police had burst in when I discovered Eric, I had squeezed off a couple of shots. I didn't feel good about it, but the story comes first. Always. Knowing Eric just made it harder.

I steeled myself before I looked at the pictures. When I eventually did, I felt just sadness. Eric's legs dangled downwards and he had his eyes closed. The folds of skin on his neck were bunched up where the rope dug in. It changed his features from the man I had known into a grotesque corpse.

I was about to close the image file when something stopped me, a feeling that there was something not quite right about the picture. I looked closely, scoured the background, looking for whatever it was that had make me think something was wrong. I could see Eric, and then the chair, the boy on the floor nearby. Then I saw what had made me stop.

My hands trembled as I printed off a copy of the picture and turned off my laptop. I scribbled a quick note for Laura and left it on the table and looked for a torch in the boxes at the end of the room, those still not unpacked. Once I found one, I headed for the door.

The street was in darkness when I arrived. I parked outside Eric's house and looked around. The pavements were scattered with cars – none of the houses had a drive – so passage into the street was limited to one in, one out. The houses nearby had blue glows flickering behind the curtains, televisions playing late into the night. As I stood there, I could hear people shouting in the distance, the sound travelling through the cool, still night.

As I stood at Eric's gate and looked up the path, I patted my pocket; I'd put some washing line in there on the way to my car. I shuddered slightly. The last time I'd been in the house I had found Eric. Crime-scene tape was stretched in front of me so I listened out for the sound of the police. There was nothing, so I ducked underneath. I was surprised that there were no police officers outside, but I knew from Laura how the force was stretched at the moment. Maybe the suicide conclusion made watching the house an expense too far.

As I walked towards the house, the wooden boards over the windows seemed to loom out of the darkness, so different from the signs of life in every other house on the street. I tried the door but it was locked this time. I had expected that.

I moved around the side of the house, looking for something left insecure. I couldn't see anything.

I went into the back garden, the green of the lawn now just a silvery sheen from the sliver of moonlight. I tried the back door handle but that was locked solid as well. I stepped back and looked over the house to find that chink, that way in.

I was about to turn away when I noticed that the bathroom window upstairs seemed to jut out slightly, as if someone had opened it and not closed it properly. It was the only window on the house without a board over it. I almost laughed. Eric had been right. He hadn't been dead a full day yet, and already it was going to ruin.

I looked around to find a ladder. There wasn't one. The drainpipe was the only option, a skill I hadn't used since I was at school.

I slipped my camera into my pocket and gripped the drainpipe firmly in my hands. It seemed solid, old-style cast steel rather than one of the modern plastic ones. I swung my legs upwards, and when I felt my feet smack against the wall I started to pull myself up, a slow creep towards the window.

I was panting as I reached it, and tried not to look down. I could feel one hand slipping on the drainpipe as I pulled at the window with the other. Once I'd opened it enough, I gripped hard on the window sill, took a deep breath, prayed, and then let my body fall towards the wall, one hand taking my weight as I reached with the other for the sill. I began to haul myself upwards, straining, grunting, until I fell into Eric's bathroom, wincing as my ribs took a dig from the taps on the small white basin.

I stood up and brushed myself down. I listened for the noise of feet outside, but there was silence. I reached into my back pocket and pulled out the small torch I had put in there. It wouldn't be brilliant, but I reckoned it would give me enough light.

I made my way slowly down the stairs, every creak loud in the empty house. My torch flickered around the plain walls in the living room, every corner full of shadows. The light landed on a photograph, the one I had seen before, and when I looked, I saw that the young girl was Mary. I turned away from it and headed for the cellar door. I felt nervous. Once I was in there, I could get shut in and there would be no other way out. I should have told Laura where I had gone.

I opened the door and it creaked loudly. I flashed my torch down the stairs. It had been dark during daylight hours, but in the middle of the night it seemed to be in darkness so much more complete than I had ever seen before.

I stepped into the doorway and began to move slowly downwards. Once I got to the cellar floor, I looked around. The police had taken away everything I had recorded in the photograph, so I would have to use fresh props. But as I flashed my torch to the ceiling, I realised that my earlier suspicions were confirmed. Eric hadn't committed suicide.

My mind flashed back to the images I had seen earlier in the day, and I remembered the style of the chair. I recalled something similar in the kitchen.

I rushed back upstairs, feeling somehow relieved to be out of there, and flashed my torch. The kitchen was as bare and unwelcome as it had been earlier, but I saw what I was looking for: a chair identical to the one that had been in the cellar with Eric.

I grabbed it and headed back down the cellar steps. I was moving quickly now, wanting to check out my suspicions, get some pictures, and then go home and clamber into bed with Laura. Safe and sound.

I shone the torch towards the ceiling and worked out which ceiling joist in the cellar had held the rope. I stood on the chair and pulled from my coat pocket the piece of washing line. I made a noose at one end, and then, as I thought back to the photographs, I tried to gauge how much rope there had been between the noose and the ceiling joist.

I stood on my tiptoes on the chair and threaded the washing line around the joist. I tried to make it the same length as the rope around Eric's neck. I knew it wasn't exact, but if I was right, it wouldn't have to be.

I stopped. I had heard a noise. It sounded like a light knocking upstairs. I stayed still, silent, tried to hear the noise again. There was nothing. But if there was someone up there, I had to move quickly. It was too late to go back now.

I jumped off the chair, but then I heard another noise. A creak. I paused again, my ears straining, but the sound didn't repeat itself.

I kept going. I went to put my camera on one of the cellar steps, so that the angle would be similar to when I had taken the pictures of Eric.

I heard a whisper, like a hiss, above me. I almost dropped the camera. I stopped and listened carefully. A soft scrape on the floor. I knew I wasn't alone. I thought about what to do, my heart beating faster, a bead of sweat popping onto my top lip. I could stay silent. But what if whoever it was didn't know I was in here and locked me in?

Why wasn't I alone? Maybe someone had been watching the house and had seen me come in. Which meant only one thing: that whoever was in the house was looking for *me*.

My breaths were coming fast now, my fingers damp as I tried to set the camera. Whatever happened, I had to get the story. I needed the picture.

I heard a soft footstep outside the cellar door.

Hands shaking, I flicked on the self-timer and put the camera down, the lens pointing towards the chair.

I stepped away to get back onto the chair, but I stalled for a moment when I heard the doorknob begin to turn. It screeched as it echoed around the cellar.

I jumped onto the chair – the flash would go off in twelve seconds – and I looked up towards the noose, my head directly underneath, my torch shining upwards. I could see the underneath of the noose, swinging from the draughts I'd caused. I smiled. I'd been right.

As I looked up, the noose was higher than me. I was taller than Eric, and the only item in the room had been the chair. If Eric had hanged himself, how had he done it? He could not have stood on the chair to put his head through the noose because his head wouldn't have reached it. It was swinging above my own head. So if he hadn't stood on the chair, and nothing else had been in the room, there were only two other options: that someone else had been into the house and moved whatever it was. Or he had been murdered, and the hanging had been staged.

I turned off my torch, and the cellar was filled with the red blinks from the self-timer. I heard the door begin to open and tried hard to stay still for the photograph. I heard the same loud crunches as feet edged their way down. Then I heard an echo, and I realised that the person wasn't alone. I sensed a pause as they noticed the red light flicker on the back of the camera and then the footsteps got quicker.

I had literally stopped breathing by the time the flash went off, the cellar lit up by dazzling light. I heard a shout by the steps, as if I had made them jump. In the flashlight, I recognised the clothing.

As they turned on their own torches, I could tell that I might have some explaining to do.

Chapter Forty-five

At least I might be able to use it in the story, I thought, as the police car rattled down the cobbled slope into the police yard.

The two officers had been surprisingly friendly. I had been a welcome distraction from a night spent on an estate street watching Eric Randle's house. They were supposed to be on the gate to keep curious onlookers away, but as the cold and boredom had crept in they had retired to their car parked further down the street. I hadn't seen them as I'd gone in, but they'd seen me.

I wasn't cuffed, and they joked with me as we walked towards the steel doors of the custody suite, but as we waited for them to open, I felt them each place a hand on my shoulders.

It was bright in the custody area, with a high mahogany counter and strip lighting, glossy posters on the walls telling prisoners of their rights.

The custody sergeant looked bored as I approached the desk. He had given up life on the streets to spend his days in the bowels of the station, processing criminals and paperwork. He glanced at me briefly when the arresting officer told him that I had been arrested for burglary – perhaps I didn't look like the average deadbeat burglar – but he went through the standard questions on auto-pilot. My answers were just as routine as my mind raced with the thought of what Laura would say when she found out.

It was when they asked me if I wanted any legal advice that my mind clicked alert. I remembered how I had found out about Eric, and then I remembered Terry McKay.

'Sam Nixon,' I said, and I waited until the sergeant flicked through the business cards to get his number.

'You might get one of his runners,' warned the sergeant.

I shook my head. 'It has to be Sam.'

He shrugged nonchalantly, and then held out a key to the arresting officer. 'Tuck him in while we wait for Nixon,' he said, and I turned to follow as I was led into a dim tiled corridor lined by thick grey doors.

Sam held Helena. She had cried herself to sleep and stayed away from the booze.

They were on their bed. Helena had said little on the way home, and nothing at all when they got there. They had done functional things, made the children their food and then put them to bed, and acted like nothing had happened. But it was there all the time, the talk they needed to have. When the children had gone to sleep, happy that Sam was at home, no one mentioning the drama of that morning, the smashed vodka bottle, the stain on the wall, Helena broke down.

Sam had stayed away from her at first, not knowing how to react, but when she looked up at him, tears streaming down her face, he'd gone to her.

He had cried, really cried, seeing something of the Helena he used to know, of the girl he'd fallen in love with, and he realised how much he had missed her.

Now, in the darkness of the bedroom, with Helena sleeping, he thought about Terry. He should have called the police when he'd found him. Or maybe an ambulance. How long had he been there, in agony? Had he left an injured man to protect Harry Parsons, or was it so he could hang on to his own job? Sam knew what he thought about Jimmy King, and now Luke. Was he so much different?

His phone rang. As he looked at it, he saw it was flashing 'Blackley custody'. He should ignore it, stay with Helena, be there for her when she awoke.

'Hello, Sam Nixon,' he said automatically when he answered. He nodded at the message and then said, 'I'll be there in five minutes.'

The metallic rumble of the lock woke me, the crisp white shirt of the custody sergeant reminding me where I was.

I was taken into an interview room, really just a spare room near the custody desk, near enough for the sergeant to hear a lawyer scream if a prisoner turned nasty. I was left on my own for a few minutes before Sam was led in.

I was shocked by his appearance. His face was covered in stubble, and his eyes were red and puffy.

He waited for the door to swing slowly shut before he said anything.

'You've impressed them,' he said, as he undid his brief-case and set a pad down on the table. He must have sensed my confusion, because he nodded towards the door and said, 'We're not in the bubble further along. They must trust you.'

I started to smile.

'So c'mon, let's get on with this and then I can go home.' He held out his hands. 'What the hell were you doing in Eric Randle's house?'

When I didn't answer straightaway, he added, 'They've told me how they found you.'

I looked at Sam, and it struck me how he hadn't said anything about Eric's death.

'Why did you come?' I asked.

'Because you asked, Mr Garrett. It's what lawyers do.'

'Or maybe you don't believe Eric killed himself.'

Sam dropped his head back and rubbed his eyes. He looked tired all of a sudden, a stranger from his usual persona of assured courtroom advocate. Then he composed himself again, took a deep breath.

'Why should I care about Eric Randle?'

I shrugged. 'Because you cared enough to send Mary Randle on to me?'

He looked at me, grim-faced. Then he leaned towards me. 'I didn't know Eric Randle until a couple of days ago, and I was quite happy with that. Now I want to go back to that state of bliss.'

I smiled at Sam, trying to gauge his thoughts. I sensed a real tiredness, but also fear, as if something was happening that he couldn't understand. Maybe there was something else to this, something more than Eric's death.

'Why did he scare you?' I asked, watching Sam's eyes, checking his reaction. 'He was just a harmless old man.'

'You're the one with questions to answer, not me,' he said, but I could sense wariness in his voice.

'Did you believe him?'

Sam sat there and watched me, and I saw him swallow, his mouth dry.

'Eric didn't kill himself,' I continued. 'He wasn't tall enough. He couldn't have reached the noose from that chair. Now, you're a lawyer, which means you're clever, which means you know that if Eric didn't kill himself, then someone else did.'

Sam didn't say anything.

'Any ideas?' I asked, my eyes wide.

Sam looked down for a second and said, 'I've seen killers go free before. If another one goes free, it's just one more in a long line. Is there a reason why I should worry?'

I cocked my head, trying to guess why he looked nervous, despite his bravado; why sweat was making his hair damp in the coolness of the interview room.

'Because this involves you, but you don't know how yet,' I answered.

Sam stood up to go, but then stopped. He stared at the door for a few moments, as if he was willing himself to walk through it. But I could tell that he couldn't.

'Sit down, Sam,' I said softly.

He didn't move at first, but then I saw exhaustion take him over and he slumped back into his seat.

I stood up and leaned against the wall. I watched Sam as he decided what to say. It was time to back off.

I nodded towards the door. 'If you can get me out of

338

here, we could talk some more. I'm starting to build up a good story.'

'But the police will find out whether Randle killed himself or not. These things are pretty hard to fake.'

I grinned. 'The first two on the scene panicked and thought they could save him. They cut him down before the crime scenes got there. So I've got the suicide photo and the re-enactment photo. The police haven't got either yet.'

'You should disclose them.'

'And so should you, but this conversation is confidential, right? You're here as my lawyer, so you can't tell the police anything unless I agree.'

Sam's lip twitched, just a little, but I saw the reality of it all sink in.

'I can breach that to save life and limb,' he said, but his tone was unconvincing.

'Whose? Eric has gone. Who's next, Sam? Who's next for Luke King?'

He blinked.

I nodded. 'That's right. He's the one person linking all of this, isn't he? He was arrested for the murder of Jess Goldie, Eric's friend. Then Eric dies. And what about Terry McKay? He wasn't the biggest fan of your boy, and the last I heard he's wound up pretty badly injured.' I saw Sam blink again. 'And the missing child was found with Eric, so I guess that there's a link, that whoever killed Eric killed that boy.' I watched Sam, but he just looked at the floor. 'Am I right?'

Sam shook his head but he didn't answer.

'You're scared, aren't you?' I said.

Sam looked up at me. 'What do you want me to say?'

I shrugged. 'Nothing really. I just want you to tell me that I should carry on digging, find out what I can before another child dies.'

Sam looked down again and shook his head. 'I can't do that and I *won't* do that.'

'Professional conscience?' I laughed. 'Something of an oxymoron with lawyers, don't you think?'

'And you reporters are a step above?'

I shook my head. 'Maybe not, but I don't pretend any differently.'

I started to pace. Sam tracked me as I went, his eyes wide open, confused. 'How will it play if I uncover Luke King as a murderer and it comes out that you could have stopped it? Do you think all the young mothers of Blackley will love you for that?'

'That's blackmail.'

'No, it isn't, because I'm going to write this up anyway. It's your quote I'm looking for.'

Sam sat there for a while, and then he stood up quickly and picked up his briefcase.

'Get a different lawyer,' he said, and then banged on the door.

He stayed looking at the door until I heard it unlocked from outside. He didn't turn back to look at me as he disappeared from view.

I had what I wanted: confirmation that something big was going on. I've met a few lawyers in my time, and one thing they don't do is storm out on clients. It seemed like I was going to have to advise myself this time around.

* * *

He stood in the shadows, his collar up. He was cold, his hands aching.

Healing hands. He looked down at them. They were shaking. It wasn't right. It wasn't supposed to turn out this way.

But he knew what had gone wrong. He had guessed the age wrong. A simple mistake. Too simple. He should have been more attentive. He had got too confident.

He could make amends, he knew that. There were others he could help.

He was looking out for the next one. And he knew just who it was going to be. He had been watching, listening, trying to work out who was getting closest, who might stop him.

He looked towards the house. He was out now, leaving her on her own. Like always. He could take the child and she would never know. He would be more careful with the sedative, and then maybe she would be there for her son more.

He turned away from the house and went back to his car. He would have to sleep in the car tonight, but tomorrow he would be gone.

Chapter Forty-six

I opened my eyes slowly when I heard a noise. The room took a while to come into focus, and it took even longer for me to realise that I was in my own bedroom. I looked to the space next to me, and I saw Laura looking at me, her hair lying over her face.

'Good morning,' I mumbled sleepily. 'Shouldn't you be at work?'

Laura didn't reply at first. She looked at me intently instead, trying to gauge my thoughts. Then she asked, 'Where did you go last night?'

'Last night?' I asked innocently, but when I saw the look of mistrust I knew I had to be truthful. 'I was researching Eric Randle.'

Laura sat up and raised her knees, wrapping her arms around them. I put my hand on her back and traced her spine with my finger.

'I shouldn't have to deal with this,' she said. She turned towards me. 'Geoff is coming for Bobby today, and you go out all night, leaving me on my own. I couldn't sleep properly.'

I went to hold her but she pushed me away.

'No,' she said, her voice thick from tiredness. 'That won't do it.'

'What will?'

She threw back the covers and climbed out of bed. 'I don't know. I'm too knackered to think.' She rummaged through the drawers before she turned back round to me, clothes in her hand. 'Where did you go?'

'I told you, researching Eric Randle.'

'Where?' She was raising her voice.

I thought about how to put this. I knew silence wasn't an option, and a lie wouldn't do much good, but I was concerned that the truth wouldn't help me too much either.

'I went to his house,' I said quietly, and waited for the barrage.

'You went to his *house*? A crime scene?' She was aghast. 'You could get yourself arrested.'

I looked up at her and grimaced.

'You got arrested?' She shook her head, pacing on the spot. Then she threw her clothes onto the bed. 'You got arrested?' she repeated. 'Fucking hell.' Then she looked at me, anger replaced by disbelief. 'What did you do?'

I chewed my lip nervously. 'When I found Eric yesterday, something about the scene bothered me. It stayed with me all day, and when I looked at the photographs again last night, I saw it.'

'What photographs?' Laura's voice was stern, her arms folded over her breasts.

'The ones I took before I called the police.'

When she raised an eyebrow, I said, 'I'm a reporter. It's what I do.'

'Show me.' It was a command, not a request.

I reached for the camera from my trouser pocket, my clothes still lying crumpled on the bedroom floor. I had told the police I was just re-creating the scene for the story, so they had given the camera back to me and told me to stay away. I scrolled through until I found the pictures from the day before. Laura looked impassive as she examined the screen, using the zoom button to search around the room, to look at Eric hanging from the ceiling.

'What's the problem?'

I took the camera back and found the picture I had taken of me on the chair.

'I made a noose of the same length,' I said, 'and the chair is the same, but look.' I pointed at the screen. 'I'm much taller than Eric. I could not have got my head into that noose by standing on that chair.'

'You mean someone helped him?' she asked, still looking at the picture of me with a noose above my head. She shuddered.

'I mean that maybe he was already dead when he was strung up there. When I looked at the picture again last night, I realised that it could have been staged, and so I went back to check.'

'And you were arrested.'

I nodded.

'What did the cops say last night when you told them?'

'I didn't. I'm saving it for my story.'

344

'So why are you telling *me*? I'm going to have to say something.'

I looked down at her body. 'You being naked made me sort of reckless.'

She smiled a little at that. 'I've got to get to work now,' she said, her voice keen.

'You can't take my camera,' I complained.

'Will you print these off for me?' she asked.

I was about to complain, when she started to leave the room, my camera in her hand.

'Okay, okay,' I said. 'I'll do it.'

She turned around and tossed the camera onto the bed. 'I can hear Bobby. I'm going to spend some time with him before I go.'

And then she was gone.

Sam woke up with a jolt. He was falling. The same dream, but stronger this time. He felt a sense of dread, worse than before. He looked down. His shirt was drenched with sweat, his face slick, his fingers tightly pressing into his leg.

He looked around. He was in his office. He had slept in his chair. He checked his watch. He could hear people moving around, talking. He caught his reflection in his window. He hadn't shaved in a couple of days, and he was in the same shirt he had worn the day before. It was creased and dirty.

He leaned forward and put his face in his hands. Just for a moment, it felt good. It was dark, and so he couldn't see anything, could feel only his own breath, hot and scared. But when he pulled his hands away, the daylight came as a stark reminder that he had another day to get through.

He wasn't sure he could do it.

Then he thought of Terry McKay. How must he be feeling, his hand ruined, dumped like rubbish at the back of the office?

Then it struck him. Behind the office. The car park. The security light. There was something he could do.

He looked at his reflection in the window again, tried to smooth down his shirt, checked that he didn't look too tired. He felt a glow, empowerment. Time to make things right.

He stood against a wall, the stone grey and jagged, and watched through the window of the house. He checked his pockets, felt his hand wrap around the cloth, soaked through with diethyl ether. He had used it so many times with children but they were usually older. He would have to be more careful.

He checked his watch. He had watched it crawl through the night, time slowed down, his car cold, just a blanket to keep him warm. His skin felt dirty, his hands clammy as he ran them over his stubble.

He looked down at his hands, turned them over, saw how the sunlight seemed to make them shine, reflected back off the strong fingers. Then he noticed the teeth marks, bright red gashes across his knuckles, raw and vivid. He clenched his fist, felt the anger burn through him.

He blew into his hand and unclenched his fist, took

a deep breath and shook his arms loose. He checked his watch again. He was ready to go.

I came out of the shower and went to the top of the stairs. Bobby had been on his own for ten minutes.

'You okay, Bobby?'

As I listened, I could hear the television playing. Kids' TV. The sound of a glockenspiel floated up towards me.

'We'll be going soon,' I shouted. 'Can you find your shoes?'

Still nothing. The power of television, I thought. I'd once tried to tell him that when I was his age there were only three channels. He'd giggled.

I rummaged through my drawers to find some clothes. I wondered what it would feel like if he wasn't there. Would the house seem too quiet?

I couldn't hear any movement downstairs. I checked my watch. He had to be ready to leave for school soon. 'How are you doing?' I shouted as I got dressed. 'You're seeing your daddy today, so you need to look your best.'

There was still no reply. Maybe it was time to turn the television off more, I thought. What was wrong with the radio, or toys?

As I pulled on my shoes, I went to the top of the stairs. 'Bobby, have you got your shoes on? I'm getting mine on, and I bet you can't beat me.'

I started to walk down the stairs, making theatrical thumps to make the shoe game fun.

'I'm on my way,' I said, but still no answer. That television would have to go off.

347

'Bobby?'

Still no response.

I started to get concerned. He should have answered by now.

Two more steps, heavy thumps of my feet.

'Bobby! Can you hear me?'

Now I knew something wasn't right.

I ran down the rest of the stairs and rushed into the living room. I looked around, at the unpacked boxes, the toys on the floor, the television blaring in the corner. He wasn't there.

I turned quickly, tried to see if he was hiding. I started to feel sick. I looked behind the sofa.

'Bobby! This isn't funny. Come out.' I snapped out the words and then ran into the kitchen. Still no sign. I flung open the door to a cupboard. The ironing board fell out. I ran back to the foot of the stairs and shouted, 'Bobby!'

No reply.

I was frantic. My hands were on my head. I could feel my heart beating fast, the adrenaline, the fear racing through me. I went to the front door and looked out. All I could see were fields, dry-stone walls, and Turners Fold in the valley below. Bobby wasn't out there.

I went back into the house, tried to stay calm, tried to think of when I had last seen him. It was only minutes before. I turned around, hoping that he might just appear from somewhere. He didn't.

'Bobby, if you're hiding it's not funny,' I shouted, my voice strained.

I put my hands over my face and slumped onto the

floor. It was my fault. I had left him unsupervised. But I had only been upstairs.

And then I heard a knocking sound, coming from the kitchen. I felt sick as soon as I heard it.

I ran into the kitchen and saw what I had missed before. That was when I moaned. The back door was open, and the breeze was making it rattle against the doorframe.

Bobby was gone.

Chapter Forty-seven

Sam walked through the office. He knew where he was headed, but as he made his way along the narrow corridor that connected all the rooms, he thought it seemed quieter than usual. The clerks were normally kicking up some noise by this time. He could hear faint murmurs, but nothing else.

As he turned into Jon Hampson's room, he saw them all in a huddle by his window. They all turned to Sam at the same time. They looked worried. Jon Hampson just stared at him, his glare hostile.

'Are you okay?' asked Sam.

They exchanged glances, unsure what to say. One of them asked, 'Is the firm in trouble?'

Sam's eyes narrowed. Most criminal firms worried about the future. Defence lawyers were an easy budget cut with no political negatives. Sam saw the worry in their eyes again. They had mortgages and children, just like everyone else, and he could tell that these were new worries.

'Why do you say that?' he asked.

The clerks all looked towards the door. 'It feels different around here this week, sort of tense,' one said.

'What have you heard?'

One of them put his hands in his pockets and fidgeted, but no one answered.

Sam felt his resolve weaken. There was more than just himself to think about. He could get a job elsewhere. He could even retrain and become a civil lawyer. The people he was looking at were crime clerks, nothing else. Civil firms didn't need police-station runners.

'I'm sure everything will be okay,' said Sam quietly, and then looked away before anyone could say anything.

He set off again. His cheeks were flushed, but he knew what he had to do.

I had the telephone in my hand, ready to dial, when I heard him. It was a giggle. I put my head back and sighed. Then I rushed to the back door. There was Geoff. My stomach turned over and I had to lean against the doorframe as they turned into the garden path.

'Hello, Jack,' shouted Bobby as he bounced on Geoff's shoulders, his laugh carrying towards me on the breeze blowing through the valley. 'Daddy's here.'

I nodded, breathing heavily. 'So I see,' I said, and I began to laugh in sheer relief.

As they got closer, I saw Geoff glare at me.

'A child shouldn't be left on his own,' he said.

'I was in the shower.'

He put Bobby down and tapped him on the bottom. 'In you go.' When Bobby had gone inside, he stepped closer. I could smell the early start on his breath. 'I'll rephrase that. You don't leave my son on his own. I could make things difficult for you. Remember, children go missing round here.'

'I thought you were collecting him from the school.'

He sneered at me. 'I wanted to see where Bobby was living, so I set off earlier. You've nothing to be ashamed of, have you?' As he said it, he looked around, took in the view, tried not to look impressed.

'It's called fresh air,' I said flippantly. 'I think he likes it.'

Geoff's cheeks went red as he glared at me.

'Don't get too cosy, northern boy. She'll get bored.'

'She? That would be Laura, I presume.'

'Don't get smart. Don't you think she's been here before? Young love?'

I looked back into the house and saw Bobby dragging a bag of clothes towards the front door.

'He's a giveaway.'

Geoff's eyes narrowed. 'Yeah, she's good at the start. We had a real good time. But she'll get bored, maybe only fuck you once a week. Maybe even less. She turned into a real old rag doll towards the end. You're the journalist. What word would you use?' He pointed at me. 'Unresponsive. That's the word. Fucking unresponsive. She knew every fleck of paint on the ceiling by the time I left.'

I could feel myself starting to get angry, but I tried not to show it, knowing that's what he wanted.

'Young mothers get tired,' I said, deadpan. 'I understand that.'

Geoff was about to respond, the skin around his eyes mottled red with anger, when Bobby came out. 'Come

352

and look at my bedroom, Daddy.' As Geoff felt Bobby tug on his hand, he looked at me and nodded, as if to say *Don't get too comfortable*.

'Let's inspect your house. I need to see if it's good enough for my son,' and then he went inside, glaring at me as he went.

When he was out of view, I heaved a sigh of relief again, my breath short. I now had a sense of what it must be like for a child of your own to go missing.

The scuffed Perspex in the bus shelter gave him cover, but he could still see her as she brushed her hair. Her hands moved slowly, just like the night before. He saw flashes of blue, a school jumper, someone moving quickly, running around. She seemed almost absent-minded.

He smiled to himself. Things would be different later. Her senses would be heightened like never before.

He looked at the other people in the bus shelter. It seemed like they were edging away from him. Maybe it was because he looked unkempt, or maybe it was something about his mood that scared them off, but they had noticed him. That wasn't good.

He tried to look natural, inconspicuous, but he felt himself tense when he saw her leave the house.

She didn't go to the car. He had seen her the night before, brought home by her husband. His car was gone, and her car was on the drive, the front all twisted and bent. She would have to walk right past him, he knew that. He knew where her son went to school, half a mile away. It was a long walk for the youngest one, but there was a shortcut by the canal, along a brick path, dotted by cast-iron moorings and overhung by bramble bushes.

He had walked the route the night before, knew where he would get a view as she made her way home. He had guessed right. She headed straight towards him. As they got closer he could hear the boys jabbering to each other, pushing, bickering. They both stepped into the road to get past the bus queue, but she didn't notice. It seemed like she didn't have the energy to tell them off. They talked to her but she wasn't listening. Her head was down, her hair lying straggly over a camel-coloured coat, her skin looked pale and blotchy, her eyes heavy. He turned away as she got near, worried that she might recognise him, but she barely glanced at him as she went past.

He smiled to himself, took a long, deep breath. He looked down at his hands, thought of mother and son. He was going to bring them closer together. It's what he did. His fingers ached as he thought of it.

He watched them walk away. His smile turned into a sneer as he thought about her unhappiness. Why was she unhappy? She had two beautiful boys. A house. Money. Why wasn't that enough?

His hands curled into fists. He knew it wasn't enough. He would make it better. He had done it before. He had changed people's lives, made them more precious, made them realise that the most valuable things come free.

He looked at his hands. They were precious. He turned them over, the fists clenched hard, and saw the bite marks again. Healing hands.

* * *

Sam rushed into the cellar, to the room at the end, past all the archived files. The door was open, he knew it would be. It was where the cleaning fluids and all the household things were kept. But in the corner was the thing Sam had come looking for: the CCTV.

Like most solicitors' firms, Parsons had been the victim of burglaries. Criminals worked out the layout of the building during their visits, when they saw the laptops and computers. The building was protected by alarms, but Harry installed security cameras as well a few years earlier, after some of the staff cars were broken into before Christmas, when the car park turned dark before everyone went home and cars were filled with presents hidden from children. A large light now illuminated the car park, and a static camera covered the area, along with ones pointed at the building, and at the front, just to see who tried the windows.

It was a simple system. It recorded the footage onto a hard disk. It wasn't great quality, but it was good enough to make out clothes and glimpses of faces. It recorded continually, and the secretaries were convinced that it was a snooping device. But it wasn't. It was just what it was: a security camera. After twenty-four hours it created a video file, numbered from one to nine. On the tenth day, it went back to one, overwriting the earlier file. Simple and maintenance-free.

He clicked on the monitor and went into the hard drive. Sam's eyes remained on the door as the machine whirred, waiting for Harry to walk in, convinced that the machine must be fitted with an alarm. The software was slow, though, and it seemed like an age before he could open the video file.

It started in late afternoon, so he had to scroll through a few hours of footage, the cursor moving across the screen, nothing to see except the flickers of the rest of the staff leaving.

Sam almost missed it. He was moving fast through the footage but the image didn't change, just an empty car park. But then he thought he saw some ghost footage, just a faint blur at the top of the screen.

He stopped and went back, saw the ghosts in reverse, and then he pressed play.

There wasn't much to see. A car pulled in and stopped for a few seconds. Then the rear door opened and someone was dragged from the car. From the clothes, Sam recognised Terry McKay. He wasn't moving in the footage. He had slumped onto the floor by the car wheels. Sam thought the car was about to drive away when some legs appeared at the top of the screen. Then the body appeared, and Sam recognised him. It was the man seen with Jimmy King at the office, bald and intimidating. Sam's breath caught as he saw the shine on another pair of shoes. As the rest of that figure came into view, Sam saw that it was Jimmy King. Both men dragged Terry McKay away from the car, their hands on his jacket as his legs made dust clouds in the gravel.

Sam put his hand over his mouth as they stood over him. Terry wasn't moving.

The two men went to leave, but then Sam saw Jimmy King stop and return to Terry. He stood over Terry, still. Sam noticed a dark patch spread on Terry's jacket. He felt sick when he realised what was going on. Jimmy King was pissing on Terry McKay as he lay there on the floor.

Sam stepped back and shook his head, shocked. He didn't feel good about himself for leaving Terry, and he would have to come to terms with that, but Jimmy King had burned off the man's hand and then pissed on him like Terry wasn't even human.

He rummaged through the drawer next to the CCTV unit until he found what he had been looking for: a blank DVD. He put his ear to the door. Still no one there. He copied the video file onto the blank disk and then left the room.

He knew where he was headed next.

Helena turned back onto the canal path, her time at the school gate cut short. Zach had been quiet during the walk. He sensed that something wasn't right, that there were tensions at home, and he didn't look back as he went through the gate. Little Henry had been the same as always, a pocket of energy, running everywhere. How would she deal with it once he was at school too and she would return to an empty house?

Her hands were thrust into her coat pockets. She had a headache, a pounding behind the eyes, and her stomach was turning cartwheels, waves of nausea sweeping over her. Alcohol withdrawal. She recognised it. She had tried to fight it before, but had always lost the battle. Maybe because when she was drunk, her life seemed so much better than it did when she was sober.

An image of Sam flashed into her head. It wasn't the

Sam who came home every night, the distant lawyer with greying hair and a suit, pompous and self-satisfied. It was the Sam she had known a decade earlier, the one who had talked about changing the world, who had made her feel warm inside with just a look, a sideways glance, the man who had once held her so tight that she wasn't sure if she'd ever want to breathe again. She fought back a tear when she remembered how he had been the night before. How she had been the night before. They'd made love, tender and emotional, like they had discovered each other again, and afterwards, she had sobbed into his chest, his hands stroking her hair until she fell asleep.

The path ahead looked hazy, the water shimmering as the low morning sun was reflected off the surface. She shielded her eyes. She could see Henry skipping ahead. She shouted out that he was getting too near the edge. As trees gave some shade for the moment, she had a better view. He looked back and waved, and then skipped off again. She clenched her jaw and walked on, not feeling good.

She didn't look to check whether there was anyone watching.

He was in complete shadow, tucked into the bushes on the other side of a bridge. The little boy had run ahead. He would have to deal with the mother first. As he peeped around the corner of damp brickwork, he saw them getting closer.

He checked along the canal bank. There was no one ahead. No pleasure barges cruising down. The opposite bank was filled by an empty mill building, the roof in pieces, the windows broken.

He heard their footsteps come under the bridge, the soft shuffle turned into a loud echo, Henry talking about his father, shouting questions back along the towpath. The responses were short and empty. She sounded like she wished he wasn't there. He'd teach her.

As Henry emerged into the sunlight first, he saw that the boy was skipping.

He dropped lower down into the bushes.

Then he saw her come out from under the bridge, her head still down, her thoughts wrapped up in herself, not focused on Henry, not watching, not caring.

He reached into his pocket, feeling for the cloth. He soaked it in diethyl ether again, handling the bottle of fluid carefully.

He stepped out from behind the bush and joined them on the canal bank, his footsteps nimble, almost silent as he made his way towards them.

Helena tried to break the day into sections as she walked on. Just get through to lunchtime, she thought. Do some housework, maybe, or just take Henry for a walk again. What about meeting Sam for lunch? If she could hold out until Sam came home, he would help her through the evening.

But her mouth felt dry and her hands weak.

She looked up, saw that Henry was still running ahead. She opened her mouth to shout, just to call him back.

She didn't get the chance.

She heard a noise, the quick rumble of feet. She started

to turn, suddenly scared, when she felt someone grab her from behind, a strong arm around her neck. Her shout turned into a scream, but it was snuffed out by a cloth, clamped tight over her face.

She began to struggle, but the arm tightened around her. She could smell something strong. It was sweet and hot.

She tried to thrash her arms, kick back with her legs, but she was held too tightly. And then she felt her legs become weak, and her arms too. Her struggle slowed down.

She saw Henry in the distance. He had turned round, was watching, eyes wide, teeth bared, his hands over his ears. She tried to reach out to him, to shout out to him, to tell him to run, but she could feel herself slipping into darkness, the view ahead fading out, as Henry blurred into the background.

The gleam from the water grew, and everything turned bright white. The last word she heard was, 'Mummy.'

Chapter Forty-eight

Laura crinkled her nose as she went down the stairs to the morgue. There was a strong smell of disinfectants, and the tiles along the stairs were cracked with age, cream at the top, green at the bottom. It seemed like all the death through the years was embedded into those walls. Pete walked behind her, trying to keep up, but he was hesitant. She turned around.

'You okay, Pete?'

He took a deep breath. 'Never liked this place.'

'Queasy?'

He shook his head. 'No, it just gives me the shivers.'

Laura tried to stop a smile. 'For a big tough thing, you're a bit of a softy.'

Pete harrumphed and walked ahead. 'Yeah, well, whatever. You better be right on this.'

Laura didn't respond. She was angry still, concerned about whether she would be accused of being too close to the press, but what if the photographs showed the truth, that Eric *couldn't* have hanged himself? A visit to the pathologist would clear up the mystery, but she was scared of being wrong.

361

They turned the corner and almost bumped into Egan, who looked preoccupied and angry.

'Everything okay, sir?' said Laura.

He looked up, was about to say something, and then walked off, his head down.

Pete and Laura exchanged glances and raised their eyebrows.

'Doesn't look good,' said Pete.

'Maybe things worked out like I said,' replied Laura, before they carried on down the steps.

They were in the basement of an old Victorian hospital on the way out of the town centre, just used for the maternity ward and the morgue now that the new hospital had been built. An odd mix, thought Laura, just deaths and births. A lift provided a quick route down for the corpses, but Pete wanted to walk down. The lift felt like there had been too many bad memories in it. The walls of the corridor were tiled in the same way as the stairs, but they were even more yellowed by age.

Pete went through the double doors which took him into an outer room, where the pathologists got scrubbed and ready. There was someone already in there.

'Doctor Pratt,' said Pete, trying too hard to be cheerful. 'Good to see you again.'

The doctor turned round to look at Pete, but then turned straight back to the sink, where he was washing his hands and arms.

'I'm not changing my mind,' he said. 'I've just told your inspector that.'

Laura looked at Pete quizzically but he nodded, just slight enough for her to see.

'We're not here for that,' said Laura.

The doctor turned around slowly and looked down at her over his glasses.

'I don't think we've met,' he said. His voice was rich and deep, the accent betraying an expensive education.

'DC McGanity,' she said. 'I'm working on the Jess Goldie murder, and we think the deaths of Eric Randle and Kyle might be connected to it.'

'The young lady who had her eyes taken out?'

Laura nodded.

Doctor Pratt shook his head. 'That was a bad one,' but Laura sensed some pleasure in his voice. Pathologists were crazy, Laura knew that, every one she had ever met had been wild in some way. Doctor Pratt nodded towards the doors leading into the post-mortem room. 'But why do you think they are connected?'

Pete looked at Laura, who took the cue.

'We don't think Eric Randle died by hanging,' Laura replied.

Pratt's hands stopped moving in the towel, and then he began to smile. 'Tell me why ever not.'

Laura took a breath. She realised that she might be on the verge of embarrassing herself.

'I don't think Eric Randle was tall enough,' she said. 'He couldn't have got his head in the noose.'

Doctor Pratt nodded, and then sighed, his hands on his hips.

'C'mon, DC McGanity,' he said. 'Come with me.'

The doctor turned to go into the post-mortem room. When Pete and Laura didn't follow immediately, he turned to them. 'C'mon, children, you're going to learn something.'

When they got into the room, Laura heard Pete take a sharp intake of breath. The post mortems had been done on Eric and Kyle, both bodies stitched back together, the Y-shaped incisions ugly across their chests. For Laura, it was the sight of the young boy that gave her a kick to her gut. He looked so small and pale against Eric Randle, too young to be cold and grey in the morgue.

She tried to stop herself but she knew it would come: an image of Bobby on the slab. She shut her eyes and tried to mentally shake it away. She remembered all the jibes at the police station about Kyle's mother. She had been to prison for shoplifting a few times, just twenty-eight-day turnarounds, broken only by nights working the streets. Kyle was the offspring of that career, but Laura had heard too many snipes from people who had just got a bit luckier. All Laura saw was a dead little boy whose life had been spread out before him, good or bad. And his mother would hurt just as much. This wasn't just another twist of fate. This was something beyond anything Laura could comprehend.

She looked away from Kyle when she saw that Pete and Doctor Pratt were standing by Eric Randle. As Laura looked down at him, she saw how peaceful he looked, his facial muscles relaxed now, no longer the tense bundle she had seen in life just a few days before. And then she noticed the marks around the neck. She began to doubt herself. She had raced to the morgue just to tell a trained pathologist what she thought, based upon Jack's guess-work from photographs and a matching chair.

She glanced up at Pete. Laura thought she detected a glazed look in his eyes, and from the clenching of his jaw she knew that he was doing his best to stop himself from fainting.

'Sorry, Pete,' she said quietly. 'Looks like I might have got it wrong.'

'Why is that?' the doctor asked, his deep bass bringing Pete round for a second.

Laura pointed at the marks on Eric's neck. 'I can see where the rope dug in.'

The doctor started to grin, and then he stood up, pompous and full of himself. 'No,' he said. 'It looks like you are right.'

Laura looked confused for a moment, and then she looked again at Eric's neck. 'Why?'

'Did you see the rope?' the doctor asked.

Laura shook her head, and then thrust her hand into her pocket. 'We've just got the photos,' and she held up the photos she had been given earlier.

The doctor nodded. 'That's good, because if you look closely you will see that the knot in the rope is a *fixed* knot.'

Laura peered into the photograph and then looked up. 'I can't tell.'

Doctor Pratt nodded. 'Well, I saw it, and I can tell you it was.'

'And that makes a difference?'

'Oh yes,' he said, enjoying the audience. Even Pete was looking more interested. 'There are two types of knot: fixed and sliding. If you imagine a fixed knot, where the knot won't move, death is caused by the weight of the body against the rope. A sliding knot, however, closes against the neck as the weight takes effect, so it's the tightening of the rope that causes death.'

'I don't understand,' said Laura, sounding confused. 'That sounds like the same thing to me.'

Doctor Pratt shook his head and smiled. 'Oh no, Detective, they are very different. Think about the actions of the rope on the neck. In a fixed-knot hanging, the rope will dig deep into the skin of the neck as the body weight takes hold, but the weight of the body will always force the rope upwards until it hits the jaw.' He paused for effect, checking that Laura was still with him. 'The rope will make deep furrows into the neck, but they will always follow the jawline, as the jawbone acts as a brake, to keep the rope around the neck.'

'And a sliding knot?' she asked.

'Ah, much different,' he said, his eyes wide with excitement. 'In a sliding knot, the knot just closes the rope as tight as possible around the neck, so that it doesn't get anywhere near the jawbone. The weight of the body actually tightens the knot, and causes the rope to literally throttle someone to death.'

Laura bent down to Eric's neck. She could see a deep furrow underneath Eric's jaw.

'So it was a fixed knot that killed him,' she said. 'I can see the line there.'

Doctor Pratt nodded. 'That is a fixed-knot mark,' he said, 'and a fixed knot was found at the scene. But is that the only mark you can see around his neck?'

Laura looked closer. And then she saw it. There was a narrower groove around the neck, deeper and lower down. She looked back at Doctor Pratt.

'That's the one,' he said, nodding. 'It wouldn't have been very noticeable at first, very pale, but later on grooves like that become brown and dry. That's why I left him until this morning.' He pointed to Eric's neck. 'That's the mark from a sliding knot, pulled tight from behind. It was death by strangulation, my girl, not hanging.'

'How do you know it was from behind?'

He pointed down to some tiny marks just above the narrow groove around Eric's neck. 'Scratch marks, made by Eric Randle as he tried to pull the rope away. The person would have to be behind him for Eric to get his fingers to the front of his neck like that.'

Laura stood up. 'So he was throttled to death using a sliding knot, but when it came to hanging Eric Randle, the killer didn't appreciate that there would be a difference and used a fixed knot. He tried to make it look like a suicide and bungled it.'

Doctor Pratt nodded. 'It looks that way.'

'And then he throws in the chair, just to complete the illusion,' said Pete, his interest distracting him from the two corpses.

Doctor Pratt said, 'That would be my guess, but that's *your* job.' He winked at Laura. 'Maybe your inspector should learn to keep his mouth shut before I've finished mine.'

Laura and Pete both understood now why Egan had looked so angry. He had proclaimed to the world that the Summer Snatcher was dead, but it seemed now like he was very much alive. And he was killing people, those who he thought could identify him.

Laura turned to Kyle. She felt her stomach turn. Kyle's life would have been bad, she guessed that. Police, drugs, jail. Maybe he wouldn't have got past forty, and he would have created victims along the way, but he had lost the chance to make it different. And even if it had been bad, it was still his life.

'What about Kyle?'

Doctor Pratt looked less happy about that. He sighed. Laura guessed that he had children of his own.

'My guess is morphine overdose. Accidental.'

'Why do you say "accidental"?'

Doctor Pratt paused for a moment, and then said, 'Because I can't find anything else. The blood's been sent to the lab, so we'll just have to see, but do you see that?' and he pointed to a small square patch of brown skin on Kyle's arm.

Laura looked closely and then looked back at Doctor Pratt.

'That's adhesive,' he said, 'from some kind of analgesic patch. A common one would be fentanyl.'

'What do they do?'

'They release morphine into the bloodstream at an even and steady rate, so it can act as a strong painkiller for a few days at a time.'

'Or even knock someone out?' she asked.

Doctor Pratt nodded. 'If the dose was strong enough, it could knock someone out for just as long.'

'But can you overdose on them?'

Doctor Pratt nodded again, taking his glasses off. 'Oh yes. These aren't like nicotine patches. They are strong anaesthetics, designed for people who are in real pain, and they do their job well. But,' and he looked thoughtful for a moment as he sought to get his words right, 'if something happens to accelerate the intake of morphine, or if the dose is wrong, then the patient can receive too much of it over a long period of time.'

'What can cause this?' asked Laura. 'A faulty patch?'

Doctor Pratt shook his head. 'More likely a faulty application by someone who doesn't know what they are doing. These patches come in different dosages. You have to apply the correct patch for the size and age of the patient. This boy was nine, so any patch would have been too much. Maybe whoever took him thought he was older and put on a bigger patch. Heat can also be a factor.'

'Heat?'

'Yes. If a patient decides to park themselves in front of a fire or next to a radiator, the heat will make the patch work much quicker, so the body absorbs the morphine at a faster rate.'

'Do you think that might have happened here?'

'Possibly. The nights are getting colder. Maybe he thought he needed to keep the boy warmer. It might be that he was getting too much morphine because he was too young, so he seemed cold, his body starting to shut down. Any attempt to keep him warm will have accelerated the morphine intake and made it worse.'

Laura stepped away. She teased at her hair with her fingers, just a distraction as she thought it through.

'But I don't remember any of the other abducted children having patches on their arms, or their blood being full of morphine.'

Doctor Pratt smiled. 'That was *living* tissue, and living blood. If you want my opinion, it's that the children will have been released when the last patch he put on was wearing off. These things don't stick on like superglue. Once it is off for a couple of hours, the skin recovers, and the fact that the children who were returned alive were awake when they were found points to the fact that the morphine effect of the patch had worn off.' He pointed down at Kyle. 'This poor little mite is dead, so he never had the chance to recover. His skin still has the adhesive on it, there is still a slight mark where the patch was taken off, just where the skin stretched, and the blood will still be full of morphine.'

Laura exhaled. 'And you told Egan all of this?'

Doctor Pratt nodded. 'I don't know if he was convinced. He wasn't happy, I know that,' and then he chuckled. 'It looks like he has made a fool of himself.'

Pete smiled and then he stopped as he thought of something else. 'Who would have access to strong painkillers?'

Laura looked puzzled for a moment. Then she realised what Pete meant.

'Someone with an ill relative,' she said, comprehension dawning.

Pete nodded, his face stern now. 'C'mon, we're going to see Billy Hunt again. Let's not have a second suspect slip away.'

Chapter Forty-nine

Sam pushed open the door into Harry's office. Harry looked up, startled.

'I'm going to the police.'

Harry didn't respond at first. He sat at his desk, his fingers steepled and resting just under his chin. His cheeks looked flushed, pensive.

He looked up at Sam slowly, had to refocus as he watched him.

'What did you say?' He said it like he was irritated.

Sam shut the door behind him.

'Terry McKay. I'm going to the police.'

'And what would you say?' Harry asked wearily.

'That Terry threatened to expose Jimmy King and had arranged to meet him.'

Harry shook his head slowly. 'And I'll say the opposite. Jimmy King was with me when Terry McKay was hurt.'

'And Luke?'

Harry nodded. 'Luke too.'

Sam shook his head angrily. 'I was there,' he said, his voice loud. 'I saw Terry. I saw what Jimmy King did to him.' He raised his eyebrows. 'Were you there, Harry?'

When Harry didn't respond, Sam sat down and stared at him. 'It wouldn't be the first time you've lied for Jimmy, would it?'

Harry swallowed and then replied, 'Think like a lawyer, Sam. That's what you are, remember. What chance would you have of proving that?'

'It doesn't always have to be about what you can prove,' Sam replied. 'Sometimes, it can be about what's right.'

'Is that what you thought when you went to law school, that it wouldn't be about proof?' Sam didn't reply, so Harry continued, 'If you think that, you're in the wrong job. It's only ever about what you can prove.'

'So why did you go to law school?' Sam replied, his voice harsh. 'For the power, because you can change a life just like that?' He clicked his fingers.

Harry leaned forward, a sneer on his face. 'You're the type who never lasts long. I've seen it too often. Came to the law to change the world.'

Sam smiled. 'The trouble with lawyers is that you don't live in the real world. You have no moral compass. Deep down, it's only ever about the money.'

'And now you talk about lawyers in the third person. Have you given it up already?' When Sam didn't reply, Harry added, 'That money affects me and my family. It gives them a good life, a better one than I had.'

Sam laughed, the noise loud in the office. 'Don't give me that impoverished speech again. I've heard it too often. And don't pretend that you did it all for Helena.'

Harry swallowed. 'And I would do it again.'

'Where did this "good father" act come from?' asked

Sam, his voice rich with sarcasm. 'Helena talks like you were never there. Remember, she called *me* yesterday, when she got into trouble, not you.'

Harry threw his pen down and stood up sharply. 'I worked hard to build this firm. All hours. All days. I gave Helena a good life.'

'But where were you?' Sam looked around. 'Here? Helena needed a father, not a lawyer.'

Harry seethed as he looked across at Sam, their eyes locked.

Then Sam smiled and pulled a disk out of his pocket. 'Maybe this will answer a few questions. See what Helena thinks of your friends then.'

Harry looked at the disk, and then at Sam. He went pale.

'What is it?' he asked, but Sam could tell that he had worked it out already.

'You've got good cameras, Harry.'

Harry's eyes widened and his cheeks turned crimson, but before he could respond, the air was broken by the ring of Sam's phone.

Sam stepped back and looked at the screen on his phone. He held it up for Harry to see. 'Your daughter,' and then he turned around to answer.

When he heard her voice, he was worried. She was crying, a soft mew.

'I've been attacked,' she said quietly.

'Where are you?'

'On the canal path,' she said, the words coming in gulps, 'between the school and home. I was walking back when I was jumped.'

Sam's nails dug deep into the back of the chair.

'What about Henry? Is he okay?'

Then he heard Helena begin to wail.

'I can't see him,' she screamed. 'He's gone.'

Sam dropped the phone, his hand trembling. He could hear Harry asking what was wrong, but it was background noise, the sound of the blood rushing through his brain the only thing he could hear. He had to swallow, just to stop himself from being sick.

He turned round to Harry. 'Something's happened.'

I turned off Johnny Cash. The first *American Recordings* album had rumbled around the room, his voice resigned to his short future, the guitar lean and raw, but it distracted me. My father had brought me up on Johnny Cash, but for once, I wasn't in the mood. I offered my father a silent apology, a quick look to the heavens, and then looked down at Eric's paintings.

They were spread across the table, a mosaic of his final years, the images that haunted him as he woke. There was no logic here. I didn't think Eric could dream the future any more than I could. But I knew that I was looking at the pictures for more than just interest now. I was looking for clues, some hint that he might have dreamt his own future, his own end.

It was the most recent paintings that troubled me. There was darkness in them. The colours were flatter, almost dirty, and they all showed the dark building.

I thought back to Jimmy King's house, and then looked again at the paintings. In silhouette, it wouldn't look much different. It was large, imposing, with two gables at the front, H-shaped. Is that what Eric had seen?

And then I remembered the outbuildings there, at the end of the long, neat lawn. A child could be hidden in one of those.

I smiled to myself. I sounded like I was starting to believe it. I knew why I was looking, why I was giving Eric the benefit of the doubt. It was because I had that same feeling that I'd had the year before, when my own father was killed, that there was something to look into. These paintings were by someone I knew, just briefly, and they had somehow led to his death. I knew there was a great story in them, but it had become more than that to me. I had seen the look in Mary Randle's eyes, that loss, that disbelief. I had the chance to somehow make it right.

I glanced towards a photograph on the wall. It was my father, playing football. He'd had a brief career as a professional in the lower leagues, before he gave it up and joined the police. I'd had it on my wall in London. It had made its way north, and I found myself nodding at it, making promises.

Luke King. He was the key. He was at the centre of all of it, I sensed it, felt it, knew it with every gut instinct I had. He was linked to Jess's death by his arrest. He was linked to Eric by the painting. He was linked to Terry McKay by Terry's own words. And he was linked to the abductions by Eric's death. But I didn't know enough about him. I decided to go to Luke's house, just to see what else I could find. I had the paintings now. I might see things I hadn't seen before.

* * *

375

'So how do we play Billy Hunt this time?' asked Pete. 'We've tried softly softly.' When Laura shot him a glance, he held his hands up. 'That's not a dig.'

Laura looked at the house and thought about that. 'We'll just play it as it comes. He'll be suspicious, but if he's talking, keep it soft.'

'You're the boss.'

Laura looked at him. 'Since when?'

'Since you keep on getting things right.'

They walked to the door together, but when they arrived, Pete hung back. The net curtain twitched even before she got her finger to the doorbell. When the door opened, it was Billy, and he looked flustered.

'Who called you? I didn't.' He stepped to one side. 'Come in, come in.'

Laura and Pete exchanged confused glances but went in anyway. As they passed the front room, they saw Billy's mother on the sofa, asleep. When they got to the back room, they saw a young woman in there, pretty, dressed in khaki trousers and white T-shirt, her short dark hair filled with red flashes. Protest chic.

But it wasn't her clothes or hair that drew Laura's attention. It was the cut above her left eye, and the purple swelling over her right eye. There was a cut to her top lip, fat and red, and swelling to the side of her cheek, just above deep scratch marks on her neck.

The woman looked at Billy, and then at Laura.

'You said you wouldn't call them,' she wailed, and she pulled her knees up to her chest. Her hands went over her face, and Laura could hear the sniffles.

'No one called us,' said Laura. 'We came to speak to

Billy.' She paused, and then asked, 'Do you want to tell us what happened?'

The girl said nothing.

'Charlie, tell them,' pleaded Billy, his eyes wide.

She looked up, wiped her hand across her cheek and winced as she made contact with the swelling.

Billy spoke for her. 'It was Dan Kinsella. He did this.'

'Dan Kinsella?' queried Laura.

'He goes to our group,' said Billy.

'The dream group?'

Billy nodded.

'So what happened?' Laura asked Charlie. 'Were you a couple?'

Charlie looked down and shook her head slowly. 'No,' she said, but she said it in a way that told Laura that maybe she had hoped differently.

'He came round yesterday morning, early,' Charlie continued. 'He seemed different, all excitable.'

'What do you mean?'

She looked up. 'Just that. He was pacing up and down and talking really fast. I mean, he's always bubbly, the life and soul, but this was different. He seemed, well, a bit desperate.'

'So what did you do yesterday?'

Charlie shrugged. 'Just chilled out. But he didn't want to go out, so we just stayed at my house.'

Laura and Pete exchanged brief looks. They'd both picked up on the timeframe, that he had gone to see Charlie at around the time that Eric was discovered, along with Kyle.

'Did he say why he didn't want to go out?' asked

Laura, now sitting next to Charlie, her voice gentle, trying to coax out the facts.

Charlie shook her head again. 'He's the sort of man you go along with. If he doesn't want to go out, he just sort of makes it seem okay.'

'He's a control freak,' interrupted Billy, his tone hostile.

Charlie shot him a look, part anger, part acceptance.

'What do you mean?' asked Laura.

'Just that,' he said, but more quietly now. 'He's only been coming to the group for a few weeks, and he acts like he runs it, knows everything there is to know about precognition, as if he has read it all in a book.'

'So what did you do all day?' Laura asked Charlie. She was worried that Billy might stop her from talking.

'Nothing much,' replied Charlie quietly. 'Just talked. About him. About me.'

'What about him? Where is he from?'

She looked embarrassed. 'I don't really know. He seems to know Blackley, but he doesn't like to talk about himself.' Then she looked up. 'His parents are dead, he told me that much, killed in a car crash. That's when he started having precog dreams, like the emotions were a trigger.'

Laura looked at Pete and nodded that he ought to go outside. He realised what that meant, that he should call it in, see what the computer had on Dan Kinsella.

Once Laura was on her own with Charlie and Billy, she asked, 'How did it get rough?'

Charlie's chin began to tremble, so Laura asked Billy if he would leave the room. She thought he was going to refuse, but when Laura smiled at him, he reluctantly agreed and went to make a drink. Once she was alone, Laura asked, 'Did you become involved last night?'

Charlie didn't respond at first, but then, as the tears started, she nodded. 'I went out to buy some wine, and I thought, well, you know, I thought something might happen.' She wiped her eyes and shook her head. 'It sounds stupid, but I thought we would, you know, kiss or something, maybe even end up in bed.'

'But that isn't what happened?'

Charlie shook her head, and then she started to sob. She covered her face as she spoke, her voice broken and high.

'He went through the bottle too quickly, so I opened another, and then he started coming on to me, but it wasn't like how I'd imagined it. He gripped my neck, became all aggressive, like he was angry with me, but I hadn't done anything wrong.'

Laura reached out and held Charlie's hands, giving them a reassuring squeeze. 'Go on,' she said quietly.

'He kept on squeezing my neck,' Charlie continued, 'really hard, and I knew I didn't want that. I had been having a dream like that, and I'd told Dan all about it, that I wake up gasping, my throat all closed up. It was like he was trying to make my dream come true. When I told him no, he said he wanted to put his hands around my throat, wanted me to feel like death was close, and that he could bring my life back.' She sniffled and wiped her eyes. 'He was so different when he was drunk.'

'What did you do?'

'I thought he was joking at first, so I laughed. But that made him angry, so he pinned me down.' Her hands went to her throat and tears started to meander down her cheeks. 'I could feel his hands on my neck.' She gulped at the memory, and then seemed to steel herself. 'I fought back. I screamed, kicked, thrashed around. I was scared. Then I bit him, really hard on his hand. He shouted out, and then he began to swear at me, loudly. Then he started to hit me.' She took a deep breath as she recalled it. 'He only stopped when the old man in the house next door banged on the wall.'

'So he left?'

Charlie nodded. 'He ran out. I haven't seen him since.'

'You've no idea at all where he lives?'

She shook her head slowly. 'We see each other at the meetings, and sometimes in town. It sounds stupid now, but he just never mentioned it.'

Laura looked back towards the kitchen. 'Why did you come here, to Billy?'

Charlie wiped her nose and sniffed heavily. 'I know he's done some strange things, that he got into trouble over that girl, but anyone who looks after his mum like Billy does can't be all bad. He never liked Dan, I knew that. I thought he was jealous, because maybe he liked me or something. I knew he liked Jess, and I thought Dan did too. It turned out that Billy was right.' She smiled. 'I think he gets lonely. He'll make someone happy one day.'

'I think his mother comes first,' said Laura.

Charlie nodded, gave a little laugh. 'For now.'

Just then, Pete came back into the room, shaking his head. 'Intel hasn't thrown anything up. There aren't any Dan Kinsellas in Blackley, as far as we know.'

Laura looked back at Charlie, who looked shocked. 'Can you describe him?'

She nodded, her eyes wide. 'I can do better than that. I've got a picture of him.' As she rummaged in her bag, she said, 'I don't think he knows I took it. It was at one of the meetings, just a couple of weeks ago.'

Laura smiled. Progress. But as she looked at the photograph, something troubled her. She had seen him somewhere before.

Just as they were getting ready to leave, Charlie smiled weakly, her eyes bleary from tears, and said, 'My mum always told me I picked men badly.'

Laura put her arm round her and guided her towards the door. 'Just be patient,' she said softly. 'Your luck will change.'

Chapter Fifty

Sam's tyres spewed out some gravel as he came to a stop, and then he ran to his house. There was a policeman by the door, taking a cigarette break. He almost stopped Sam from going in. The glare from Sam made him give way.

The police activity was less than Sam expected. There was a female officer in uniform in the kitchen, making drinks. Helena was lying down on the sofa, a cold cloth over her head. There were two uniformed officers with her. Sam looked back into the kitchen. He saw that some of the empty vodka bottles were lined up on the worktop, taken out of the recycling bin. When he looked into the policewoman's eyes, he saw pity.

He turned around and walked into the living room. He went straight over to Helena and knelt beside her. He gripped her hand. Helena's mother was there too, sitting in a chair by the window, sobbing quietly into a lace handkerchief.

'What's going on?' he demanded.

The two policemen glanced at each other, and then one said, 'Can we speak to you in private, Mr Nixon?'

'Why not here?'

They shrugged and then gestured towards a woman in black jeans with purple tints in her hair, standing in the corner of the room. 'This is Madeleine Chilton from Blackley Social Services. She might be able to help.'

Sam felt his head go light. Social Services. His family?

He stood up and nodded. He noticed how Helena had just rolled over.

Sam went into the dining room, Madeleine just behind him. When they were out of Helena's hearing, Madeleine said, 'We think Henry might have just run away, frightened.'

Sam was confused. 'Why? Helena called me. She told me that she had been attacked.'

The two policemen had come into the room. They glanced quickly at Madeleine and then looked down.

'The school has been concerned about your eldest son for a while now,' said Madeleine quietly. 'He has been arriving at school unkempt, sometimes without his coat in winter, and often complains of being hungry. They tried to speak to your wife about it, but she seemed drunk.'

Sam stepped away, angry now. 'What has this got to do with Helena being attacked, and Henry going missing?' He went towards her, his eyes wild. 'What is being done to find my son?' he shouted, every word spelled out slowly.

Madeleine swallowed, cleaned her front teeth with her tongue. 'When the police arrived,' she said, 'your wife seemed confused, disorientated. There were no injuries.'

'What, you think she made all this up?'

Madeleine's cheeks started to flush. 'We think she may have collapsed, and then Henry ran away, frightened. This is being treated as a lost child, not an abduction.'

The two officers stepped in. 'We know about your wife's drink-driving yesterday, Mr Nixon,' said one, 'and all the evidence says that she has a serious drink problem. We think that might be connected to whatever went on this morning.'

Sam stepped forward, breathing hard, his voice deep and low. 'Is this because you fucking clowns have told the world that the kiddy snatcher is dead, and you want to keep this quiet?'

The two officers didn't answer.

Sam put his hands on hips and laughed out loud, bitter and angry. 'I do not fucking believe it. You can think what you like about Helena, but she has always been honest.'

'Did you know she was drinking so heavily?' asked Madeleine.

That stopped him dead. He did know she was drinking heavily, but Sam had also known enough alcoholics to realise that their lives are all about lying, an endless self-delusion that they are in control. He took a deep breath, and then said, 'My son is being left out there with some madman because you fucking idiots are trying to save face.'

'Calm down, Mr Nixon, please.' Madeleine's voice became firmer.

Sam stepped away and went back into the living room. He stood over Helena. 'Do you know what they are saying?' he shouted.

Helena stayed turned away from him.

'They are saying it is all your fault.'

Sam turned to Helena's mother. 'Do you believe your daughter?'

'Please stay calm,' Mrs Parsons replied, her voice soft and polished. 'For Helena's sake. There are people out there looking for Henry.'

Sam turned around, saw all the faces looking at him. 'So this is it?' he said, as he felt his own tears well up.

The police officers looked at the floor.

Sam glanced around the room, his eyes darting from person to person, trying to see some hope, just a glimmer.

Then he noticed something. Not everyone was there.

'Where's Harry?'

Helena's mother shook her head slowly. 'He had to go somewhere,' she said.

And then it all came crashing in on Sam.

Harry wasn't there. His grandson had gone missing, and he had somewhere else to be. Sam knew straight-away where he had gone: to Luke King's house.

The morning briefing was coming to an end as Laura and Pete rushed in. Egan squeezed past them to make his way to his office, and Laura thought he looked red and flustered. She guessed that it hadn't been the best of mornings for him, finding out that Eric's suicide was in fact a murder.

Pete sensed the discomfort in the air, Laura could tell that from the gleam in his eyes. There were a few comments of 'Good breakfast?' and 'Have you two shacked up?' as they made their way through the crowd to their desks, still cluttered with unchecked witness reports.

Laura looked back towards where Egan had gone. 'I'm going to see him,' she said to Pete eventually.

When Pete started to follow her, Laura shook her head. 'On my own. I didn't join the police to score points. I did it to catch crooks.'

She made her way over and to Egan's door and knocked lightly. She heard a mumbled 'yes' from inside, and when she went in, Egan was looking through some paperwork. 'Hello, sir, I just wanted to have a word.'

He sat back and looked up at her. Laura almost felt sorry for him. He had jumped to a conclusion and had got it wrong, but she knew that everyone made a mistake sometimes. He nodded to a chair in front of his desk.

'What can I do for you?' he asked.

She sat down. 'I want your permission to investigate an unusual angle.'

He nodded. 'I'm listening.'

'In Jess Goldie's house,' she said, 'we found some diaries. Jess thought she had premonitions, and she kept a diary of them.'

The corners of Egan's mouth flickered.

'She wasn't the only one,' Laura continued. 'She used to go to a club where people shared their premonitions. Eric Randle went there too.'

Egan started to smirk, looking like he was grateful for the light relief. 'Can't see you and Dawson as Mulder and Scully.'

Laura took a deep breath, controlled her frustration,

and then said, 'I think her murder might be connected to someone at the club. There's someone called Dan Kinsella who goes there, or at least that's the name he uses. We can't find any trace of him. He knows both Jess and Eric, and yesterday, not long after Eric died, he turned up at a woman's house in a strange mood. He ended up assaulting her, a woman called Charlie. She thought he was going to kill her.'

Egan was too busy smirking to speak, so Laura continued, 'It was something Charlie said that got me thinking. Or, rather, that he said.' Laura had the feeling that Egan wasn't paying attention. She ploughed on. 'Charlie has been having dreams of being strangled, gasping when she wakes up. This guy said he wanted to strangle her. He said he wanted to make her dream come true.'

'You're running out of time,' Egan said, the smirk disappearing, his mood growing impatient.

'This isn't supernatural shit, sir. This is just some guy getting his kicks in a sick way. Jess Goldie had written a dream down, and it described just how she was found. This guy from the club, well, he turns up at this Charlie's house at around the time that Eric Randle was being strung up. She said he was jumpy and excitable, different to normal.' Laura exhaled loudly. 'I know it's far-fetched, but maybe he's killing people from the group in the way they have described.'

'Why would he?'

'Because he can? Because it's more fun that way? He gets the people from the group to set up their own death by talking about it.'

Egan raised his eyebrows. 'Is that it?'

Laura sighed. 'I just thought it was worth looking at.' She sounded weary.

Egan pulled at his lip, and Laura watched as his cheeks turned crimson. 'We'll make ourselves a laughing stock,' he said quietly. He pointed at his shoulders. 'I'm not wearing a uniform, but there are invisible pips on here. With that comes responsibility. I'm not going to show that by turning the force into the Ghostbusters.'

'I'm not saying make it a major line of inquiry, sir. We don't even have to tell anyone in there. I'll make some discreet inquiries. If there's nothing in it, we know we checked it out.'

He looked towards his door, and Laura could tell that he was thinking of the reactions of the others out there. 'I was told you had promise when you joined us. Maybe we need to get you away from Dawson.' He nodded, enjoying the power for a moment. 'For now, I'll allow it, but no more than you and Pete, and report back only to me.'

Laura smiled. 'Thank you, sir, but, for now, can we keep Pete Dawson out of it?'

Egan looked at her, up and down, and then he smirked. 'Yes, okay,' and then he looked down at the folder he had been reading.

Laura understood the signal. He had finished with her.

'Thank you, sir,' she said, and when he didn't look up, she left the room.

By the time she got back to her desk, Pete was talking to another officer, his face full of surprise.

388

'Something's going on,' she said. 'Is there some news?'

Pete turned around. 'Just a bit of a twist,' he said. 'Sam Nixon's kid has disappeared.'

'The lawyer?' When Pete nodded, she asked, 'What's the story there?'

'It depends on who you ask. The kid's mother says that she was grabbed from behind, and when she came to, the kid had gone. The cops at the scene aren't so sure. She was hauled in for drink driving yesterday, and there are enough vodka bottles in their house to keep the Russian navy happy.'

'They think that she was drunk and lost him?'

'They don't know, but it's the best guess.'

'It's another link, though.'

'To what?'

Laura shook her head. 'To *whom*. Another link to Eric Randle, except this one goes back towards Luke King.'

'What are you thinking?'

She shook her head again. 'I don't know, except that we seem to be going round in a circle, ending up back at the start all the time.'

'Perhaps that's where we ought to be then. What did Egan say?'

'He told me to leave the dreams alone,' she said, and then turned to walk away. She felt bad about lying to Pete – she liked him – but his desire to get a small win over Egan had become too wearing.

'Where are you going?'

'Just the little girls' room, if that's okay?'

Pete looked away, his face suddenly red.

As Laura walked towards the toilets, she pulled out

her phone. Once inside, she checked the cubicles. She was on her own. She pressed the speed dial and waited for an answer.

I sat in my car and looked through my notes.

I was near to Jimmy King's house, parked in the same place as before, out of the way, the country lanes still dappled by late summer sunshine shining through the trees. It didn't seem like the right scenery for investigating murders.

But I suspected that there was a killer in that house.

I had some of Eric's recent paintings with me. The sky was almost black in them, with just the bright moon to make the silhouette, the building dark and impressive.

I cast my mind back to my last trip to the King house. I remembered the view of the front of the house, and I realised that it was the same in the picture. The gables on either side of a large church door. Had Eric painted Jimmy King's house?

But why? Was it just a coincidence?

Then I thought of the abducted children. They had to be kept somewhere, and if Eric was murdered it was for a reason. The murder was connected to the abducted children, and so were the paintings.

I stepped out of the car and rolled up the picture into my pocket. I checked I had my camera with me. If I could get a picture of the King house that was similar to the painting, then my story had some shape.

My phone rang.

We didn't speak for long. I told Laura where I was,

and what I was going to do. She told me to wait. We could spend lunch together. She didn't seem to mind that it would be up a tree, looking into Jimmy King's garden.

Chapter Fifty-one

Sam stopped his car at the entrance to Jimmy King's house. The driveway looked busy, filled with Jimmy's cars, his Bentley and a Porsche. Then he saw Harry Parsons' car, a black BMW M5.

Sam closed his eyes and gripped the wheel hard. He had driven to Jimmy King's house expecting Harry to be there, but praying that he was wrong, that Harry would be on his way to be with his daughter.

Sam felt a sob bubble in his throat as the words of Luke King came back to him, that he enjoyed killing, and that he would do it again. He remembered the gloating look in his eye, the pleasure he got from passing on the news. A cold-blooded killer lived in that house, and Sam's son was missing.

He jabbed at the button on the intercom, and when the voice came over the speaker, Sam told him that he had better open the gates or he was going to drive through them.

There was a pause, and then Sam heard the lock click, and the gates began to slowly open.

*   *   *

I had returned to the same vantage point as before, in a tree overlooking Jimmy King's house. As I tried to keep my balance, I scanned the grounds with my zoom lens, looking for people who might be looking out for someone like me.

I was drawn to the small collection of outbuildings at the bottom of the long garden. There was an old tumble-down shed, a do-it-yourself bargain shack, and next to that there was a concrete garage, squat and square, with large green double doors, perhaps used to house the mower.

As I looked, I saw someone walk along the lawn. It was the same man I had seen on my previous visit. As I watched him, I saw him go to the garage. He looked around as he got there, and then opened the door, just a chink, before he slipped inside.

I took some photographs and started to climb down. I had some shots, but I knew I needed more. I felt a surge of excitement, I knew that Jimmy's house matched the one in Eric's painting. I had to get closer.

I would wait for Laura out of sight, show her the photographs on the camera screen. But then something caught my eye. Movement on the drive, fast and angry.

I raised the camera to my eye once more. It was Sam Nixon. That made me stop. Was Luke King in trouble again?

I made myself comfortable in the tree. Perhaps the day was going to be longer than I'd thought.

As Sam walked quickly to the front door, Jimmy King came out and tried to stop him.

'Stop there, Mr Nixon,' he said, his voice cold and flat, his arm outstretched.

Sam ignored him and just kept on going. Jimmy King was pushed almost to the floor as Sam got into the house.

'I'm looking for my son,' Sam snarled back.

Jimmy King went pale, but ran in front of Sam. He jabbed his fingers into Sam's chest. 'Just you wait there,' he said. His voice had turned mean, less robotic.

Sam got up close to him, until he knew Jimmy could feel his angry breath on his face. 'Why is Harry here?' he asked menacingly.

Jimmy didn't answer. He stared at Sam, and Sam could see the doubts flicker in his eyes. And, just for a second, he saw fear.

But then Sam heard a familiar voice ask, 'How are things at home, Sam?'

It was Harry, standing in the room at the end of the hall, a bright conservatory that looked out over the garden. His hands were clasped in front of him, and he looked poised, controlled. But Sam heard the tremor in his voice.

Sam rushed towards him.

'Why are you here?' Sam was angry, but as he got closer he saw the worry in Harry's eyes, his eyes red, his skin pale and drawn. There were beads of sweat on his forehead.

Harry took a deep breath. 'Jimmy and I go back a long way,' he said quietly. 'I thought he could help.'

Sam didn't say anything. He just got closer.

Harry looked down, his lips twitching as he thought of something to say.

Then Sam became aware of movement from the stairs. As he looked, he saw it was Luke.

'Are you here because of me?' said Luke, a cool smirk on his face.

Sam's mind went blank for a moment, the shock of seeing Luke making his mouth go dry, his palms slick, but then, as Luke came down the stairs, Sam went towards him.

'Where is he?' Sam roared.

Luke smiled. 'Who do you mean?'

Sam felt his chest go tight with anger, and he gripped Luke's shirt, propelled him backwards, banged him hard into the wall. Luke blinked in pain, but the smile didn't fade.

'My son,' hissed Sam as he peppered Luke's face with spittle. He pushed his hands towards Luke's neck. 'What have you done with him?'

Sam felt a hand grab his arm and pull him back. It was strong, insistent. When he looked around, it was Jimmy.

'Be careful who you accuse,' he growled, his voice full of threat. 'Luke has been at home all morning.'

Sam laughed loudly, manically. 'Another cast-iron alibi,' he screeched. 'Just like before, when you bastards fitted up Terry McKay.'

Harry gave out a small cough as if to steady himself, and then he said, 'Terry McKay is a drunk and a liar. His word means nothing.'

'No, what you mean is that his *life* meant nothing. He was just some drunk that you could fit up just to keep this murdering bastard out of jail.'

'Who said I was a murderer?' asked Luke quietly, calmly.

Sam pushed him back against the wall, trying to hurt him. Luke didn't flinch.

'You did,' hissed Sam, and banged Luke's head into the wall again. 'You told me how you killed that girl, and how much you enjoyed it.'

Luke raised his eyebrows. 'That was confidential, right?'

Sam shook his head slowly. 'I don't care what the rules say. I want my son back, and I know you have something to do with it.' He squeezed Luke's neck tighter. 'What's wrong, the noose getting tighter?'

'You're not helping, Sam,' said Harry. His voice was getting higher, the panic evident.

'And neither are you,' said Sam, and then he released Luke, who coughed and bent over as he tried to regain his breath.

Sam went towards Harry, his eyes blazing with anger.

'You tried to fit up Terry McKay. How many other times have you helped him out?' He pointed back to Luke as he said it, then turned towards Jimmy. 'And how will this play in the golf-club bar? You'll be tainted goods. You'll become easy meat for the tenants who want to sue, happy to go to the press. You'll have to run this place from what you squeeze from those sods who can't afford to move.'

Sam turned away, but then he felt a blow from behind, hard, straight into his kidneys. He cried out and fell to his knees, the breath knocked from him. When he looked up, he saw Jimmy glaring down at him, his fist clenched, his teeth bared.

'Never quite stopped being the bully landlord, did you, Jimmy?' gasped Sam, his hand clutching his back. 'Are you going to burn my hand off as well, you sick bastard? What about pissing on me? Are you going to stand over me and piss on me like you did Terry McKay?'

Jimmy halted at that, surprised.

Sam grinned. 'I've watched the video. Has Harry told you that I've got it all saved? Records *everything*.' Sam pointed at Luke. 'Your son told me that he had killed Jess Goldie. Worse than that, he said he enjoyed it. Maybe he even killed Eric Randle.'

Sam took a few deep breaths before continuing, looking at Harry. 'And now you want to protect him? He is a killer, but now it's more lies, one more false alibi.' Sam shook his head in frustration, in anger. 'It's your grandson, Harry. Doesn't that mean *anything*?'

Harry swallowed and then he sat down.

Everyone turned round when they heard a woman's voice.

'Luke was here all morning,' the voice said.

As Sam looked up the stairs, he saw a woman coming down. He knew it was Luke's mother; he had seen her at family functions. Luke had her cheekbones, delicate and defined, but her eyes were red, ringed by dark circles. 'Luke had nothing to do with your son going missing,' she said.

'Why should I believe you?' asked Sam bitterly. 'You would do anything to protect your son.'

She came towards Sam and took his hands in hers, looked into his eyes, and said calmly, 'But I wouldn't do anything to hurt yours. I hope you find your son, but if you are searching for him, stop wasting your time looking at Luke.'

'Shut up,' snarled Jimmy. 'You stupid bitch. Keep your fucking mouth shut.'

She shook her head slowly. 'I've had enough of lying. He's gone too far now. A child has died. I won't let that happen to another one.' She squeezed Sam's hand, and said, 'We are doing what we can. Trust me.' And then she walked away.

As she went, Sam looked around at Jimmy. He had a different expression in his eyes. The anger was gone, replaced by fear. And, from the way his gaze followed her, Sam guessed it came from something his wife had said.

Harry swallowed hard, and it was panic Sam saw in his eyes, while Luke looked calm, unconcerned.

'So where am I looking, Luke?' asked Sam quietly, the menace soft but obvious. 'What is this all about?' Sam looked at Jimmy, and then at Harry. 'Do I look again at Terry McKay? What about the girl who died, the one Terry lied about? Do I look there?'

'If you say anything,' said Harry, 'I'll lose everything. But don't think about me. Think about Helena. It'll destroy her.'

'Go see her now, Harry. She's already destroyed.' Sam looked at all of them. Harry looked away. Jimmy met his gaze, but he looked angry. Luke's smugness faltered, just for a moment, but when it came back it was mixed with arrogance.

'You'll stick by Jimmy, even when your own grandson is at stake?' asked Sam, as he looked at Harry.

Harry sat down on a kitchen stool and put his head in his hands. Sam had his answer.

'Shame on you, Harry,' Sam spat.

He turned around quickly and left the house.

The hall stayed silent for a few moments, but it was Luke who broke the deadlock. He looked at his father and asked, 'So now what are you going to do?'

Chapter Fifty-two

I was waiting by my car when Laura arrived. When she came towards me, I greeted her with a kiss. 'What's the game?'

She stepped back in mock surprise. 'Jack, how could you?'

I smiled at her. 'You make it hard for me to say no, but that's the answer until you say we're working together, sharing information.'

Laura came forward and kissed me this time. 'You're too suspicious.' When I didn't respond, she said, 'Okay, like you said, quid pro quo.' She put her hands on her hips and then said, 'Egan won't look at the dream club as a line of inquiry. Not officially, anyway.'

'So you're it?'

She shrugged her shoulders and grinned. 'Quite a little task force, don't you think?'

'It's powerful,' I agreed, 'but if you've come to me, it's because you need me, so I'm in charge.' I tilted my head in the direction of the King house. 'Follow me.'

We set off walking towards the King house, looking just like a young couple going for a stroll. I didn't ask much as we went, just about the post-mortem results and Egan's response. As we got near to the King house, I veered off the path and headed towards the tree that I'd climbed before.

'Where are you going, Jack Garrett?'

The full name. That usually meant trouble.

'I'm going to have a look around.'

'Why don't you try the front door?'

I shook my head and grinned. 'Sometimes you show a *distinct* lack of imagination.'

Laura looked like she was about to walk away.

'If I get in difficulty, you leave. No one knows you are here,' I told her.

'What are you going to do?' Laura asked.

'If I tell you, will you try to stop me?'

'Probably.'

'So you'll understand why I'm not telling you.'

I got to the tree, but kept on going. Laura stayed with me, but I could tell she was getting nervous.

Jimmy King's house was surrounded by a high brick wall, so that his property sat in the countryside as if it had been dropped there. I made my way quickly to the back, to the wall just behind the outbuildings I had seen earlier. Once there, we seemed to be hidden.

I turned to Laura.

'Eric Randle painted something not too long ago, a picture of a house with two gables at the front. This case keeps on coming back here, and when you look at Jimmy King's house, it has two gables at the front. Now, it isn't that accurate when compared to the painting, but it's worth a look, and I'm starting down here.'

'No, Jack, you can't go in there. King will have security, he'll have cameras. And from what I've heard, he's a violent man.'

'But what if I'm right? If I am, the last place the camera will point is down here.'

'Jimmy King isn't the murderer, or the person abducting children.'

I nodded. 'I know, but he doesn't seem keen on us finding the real culprit.'

'It's "me", not "us". I catch them, you report them.'

'Sometimes we have to swap positions. I'll tell you what I find afterwards.'

I went to put my hands on top of the wall, but it was too high for me. I looked around for a toehold, but then I felt Laura's hand on my arm.

'Stop, Jack, there's something you don't know.' When I looked at her, she continued, 'Sam Nixon's son went missing this morning. It looks like an abduction.'

I opened my mouth in surprise. I looked at the wall, and then remembered what I had seen not long before: Sam Nixon at the house.

'You might foul up a crime scene if you go in there, if you think there is any connection with the abductions.'

'Or catch a killer,' I said, and then jammed my foot into a toehold in the bricks. I leaned against a nearby tree and then threw myself at the wall. I pulled myself up until my stomach was on top and I could see into the garden. As I balanced there, I looked down at Laura and asked, 'What would you arrest me for if I'm caught?'

'Being found on enclosed premises, as soon as you

402

drop down on the other side,' she said. 'Just a fine in all likelihood. We can sell some of your vinyls to pay it.'

'And if I get inside this building?'

Laura raised her eyebrows. 'Then you'll be a burglar, and for that I might just have the house to myself for a few months.'

I winked. 'You'd better not miss the arrest then,' I said, and then I dropped over the wall.

I knelt down for a few minutes after I landed. I was in long grass, straggly and unkempt, the patch behind the fence that was never cut. I listened out for a noise, anything to tell me I'd been heard. It seemed silent.

I wondered whether I had done the right thing. I would find it hard to justify being there. Freedom of the press wouldn't cover me, and it would make things difficult for Laura.

But when I thought about Sam Nixon's missing boy, and the lost look in Mary Randle's eyes, I realised that I had to go on.

I looked around for a window, some other way in, but all I could see was pebbledash, covered in lichen blown down from the trees. I went to the back of the building and edged along. My footsteps made soft swishing noises in the grass, but to me it sounded loud, revealing, all the time waiting for someone to appear around the corner, some hired thug or the police.

I got to the first corner without any problems. I put my head slowly around the side, ready to duck back if there was someone there. As the garden came into view, I realised that I could see all the way down to the house.

I felt a jolt, a nervous jump. That meant anyone in the house could see all the way down to *me*.

The building I was leaning against was next to an old wooden shed, and there was a small gap between, maybe only a foot wide. I could squeeze in, just, and it gave me the best chance. It created a shadow, and if I saw movement, I could just stay still. But it also gave me my worst chance, because if someone blocked off the ends, I was trapped.

I took a deep breath and thought about what to do. It didn't take me long to decide. To go round would leave me too exposed.

I squeezed in between the shed and the garage and began to shuffle along. I stumbled on some old planks left in the long grasses. They clattered together, the noise echoing along the gap. I stopped to see if anyone came to inspect. No one did.

I carried on, my hands scraping the side of the building, the peddledash unblunted by the wind and rain, protected by the old shed. It felt sharp and raw.

I found myself at the end of a long lawn, green stripes that marked out Jimmy King's country dream, surrounded by flowerbeds, lovingly tended. That was all just framing for the house at the end, the bricks bright and red, the ivy taking over the front, not the back. The walls seemed higher now that I was in the garden, and I knew that I would have little chance to escape if anyone came towards me. I thought briefly of Terry McKay, but I shook the image away.

I looked round the corner, along the front of the outbuilding. The door was old wood, with green flaky paint and dusty windows. I could see that there was a padlock on it, but it looked rusty and weak. I strained to hear sounds from inside. I thought I could hear faint noises, the odd rustle. I pulled my ear away and wondered if I'd just imagined it. Was Sam Nixon's son in there?

I looked again at the padlock. It looked breakable.

I scoured the ground for something to use as leverage. There was nothing, but then I remembered that I was only trying to write a story. *Don't break in, don't get caught, don't go to prison.* I thought about Laura on the other side of the wall. What was she doing right now?

My nerves made my breath come quickly and sweat prickled my top lip. My heart took over from the sounds of the countryside.

I heard a snap, the sound of a footstep. I whirled around and saw nothing. Only the flutter of a bird's wings broke the scene.

It was too quiet. I didn't like it.

There was a window next to the door. I knelt down and crawled underneath it, tried to stay silent, listened out for any whimper, any shout, any threat. I heard nothing. I was in full view of the house now. I couldn't see any movement in there, but I knew that could change in an instant.

I felt in my pocket for my camera, just to reassure myself that I was equipped, and then realised that if I was going to go in, it had to be then.

I rattled the padlock, and was surprised to see the latch swing open. The padlock had been hanging loose.

All I could hear was the light breeze brushing the leaves of the trees.

I stood up, just so that I could get a grip on the door. I moved to one side, but realised that I was in front of the window. All I could see was myself, reflected back. I didn't know whether I could be seen by anyone inside. I nudged the clasp to one side and started to pull on the wooden door. It swung towards me slowly, the hinges making a steady whine. I was still hunched, but as the door opened enough for me to get in, I slipped inside.

I pulled the door closed behind me. As I gave my eyes a chance to adjust to the darkness, my nose was filled with gardening smells: creosote, fertiliser bags, mown grass-heads left to go dry on the floor.

As the interior started to come into view, like buildings appearing from the fog, I saw that it looked ordinary. Tools lined the walls – spades, forks, hoes, and shelves of lawn treatments and weed-killers. I reached for my camera, ready to take a picture once the darkness cleared, when I heard movement behind me.

I turned towards where I thought it had come from, my throat tight now, knowing that I was not alone. I was about to say something when I sensed a sudden movement behind me. A strong arm grabbed me from behind, strapped tight across my chest, and I could feel the heat of someone's breath on my ear. Then a hand went across my mouth, and I knew I couldn't shout out for Laura.

Chapter Fifty-three

Laura paced on the other side of the fence, angry, nervous, worried.

She checked her watch. He had been over the fence for more than five minutes. If there had been nothing there, he would have been back now. If he had been caught, she was sure he would have made a noise.

She looked back towards the wall and stamped her foot in frustration. They had both made a big investment in each other, and if he was in trouble, she was going to help him. But she could put her job in jeopardy if she was caught effecting an illegal search of some local big-shot's property. And anyway, she was wearing a new grey suit. It wasn't built for climbing over walls.

Laura paced in a tight circle, her hand pulling her hair to the top of her head. She looked skyward, as if the answer might be printed on a cloud. Then she let her hair tumble down and sighed. She had no choice, she knew that.

She hitched up her trousers and got in the same way as Jack, by digging her toe into the wall, using the tree to lever herself up, and then clambering over the wall.

When she landed, she looked down. She brushed off some brick dust, but no damage.

She edged along the side of the shed, assuming that Jack had gone the same way, keeping an eye out for movement from Jimmy King's house. It seemed quiet, no one keen to enjoy the late-afternoon sun.

As she got to the front of the shed, she listened out. She felt her stomach take a lurch when she thought she could hear murmurs, whispers from inside. Her mouth went dry. Someone had Jack.

Her mind filled with images of him, hurt, trapped, scared. She swallowed as she thought of him.

She looked along and saw that the door to the main outbuilding was open a crack. That was where the sounds were coming from.

She crept towards the door, keeping her head down, below the level of the window. She listened out again, and she could hear a voice. And it wasn't Jack's. She reached out for the door and gripped the frame, closing her eyes in silent prayer. She put her warrant card in her hand, the sight of a police crest might be enough to buy her some crucial seconds.

She flung open the door and leaped into the building, her warrant card held out in front of her. She was about to shout 'Police!' when she stopped, her mouth open in shock.

Danut, the gardener, was there. Laura remembered him from her visit with Pete. He was sitting down and facing Jack. Danut turned round quickly, and he looked just as shocked to see her.

Jack didn't. He grinned and held up his cup. 'What

took you so long?' he said, and then he turned to Danut. 'Have you got an extra cup?'

Laura relaxed and shook her head in disbelief. She hoped for Jack's sake that her suit was fully intact.

I tried to smile an apology at Laura. I looked towards Danut and said, 'This is Laura. She's my partner.'

Danut looked at Laura, and then back at me. Wariness crept into his eyes. 'You told me that you are reporter. But she is police,' he said. 'She came here before, when Luke was at police station.'

I looked at Laura's warrant card, still in her hand. There was no point in denying it.

'She is police,' I said, 'but she hasn't come to arrest you.'

Danut's eyes flickered between us both as he stayed silent. He didn't look convinced, and I saw that Laura had her hands on her hips.

'Tell Laura what you've told me,' I said to Danut.

He looked at me nervously, but I nodded and smiled, encouraging him to carry on.

Laura sat down on a metal garden chair.

'On that morning,' Danut began, his English broken, the Romanian accent making his speech come out like gun-bursts, 'when you came with your colleague, I had taken car to valet.'

Laura nodded. 'You told me then.'

Danut grimaced. 'Mr King not happy with that. He almost fire me, but Mrs King stopped him.'

'Why would he be angry?' asked Laura.

'Because if he fire me, he knows that I tell police everything.'

409

Laura glanced at me quickly, and I could see her interest quickening.

'What is everything?' she asked, her voice slower now, quieter.

Danut looked down. He appeared ashamed.

'When I take car for valet,' he said, 'I not know about dead girl, or else I would not do it. But I did it.'

'Was it Luke who asked you?'

'Yes. He was firm about it. He say must get car clean properly.'

'What could you see in the car?' I prompted. He had told me his story, but I wanted Laura to hear it from his mouth.

He looked at Laura, and then down at the floor. He chewed his lip, made dust circles with his feet. When he spoke, his words came out quietly.

'I see blood,' he said.

'Where?' asked Laura. Her anger had been replaced by keenness. She leaned forward, her eyes narrowed.

'On the steering wheel, and on the driver seat.'

Laura and I exchanged glances. I nodded at her.

'How do I know that you aren't covering for yourself?' she asked.

Danut held his hands out, his shoulders bunched up into a shrug, his face full of regret. 'You don't, but I am telling you truth.'

Laura didn't respond at first. I could sense that she was weighing up Danut's tale against her gut instinct. It was that instinct that separated good cops from bad ones.

'What time did Luke get in that night?' she asked.

Danut shook his head slowly and wagged his finger. 'Luke was in house all night.'

'But you said it was Luke who asked you to get the car valeted.'

Danut nodded. 'He did, but he was not driver. His brother was driver.'

Laura's eyes widened. 'Brother?'

Danut nodded again. 'Luke, he have an older brother. Mr and Mrs King don't let him come to house, but Luke, he worship him. So Thomas comes to house when Mr and Mrs King out. Thomas take car, and he bring it back.'

'What time?'

Danut exhaled, and then shrugged. 'Middle of night. He drove Audi back, I heard it, and then drove away in his own car.'

I looked at Laura. Her eyes were distant now, thinking hard, looking towards the roof. My own thoughts started to come in fast bursts, ricocheting around my head.

It was Laura who spoke first. 'Where is Thomas?'

Danut shrugged. 'He live in Blackley. Work too.'

'What as?'

'Thomas is doctor.'

'Doctor?' said Laura incredulously.

Danut nodded.

Laura and I looked at each other. Why was Thomas King barred from his own family home?

Laura was pulling on her lip, lost in thought.

'What are you thinking?' I asked.

She looked at me, and then at Danut. She turned away as she thought and looked at the floor. When she looked back at me, she asked, 'Do you know a Dan Kinsella?'

I shook my head slowly, Danut as well. But the name sounded familiar. My mind rushed back through the previous few days, as I tried to work out where I had heard it.

Then it came back to me. A smile. Blond hair. The dream meeting.

'He went to the same group as Eric,' I said excitedly. 'He was there the other night. Is he connected?'

'How did he seem?'

'He seemed okay. Pretty friendly, engaging.'

Laura went into her pocket and pulled out a photograph. She handed it to me.

I nodded as I saw it. 'Yeah, that's him.' I passed it back. 'Why?'

Laura didn't answer. Instead, she passed the photograph to Danut. As he looked at it, he looked at Laura, and then at me. Then he nodded, slowly.

'What kind of game is this?' He looked angry, defensive.

'Do you recognise him?' asked Laura.

He nodded curtly and handed the photograph back. 'You know I do.'

'Who is it?'

'You know who it is. That's Thomas King, Luke's brother.'

Laura looked at me and then looked grim-faced. Straightaway, we both knew what the other was thinking. We were going to see Thomas King.

Chapter Fifty-four

We walked quickly away from Jimmy King's house. Danut had kept a lookout, and we got out the same way we had got in, by scrambling over the wall. Laura was quiet.

'How did you know Dan Kinsella was really Luke King's brother?' I asked.

She swept her hair back over her ears and said, 'Part guesswork, part memory, but it sort of fitted. Was there a girl at the meeting who seemed to be with Thomas King?'

I thought back, remembered the girl with red flashes in her hair. 'Yeah, nice girl. Charlie I think her name was. I got the vibe that she and Thomas might have been getting it together.'

Laura smiled, but it seemed a sad one. 'It seemed like Charlie read the same signals as you.'

'You make it sound like there's a postscript.'

'He went to see her yesterday, maybe after he strung up Eric Randle. They spent the day together, but when she expected it to get all loved up, he turned nasty.' She flashed a look at me to let me know that this was all off the record. When I nodded my agreement, she carried on. 'He told her that he wanted to make her dream come true. The problem was that her dream had been one of waking up breathless, like she was being strangled. He started to grip her around her neck, but this was more than play-fighting. She had to fight him off. She's still got the marks to prove it.'

'So you deduced that Dan Kinsella was really Thomas King from that? I'm impressed.'

She smiled. 'I wish it was that simple. Jess, the girl found tied to her chair. Well, she kept a dream diary, or sometimes wrote her dreams down on pieces of paper, those that she thought were premonitions.'

'And there was one just like her death scene?'

'Not far from it.'

'Like Eric had painted it?'

Laura smiled. 'Looks like we had the psychics of Blackley lining up to predict it.'

'Wow, you did well to keep that away from the press.'

She smiled ruefully. 'Let's just say that the force isn't as receptive to the idea as I am.' She sighed heavily. 'So it looked like the killer was someone from the group, because whoever was killing the group members was doing it in ways they had already predicted.'

'That's sick.'

Laura shook her head. 'No, it's just a game for him, a tease. Thomas King isn't doing this to be sick. He's doing it because it's fun.'

'And to protect himself,' I added. 'Kyle's body confirmed the connection with the abductions. It looks like Thomas was attracted to the group because Eric Randle

414

got himself involved with the family of a missing boy after one of his dreams. It looks like it piqued Thomas's interest, and so he joined the group to find out more. He stayed in the group because it was a way of deflecting attention, making him look like a potential victim, not the perpetrator.' Then I thought of something. 'What about the way Eric died?' I asked.

She looked at me with interest. 'You tell me. Did you hear anything?'

I thought back to the meeting, and all the different accounts I had heard. I had made some notes, but they were general, more about the moods, the people. But then I remembered Billy Hunt.

'There was someone who talked about an old tramp hanging. Someone called Billy Hunt. Eric had even had a dream like that, where there was something around his throat and he couldn't move.'

Laura nodded. 'I've met Billy. But I think Thomas got lucky with that one. It seems that his attempt at sedating young Kyle went wrong, so when he dumped the body he was able to put the blame on Eric, or so he thought, and still fulfil Billy Hunt's dream.'

'But he went to Charlie's all wired because he'd just killed Eric?'

'And because Kyle had died,' Laura agreed. 'That was an accident. Remember the cards I told you about: healing hands. He told Charlie he wanted to kill her and bring her back to life. He thinks he is doing the same with families, bringing mothers and sons back together. Kyle wasn't meant to die.'

'So when you were speaking to Danut,' I asked, 'you

thought that it must be someone from the group, because they knew the dreams, and that Dan Kinsella looked the likeliest because of what he said to Charlie about making her dream come true?'

Laura nodded.

'And so when you heard that Thomas King had returned that Audi with blood on it, the one that had been near to Jess's house, you figured that if it must be Thomas King, and that it must also be Dan Kinsella, the obvious thing is that they are one and the same person?'

Laura nodded, but she smiled this time. 'But it wasn't just that,' she said.

I raised my eyebrows. 'Go on.'

'There's a huge family picture in the hallway of the house. I saw it when I was there a few days ago. When Charlie gave me a photo of Dan Kinsella, I knew he looked familiar, but I couldn't place him. As soon as Danut mentioned Thomas King, my mind flashed back to the family portrait, and I realised why I recognised Dan Kinsella. He was really Thomas King.'

I smiled, impressed. I thought then about Sam and his missing child. 'Why has Thomas taken Sam's son?'

Laura exhaled loudly at that question. 'I don't know if he has, but remember that Sam Nixon acted for Luke King. Maybe Sam got too interested in what Luke had to say.'

'Do you think Luke had anything to do with Jess's death?'

Laura shook her head. 'Not with the death. But I think he knows about it, and I think he is trying to protect his brother. They've got a sign above the door, engraved into stone. *Strength in Unity*. It looks like it's the King family against the world.'

'And Luke does it by making himself suspect number one?'

Laura gave a thin smile. 'We can moralise all we like, but sometimes we will do anything to protect our own.'

I looked away at that. My father had once told me how he had allowed someone to get away with murder because to speak out would have made it hard for him and his young family. Morality can be complex.

'But Thomas King is out of control now,' I said. 'A child died, which was not how it was supposed to be. So he killed Eric. Then he tried to kill Charlie.'

'That was sexual. He was excitable all day, but once things turned smoochy it tipped him over the edge.'

'It wasn't sexual before?'

'No, not at any point. None of the children who were abducted were molested, as far as we know. That was just delusional, some conceit of his, that he could change people's lives. Jess wasn't sexually assaulted. She just got in his way when she saw something in a dream. Maybe she told it to the group and Thomas thought it was too close to the truth. If he was discovered, it would put a stop to his good work, so it was a cold and rational decision to kill her in the way that he did. His desire to hurt Charlie wasn't rational. It was drink mixed with desire, and the real Thomas King bubbled to the surface.'

'And so, if he has taken Sam Nixon's boy?'

Laura's expression was grim. 'Henry is in real danger, because he's a hostage.'

'For what outcome?'.

'That's why he is in danger, because Thomas doesn't know yet. Thomas King is imploding, and Sam's son is the subject in his final message.'

'A blaze of glory?'

Laura nodded grimly. 'It's always the way. Think of Thomas Hamilton in Dunblane, Michael Ryan in Hungerford, the Columbine boys. When they know they have reached the point of no return, it only ever results in death, and that includes anyone who gets in the way.'

'So what next?'

'We are not going to move on anyone from the King family until we have something firm. We're still waiting for the forensic hits from the scene.'

'Why are they taking so long?'

'Money. They can pay more to bring the results through quicker, like a queue-jump, but the department has run itself skint on the child abductions through the summer.'

'And Sam's son is still missing?'

Laura nodded. 'They think he wandered off after Sam's wife passed out.'

'Sam doesn't, because he was here, and I know where I'm going.'

'Where?'

'I'm going to see a doctor.'

Chapter Fifty-five

Sam went straight to Alison's office. She wasn't in, but Sam didn't care either way. He was going to search her office.

Her desk was small and functional, just chipboard and vinyl, with a computer on top and three drawers. A filing cabinet filled one corner of the room.

He went to the top drawer first, flinging it open, some of the contents jumping out onto the floor. But it was all junk, just pens and paper clips, loose pieces of paper. The second drawer was just the same, except that there were some training notes and copies of the Law Society *Gazette*, just headlines of gloom about less money.

He kicked the drawer shut and yanked hard on the bottom drawer. Nothing. Just Alison's court kit. Hair bands, an umbrella, some perfume.

He stood up and looked around. Terry's file must be here somewhere. If he could find it, he might be able to force Harry into giving up Thomas King. If he won't do it for Henry, he might do it to save himself.

Then he saw a Post-it note stuck to the monitor. Just two numbers on it: 14. He knew what it meant: the end digits to her computer password, as it changed every two months. He knew her password as he had shown her round the system. Blondie. And there was 14 at the end.

He turned on her monitor and logged in. As the system booted into life, he went to the filing cabinet.

Alison's files were in alphabetical order, and as Sam went through them he threw them onto the floor, just so he didn't miss any. He went through each drawer, and still he couldn't find Terry McKay's file.

He went back to the computer monitor. He checked in her documents folder. As he sat down in her chair, his eyes scanned quickly through the files and folders. Again, nothing.

He clicked on Outlook. He went back a week and read Alison's emails. Some were work-related, but many were quick messages to meet for lunch or for a meal. He read those carefully. Were there code names here? What name would Harry use?

He sat back and rubbed his eyes. He couldn't see anything in the messages. He stood up quickly and went to leave the room. Maybe he would have a chance to look in Harry's office. Before he got to the door, he realised there was someone standing there. It was Alison.

'What the hell are you doing now?' she asked, aghast.

'Where is it?' he shouted.

Her cheeks reddened. 'Where is what?'

'Terry McKay's file. His murder file. You took it.'

'Why would I do that?'

'To jump the queue,' Sam scoffed. 'To keep in with Harry.'

'Oh, for Christ's sake!' she yelled. 'Listen to yourself.'

Sam stepped closer. 'Do you know where it is?'

Alison shook her head. 'No, I do not know where it is, and why should I help you?'

'Because my son is missing.'

She paused at that, and when she spoke, her voice was quiet. 'I do not know what you think I have been up to, but the threat in this place isn't from me.'

'What do you mean?' Sam stepped closer.

Alison swallowed and looked nervous.

'Alison? Tell me. I need to know. My son is in danger.'

She looked down at the files on the floor, at the intense look in Sam's eyes, and thought about walking away. But she spotted something else in his eyes: a plea for help.

'Jon Hampson,' she said quietly. 'I keep seeing him with Harry, and I saw him coming out of your office the other morning. He looked furtive.'

Sam was surprised. 'Jon? Why would he want it? He's just a clerk.'

'I don't know, but he's the one with Harry's ear, not me.'

Sam tried to think, to work out why Jon would be a threat.

'I heard him talking with Jimmy King when he was here the other day,' Alison said, nervously. 'They mentioned Terry's case.'

It all came in at Sam in a rush. He felt his hands tremble. Jon Hampson, former senior detective, now a senior clerk at Parsons & Co. He thought about the date of the murder, and how long Jon had been at the firm. He must have retired not long after Terry McKay was arrested for murder, the case left unsolved, no one else suspected. Jon Hampson ended up at Parsons & Co – nothing unusual in that – but it seemed from his lifestyle that he enjoyed a very good income, certainly a lot more than most solicitors' clerks.

Sam rushed into Jon Hampson's room. Jon was there, working through some files. Sam was angry, his eyes wild. 'You knew, didn't you?' he shouted accusingly.

'I knew what?' Jon stood up, walked towards him.

'You knew all about Terry McKay.' As Jon stayed silent, Sam shouted, 'You bastard. You fucking bastard. You knew all along. And you were watching me, reporting back to Harry.'

Jon didn't move, so Sam got nearer to him, his breath close enough for Jon to feel the heat. 'What did you say you wanted, a piece of the pie?'

Jon took a deep breath, and Sam noticed that his cheeks were red.

'I didn't really know anything,' he said quietly. Gone was the brashness from the bar a few days earlier. 'I had my suspicions. McKay had said something different on the way in to the station. He was drunk though, so we couldn't have used it. Egan was angry, thought Harry had got him to change his story. We just didn't know why.'

'Egan?'

Jon nodded. 'I wasn't the SIO. We were both on the team though.'

'So what did you do?'

Jon looked uneasy. 'Not much. There was no proof of anything, so I just let Harry think that I knew something. He offered me a job when I retired.'

422

'Made you too well-off to say anything?'

Jon smiled unpleasantly.

'You let him buy your silence,' accused Sam.

Jon nodded. 'And worth every penny. I gave most of my waking hours to the police. All I had to show for it was a semi-detached bungalow and a poxy pension, while all the time fat cats like Harry grew richer. Why didn't I deserve some?'

'You had something of value,' Sam said, his voice getting louder, bringing the secretaries out of their rooms. 'Integrity. A clean conscience.'

Jon sneered. 'And now I've got a holiday home and a nest egg. So go fuck off with your conscience,' and he stormed out of the room.

Sam was going to follow him, confront him further, but then he realised that it wouldn't change anything. But maybe Egan would help more.

Sam walked quickly into the cobbled yard of the police station and saw Egan waiting at the back wall, just where he'd said he would be. Sam was panting by the time he reached him.

'What's this cloak-and-dagger shit, Mr Nixon? We're sort of busy right now.'

Sam caught his breath and then said, 'Me too. I am trying to find my son.'

Egan didn't respond.

'Terry McKay was once arrested for murder,' said Sam. 'Who do you think did it?'

Sam could see that Egan didn't want to answer at first, that he didn't need reminding of which murder it was. After a few seconds of pursing his lips, he said, 'Terry McKay was the only suspect.'

'That's not the question I asked, Inspector.'

'I'm not in the witness box,' retorted Egan.

'You might be, if you don't help me.'

Egan stared at Sam for a while, and then softened, maybe remembering that Sam's son was missing.

'I didn't think McKay had done it,' said Egan. 'Terry McKay is a drunk and he's a thief, but he is not a murderer. You know what people like him are like. They steal, they get caught, they admit it, and they go to court. They are a nuisance, but just the everyday part of being a copper. I've never known him hurt anyone.'

'So why was he arrested?'

'We got some information,' said Egan, a smile flitting across his face. 'It was enough to lead us to him. He had the purse, and his story was a crock of shite.'

'Who tipped you off?'

Egan smiled. 'You know I won't tell you that.'

Sam guessed straightaway who it had been: someone connected with Jimmy King.

'But you didn't charge him.'

'That wasn't our decision. That was the CPS. You know how it works.'

'But everyone thinks he got away with it,' said Sam.

'He had an alibi.'

Sam looked surprised. 'How come?'

'He was wanted for shoplifting,' said Egan. 'It had been caught on CCTV, a booze theft, and had happened at the same time as the murder, but a mile away.' His eyes narrowed. 'Whoever called it in, hadn't counted on

424

that. Maybe they'd seen him sleeping off the stolen sherry later and assumed he had been like that all day.'

'Who was she, the dead girl?' asked Sam, his mind busy with what he had just been told.

At that, Egan smirked. 'Ask your client.'

Sam paused, confused. 'What do you mean?'

'She was Luke King's fiancée. Or, should I say, *ex*-fiancée. Debbie Harris. She'd dumped him a few weeks before.'

Sam looked up, took some deep breaths. There were too many things coming together.

'I didn't know she was Luke King's girlfriend,' said Sam quietly.

'Is there any reason why you should have done?'

Sam shook his head slowly, and then asked, 'Was he ever a suspect?'

Egan thought for a moment, and Sam could tell that he was thinking back. 'He had an alibi too.'

Sam raised his eyebrows.

'Your boss,' continued Egan. 'He was at dinner with his family, celebrating some land deal Jimmy had organised. Parsons was there.'

Sam turned away and started to pace as he thought about Harry's involvement, and what he had been told by Terry McKay. And what Luke King had told him. It was all moving fast now, too fast.

'I think my son's disappearance is connected with the King family,' said Sam eventually.

Egan nodded. 'I know you do. I can tell that.'

'Are you looking there?'

Egan hesitated. Sam could tell there was more he could

say, but he replied simply, 'I am not in charge of that investigation.'

Sam looked at the floor, saw that it rippled and moved in front of his eyes. He wasn't in control, he knew that. He turned to run out of the yard. He wasn't looking where he was going, and he ran straight into the path of a 1973 Triumph Stag in Calypso Red.

I had to slam the brakes on to avoid Sam Nixon. I stopped just in front of him, his hands resting on the bonnet, a wild look in his eyes.

I put my head out of the window. 'Sorry about that.'

Sam didn't respond, he just stared at me through the windscreen.

'It's okay, Sam. It's okay.' I knew that it wasn't.

Sam put his head down, his forearms now over the bonnet, so I got out. I glanced at Laura, who had been driving just behind me, and raised my eyebrows. She got out of her car and joined me.

'What's going on, Sam?' I asked.

His eyes looked haunted, his face drained of colour. He didn't answer.

'I think Thomas King has something to do with the disappearance of your son,' I said.

Sam's eyes started to focus on me, some colour returning to his face. 'Thomas?' he asked.

I nodded. 'Luke's older brother. He's a doctor, here in Blackley.' And then I filled him in on all we had found out over the previous few days, about the dream meetings, about Eric Randle's paintings, about Jess's dream diary. He knew some of it, but not the full picture.

'But Luke King told me he'd done it,' said Sam, lamely.

I glanced over at Laura, and she looked like she had guessed that response. No comment to questions only ever meant one of three things: guilt, or they'd done something even worse, or they were covering for someone else. I looked back at Sam. 'It looks like he was covering for his brother.'

And then Sam told me the full story of Terry McKay. 'I thought it was Luke the family were protecting,' he said. 'It must have been Thomas all along. Egan just told me that Harry Parsons alibied the whole family when Debbie Harris was murdered. That must have included Thomas.'

'And, if Terry was right,' I added, 'Luke must have given him the purse to set him up, but they didn't know about the shoplifting. The story about someone else giving Terry the purse was the back-up story, just in case the police believed him and wanted to use him as a witness. It was Harry who told him what to say.'

I looked round at Laura as she asked, 'But why kill Debbie Harris?'

It was Sam who answered. 'She'd broken off her engagement to Luke a few weeks before. Luke's a pathetic person. Maybe he was hurting, maybe he had said that he wished she was dead. Thomas made it all better.'

'Healing hands,' I added.

Laura nodded. When Sam looked confused, Laura said, 'He's been leaving calling cards with the children when they are returned. Healing hands.'

Sam looked angry. 'I want to find Thomas King. I want to be there when you find my son.'

'We have procedures, Sam, you know that,' said Laura.

'Fuck procedures.'

'Come with me,' I said. And as he climbed into my car, I said to Laura, 'I'll keep an eye on him.' As I pulled away, I saw that Laura was watching me, her hands on her hips. I knew that she wouldn't be far behind me.

Chapter Fifty-six

We were quiet all the way to Thomas King's surgery. It was on one of the roads out of Blackley, on the ground floor of a redbrick Victorian semi, the road choked by traffic all around it as rush hour started to take hold. A collection of brass nameplates on the wall gave it away, and the colourful Family Health posters in the window.

As we made our way to the door, I saw Sam straighten his tie.

'Are you okay?' I asked him. I cursed myself silently. Silly question.

He looked at me, his reactions slow, and then he shook his head. 'Not really,' he said.

I saw Thomas King's name on one of the brass nameplates before I opened the door into the reception area. It was quiet. The only person in there was an old woman perched on a chair in the corner, with a shopping basket, black PVC on wheels, rested against her knees. She wore a patterned woollen hat and her glasses were thick, which made her eyes look large.

I smiled at her, and her eyes glowed with pleasure as she smiled back.

The receptionist sat behind a high wooden counter, so that she couldn't been seen, invisible to me until I got right up to her. She looked irritated when I knocked on the counter.

'I need to see Doctor King,' I said. 'I'm a reporter and I would like to ask him some questions.'

Her eyes fluttered nervously and then she gestured towards a seat. 'Doctor Newby will be out in a couple of minutes.'

'No, Doctor King,' I said.

'Doctor King isn't here,' she said, but before I could ask why, she walked quickly into another room. The old woman leaned forwards and said, 'Doctor King was lovely,' her smile sweet, painted pink lips hiding the worn yellow of her teeth.

I smiled politely, but Sam turned round and asked, 'Was?'

The old woman nodded, still smiling. 'He left. Such a nice man.' She wiggled her finger playfully. 'Healing hands, he used to say.'

She chuckled louder this time, her hat bobbing as she shuffled in her seat, but I could tell from Sam's expression that he and I were both thinking the same thing.

Then a door opened, and a man with a short grey beard and a chisel parting appeared. Doctor Newby, I presumed.

Bruce Newby looked nervous behind his desk. His hands fidgeted as he straightened his tie and brushed his legs. From his purple cheeks and the redness in his eyes, I got the feeling that being a doctor in a small Lancashire town came with more pressures than I expected.

'Why do you want to speak to Doctor King?' he asked. He tried to sound confident, but I heard the nervousness.

'I'm sorry,' I said, 'but our questions are for him. Why did he leave?' I smiled politely.

Doctor Newby looked to his right, as if some help might miraculously appear on the wall.

'I don't think I can assist you,' he said quietly, his voice trembling.

'That's fine, Doctor,' I said, and stood up to go. 'Sorry to have bothered you,' and I smiled and turned towards the door. Sam looked confused, but then he realised what I was doing when I said, 'It was only Doctor King we wanted, but the police are on their way, and they'll be more insistent than me. They'll want to go through your drug stocks. You do keep drugs here, don't you?'

'They can't do that,' he spluttered.

'Do you want to test the theory?'

I saw Doctor Newby waver and lick his lips. I went to walk through the door when he blurted out, 'We caught him stealing drugs.'

When I turned round, I saw that his eyes were filled with regret. 'He was a good doctor. The old dears around here loved him. Whenever they were near the end, they asked for him. He did more than most doctors. He spent time with them, he listened to them, made them feel better in the last days of their life.'

'What did he steal?' I asked.

'Diamorphine. Pethidine.'

'Seems like he was hot on painkillers,' I said.

'Diamorphine,' said Sam. 'That's heroin.'

Doctor Newby nodded. 'In its street form, yes. But this was medicinal stuff, used as painkiller.'

'What was he doing with it?'

The doctor shuffled in his seat and swallowed. He looked like he was trying to find a way of avoiding the question, but he realised that there wasn't one. 'He told me that he had become addicted to it,' he said quietly.

'So what did you do?' I asked. 'Send him to rehab?'

Doctor Newby didn't answer straightaway. He looked around the room once more, straightened his tie again. We sat there and let the silence grow. After a minute, he said, 'We had to let him go.'

'Why?' I pressed. 'What else was there?'

His eyelids flickered. 'Nothing.'

I cocked my head, gave a wry smile. 'C'mon, Doctor Newby. You don't let young doctors leave just because they have a drug problem. That can be cured. You are the caring profession, after all.' I raised my eyebrows. 'Would the GMC like to look at his patients' files?'

The doctor looked down at that, and I thought I could see tears in his eyes. I glanced at Sam, and I saw that he looked worried. There was something more going on than we'd thought.

Sam intervened. 'I'm a lawyer. Would you like some legal advice? Free of charge?'

'Do I need it?'

'Ask me and find out. You'll be my client, and everything will be confidential.'

'What about the reporter?' he asked, and pointed at me,

'This is off the record,' I said.

Doctor Newby thought for a moment, and by the

time he nodded his assent, it looked like he had aged ten years.

'I think he might have been over-prescribing,' he said quietly. He cleared his throat. 'Even though some of his patients were old, a lot were in good health. Some of the deaths were a surprise.'

'And you think he might have over-prescribed painkillers?' I asked.

Doctor Newby swallowed and straightened his tie again. Then he nodded.

'Wouldn't that show up in the post mortem?' I asked.

'What post mortem?' said the doctor, and he laughed ironically. 'These were old people, with their GP saying that they had died of natural causes. The death certificate was counter-signed by a surgery near the town hall – we have a reciprocal arrangement – and they were cremated mostly.'

'And you are suspicious?'

His lips tightened, as if he couldn't bring himself to say it. 'We didn't notice. It was the other surgery that commented, at a Rotary Club dinner, just as a joke. One of the doctors said that they called him Doctor Death behind his back. And there was a solicitor at the dinner. He pulled me to one side, told me that one of his clients had left a large legacy to Doctor King in a will that she had drafted herself, when the solicitor had drafted all the earlier ones. He was doing the probate, but he was worried it was a forgery.'

'So what did you do?' I asked.

'I told him to leave, said that I thought he had been stealing drugs.' He looked down.

'Did he deny it?'

Doctor Newby shook his head. 'He just went. Hardly said a word.'

'How long ago was this?'

The doctor stroked his beard. 'Earlier this year. Before the summer.'

Around the time that children started to disappear, I thought. Was this the catalyst, the event that had sent him on a more extreme mission?

'Do you have his address?' I asked.

The doctor nodded, and then scribbled an address on his pad, with some directions. 'I don't know if he still lives there,' he said.

We stood up to go, but then something occurred to me. King was abducting children to bring them closer to their parents. If he had killed elderly patients, what would be the reason?

'The patients who died,' I asked. 'What were their family lives like?'

Doctor Newby looked at me, puzzled. Then he thought back to the men and women who had just been appointment cards a few months earlier. 'They lived in care homes. This isn't an affluent town, and so if anyone gets a good education, they leave. Once their parents end up in a care home, the children don't visit any more, because then someone else is there to spare them the long drive from wherever.'

'So they weren't people who received many visitors?'

Doctor Newby held out his hands and looked confused. 'I don't know, but many of our elderly patients are lonely.'

'Because their children lived lives that were too busy to fit them into the schedule?'

The doctor nodded. 'Something like that, I suppose, but not neglected. Just sort of forgotten.'

I glanced at Sam, and I saw that he knew why I had asked the questions. Healing hands. Sometimes you have to lose something to realise how much you needed it. But was it unsatisfying with the elderly, because you can only cause hurt, not heal? All he could do was watch the families squabble about inheritance and blame each other for allowing their parent to die forgotten. Is that why he turned to children, because he could make things better?

We turned to leave, but Doctor Newby stopped us. 'I didn't know,' he said, his eyes filled with worry. 'If I had, I would have stopped it.'

'He was a doctor, right?' I said. 'He helped, not harmed.'

The doctor looked down and nodded.

When we left, the old woman was still sitting there patiently. She smiled as we went.

'I hope you find Doctor King,' she said. 'He is a nice man, a very good doctor.'

I smiled back. 'We'll find him.'

Chapter Fifty-seven

Sam was animated as we drove away from the surgery, an address and directions tucked into my pocket.

'It is classic psychopathic behaviour,' he said, his voice loud and tense. 'Medicine and psychopaths. They get drawn to each other all the time, like opposite poles, one made for help, the other for harm.'

'How do you know that?' I asked.

'I'm a criminal solicitor,' he said, his tone weary. 'I've had to deal with psychopaths, get reports on them, to help out in trials or sentencing.'

'To try and keep them out of jail,' I said, before I had a chance to stop myself. I cursed when I saw Sam's face fall, a sudden acceptance of what he'd always known, that if Thomas King had kidnapped his son, someone just like him would try to make sure that he was free to do it again.

'I'm sorry,' I said in apology. 'I didn't mean anything.'

Sam raised his hand and looked away. 'I know what people think. Don't think I haven't thought it myself.'

'Why is it classic psychopathic behaviour?' I asked, trying to retrieve the situation.

'It's the power. Psychopaths are arrogant, probably the most arrogant people alive. They assume that they are better than everyone else, that they have been empowered with some special gift. And what better gift is there than the power to save people, to prolong their lives?'

'Or to end them?' I added.

Sam nodded grimly. 'Being a doctor brings status, admiration, but above all else, it brings power. You heard what Doctor Newby said. He was killing pensioners, with his beautiful bedside manner, maybe even watching them die. He could end their pain, or maybe he just got off on watching old people slip away.'

'And that's why he abducts children.'

Sam didn't answer, so I continued, 'He likes the return.' When Sam looked at me, confused, I said, 'It's the healing hands thing. All the kids taken were neglected.' When I saw Sam jolt, I added quickly, 'Not in any bad way, like abused or anything, but just left to wander the streets late at night, no supervision or care. We are talking about his perception, not what might be true. He takes them, keeps them, looks after them, and all the time the parents are worried, guilty, feeling that they have let their children down. The parents remember how much they love them and so what happens when the child is returned?'

Sam nodded, his mouth set firm. 'Loved all over again.'

'As far as the child is concerned,' I said, 'it might feel like it's for the first time. He's now treasured, loved.'

'That's a bold assessment,' said Sam, swallowing.

'I interviewed one of the parents,' I said, 'and do you know what she said? She told me that it had come as a blessing, that she only realised how much she had when he had been taken away from her.'

'Healing hands,' said Sam slowly, as the truth of what I said dawned on him. 'So he took the kids so he could keep them, relish the parents' pain, and then enjoy the pleasure of the return?'

I nodded. 'Then it went wrong with the last one – Kyle. The child overdosed on sedative.'

'But why kill Eric, and blame it on him?'

'His dreams. You remember what Eric told you, that he had dreams and they came true. He'd contacted the police, but they didn't want to know.' I shrugged. 'You can hardly blame them for that, but it made Eric get in touch with the families he had been dreaming about. Maybe it worried Thomas, he was scared that Eric would discover something, would stop his good work, so perhaps he watched him to find out where he went. Once he discovered the group, all he had to do was go along, pretend to be precognitive, and he could pick people off whenever he thought they were getting too close.'

Sam thought about that, and then his mind went back to Jimmy King. 'The family knew about him,' he said.

'How do you know that?' I asked. I felt a tremor in my stomach. I knew how much it was tearing up Sam, but I also knew how big a story it would be if I could get it into print.

Sam took a deep breath. 'When Luke told me that he had killed that girl, Jess Goldie, he was brought to see me by his father, and Harry Parsons was there. Maybe they knew the car would have been seen, so Luke confessed

438

to the killing, and, worse than that, he told me that he had enjoyed it, that he would do it all over again.

'They all knew what I would do,' Sam continued. 'I would do my job, advise him to stay quiet. Harry probably guessed that Luke would become suspect number one.'

'But then Eric kept interfering,' I said.

Sam nodded. He paused to examine his nails, looked like he was thinking what to say next. 'I suppose Eric made it even easier for them, except that he had met Thomas, and Thomas wanted to control the situation. He made it messy.' Sam looked confused. 'But why would Harry get involved?'

'Do you remember that you told me about the murder of Luke King's fiancée, when Terry McKay lied to the police?'

Sam nodded.

'Maybe once Harry got involved, he couldn't get out,' I continued. 'Perhaps he didn't know at first; Luke King would have been a natural suspect, as he was the dead girl's jilted fiancé. Did Jimmy persuade Harry that he was keeping Luke from being a suspect, when in fact it was much worse than that?' I shrugged. 'It doesn't matter how you arrive in the plot, once you're in, there's no out.'

'They go right back to their childhoods,' said Sam. 'They grew up in a children's home together, and they have this special bond from then. Perhaps Harry saw it as a one-off favour, but of course Jimmy King isn't a one-off sort of person.'

'And now Jimmy has Harry whenever he needs him?' I queried.

Sam nodded. 'But Harry is retiring soon, and so he passed Luke on to me. Harry was making sure that Jimmy still had someone there for him after he'd gone.' Sam swallowed and then exhaled heavily. 'I acted in accordance with my client's instructions. I did my legal duty.' And when I didn't respond, he added, 'And look at where it's taken me, looking for my lost son.'

I tried to offer some comfort. 'You didn't know Luke was covering for his brother.'

Sam covered his face, and I saw his nails dig into his skin. 'Thomas is in meltdown,' he said through his hands. 'He's losing control, and psychopaths are driven by control.'

I looked at Sam, and I saw that he had his jaw clenched tightly, panic in his eyes.

'We need to get there quickly,' he said, his voice barely audible. 'He's taken Henry as an act of revenge, not pleasure.'

I gritted my teeth and increased the pressure on the pedal. I knew what Sam meant: that if it was revenge, Thomas would not return Henry. Not unless we got there first.

Chapter Fifty-eight

Thomas King's home wasn't what I expected.

'He doesn't bring the children here,' I said immediately.

As Sam looked up, he agreed.

There were stone steps that led up to latticed glass doors. As I climbed and looked through the glass, I could see that the building was made up of flats. There was a column of doorbells with names next to them. Thomas was at the top. Flat 10. He obviously lived on the top floor. I looked through the doors, my hands cupped around my eyes to give me a better view. No sign of a lift.

I stepped back and shielded my eyes against the streetlight; the day was moving into dusk and the sky was turning deep pink on its western fringes. As I looked up, I saw that the top floor was an attic apartment, with two narrow windows looking out over bowling greens. The location was good, tall buildings in a long line with views over the hills, but I had expected more grandeur for the home of a young doctor.

'He couldn't bring a child into here and go unnoticed,' I said. 'Too many stairs, an uncarpeted hallway, too much risk of the child waking up and making a noise.'

'So where should we look?' asked Sam.

I pointed through the door. 'We start in there and see where it takes us.'

I jabbed a doorbell, one of the ones lower down. A frail voice came over the intercom. 'Hello?'

'Good evening, madam. I'm from Blackley Police. We need to speak to you about something you might have seen this morning from your window.'

I knew that I was moving into dangerous territory, impersonating the police, but Sam said nothing. We heard a buzz and went inside.

The hallway smelled of stewed cabbage, none of the exotic spices you might find in a trendier apartment block. The hall floor was dark wood, laid in herring-bone style, with a dark brown carpet running down the middle of the stairs. It was warm, as if everyone had the heating on full. I could hear a television blaring loudly, it sounded like the news.

As we made our way up the stairs, a door opened in front of us. A frail old lady appeared, supported by a stick, hunched over and bow-legged.

'I'm sorry, madam,' I said, my voice reassuring, 'but we got the number wrong. It's the next one up we need.'

The old lady smiled and turned to go back into her flat, and we kept on going up, until after three flights of stairs we came to the top landing. There were more flats on that floor, but at the end we could see a door with a frosted glass panel and a number 10 on the wall next to it. The attic flat. I looked round at Sam. He was expressionless, and so I knocked on the door, three quick raps.

We said nothing as we waited, but when there was still silence a few seconds later, I knocked again. Still nothing.

'Let's break in,' offered Sam.

'Won't it make anything we find inadmissible?' I asked, unsure. 'He'll get away with it.'

Sam shook his head. 'This isn't America. We still allow the occasional abuse of power if it throws up something useful. And anyway, you're missing the obvious point.'

'Which is?' I queried.

Sam raised his elbow. 'You're talking about police powers. We're civilians.' And before I could stop him, he smashed his elbow into the top pane, by the Yale lock, the crash of glass loud along the landing.

I saw blood creep along the cloth of his suit, a piece of glass stuck into his arm, but still he reached through and turned the lock.

The door swung open.

'We'll be trespassing if you go in there,' I said, a final note of caution.

'And my son will still be missing,' he replied, and stepped into the flat.

Thomas King paced as he looked at Henry, saw that he still had his face buried in his arms, but now he was turned into the corner.

'Are you listening?' whispered Thomas, the hiss loud in the cold room. 'They should love you more than this. You understand that, don't you?'

The little boy didn't look up.

'Why aren't you listening?' Thomas shouted, and he stepped forward quickly. Henry curled into a ball and squealed in terror.

Thomas held out his hand, which shook slightly in the shadow from the small lamp, and knelt down. Henry tried to move away but he was pressed up against the wall.

'They know now what it feels like to be without you,' he said. 'How they miss your laughs, your tears.' He stroked the boy's hair gently. He felt a tear trickle down his own cheek. There wasn't long left.

I shielded my nose with my arm as we entered the hallway of Thomas King's flat. One side was lined with shopping bags, piled high on top of each other. Flies buzzed the air over them and I grimaced at the stench. I looked inside one of them. It contained food, bread, now mouldy, and when I looked in another I saw meat. It was crawling, small white maggots writhing in the bag.

'Jesus Christ,' I muttered. 'You hear about old men who get like this, when they finally lose grip on reality, but Thomas King is young.'

'He knows his life is on a timer,' said Sam. 'He's known it for some time,' and then he went into the living room. I took some photographs of the hallway, and then followed him.

When I went into the room, I was taken aback. The carpet was virtually invisible. It was covered in papers. Newspapers, old calendars, medical journals, magazines. And among those, scribbled notes, drawings. I picked up a piece of paper. It was a ramble, just words written randomly, like a list of grievances, no punctuation, the paper scored heavily where he had obviously dug in hard with the pen. I put it into my pocket and then took more photographs of the room.

Sam scurried through the papers, looking for something, a sign, a clue. He turned towards some drawers and began to root through those. Then I whirled round as he shouted out, 'What are these?'

Sam was holding up a small shoebox. He had taken off the lid and was looking into it.

'What have you got?' I asked, and stepped closer.

Sam reached into the box and pulled something out, small and white. It was a business card, showing large hands over a small head. As Sam held out the box, I saw that there were more in there, a whole batch.

'Shit!' he said.

I whistled. 'The final confirmation.' I took a picture on my phone and sent it to Laura.

Sam paled. 'We can't wait for the police to arrive,' he said, the box on the floor now, his fingers moving frantically, skimming over paperwork, brochures, old magazines. He was scattering them on the ground.

'Do you know what you are looking for?' I asked.

Sam shook his head. 'If he hasn't brought Henry here, then he has access to somewhere else. There might be something here somewhere. Keep looking.'

We pulled all the drawers out, Sam tipping the contents of the bottom one onto the floor, and then he was on his knees, pushing papers around. There were bank statements, travel journals, maps.

'What's this?' he said.

I turned round and saw him with a small black notebook. He opened it and read out loud, '*Jess Goldie. Dream Journal 2.*'

We both looked at each other. As he leafed through it, I thought he was going to keel over.

'Are you okay?' I asked.

'Listen to this,' he said, his voice quiet, and then he started to read. '*Boy scared, struggling. See him with someone. Know him. Man, young, but can't place him. He's doing something bad. Shouting for mother. Can hear crying. Know him, so familiar, but face always turned away. Heart breaks. Young boy, so hurt.*'

'How old is that entry?' I asked.

'Ten days ago,' he said, and I could tell that we both realised what it meant.

I watched Sam as he flicked through quickly, trying to make sense of the other entries, when I was distracted by something.

I stepped forward to a large wooden bureau that stood against a wall, the top filled with books, the parts below pulled out to make a writing desk. It was what was on top that made me go quiet. I rested my hand on Sam's shoulder.

'Just stop,' I said.

He looked round, his eyes wide. 'What is it?'

I pointed to a picture frame, with an old black and white picture inside. It showed a large house, with twin gables on the front, three storeys, and a large church door in the centre.

'Where is that?' I asked.

Sam looked at the picture, and then back at me. 'It's where Harry grew up, his old children's home. There's the same picture in the office.'

'And Jimmy King?'

Sam nodded. 'He modelled his own home on it when he had it built a few years ago.'

I felt sick. I had been looking in the wrong place all this time.

'Is it still there?' I asked.

'For now. Jimmy bought up the streets a few years ago. He's waiting for planning permission to build new houses there. Why?'

I pulled out the painting that had taken me to the King house earlier that day, the one that had led me to Danut, then to the surgery, and to Thomas King's flat. I showed it to Sam.

'Eric painted it not long before he died,' I said.

Sam looked at it, and recognised the shape straight-away. It was the same outline. The two gables, peaked high in front of a bright moon.

And then we both turned to rush for the door, our feet crunching on the broken glass.

Chapter Fifty-nine

We raced through Blackley, the Stag's engine echoing loudly, the town centre going past in a blur, just shop shutters and traffic lights, and started to climb one of Blackley's steep hills. The moon lit up the sky ahead, but it was mostly hidden behind the shadow of the viaduct, the dark arches in silver silhouette.

'Tell me more about this place,' I asked.

Sam didn't answer at first, just gripped the door handle as I dropped down a gear to take us faster up the rise. When he spoke eventually, his voice was quieter, more measured.

'It was called the Four Gables,' he said. 'Two at the front, two at the back. Harry and Jimmy grew up there. Neither knew their parents. All they remember is the Four Gables. The kids grew up scared, so Helena said. The carers were a mean bunch. Used to lock the kids in their rooms so they wouldn't get into trouble. No visitors were allowed, and all the staff had canes.' He shook his head. 'It was a long time ago, things were different then, but for Christ's sake, they were just children. That should have counted for something.'

'It made them the people they are.'

Sam laughed harshly. 'That's the problem. Harry is cold. I've never seen him show any affection, not once, and I'm not sure I even know the man. He has a shield, and no one gets near him.'

I thought back to my own upbringing, my father's strength, my mother's fun. 'Sounds like it robbed him of his childhood, but it must have been hard for so many people back then. Postwar, poverty, no luxuries.'

'It's important,' said Sam, through gritted teeth, 'because they went on to have children of their own and they had had no parent to learn from, just a set of dictators. My wife had a Four Gables child as her father, and she is one of the loneliest people I know. Thomas King is the same, and he has my son.'

I didn't answer. I watched the road ahead, just a blur of streetlights. A flash went off behind me. A speed camera, bright in the mirrors.

I thought about the Four Gables. It gave some sense to Thomas's actions: he was reminding parents to love their children. He just didn't have the emotional capacity to channel his intentions better. Victims just create more victims. A vicious circle.

Sam's voice interrupted my thoughts.

'Four Gables had a motto,' he said. '*Strength in Unity.* Harry takes it literally, thinks it is his family against the world. It's even on a sign in his hallway. Jimmy must be the same. Helena knows how it works. The family sticks together through everything, that was the plan, but Helena saw it differently. It was all about doing what Harry wanted, without question. It looks like Jimmy's kids were more devoted. Luke lied for Thomas. Thomas killed the girl who dumped Luke. Jimmy arranged alibis. It was the Kings looking after themselves at everyone else's expense.'

We hit a dip in the road, and sparks flew from the exhaust as the suspension bottomed out.

I felt the noise of the car take on a different sound as we hit the rutted streets near to our destination. The area was awaiting demolition, just streets of empty houses, waiting for planning permission to build new estates with curving streets and open driveways. As we crossed parallel terraces, we saw that they were all boarded up. We glanced quickly down each one, looking for the Four Gables.

We saw it on the last street, before our way was blocked off by the railway. I screeched to a halt.

Sam was about to leap out when I placed my hand on his arm.

'We need to surprise him. Don't give him time to get away.'

Sam looked at me as I said it, and I thought he was going to shrug me off, but instead he nodded. I went back two streets and we both stepped out. I felt my pocket for my camera.

It was the silence that struck me first. The streets and houses were empty as we walked and my nerves were keen. I whirled round at any sound; the rustle of paper that blew along the pavement, the tapping of an old telephone cable against the front of a deserted house. Sam had a torch, although the streetlights provided enough light to see. But it wasn't just the streets that made me nervous. It was the alleyways that ran between the streets, with no lighting to show who might be there. The windows were all boarded up, but some of the boards hung down where someone had gone in to steal the copper piping.

I tried to see into the shadows, but Sam walked forward, didn't give me time, as he took us towards the Four Gables.

As I turned a corner, I paused. It was in front of us, at the end of the street, the last house before a high brick wall, a dark block next to the dead end. The twin gables were high, with Gothic peaks that scratched at the stars, the moon behind making the roof shine like sheet metal.

I turned to Sam. 'Do you think Henry is there?'

He didn't answer. He was looking at the Four Gables. 'Sam?'

He looked round at me, his eyes wide with fear. 'I don't know what I'm going to find in there. What if we find Henry and he's . . .' and then I saw his eyes fill with tears as he realised he couldn't say the word.

'We'll find him,' I said, although I wasn't sure I believed it.

He started to walk, speeding up until he was running, his footsteps like loud clicks in the empty street. My heart jumped as I heard a noise behind me. I looked round. There was nothing there. I ran to catch up with Sam.

We stopped in front of the Four Gables. The church doors were heavy and black, studded with metal. I pointed to an engraved stone above them. I could make out the words.

'*Strength in Unity*,' I whispered, the words sounding loud. 'It was the first thing they saw when they arrived.'

'And the last thing they saw when they left.'

I looked around and realised that getting in wouldn't be easy. The rest of the houses on the street were protected only by chipboard and Jimmy King's reputation, but the Four Gables was different. The windows had metal shutters and entry was blocked by fences, six feet high, joined together by padlocked chains. I looked along for a weak point.

'The only way is over,' I whispered.

'And if he's in there, he'll hear us.'

My nerves tingled. I glanced along the street. I thought I saw someone slink back into a shadow, but it could have been my imagination running wild.

Then I definitely heard something. A rumble. The chains began to jingle against the fence.

'Smoke and mirrors,' I whispered quickly.

Sam looked at me, confused, but then he heard the same thing I had. He looked at the fence and then back at me and nodded.

The noise got louder. I could feel it in my feet, and then it grew louder still, turning into a steady rattle. It was a train, and it would pass just behind the house before it rumbled over the viaduct and weaved its way through the cotton valleys of Lancashire. More importantly, it would hide the noise we would make.

We both looked at each other and then jumped at the fence. The sections clanged against each other, but it was the steady rhythm of the train that filled our ears, and as we dropped down on the other side we heard it fade away as it started to cross the viaduct.

We were in.

*   *   *

Laura burst into Egan's office, Dawson just behind her.

Egan looked up from his papers. 'He's teaching you bad habits,' he said, irritated. 'Try knocking next time.'

'We've got him.'

'*Him*? Who is *him*?'

'The abductor. The murderer. Both.'

Egan sat back and folded his arms. 'What are you talking about?'

'Thomas King is your killer,' said Pete, 'and Thomas King is the person who has been abducting children all summer.'

Egan laughed scornfully. 'Thomas King?'

Pete nodded. 'Luke King's older brother.'

'I know who he is. I thought you were all set on the younger brother.'

'Thomas King has these,' said Laura, and she showed Egan her phone, with the picture of the calling cards piled up in the box.

Egan stopped laughing.

Pete's eyes widened. 'So what are you going to do? We've given you a lead.'

Egan didn't answer. He looked at Pete, his face filled with uncertainty.

'Where did you get those?' he asked, but his voice was quieter now.

'Sam Nixon,' said Laura quickly. 'The cards were in Thomas King's flat. A boxful.'

Egan exhaled loudly and then pulled on his lip.

'We have to move, sir, before any other children are taken.'

'I know that,' said Egan, his voice filled with resignation. 'Where is Sam Nixon now?'

'On his way to the Four Gables,' replied Laura.

Egan scowled. 'Why is he going there?'

'Because he thinks Thomas is there.' And then Laura told Egan all that they had found out. About Thomas King attending the dream meetings. She told him what Danut had said, that Thomas King had been in the Audi that night, and that there had been blood in the car. She told him that Doctor Thomas King had left his job because of an unusually high number of patient deaths. And that Eric Randle had dreamt of the Four Gables.

Egan stood up and walked quickly towards the door. 'C'mon, Dawson, you're coming with me.'

'Where to?'

'To Jimmy King's house. If you've both fucked up, I want you to be there to apologise in person. And you,' and he pointed at Laura, 'get some people up to the Four Gables. If Thomas King is there, bring him in.'

As Egan left the room, Pete and Laura grinned to themselves, and then followed.

We stood in front of the doors.

'Get your torch out,' I whispered.

'But he'll see us.'

'We want him to, now that we're in, because it might make him move, and we'll be near enough to hear where he goes.'

I heard Sam reach into his pocket, and then when he clicked the torch on, he asked, 'Do you think this is the best way in?'

454

As he swung his beam around, I looked up. The door-frame was covered in dirt and there were cobwebs on the door, but I saw that it looked cleaner around the handle, as if it had been used more recently.

'It might be the only way in,' I replied.

My gut churned with nerves. Sam was deathly quiet. Then I heard a noise, a rustle. We both stood and held our breath, listened, and then we heard another rustle. It was something moving quickly, lightly. Then something ran across my foot. I jumped back, startled. 'Shit!' I exclaimed, my heart beating fast, and then I laughed, a mix of embarrassment and relief. 'It must have been a rat or something.'

Sam said nothing. He looked scared. Not because of what might happen to him, I suspected, but of what he might find in there.

I reached out and pushed at the door.

The hinges were stiff, and at first I didn't think the doors were going to shift, but slowly, noisily, they opened into a large hallway. Stones on the floor made screeching noises as the door passed over them.

Sam leaned in and flashed his torch inside. The ceiling was high, with dirty walls, once whitewashed, now grubby from decades of disuse, decorated by graffiti. 'Tez', 'Baz', 'Jules 84', 'Tracy 4 Kenny'. The stairs swept upwards from the centre of the hallway, grand and imposing, and then split to landings on both sides. I looked forward and saw doorways, just dark shadows.

'Shit,' I heard Sam whisper.

'What is it?'

'It is just like Jimmy King's house. He really has built a replica to live in.'

Sam swept his torch around the hallway again. I could hear a dripping noise, a steady sound that echoed. Our feet crunched on stones and broken bottles, loud like gunfire.

'If it is an absolute copy, Thomas will know his way around.'

Sam looked at me, his face dark and eerie. 'I know that,' he said quietly, and then edged forward.

Our feet shuffled along on loose chippings, our clothes brushed against the dust and grime on the walls. I twitched my nose at the smell, of damp and mould. Sam shone his torch into the first room, one of the two at the front. Once a splendid living room, with a plaster rose on the high ceiling and a large stone fireplace, it looked abandoned now. There was a desk in one corner, with a drawer on the floor, dusty and neglected.

We went further along the hall, to the next room. It was the kitchen, with a large stainless-steel table and cupboards around the room. I felt jumpy. I was waiting for the blow all the time, for someone to step out of the shadows. We were about to step away when I thought I saw something.

'Sam, get your torch in here again.'

'What is it?' I heard him say in my ear. Then, as he shone the torch, he saw it too. 'Shit,' he said, and he grabbed my shoulder, his fingers digging into me. 'He's here.' I heard him slump back against the doorframe, as if to stop himself from falling.

I licked my lips, my mouth now completely dried up. I clenched my fist and I felt my fingernails dig deep into my palms.

'We have to keep going,' said Sam, his voice hoarse with emotion.

I didn't have to answer.

'Where next?' I asked instead, but it was Sam who answered the question by turning around.

My hands felt slick, my breathing fast, sweat prickling across my forehead. Where was Laura? I thought, as we moved back into the hallway. As Sam moved on, the kitchen went dark again. I wanted to have just one last look. But I didn't need to. I had seen it, I'd known what it was straightaway.

It was in the corner of the room, in the shadows, cobwebs dancing above it. It was Henry's coat, just as Sam had described it. Navy blue with white stripes along the arm.

I followed Sam into the cold and darkness of the house.

Chapter Sixty

Thomas King watched the torchlight as it flashed around the hallway, sweeping its beam in rapid arcs, like fingers, pointing, accusing. His eyes were dark through the spindles of the landing rail.

He had heard them come in. At night, if the day had been warm and the skies were clear, he could hear clicks and bangs as the house cooled and shrank. This was different, though. These were murmurs, whispers.

As he watched them, they looked familiar, a recent memory that he couldn't place. His hands gripped the wooden rail. He was outnumbered, but he felt strong, his fingers taut, his arms muscled, ready for the fight. He looked at his hands. They'd healed, saved, released. Now they were ready to kill again.

He looked back along the landing, into the darkness of the bedrooms. It was totally black, but he knew the way, had traced it himself all year, knew every corner, every doorframe, waiting for this moment.

Thomas watched the beam dance around, and then saw it point upwards, towards the stairs. They were coming his way.

He crept along the landing. The house had rooms all around on the first floor, so that doorways surrounded the open stairway, but there were doors that connected all the rooms as well, so that there were three exits to each room. Whichever way they came in, there would be another way out.

The boy was in a small room at the back, the window blocked up. The door opened softly, and he flicked on his cigarette lighter as he bent down. Thomas swallowed when he saw him. Henry was cowering on the old mattress in the corner of the room. He looked frightened, unhappy, the rag around his mouth stained by tears. The other children had looked peaceful, contented, wrapped up in their sleep. There was nothing so peaceful as a child asleep.

Thomas looked away. He couldn't stand seeing him. It was supposed to be different to this.

Then he stopped, his ear cocked. They were getting closer.

He felt for the metal bar in his waistband, solid and heavy.

He looked over at the boy. He had to deal with him first. He clicked off his lighter and moved towards him.

We climbed the stairs slowly. They creaked, the carpet gone, just the bare boards visible. I thought I could hear noises, the sounds of children crying, but I knew it was my mind playing tricks on me, the memories of too many broken childhoods embedded into the walls.

As we went upwards, I sensed Sam getting edgier. He looked around constantly. He was fidgety, uneasy.

459

I looked back. As our torchlight went up, the ground floor returned to darkness, the doorways became shifting shadows.

Sam stopped.

'Are you all right?' I asked, my voice a loud whisper.

'I've been here before,' he said. I could hear a tremble in his voice.

'When?'

He shook his head. 'I don't know.'

As we got higher, the doorways into the upstairs rooms began to appear. My mouth was dry, my breaths shallow, my stomach turning over. I could sense someone was watching me, thought I could hear their breaths, but I couldn't see anybody.

Sam stopped again. I looked at him. Something wasn't right. His breaths came fast.

'Sam, are you all right?'

He didn't answer but he peered ahead instead. When he turned around to look at me, the beam catching his eyes, he looked petrified.

'I know when I've been here,' he said slowly. I could hear the fear in every word.

I was surprised. 'When?'

'I've dreamt it.'

'What do you mean?' I swallowed.

'Just that,' he said. 'But I don't believe in any of that. But this, here, I've seen it before. I've been having dreams. No, not dreams. *A* dream. It wakes me up most mornings. Doors, lots of doors, and a child crying, going on and on and on.'

'You too?' I asked, incredulous.

When Sam didn't answer, I barked at him, 'How does it end?'

He looked towards me, and I could see that he was scared. 'Falling,' he said. 'It always ends with falling.'

I was thinking about what to say when Sam thrust the torch into my hand and turned back down the stairs. Before I could stop him, he began to run.

I went to follow him, but I sensed that he didn't want to wait. And the story wasn't with Sam. It was in the house, I knew that. I wanted to leave. I could feel a threat wherever I turned, hiding in the dark, and I was scared. But then I thought about Henry, about Bobby, about how I would feel if it was him in here. I shone the torch after Sam so he could make out his exit.

Then I was alone.

Harry was standing by the front door, looking out over the driveway. Helena was in the room at the back of the house, with Madeleine from Social Services and the police Family Liaison Officer. Harry heard his wife approach from behind. He didn't turn around. He could feel a prickle of sweat on his forehead, and his fists were clenched hard.

She cleared her throat nervously and asked, 'What do we do now?'

Harry clenched his jaw, looked towards the back room. He could see along the hall to where Helena was sitting, her head in her hands, a tissue clenched in her fist. He was scared for the first time ever. And when he thought of Thomas King, he became angry.

'We find Henry,' he said quietly.

She didn't answer at first, but when she asked, 'How?' she sounded shrill, hysterical. He could hear the tears in her voice. 'By sticking by Jimmy? *Strength in Unity*?'

Harry looked down. 'We don't know for sure,' he said quietly.

She hit him, a slap on his shoulder, and then another. He glanced towards the back room, heard some movement as Madeleine looked around the door. 'You can't see it, can you?' she hissed at him, tears running down her face. 'There was never any unity. It was just Jimmy, nothing else. What has he ever given you? Nothing, that's the answer. He uses that stupid motto to get you to do what he wants. It's not unity. It's Jimmy using you, and you can't bloody see it.'

'I'll go to jail,' he said.

'That's a small price to pay,' she replied, and then walked back to the living room.

He watched her go and then turned back to the window. As he heard her talk to the police, he closed his eyes.

As I reached the top of the stairs, I flashed the torch along. There were two landings, each with a rail overlooking the stairs. Four doorways went onto each one, dark, no clue as to what might be on the other side. There was a door in front of me, and I noticed it was ajar, just a sliver of darkness. As I flashed the torch towards it, I thought I saw movement.

My stomach lurched. I swallowed, not sure if someone was on the other side. I reached out with my hand and pushed. The door swung open slowly. It creaked. The noise echoed around the empty hallway.

I paused for a moment, wondered whether I should proceed. But then I realised that if someone was there, I didn't have a choice.

I pushed the door open the rest of the way, feeling my stomach flutter as I waited for someone to fly out, ready for a fight. There was nothing.

I stepped into the doorway and put my back against the wall, lighting up the room with the torch. It was large, with a high ceiling and long sash windows. The ones at the back of the house weren't boarded up, and I could see the lights from the streets on the other side of the railway lines. There was dampness in the air, and when I ran my hand along the wall, it came back with moisture on it.

The room was empty, apart from an abandoned steel bed in one corner, cobwebs joining the rails. I could see gaps in the floor where people had ripped up the floorboards to steal the central heating pipes. I pointed the torch towards them and I could see dust and cables, and a space deep enough to break a leg in.

I shone the torch towards the other side of the room, and I saw that there was another door there, leading into the room next to this one. And it was open.

I could hear my heartbeat, fast like a drum-roll. I stepped into the room, looking out for the gaps in the floor, the floorboards groaning under me.

Then I heard something. A yelp. A cry. And then the sound of movement. I felt goose bumps jump out on my arms and a chill that made me tremble.

I wasn't alone.

Chapter Sixty-one

I knew it was a trap, could sense it. The open doors were leading me forwards. I had heard a young boy cry out. He knew I would follow.

I shone the torch into the next room. There was no one there. I flashed the torch across the floor. There was only one gap, right in the middle. The torch reflected off a window but I couldn't see anything outside. I looked across and saw what I expected to see: another open door.

He wasn't going to make me go through it.

'Thomas King!' I shouted. 'It's over. Let Henry go.'

My voice echoed back at me.

I paused, listened, waited for a reply. Thomas King was here somewhere.

I realised that the only chance I had was to meet him on the same terms: both in darkness. I clicked off the torch.

I paused, waited for my eyes to adjust. I could only make out the window, the moonlight turning it into a silver rectangle. Then I thought I could see some movement outside, a shadow, just a flicker. I edged along the wall, all the time listening out for some clue as to where he might be. I held my breath so I wouldn't miss any sounds, but all I could hear was the rush of blood through my head. My hands drew perspiration smears along the wall.

I tried to focus on the door. I guessed that he would come from there.

Then I saw the blue flicker, strobing bright. It looked like Laura was on her way.

Thomas King tightened his grip around the metal bar. Then the torch went out and he clenched his jaw. The intruder was in the next room.

He closed his eyes, trying to focus on what he knew he had to do. He imagined the bar swinging, tried to think about how it would feel as it struck. The noise. A soft thud. Hammer on fruit.

He let out a long breath. He was ready.

He slid through the door, his movement fluid, slick, silent. His hands felt strong. He could hear noises, soft scrapes of the intruder's feet on the floor.

He tightened his grip and took a step. He knew there was only one rule of surprise attack: hit first, and hit hard.

He crept along the wall. He could sense the intruder on the other side of the room. He was opposite him, his footfalls gentle on the debris on the floor, silent, his breaths shallow and light.

He flattened himself against the wall and waited. Then he saw the blue flashes.

I rushed to the window to get a better look at what I had seen outside. My footsteps sounded loud in the room. The blue flashes got brighter and I saw a small shape. As I pressed my face to the window, I realised that it was a boy. *Henry.* He was on the fire escape. A surge of relief threatened to overwhelm me.

I looked upwards, searching for the clasp so I could open the window. And then I looked down, and I saw the blue light on my clothes, making me visible to anyone who might be looking.

I heard a noise. I swung towards it. Something scurried across the floor. It was black and small. Another rat.

I exhaled, my heart beating fast. Then something else moved, something bigger, faster. I felt the tightness in my chest, the hairs standing proud on my arms. I fumbled for my torch and turned it back on.

It was behind me.

I whirled round, my throat tight, a shout trapped in it.

I stepped backwards, tried to get out of the way. My feet scrambled over loose floorboards. My torch flashed around the room as I stumbled. The figure moved towards me, something in his hand.

I moved back quickly, tried to turn to run. I heard the figure cry out loud. The torch beam picked out something moving through the air, swinging towards me.

I raised my arm to block it, back-pedalling now. Still it came at me. I saw the silver flicker and then I felt pain in my arm. My view exploded with flashing lights. There was another swing and the sounds went faint, my head dull. I felt myself falling, my torch lighting up the ceiling as I went backwards.

Then it went dark.

Chapter Sixty-two

As Laura's car turned into the street, she saw Sam. She leaped out as the car skidded to a halt, the blue flashes bouncing between the houses.

'What's happening?' she asked.

Sam looked back towards the Four Gables. His eyes were wide, frantic. 'He's in there. Thomas King. He's got Henry.'

'Where's Jack?'

Sam looked towards the high wall at the end of the street that made it a dead end. He didn't answer.

'Sam! Where is Jack?' Her voice was shrill.

Sam looked towards her again, and then back to the house. 'He's in there too.'

'Is anyone else in there?'

Sam shook his head.

Laura looked back towards the house, at the high gables, the shadows, the menace, and she sensed something wasn't right.

Then she turned around as she saw another car come onto the street, two police cars behind. As the driver got out, she recognised Jimmy King straightaway.

He jumped out of the car and rushed over to her, his face red, his eyes angry.

'This is my property. What are you doing here?'

Before she could answer, Laura heard a noise, a scramble. It was Sam, and he was clambering over the wall.

She rushed over, tried to grab his leg, but he had dropped over the other side.

She looked around, reckoned she could get a foothold in the wall, and then tried to go the same way as Sam. She scrambled up, and when she got to the top of the wall and looked over, she felt dizzy.

The wall was around eight feet high, but on the other side the ground fell away, just a steep, grassy slope towards the town centre. She couldn't see Sam. Then some movement caught her eye. The top of the slope went towards the viaduct that stretched out in front of her, with its high, dark arches. She could see Sam scrambling towards it.

She dropped back down to the street. 'Shit!'

And then she heard the cry. It was a child. A muffled scream. And then running, fast steps.

She made a grab for the top of the fence.

He threw down the metal bar and ran. He had to move quickly.

He pulled up the sash window and jumped onto the fire escape. He grabbed the boy, felt him struggle in his arms. The metal steps creaked as they took his weight. He tried to run, but the steps swayed as the bolts banged in and out of the wall. A couple came loose and he pitched to one side, felt himself lurch over the rail. For a second he seemed to hang there, looking down over the drop, but the stairs just righted themselves before they both went over, the metal clanging back against the walls.

He gripped the boy tighter and started to run again, his shoes making heavy clangs as he went. He saw a torch below, voices shouting up at him.

He looked around, saw that he couldn't go back into the house, more torches were flashing in there. The way down the fire escape was blocked. There was only one way to go.

There was a perimeter wall to the side, high from the floor, level with the fire escape, two bricks wide. It ran all along the side of the house. On one side was a slope down to the town centre, steep and grassy, and on the other was the yard that acted as a border behind the Four Gables. The wall would take him to the railway lines at the back of the house.

He sucked in the night air. The wind was picking up. He could taste the fields on his tongue.

He waited for the rush of police up the fire escape. There wasn't one. No big search team.

That gave him a chance.

He tucked the boy under his arm and stepped onto the wall. The boy struggled. It made him sway, and he saw how the ground dropped away on one side. He closed his eyes. He held the boy tighter, whispered into his ear. Then he began to walk.

He looked straight ahead. He could hear the voices below, people screaming at him to stop, to let the boy go.

He just held the boy tighter to him. He could feel the edges of the bricks under his shoes, just one slip from a long fall. He didn't stop.

The wall ended where he knew it would: at the tracks. He looked down. The rails ran below him, a long drop down.

He looked back, saw the torches shining up at him. He realised that there was only one way to go.

He whispered in the boy's ear, just a promise that it would soon all be over. And then he jumped.

I rubbed my head. My fingers were sticky and damp and my forehead felt cold. I was cut, maybe badly. The building swayed as I tried to stand. I thought I heard Laura's voice.

Then I could sense her next to me, saw the torch shine at me.

'Are you okay, Jack?'

I groaned back at her. My vision was still speckled red, but the sounds were coming back.

'The bastard hit me,' I said, my hand on my head. 'Some kind of weapon.' I took a deep breath. 'I saw something flash towards me, but when I stepped back, I tripped in a hole in the floor. It didn't catch me full on.'

'How do you feel?'

'Groggy,' I said, my voice hoarse, 'but I'm still here.'

I heard her sigh, and when she spoke her voice sounded thick. 'I thought he'd hurt you, Jack,' she said, and I felt her arms wrap around me, smelled her hair as she buried her head into my neck.

I ran my finger down her cheek and kissed her on

the top of her head. 'If I could see you, I would get a better aim,' I said, and then I started to stand. My ankle buckled slightly when I got up, but I could tell it was just sore, not broken.

Then we both heard the shouting outside.

'Who is that?' I asked, suddenly alert.

'Back-up.'

'He's getting away,' I said. 'He's got Henry.'

I stumbled towards the window and clambered onto the fire escape. It swayed under my feet.

'Jack, come in. You're not well enough.'

I looked and saw a figure moving in the shadows, scurrying along the railway lines. I didn't look back. I stepped onto the wall, the only way I could see to get there. I tried not to look down, feeling myself go dizzy every time I got a flash of the ground, and began to move quickly. I heard Laura curse me as she followed.

Chapter Sixty-three

Thomas held on to the boy, his hand around his mouth, on his knees after the jump. He could feel small kicks against his shins so he clasped his hands around the boy's jaw and squeezed hard.

He peered into the moonlight, tried to see if anyone was there, looking for a shadow, some movement. There was nothing. He could hear the shouts behind, the scramble of feet.

He looked down, saw the boy's eyes look up at him, frightened, pleading, dark orbs above the gag.

He moved his hand and looked away. He couldn't stand it. He started to rock, squeezed the boy harder, felt him struggle in his grasp. He looked up at the stars. They seemed to move, like pulses of light, merging and swaying, the sky shimmering as he stared upwards.

'Nearly over,' he whispered. He felt tears in his eyes. 'No more pain,' he cooed.

He looked back quickly, listened to the sounds of the chase again. The moon seemed to glow more than before, like a beacon. The shouts got louder.

He stood up, tears running down his face, the boy

writing in his grip. He looked up at the stars once more, saw them swap positions, darting around the sky. He closed his eyes quickly, screwed them up tight, but he could still hear the shouts, the noise of hate, loud, strident, in pursuit.

He opened his eyes, saw how the moonlight gave the edge of the viaduct a silvery glow, like a stardust fringe, the foil in a banknote. Then he saw the lights of Blackley in the distance, on the other side of the valley. Sanctuary. Escape.

He felt suddenly calm. He looked down at the boy and smiled at him, hugged him, ignored the struggle and the kicks, kissed him gently on the top of his head.

Then he started to run, heading across the viaduct.

Sam crouched down against the viaduct wall, half-way along its length. The wall was only thigh-high, so he had to get down low as he tried to hide in the shadows by the railway lines. On the other side of the wall there was just a drop to the road below, a hundred feet, the cars like toys, the people on the street like tiny flickers, the lines of orange streetlights making the roofs look like sweet wrappers.

He was scared. He remembered his dreams. They were why he was here, but he didn't believe them. He was too logical. Law wasn't about dreams, it was about facts, about rules, bold and clear. Evidence.

But he had dreamt of this moment. Over and over. The shadows. The house. Most of all, he remembered how it ended. The fall.

What if he was wrong, though? Where would Thomas

take Henry, if not here? Or what if he made the fall come true by being there, a self-fulfilling prophecy?

Then his stomach turned over as he saw the figure running towards him. It was Thomas King, he knew that. And there was something in Thomas's arms, something small, moving. It was Henry. He could tell from the ruffle of his hair silhouetted by the street-lights behind them, from the cry he could hear above the footsteps. He fought to stop himself from bursting forward, but he knew he couldn't. The viaduct was only two tracks wide, no space between the track and the wall; a sudden movement might make Thomas react. The drop was dizzying. If they went over, there was no chance of survival. Instead, he lay down flat, tried to make himself disappear into the shadows. He could sense Henry's fear, and he fought against it. He would wait until they passed him so he could take Thomas out quickly. He thought back to his rugby days. Shoulder into the ribs, side-on, drive upwards.

Then he felt something under his feet. A tingle, which grew into a rumble.

He looked over his shoulder. He could see the lights in the distance. A train. It was on his side of the tracks.

He would have to move, show himself.

Or he could wait, just as long as he could.

He closed his eyes and prayed, just a short one, the first real one for years. And then he tensed himself, ready to pounce.

Thomas could only hear his own breaths in his ears, panting hard, his legs aching, the boy getting heavy.

474

Then he saw the lights ahead, twin beams. He knew what they were. A train. Heading straight for him.

He stopped and looked back. He saw the intruder from the house, cast in the streetlights on the other side of the tracks. Thomas recognised him now, his mind going back to the dream meeting. It was the reporter, the one invited by Eric. And from the blue lights, he realised the other person must be a police officer.

He wasn't going to be caught, not after all this. He wanted to be remembered for how he had brought families back together, not reviled from a prison cell.

They were running towards him. And then he saw someone else appear on the railway lines behind them. As soon as he saw the figure, he knew who it was. He recognised him from the way he held his shoulders back as he walked, from the rigid swing of his arms.

He stopped. *Strength in Unity*. Their unity. Maybe it was going to end the right way.

But he sensed the anger in his father's walk, the disapproval, another burst of his temper. He remembered what that was like. It came back to him in flashes. Blood on his face, his father's hand coming down on him again and again, his own screams loud in his ears.

He looked back to the train. It was almost on the viaduct now. He took deep breaths, wrapped both arms around the boy, felt the child's heartbeat, heard the fear in his muffled sobs.

It wasn't meant to turn out like this.

He turned away from his father and started to run.

*　*　*

My heart was pounding hard against my chest as we ran, Laura just ahead, panicking. I knew why: in the light of the oncoming train, I could see Thomas King, and there was something moving in his arms. Thomas was heading for the train, and running fast. He was silhouetted against the lights, all the time his shadow getting bigger.

As we ran, I glanced to the side, saw the drop down to the street, the lines of orange lights. I felt dizzy, the roofs started to blur together. Too high, I told myself. I looked ahead, tried not to think of it, and saw the moon bright and large, the stars twinkling like rhinestones.

We made good ground along the gravel, trying not to trip on the sleepers, but as we got closer to Thomas, the lights on the train got closer. I could feel the rumble in my shoes, could hear the sound of the horn. Then, as I watched Thomas running forward, I realised that he wasn't hoping to avoid the train. He was heading straight for it. This was it. The end. It would end like they all do, in that final message, the killer's grand gesture.

I began to shout his name, my voice hoarse, screaming. It was lost in the sound of the train.

My breaths echoed loud in my head as I ran, as my feet pounded on the gravel. The ground was uneven so I was jolted, stumbled, but I carried on, desperate, urgent. Laura was in front of me, running hard, her long athletic legs covering the ground, avoiding the tracks.

We were gaining on him. The boy looked limp in his arms, but still the train got nearer. He wasn't slowing down.

I pushed harder, Laura too. She was screaming, 'Stop,

Thomas, stop,' but still he ran. She sounded frantic, scared. Thomas's head was back now. He was going as fast as he could.

I stumbled on a dip in the ground and went to my knees. Laura looked back for a second but I screamed at her to keep going. But it slowed her down a fraction, and Thomas stretched the gap by a few yards. I scrambled back to my feet and set off again. My breaths got faster, I was running as hard as I could, and I could feel the panic rising. He was going to let the train hit him, he was running at it to shorten the braking distance, Henry in his arms.

The train lights were getting bigger as I ran, the bright yellow circles widening, the brakes screeching on the rails.

'Thomas, don't!' screamed Laura.

He didn't look back. He had the boy clasped into his chest, I could see his little legs kicking frantically, scared, getting ready for the collision.

I could hear a noise, and I thought it was Thomas. But then I realised it was Laura, screaming as she braced herself for the hit.

Sam could hear the train getting nearer behind him. The lines hummed with its approach. Thomas was still running towards him, the lights from the train reflecting off Henry's face, white and scared, his eyes wide.

Sam flashed a look over his shoulder. It was close, hurtling towards him. He looked back and saw the gleam in Thomas's eye. He was looking straight forward, at the train. Sam almost stepped out of the shadows, but he had to wait.

Thomas was stumbling as he ran, and Sam thought he heard him scream.

The rumble under Sam's feet became stronger. Thomas was twenty yards away, getting closer all the time. The train sounded its horn, the brakes squealed. It was close, he thought he could feel its draught. The sound of the horn filled his head, but all the time he was watching Thomas. Ten yards away, almost on him. He saw him raise an arm to his face, bracing himself for the crash. He couldn't hear anything, just the wheels along the rails behind him, screaming at him. Henry's eyes were wide with fear, bright in the headlights.

Sam stood up from his crouch. He caught a flash of the train's headlights in his eyes, bright and blinding. He ran at Thomas. His legs pumped hard into the gravel, screaming, teeth bared.

He felt his shoulder slam into Thomas's ribs, felt them crunch, heard him grunt with pain, with surprise. His arms wrapped around Henry. His legs kept on driving, sliding in the gravel. And then they were falling.

Chapter Sixty-four

Thomas King was still on his back when we caught up with him, the train now disappearing into the distance. He was wincing, holding his ribs. Sam was near him, holding tightly on to Henry. The boy's little arms were clutching Sam hard, his head buried into his father's neck.

'It's okay,' whispered Sam, 'it's okay.'

'It's all over, Thomas,' said Laura, her hands on her knees as she leaned over him, speaking in between deep breaths. 'You are under arrest for the murder of Jess Goldie, and multiple abductions of children this summer.' She stood up straight, sucked in lungfuls of air, all of it clean and crisp, straight off the Pennines. 'You have the right to remain silent. But if you do not mention when questioned . . .'

'Give it a rest,' he snapped. He rolled over and gasped. 'That bastard has broken my ribs. Aren't you going to arrest him?'

Laura grabbed Thomas by the arm and shoved her knee into his back. 'No,' she said, and then shrugged. 'Sue me.'

I heard a crunch of gravel next to me. As I looked, I saw it was Jimmy King. He was out of breath, his eyes wild.

'What the fuck . . .?' he started to say, but he seemed to run out of words.

When Thomas saw who it was, he looked back at the ground, his face jammed into the gravel. He stayed like that for a few seconds as Laura tried to contact Pete on the radio, but then he recovered and looked up at his father. 'What next for us?' he asked, grunting as Laura pressed harder.

Jimmy flinched but said nothing.

'Looks like there isn't an "us" any more,' I intervened, my words coming out between gasps as I sucked in air.

Jimmy whirled round and looked at me, his lip curled in distaste but lost for words.

'Looks like it's just you now, Thomas,' I said. '*Strength in Unity*?' I laughed, mocking Jimmy, trying to provoke him into a quote. 'Only goes so far.' I waited for Jimmy to intervene, to maybe get physical, but he didn't. I saw confusion in his eyes.

I knelt down to Thomas's face and spoke softly. 'Tell me, what was it all about?'

'Not now, Jack,' Laura warned me.

I didn't listen. 'Why not now?' I continued, my voice harsh. 'What's next, Thomas? A few months of shots of you in handcuffs, maybe one taken through the prison-van window. You'll be a demon, Thomas: the child snatcher, a cold-blooded murderer.'

Laura glared at me.

'Speak to me, Thomas,' I yelled. 'Tell me why.'

'Do you think I care what the public think?' he replied, spitting the words out. 'Moralising idiots. They'll demonise me, but let their own children roam the streets all night, taking drugs and drinking. I used to see them in the surgery, begging for their methadone script or for a sick note for the social, their children skinny and miserable next to them. And you call *me* the demon.'

'Until your healing hands saved them?' I queried. 'I can understand that. You didn't harm any children, not on purpose, but what about Jess, and Eric? Was that to keep them from finding you out?'

'I saved more than I lost,' he said. Then he sighed. 'Look, they would have stopped me. Would you have wanted that? Go and ask the children how they feel now. Happy, I reckon.'

'Be quiet.'

I looked round. It was Jimmy, his face white, his fists clenching and unclenching.

Thomas glared at his father. 'What's wrong? Feel sorry for the deluded?' Then he laughed. 'They actually believed they dreamt the future.'

'Didn't they?' I said. 'They predicted their own deaths?'

Thomas shook his head and then spat the words out. 'No, they *created* their own deaths. I was going to kill them anyway; they were getting too close. They just provided the method.'

I thought back to Eric, and to his daughter, her tears, and held on to my anger.

'Why?' I asked. 'You were a doctor. You could have done so much good.'

Thomas tried to sit up, but Laura pushed him back

down. 'Do you know any doctors?' he asked. 'They want to be the difference between life and death. Some choose life. Some choose death. It's nothing new. Go to the history books. You'll find doctors who kill all the time, so stop judging.' He looked back at Laura. 'So Supercop is going to take me in now?' He seemed happy. 'Just tell everyone that I made lives better.'

I stood up and turned to Jimmy. 'Some dynasty you've built here, Mr King. Would you care to comment?'

Jimmy stepped up to me. I could see the rage in his face, his features screwed up, his eyes glaring at me. I met his gaze, wanting to provoke a reaction.

But before he could react, we both heard a noise behind us. It was Laura. Thomas had turned her over, thrown her onto the tracks, and he was scrabbling away, heading for the low viaduct wall, screeching, expecting to go over the edge.

Laura reacted first. She ran at him, leaping forward, rugby-style, her arm outstretched. She clipped his heel and he stumbled. He tried to scuttle away but Laura scrambled forward and grabbed his arm. They were just a few feet away from the edge. He turned around and swung a punch at Laura, catching her in the face. She grunted in pain, but still held on. Thomas tried to get to the edge again. I ran to help and grabbed his other arm. My mind was racing, panicking. I knew that Laura would hold on.

'Let him go,' I hissed at Laura.

He thrashed around, his eyes wide, desperate to get to the edge. He was strong, and we were dragged with him. The wall was low and I saw where the ground gave way to empty space, where it fell away to the road far below, and my stomach lurched.

'Thomas, stop!' I shouted.

The town was suddenly loud below us, cars driving under the arches, music coming from a nearby pub. I heard someone shout. Thomas stumbled forward and fell onto the wall. Laura pulled back hard, but I fell with him. The air was knocked out of me, my head just over the edge. The town below me swirled; there was nothing between me and the ground. I let go of Thomas and tried to scramble backwards, but Laura was still holding on to his arm. He was trying to go over the edge, kicking out at Laura. He caught her in the face and she winced, but then she jammed her heels into the gravel and screeched with effort, but she skidded and was pulled with him.

Thomas screamed, loud in the night, and then threw himself forward. Laura screamed with him as she held on to his arm.

He went over the edge. She was slammed into the wall, the impact knocking the wind out of her as her ribs took both their weight. But she held on to him.

Thomas's legs kicked into the air, nothing underneath them except a hundred feet of air and the hardness of the road.

Laura shrieked and gripped harder, trying to lean backwards. I leaned forward to try to grab Thomas's other arm, to help her take the strain. The streetlights became a blur, but Laura mustn't go with him. I could feel her slipping, her arm bent over the top of the wall. Laura glanced at me, a desperate look.

I reached out into space and grabbed his arm with

one hand, feeling my stomach lurch as my knees slipped on the wall and I felt myself fall forward. Laura screamed 'No!' I grabbed the edge with my free hand. He was swinging and kicking, trying to wriggle free.

We were straining to hold on to him.

'Thomas, don't do it,' I shouted. 'Come back up. Explain yourself.'

Thomas didn't answer, but then after a few seconds, I felt his struggles stop. He swung in our arms for a few seconds, and then I heard him shout, 'Help me,' his voice desperate.

Laura pulled backwards hard, and I went with her, kneeling on top of the wall, just one hand gripped to the edge to stop me from falling.

He was heavy. I could feel my fingers slipping on the wall. Then I realised that his hand had gripped my sleeve. If he fell, he was going to take me with him.

I looked at Jimmy, a desperate plea. He didn't move.

'Thomas! Jam your feet into the wall,' I shouted, gasping.

'I'm trying,' Thomas shrieked.

He was twisting and spinning in our grip. Laura was straining to hold on, but then he shouted, 'I've got it, I've got it.'

His weight was taken up by his feet against the viaduct wall, his shoes finding a minute ledge, maybe just a crack in a stone.

'We'll start to pull you,' said Laura, her teeth gritted.

We both leaned backwards and I felt Thomas get higher. I was able to slide down to the track, still holding on to his arm.

Laura turned back towards Sam and shouted, 'Help us!'

He didn't move.

'Sam!'

The streetlights caught him hugging his son, but it didn't seem like he'd heard.

She shouted back to Thomas, 'We're going to pull you up,' the words coming out in gasps. 'Find a foot-hold, help us, clamber up. We'll take your weight.'

Thomas didn't answer at first, but then I heard a quiet, 'Let me go.' There was another pause, and then he shouted louder, 'Let me go!'

He started to thrash around in our arms. Laura slipped towards Thomas, sent some small stones over the edge. We didn't hear them hit the ground. I was jolted around, and I heard Laura's feet skid in the gravel.

'Hold on,' I hissed at her. 'Don't you dare go over with him.'

Laura leaned back. I gritted my teeth with exertion, all the time my arms were being pulled around as Thomas tried to free himself, and pulled hard.

Laura took a step backwards.

'C'mon!' I shouted. 'Don't let it be his way.'

Thomas's head appeared at the top of the wall. His face was red, his eyes frightened. We started to pull backwards again, dragging his chest across the top of the wall, and then his knees.

We relaxed for a moment, panting, and then we felt a sudden movement. Thomas was trying to get to his feet on the wall. He pulled Laura towards him, and then he roared with the effort and stood up, his head back, his arms stretched out in front of him, straining against our grip. Then he leaned back.

'You save people, don't you?' Thomas said, the words coming out in exhausted gulps.

'Not now,' replied Laura, her feet against the wall, her voice hoarse with effort. She had her hand around his wrist. I tried to yank him, but he was strong.

'That's why we're the same, you and I,' he said quietly. 'We save people.'

Laura started to screech with effort. 'Thomas, no!'

'C'mon, Thomas, stop it!' I yelled. I turned round to Jimmy. 'Help us!' My feet were losing grip in the gravel.

Jimmy looked at me for a second, and then at his son. He took a deep breath, and he shook his head. I thought I saw a tear. And then he turned and started to walk away.

'King!' I screamed after him. 'It's your son.'

Then Laura screamed. 'No, Thomas!'

I looked along her arm and I saw that he was trying to pull his arm out of Laura's grip. She was struggling to hold onto him. Her hands were slick with sweat, and they slipped towards his wrist.

Laura lunged to grab at him. I went with her, saw the ground flash up at me as I leaned over, the lines on the road, the gardens of nearby houses, it all swirled around below as I felt the air knocked out of me as my ribs hit the wall. I lost my grip.

Laura screamed as she tried to pull Thomas back. But he was leaning backwards, making her grip take his entire weight. I heard Laura scream again and I could see her fingers start to slip.

'I just wanted you to see that you could have stopped it, but failed,' he said.

'Let him go,' I shouted. I couldn't grab him. He was leaning back over the drop. I grabbed hold of her waist, just to make sure she didn't go with him.

Laura shook her head, straining to hold on to him. I saw desperation in her eyes. I looked at Thomas. He was smiling. He leaned back, one hand free, splayed outwards, his eyes looking upwards. Laura's hand began to slide over his hand, her grip loosening, her eyes screwed up with the effort.

'Sam!' she screeched, asking for help. Still Sam didn't move.

I heard her cry out, a moan, desperate. I watched his fingers slip through her grip, her hand slick with sweat. Then she flew backwards as she finally let go, landing hard on the gravel, me alongside her.

Laura wailed. I looked up. For a moment, Thomas just seemed to hang there, leaning back, nothing beneath him but the ground. Gravity had no effect; time slowed down. I saw him smile. He put his arms out, crucifixion-style, and looked upwards. Then he started to fall.

I shuddered as I heard the impact, a thud and a crack as he hit the road. There was silence for a moment. And then we heard the screams from the people below.

I put my head down on the wall. I was panting with exertion, with fear. Laura seemed distraught, as if she had failed. Then I felt her arms go over me, and she began to sob, and I could tell this time that her tears were different. They were tears of relief.

Chapter Sixty-five

Laura woke me with a start, made me jump.

'Are you okay?'

She sat up, put her head on her knees, sucked in breaths hard.

'Laura, what's wrong?'

She looked round, and then after a few sharp breaths, she laughed softly to herself.

'Just a dream,' she said, and then she lay back. 'It was about Bobby,' she said. 'He wasn't there, had been taken away from me.'

I put my arm over her. 'That won't happen,' I said.

Laura winced when my hand touched her swollen cheek, the result of Thomas King's blows. 'How is your face?' I asked.

'Not ready for you yet, if that's what you mean.'

I laughed and pulled her closer to me.

We were in our own bed, and the excitement of the previous few days seemed like a different lifetime.

It was Sunday morning. I had spent the whole of Saturday writing a feature. I had worked out an exclusive with one of the big Sundays, the fee large enough to get us through the next year. Laura had spent the day in briefings. She'd let Egan take some credit. She hadn't minded. He'd at least let her follow the trail when others might have said no. He hadn't said much to her, but she spotted the look of gratitude afterwards.

It was Mary Randle's face that I had enjoyed the most, though. She looked like we'd given her father back to her. He was no longer the child-killer who'd taken the coward's way out. He was the victim, and with that, Mary no longer had to be ashamed.

'So what next?' I asked.

'We're going to relax,' Laura whispered. 'Bobby will be back from Geoff's later, so let's just enjoy some peace.' She looked at me. 'Do you think there'll ever be a quiet time in Lancashire?'

I stroked her hair. 'It's actually quite boring up here. Once things settle down, you'll miss this excitement.'

She nestled back into my chest. 'I'd like boring,' she said, 'just for a while.'

Harry was looking out of his window when Sam walked into his office. Sam knew he would be there, even on a Sunday. As he looked round, Sam held up an envelope.

'What's that?' he said.

'My resignation,' Sam replied.

Harry turned back to the window.

'So is that it?' asked Sam.

'What do you want?' said Harry, turning round. 'This firm will go on. There are plenty more Sam Nixons out there.'

Sam threw the envelope onto the desk. 'Go fuck yourself, Harry,' and then he went to leave the room.

Before he got to the door, he heard Harry say, 'I'm sorry.'

Sam stopped. 'What did you say?'

Harry sat at his desk. He took a deep breath. 'I'm sorry, Sam. I made a mistake a few years ago, got myself in too deep to help a friend.'

'If he was a real friend, he wouldn't have asked.'

Harry waved that away. 'I can live with my mistake. If that makes me a bad person, so be it. But I shouldn't have dragged Henry into it. For that, I'm sorry.'

'It almost cost Henry his life.'

Harry looked down at that. Sam saw him take a breath and compose himself.

'I know that,' he said quietly.

'But even when Henry was in danger,' Sam continued, his eyes blazing, 'you still wouldn't give into him. Do you know what sort of person that makes you?'

Harry steepled his fingers under his nose. 'The police are investigating the story Terry gave. If they think they can build a case, they'll arrest me.'

Sam smiled, but there was little pleasure in his eyes. 'You'll go to prison.'

'I grew up in the Four Gables. I'll survive.'

Sam shook his head. 'Things are different now. You've gone soft, and people have got meaner.'

Sam went for the door again. As he got there, he heard Harry ask, 'How's Helena? And Henry?'

As Sam shut the door, he said, 'Better – no thanks to you.'

* * *

490

Laura and I were standing in our doorway, waiting for Bobby to come back. She had her arms wrapped around me, her face buried into my jumper. I could smell her hair, warm, soft, just her. The sun shone over the fields, the remnants of the morning dew making the grass twinkle. The breeze was fresh and clean.

I looked along the lane as I heard the rumble of a car. When it stopped, I felt Laura pull away from me. Then I heard a familiar shout. It was Bobby.

He ran through the gate and into Laura's arms, screaming with delight as she whirled him round, his feet kicking outwards.

Geoff appeared at the gate. He had a half-smile on his lips, but the look in his eyes was hostile.

Laura turned back towards him. 'Do you want a drink before you go back?'

He looked back towards his car, and then at our house. He nodded, looking at me all the time. 'Okay,' he said.

Laura went past me, holding on to Bobby, and I saw the delight in her eyes. In Bobby's too.

I went back into the house. Bobby ran up the stairs to his bedroom, to get a toy to show Geoff. Laura went with him, wanting to hear the tale of his weekend in London.

I heard Geoff wipe his feet on the mat. He was a visitor, he knew that.

As I filled the kettle, I heard Geoff come into the kitchen.

'I've read about your fun,' he said tersely. 'How do you think Bobby would have reacted if you got his mother killed?'

491

I turned around. 'It wasn't down to me. It was police work. You know how it is.'

He scowled. 'It shouldn't work like that, not around my son.' He reached into his pocket and put a brown envelope on the worktop. 'You lovebirds might want to read that.'

I looked at it. It was small, with an address window, official looking. Addressed to Jack Garrett and Laura McGanity.

'What is it?'

Geoff grinned at me. 'Open it.'

I slipped my finger under the flap slowly and opened it. It was a letter. As I looked at the letter-head, I realised it was from a firm of solicitors, family law specialists. As I read, I could hear Laura laughing with Bobby.

'What the fuck are you playing at?' I hissed at him.

'Bobby is going to come to live with me,' he said. 'Read the letter. You can either agree, or I go to court.'

'How did you get this done over the weekend?'

He smirked. 'I have friends.'

'Bobby should be with his mother,' I said, my voice low, trying not to let Laura hear.

Geoff's smirk turned into a sneer. 'He can be with his mother. Back in London, near his family, grandparents and uncles and cousins. If Laura moves back to London, I'll drop the application.'

'You bastard!'

He nodded at me. 'You better believe it.'

We both turned round when we heard Laura come into the room.

'Are you boys getting on?' she said, Bobby giggling in her arms.

I looked at the letter again, and knew how much it would hurt her.

I slipped the letter into my pocket. I didn't want Laura to see it just yet. Let her enjoy Bobby for a while first. Too many children had been taken from their mothers.

Read on for an extract from Neil White's novel, *Last Rites*, out now.

Chapter One

Abigail Hobbs looked up and shivered as she opened the door to her stone cottage. The wind was blowing hard from the west, October ending with a snarl, the first bad mood of winter. It roared along the sides of Pendle Hill, a huge mound of millstone grit covered in grass and heather. The hill dominated the surroundings, dark and gloomy, and kept the sunlight from her windows. She pulled her coat to her chest and flipped the collar to her ears. She was too old for mornings like this.

'Tibbs? Tibbs?'

She couldn't find her cat, a grey British Shorthair, all smile and floppy paws. He was always there when she woke, waiting on her windowsill, blinking at her. But not that morning.

'Tibbs?'

She looked around. Still nothing. Her voice wasn't as strong as it had once been, and it died on the breeze, but she knew something wasn't right.

Abigail stepped onto the path, the stones sunken and uneven, and listened out. She could hear something, but at first she thought it was the wind. A knocking sound; a fast rattle. She edged along the path, her slippers making slapping noises on the stones. There was the noise again, like metal banging against wood. And there was something else. A crying sound, distressed.

'Tibbs?'

Abigail got nearer to the end of the house, long grass trailing against her ankles. The noise seemed louder. She called out again. The sound was still there.

She reached an old outhouse, a brick add-on to the cottage that was used to store garden tools. The door was banging, the metal latch clattering, and as her footsteps got closer, the crying got louder.

'Tibbs, wait there. What have you done?'

She pulled on the outhouse door but it didn't give at first. It felt stiff, like someone was holding the other side. She could feel the vibrations in the door, the cries from inside louder now. She yanked at the door, and then as it opened she saw Tibbs, her cat, suspended in mid-air, struggling, thrashing, something wrapped around him.

Abigail was confused. She reached out, went towards him, but then there was a flash, a loud bang. Something wet hit her in the face, sharp and small, making her stumble backwards, losing her balance. As she fell, she saw that Tibbs was no longer there.

Chapter Two

I didn't hear my phone at first.

I was walking up the steep hill to my house, legs working hard, chin tucked into my scarf to keep out the cold. The morning walk was my break from the mundane, where I could forget about the bickering at home or the long stretch of the day ahead. The air in the Lancashire hills woke me up, crisp and fresh, so different from when cotton ruled the valleys, when the giant chimneys filled the towns with smoke and every life centred on the huge redbrick mills clustered around the canal.

My walk wasn't just about the cold in my face though. The last year had seen too many chocolate runs or long nights in with takeaway and wine, and we'd both put on weight. We'd settled into each other. Maybe too much.

I turned as I walked and looked back on what had made me: Turners Fold – a tired old collection of steep terraced streets, cobbled scars in the lush green view, like a museum of lost industry. But for me it was more than just that. As I looked, I saw all the haunts of my childhood. The park where I'd braved my first kiss, the sweeping crescents of the estate where I'd grown up, the school that had educated me so I could leave the town, which I did for a while, but the lure of home brought me back.

I smiled at the view. The mills were all empty now, the chimneys cleaned up, the buildings redeveloped as offices and apartments, or just left to crumble as grass grew through the floor and the windows fell in. But the town glowed from October dew and stood in silhouette against the sun spreading from the east, making me forget the bitterness of the wind.

I turned back and saw my house ahead, halfway up the hill, dry-stone walls lining the road, the old slate tiles and stubby chimney set against the fields behind. I thought I saw Laura through the window, just a shadow as she moved about inside. I waved but she didn't wave back.

Then I heard my phone, the ringtone set to the horns of 'Ring of Fire', an old Johnny Cash tune. I flipped it open and recognised the number. Sam Nixon, a local defence lawyer. He didn't call me that often and so he must have something good for me.

'Hi Sam,' I said, as I went into the house.

Laura looked up as I answered, but I turned away. She was making Bobby his breakfast but I could tell that she was listening.

I listened to Sam, and then said, 'Okay, I'll see you then,' and closed my phone. I turned to Laura and tried to look innocent.

'What did Sam Nixon want?' she asked.

I sneaked my arm around her to pinch one of Bobby's soldiers. 'He said he would tell me when I got there.'

'Don't get mixed up in anything stupid,' said Laura, and when I glanced back I saw her eyes flash me a warning.

'What do you mean?'

'You know what I mean,' she said wearily. 'Defence lawyers can mean trouble. Most don't see the line that separates their client from themselves.'

'Sam's not like that,' I replied. 'And you know how it works.'

And Laura did know. As a detective in the local police force, she saw too much of her hard work undone by crafty defence work, silence or lies peddled in the name of human rights. My side of crime was different. I sat at the side of the courtroom, writing up cases for the local paper, usually just sidebar stuff. I'd done some feature work, even used to do freelance in London, but it was too uncertain, sometimes dangerous, and it wasn't a good time for me to take risks.

Laura sighed heavily and gave Bobby a kiss on the top of his head. 'Not now, Jack,' she said. 'We can't afford to mess this up, not so near the end.'

I turned away and walked into the kitchen, a small windowless room partitioned off from the living room. I didn't want an argument, not so early.

Laura came into the kitchen behind me. 'Jack, talk to me.'

I turned around, the kettle in my hand. 'It's all we talk about these days,' I replied sullenly.

'I just don't want you getting wrapped up in anything stupid, that's all,' said Laura.

'I know, I heard you,' I replied. 'Our lives are on hold, just so we don't upset your ex-fucking-husband.' The words came out harsher than I intended.

'Do you think I'm enjoying it?' she snapped back at me. 'Waiting for someone else to decide who my son can live with? Is that what I had in mind when I moved up here?'

I paused and took a deep breath. 'I'm sorry,' I said, putting the kettle down and holding my arms out to her, trying to pull her towards me. 'I wasn't having a go. I know it's harder for you.'

Laura shrugged me off. 'No, you don't know how it is for me,' she said angrily. 'I'm the one who has made the sacrifices. I moved north with you, with my son, made a new life for us. No, hang on, that's wrong. I moved north *for* you, and sometimes I just wonder whether I did the right thing or whether we should have stayed in London, where I wouldn't get the fucking martyr treatment every time the situation gets a bit inconvenient.'

I looked to the ceiling. We'd had the same row too many times now, but I knew it wasn't us. We were good together, in those quiet moments we shared, when the custody battle for Bobby was forgotten for a few hours and we got the chance to relax – but those moments were getting further apart.

'Look, it's okay,' I said. 'Sam just said he had a story for me.' When Laura didn't look convinced, I added, 'It will be nothing. Some tip, an overnight case or something.'

'So why didn't you just say that?' she said, before she turned and walked away.

I sighed heavily, all the pleasure from the walk now evaporated. How had we got to this? And so quickly.

I went back into the living room and saw that Laura was getting Bobby's school bag ready. Bobby was silent, eating his breakfast slowly. He had been here before with his father – Laura's ex-husband – and he deserved more than that. He was the sweetest boy, just six years old, with Laura's brightness and Geoff's height, but how did you stop a child getting hurt?

It wasn't us, though, I knew that. It was the situation, Laura's ex-husband fighting to take him back south, to her native London. He claimed that it was for Bobby's benefit, that Laura's police work made his home life chaotic, but it had never been about Bobby. It was all about me, Laura's new man, stranger in the nest, the one who made her happy, who had made her give up her London career and settle instead in a small northern town, a detective job in nearby Blackley replacing the London Met. So now we had the fortnightly trip to some motorway services near Birmingham for Bobby's handover, Laura quiet all the way home, only really happy again when he was collected two days later.

Laura looked up at me, Bobby's bag in her hand. I tried a smile.

'C'mon Bobby,' she said, turning away from me. 'Finish your breakfast. We need to go.'

Chapter Three

Inspector Rod Lucas dusted down his tatty brown corduroys, slammed the door on his battered old Land Rover, and looked at the scene.

The cottage was just as he expected it. Like most houses in the shadow of Pendle Hill, it was set back from the road, dark grey stone against the sweep of green fields stretching away behind it, the slate roof low and overhanging.

He looked up at the hill, the exposed, barren summit making him feel cold. He pulled on an old waxed jacket and turned away, thought about Abigail Hobbs instead, still in hospital, burns on her face and stitches in her head from when she'd hit the stone floor. He knew that it wasn't the physical injuries that would hurt her the most. It would be the emotional scars that would last.

The two constables by the door straightened as he approached, both young women, their hands thrust into the pockets of their luminous green coats, their hips made to look big by the large belts around their waists. He glanced down at his own clothes. He lived in a barn conversion, access gained by a mud track overhung by branches, and he had been pruning a tree when he'd got the call. His hands were still covered in dirt and he hadn't changed into his uniform. He would oversee the scene, and then go back to his garden.

'How bad is it?' he asked, his voice quiet, a slow Pennine drawl.

The two officers exchanged glances. 'It's not nice, sir,' said the older of the two.

'Are Scenes of Crime on their way?' he asked.

'As soon as they can,' came the reply.

Lucas knew what that meant: that this was a rural area, a few miles from the nearest town. Scenes of Crime would be busy with more urban crimes: burglaries, glassings. They'd come out here when the day warmed up and they fancied a drive in the country.

He looked around. Brambles overhung the path and the paint on the windows looked flaky and old. The windows didn't give away many secrets though.

'Third time in two weeks,' he said to himself.

'Is that why you're here, sir?' asked the other constable. 'An inspector, I mean. Is it more serious now?'

'Someone has been hurt,' Rod replied. 'It's gone beyond routine vandalism.'

'So what do you think?' she asked. 'Kids?'

He looked around, noticed the small track that meandered down to the cottage from the main road, grass grown over the stones so that it was sinking back into the land as the years passed. 'No,' said Rod. 'It's too far from everywhere else, so getting away would take too long. It would increase the chance of getting caught. This is something else, some kind of a message.'

'But why her?'

Lucas's lips twitched. 'I don't know. Why any of them?' He straightened himself, and when he asked where it had happened he was pointed towards an old outhouse along the path. As he set off walking, he felt his trousers become damp from the trailing grasses. He swept back his thinning hair, his head golden with freckles, grey sideburns reaching down to his jaw-line.

He slowed down as he got near to the outhouse. The remains of the cat were still scattered over the path, the tiny severed head by the door, its mouth open, the sharp little teeth set in a final grimace.

He pushed at the door with a pen, careful not to leave any forensic traces, and saw the wire hanging from the latch. Just like the others, the wire led to a small metal pipe, filled with gunpowder. Once the door opened, it pulled at the wire, which set off a small blasting cap and exploded the pipe. In the other attacks, the pipe had been left on the floor. This time it had been strapped to Abigail's cat and suspended from the top of the door by a clothes line. This was more than just kids, he knew that.

He let the door close slowly as he turned away, the rusted hinges creaking, and walked back to the house, deep in thought. The constables by the door stepped aside as he went to go into the house, curious to find out more about Abigail, but he caught their exchange of glances, the raised eyebrows.

'What is it?' he asked.

They both looked at each other again, unsure what to say, and so Rod Lucas brushed past them and pushed at the door. It opened slowly, the interior dark, and as he peered in, his eyes adjusting to the gloom, he whistled.

'What the hell?' he muttered to himself, and then stepped inside.

Chapter Four

I was heading for Sam Nixon's office, walking quickly through Blackley along the paved precinct, chain stores on one side and the entrance to an indoor mall on the other. Victorian shop-fronts used to line the street, back when the town was the glamorous big brother to Turners Fold, but the area had tried to shake off its past a few decades earlier. The modern town plan that had come along in its place looked tired already. Not many people walked the streets, just earnest young college students and shop assistants clicking their way to work in high heels.

I could see Sam watching my approach. His office was above a print shop, accessed through a glass door at the bottom of some stairs, his name spelled out in gold leaf. His clients congregated there sometimes, somewhere quiet and warm to swap dealer names, but Sam's wife, Helena, acted as the bouncer. She used to be a lawyer herself, straw-blonde with stick-thin arms and a pinched nose, but years out bringing up children and being on the wrong end of a breath test turned her against it. Instead, she managed the paperwork, the money, and allowed Sam to do the law.

I exchanged quick greetings with Helena, just a peck on the cheek. Her face was cold, her complexion pale.

'How's business?' I asked.

Helena grimaced. 'Crime's no game for a sole practitioner.'

'Not busy?'

She laughed, but it sounded bitter. 'People through the door are not the problem. Getting a decent rate of pay for it, that's the problem.'

I didn't respond. I reckoned our views on decent pay might be different. Instead, I let Helena show me through the reception area and into Sam's office, a large room with just a chipboard desk and worn-out chairs bought in a clearance sale. The desk was busy with files, the dark blue of *Blackstone's*, Sam's preferred legal reference, acting as a paperweight, but the room felt bare and cold. Sam Nixon & Co. hadn't brought in enough money to think about comfort.

Sam stood up as I entered, smiling, his hand out to shake. 'Hello Jack, good to see you.'

I shook his hand and noticed the tiredness behind his smile. Sam looked like business was tough. He wasn't much older than me, both of us moving through our mid-thirties, but his face looked filled with worry, his hair was working its way backwards quickly, and whatever was left was sprinkled with grey. He had lost weight and lines had started to appear around his eyes.

Sam Nixon fed me stories, often just a nod as he came into court, a tip that a case was worth hanging around for. My write-ups shamed his clients, but it kept his

13

name in the paper and a steady footfall through his door. For me, it was my job. For Sam, it was free publicity.

'How's Laura?' he asked.

'She's on CRT.'

'Good hours for the family,' said Sam, nodding his approval.

I smiled, played the happy boyfriend for a moment, aware that there were other people in the room.

Laura was a detective on the Custody Reception Team at Blackley Police, who dealt with the overnighters, the burglars and the domestic bullies. The nightshift officers would be long gone to their beds, leaving behind a disgruntled prisoner and a bundle of paperwork, and Laura's team had to sort it out. It gave her regular hours, but it meant she spent most days interviewing hostile prisoners in the belly of the old police station, where the smell of the cells, sweat and vomit, seeped into her clothes.

I was suspicious of Sam. If a criminal lawyer asked me first about the welfare of my detective girlfriend, I assumed that he didn't want her around.

'You know what Blackley is like,' I said. 'It's full of criminals. They keep her busy.'

'Blame it on the lawyers for setting them free,' Sam replied.

As he was talking, I turned towards the other people in the room, a middle-aged couple perched uncomfortably on chairs. I recognised them immediately. Their faces had filled the local news for the last week. I looked back at Sam, who seemed nervous now.

'Jack, this is Ray and Lucy Goode,' he said.

I smiled a polite greeting, but I knew who they were. Their daughter had made the headlines, a pretty young teacher, the photograph from the school prospectus showing her with straight auburn hair and freckles like splashes. Sarah had a boyfriend, Luke, a fitness instructor at her gym. It was normal girl–boy stuff, until Luke had been stabbed to death in her bed a week earlier and Sarah had disappeared.

It had played out in the local paper for a few days, had even brushed the nationals, but the television got the best angle – the news conferences, Mr and Mrs Goode tearful and scared, begging for Sarah to come home – but then it went quiet when there was nothing new to report. I'd guessed the subtext: it was officially a missing persons investigation, but, for the police, Sarah Goode was a murderer on the run.

'This is Jack Garrett,' Sam said. 'Our local hotshot reporter.' When I didn't respond, he added, 'They want to speak to you. Is that okay?'

I nodded at them politely, but then I asked Sam, 'Why me?'

Sam looked embarrassed. 'It's probably for the best if they tell you about it.' He went towards the door. 'I'll be in the next room if you need me.'

I watched him go, surprised, and wondered why he didn't want to be a part of it. When the door clicked shut, Sam left behind an uncomfortable silence, broken only by the ticking clock on the wall and the creaks of the chairs as Mr and Mrs Goode shuffled nervously.

I tried to weigh them up. They were in their fifties. She was in a blue suit, knee-length skirt and blazer, navy blue with gold buttons, her hair in tight grey curls. He looked uncomfortable in a dated brown suit, as if he hadn't worn one for a long time, and I could see the shirt collar digging into his neck. His sandy hair had receded to just wisps of a comb-over.

'This is about Sarah, I presume?' I said.

They glanced at each other, and I saw a nod, a look of comfort. It was Mrs Goode who took the lead.

'Yes, it's about our daughter,' she said. Her voice was firm, but the way their knees touched told me that they needed each other for support. She licked her lips and repositioned her bag on her lap. Then she said, 'We want you to help us find her.'

It was said simply, as if she assumed I would be interested.

I wasn't. I didn't write features any more. I'd sacrificed that for family harmony, for our bright future.

I tried to sound sympathetic. 'I'm sorry, but that's not the sort of journalism I do, the campaign stuff. I write up court hearings, that's all.'

'But you used to do more than that,' said Mrs Goode. 'Mr Nixon told me about some of the stories you wrote.'

'That was then. And I'm a reporter, not a private detective.'

'But we thought it would be a good story if you found her,' she pressed.

I shook my head slowly. 'I don't see a story, not the type I write.'

They looked down, disappointed. Mrs Goode clenched her jaw and a tear dripped onto her eyelashes.

It was Mr Goode who spoke next. 'Not even if you found her first?' His voice was quiet, hesitant.

I gave him a smile filled with fake regret. 'The police will have to speak to her before me, and if Sarah is charged I won't be able to write anything that might affect the case. It's called *sub judice*. It would just sit on an editor's desk for six months, maybe longer.'

'There might not be a court case,' Mrs Goode said, her eyes imploring. 'If you could find her and bring her in, once we know what she is going to say, she might have a defence.'

My eyes narrowed at that. 'What about Sam Nixon?' I asked. 'Will he speak to Sarah before she goes to the police?'

Mrs Goode looked down and didn't answer. That told me all I needed to know. It wasn't about a story, it was about Sarah's parents getting her story straight first, before she handed herself in.

'I'm sorry, I really am,' I said as I headed for the door, 'but I don't see a story, not yet anyway.'

They both turned to each other and exchanged desperate looks. Mrs Goode put her hand over Mr Goode's hand and squeezed it. He looked like he was about to break down. It stalled me.

Mrs Goode turned back to me. 'Thank you for coming down, Mr Garrett,' she said softly. 'At least you listened.'

'How much have you told the police?' I asked.

'Whatever they wanted to know.'

I sighed. 'If they can't find Sarah, I don't see how I can,' I said, and this time the regret was genuine.

17

As I left the room I saw that Sam was waiting in one of the reception chairs. 'How was it?' he asked.

'You know damn well how it was,' I said.

'What do you mean?' Sam replied, as he picked at his fingers and tried to look innocent.

'They came to you because they know the police want to arrest her for murder,' I said. 'Is that right?'

Sam started to say something, but then he stopped himself. He nodded and tried to shrug an apology instead, but then he realised that it was pointless.

'They're decent people,' he said. 'They're worried about their daughter.'

'And someone is dead,' I replied harshly. 'His family will be decent people too.' Sam looked down, so I continued, 'They need someone to help them find her, but they can't afford a private investigator and they thought I would come cheap. About right?'

'But it would be a good story if you could find her.'

'I wish it was like that, Sam, because I need the money – Laura's lawyers are taking most of what we have – but you don't understand journalism. I deal in court titbits, pub talk.' Sam looked confused, so I said, 'My point made. Papers want the pub tales: *Man Bites Dog*, that type of thing. This is feature stuff, an in-depth analysis, and I can't afford to take the gamble of someone being interested. And anyway, if I find her, *I'm* the story, and that's not how I want it right now.'

Sam nodded in apology. 'I'm sorry, Jack. They came to me for help. They're desperate people, and they're good people. You were the only avenue I could think of.'

I sighed. 'So what's your interest?'

Sam looked sheepish at that. 'We're struggling, Jack,' he said. 'We've got the work coming in, but it's all small stuff. Shoplifts, car breaks, Saturday night bust-ups. It's turnover work, but the bills come in faster than the clients.'

'You need a murder to put you in the big league,' I said, acknowledging his admission, and then nodded back towards the room I had just been in. 'And so you need their daughter in a cell.'

Sam looked ashamed, but he added, 'This is my living. I didn't kill that man, and someone has to represent her. Why not me?'

I thought about Mr and Mrs Goode and the look they both had – confused, helpless, wanting help. 'I think they want a bit more,' I said, and headed for the exit. 'Thanks for the tip, Sam, but I can't see a story in it.'

Sam didn't answer, and so I was back on the street, heading towards the Magistrates Court, ready for another day of routine crime stories.

Chapter Five

As Rod Lucas pushed open the door to Abigail's cottage, the smell hit him first. It was strong, sort of smoky. Incense-burners, he guessed. His eldest daughter had gone through a phase of burning them in her room. It helped her sleep, or so she claimed at the time. It was to cover up the smell of cigarettes, he learned later. She was away at university now, and her twenty-a-day habit was one of a list of concerns.

But he remembered the cloying smell, the way it made him cough and wrinkle his nose. He could understand an experimental teenager burning them, but why a pensioner living in a remote cottage?

He looked around. Rod had expected chintz: patterned sofas, high-backed chairs, china ornaments everywhere and pictures of grandchildren, but the cottage wasn't like that. The walls were painted black, with thick red cloth covering the windows and tall mirrors on the walls, ornate and Gothic. There were candles everywhere – on the mantelpiece, the sideboards, the windowsills – everything from deeply scented ones in small jars to large black altar candles.

He saw a rug pushed up against the wall, revealing the stone floor, large slabs worn smooth over the years. His eyes widened when he saw why it had been moved, and what was in its place, the thing that dominated the space.

White lines criss-crossed the room, jagged and uneven, made up of something sprinkled onto the floor, like small white grains. There was a table and chair set in the middle of it all, as if the old lady sat in it when she was alone. Lucas stooped down to dab his finger into the lines. He tasted it. Salt.

The lines made a shape. It wasn't perfect, as if it had been done in a rush, but he could make it out: a five-pointed star, with things placed at each point. A small posy of flowers; a large red candle; a sea-shell.

Rod thought back to the explosive device. Why would anyone target this woman? Was her lifestyle the reason? This was the third explosion like this, but no one had reported anything strange in the other houses. Or maybe they just hadn't looked hard enough.

He would go to the hospital next. Maybe Abigail could provide the answers.

I shuffled on the bench at the side of the Magistrates Court in Blackley as I tried to get comfortable. It was still before ten and the court hadn't started yet, although I could hear the corridor getting busier. I looked up to the ceiling, at the flaking paint, and wondered how I had got to this point. I used to write crime features for the nationals when I was a freelancer in London, had always had the dream of writing a book, maybe ghostwriting a gangster memoir. Now, I churned out the small stories: incidents of local shame, drunken fights, domestic violence, sexual misbehaviour. The local paper paid me for each story rather than a salary, so if the crime scene went quiet, or if the police started another new initiative to keep people away from courts, then I didn't get paid. I worked my own hours, though, and it still left me to peddle the better stories to the nationals, but I used to do so much more.

But I knew that Laura was right. The stories were steady work and provided a stable home. Laura was doing the same, working regular hours, no shifts, so that we were home each evening, and there was nothing for the judge to criticise when the trial for Bobby's custody started.

I looked around the courtroom, empty apart from the prosecutor at the front, sorting out his pile of files, ready for the morning slog. The defence would arrive soon, wanting their papers for the overnight clients.

'Anything decent for me?' I asked.

The prosecutor looked up. 'Uh-huh?'

He was one of the old guard; when the mood was right he was effective, but most days his job was just a plough through Blackley's grime.

'Anything to report?' I asked. 'I'm not here because I like your suit.'

He smiled at that, just a glimmer. 'Just the usual,' he said. 'We've got a drink-driving teacher, crashed his car leaving school, if that's any good.'

I raised my eyebrows. Another reputation ruined, but his shame was his problem. My mortgage was mine.

'Don't get too excited, though,' said the prosecutor.

'Mick Boreman's defending. There'll be no guilty plea today.'

'Too middle class to be guilty?' I queried.

'Something like that.'

I exhaled and sat back. I couldn't write the story properly until he was convicted. It was good for a paragraph reporting his name and profession, but not much else.

I thought about Mr and Mrs Goode as I waited for court to start. Was I right to turn down their request? Looking for Sarah would be a break from the mundane, and it might be a good feature to have written up and ready just in case she was caught and convicted. But then I thought about the bills that dropped onto the mat most mornings, how we needed the steady production line of small tales from the courtroom just to keep ahead of those, and if Geoff went all the way with his custody case then Laura's lawyers would soak up the rest, and quite a bit more.

The tapping of my pen got faster.

The family future was nearly resolved though. Anything I wrote now would be published later, long after the custody case had finished, and if the court was going to be quiet then it might be worth looking into Sarah's case, just to see if there was something to grab the headline. I could write the feature at night, after Laura had gone to bed.

I felt some guilt creep up on me as I thought of Laura, but I dismissed it, perhaps too quickly. I was a reporter; selling stories was what I did.

I put my notepad back in my pocket and rushed out of the courtroom.

Killer ReadS.com

The one-stop shop for the best in crime and thriller fiction

Be the first to get your hands on the **latest releases**, **exclusive interviews** and **sneak previews** from your favourite authors.

Browse the site and sign up to the newsletter for our pick of the **hottest** articles as well as a chance to **win** our monthly competition!

Writing so good it's criminal